IREX

by
Carl Rackman

Cover photo credit: Rangzen, Dreamstime.com
https://www.dreamstime.com/stock-photo-rigging-tall-sailing-ship-rain-thunderstorm-greenish-clouds-image63319017

Cover design by Jo Purusram

ISBN 978-09956393-3-1

Published by Rackman Books
Kingsmead Camberley GU16 6LX
info@rackmanbooks.com

This is for my three wonderful girls.
Irex would never have existed without you.
Thank you. CR

Preface

Irex is a historical mystery/suspense thriller following the characters and events aboard an ill-fated sailing ship whilst on its maiden voyage, told from the point of view of the ship's troubled captain. It is based on an actual event, the wreck of the sailing vessel *Irex* off the Isle of Wight in January 1890; however, the story is entirely fictitious, as are the characters and events contained therein.

A parallel narrative follows a fictional investigation several weeks later as a coroner tries to unravel the mysterious chain of events that led to its sinking, while trying to find out why his inquest is facing stiff opposition from powerful forces in the British Establishment.

Prologue

Isle of Wight
Monday, 3rd February 1890

The cab pulled up on the cobbled street outside the Newport law courts with a clatter of hooves. The horse's huffing accompanied the driver's muttered imprecations at the miserable weather.

Frederick Blake, the Hampshire County Coroner, alighted from the carriage, stiff from travel, the cab rocking with his heavy movements. He had left Winchester at half past four that morning in midwinter darkness, transferring from coach to train to ferry to train again, and finally to this cab. He endured icy fog at one extreme to the present fusillades of rain driven by a biting wind. To say he was merely cold was a grave disservice to the bone-chilled discomfort he felt. He spared a thought for the cabbie, exposed to the elements, and pressed a generous sixpence into the man's half-frozen hand.

Blake was a tall man, and his black greatcoat flapped around him as he retrieved his case and replaced his hat, defying the gusts that still assaulted the island. He negotiated the stone steps of the law courts, his stiff gait and billowing apparel presenting a brooding aspect which belied both the man and his purpose.

Once inside, Blake shook off his greatcoat. The interior of the court house was warm and dry, with the musty, institutional odour typical of all Her Majesty's official buildings.

The reception clerk took his coat and withdrew to the cloakroom behind him. As he returned he carried a waft of warm air and aromatic tobacco smoke with him from the back office.

"Mr Blake, sir, please follow me. Mr Peabody and the other gentlemen will receive you in Court Room Number One."

The young man led him through the double doors that opened into an austere, parquet-floored corridor. Windows lined the wall to the outside, while polished doors stood at spaced intervals down the inside wall. A few desultory figures, probably attorneys or reporters, graced the benches in between.

Through the windows, the gusts of the waning January storms still pulled the stripped branches of the trees this way and that. The island had been mauled by a succession of violent storms throughout the month. Violence, of course, was the sole reason for Mr Blake's presence in Newport at all – men had died, and it was his appointed duty to investigate the matter to Her Majesty's satisfaction.

The young clerk knocked lightly at the oak doors, then opened them into the green-trimmed courtroom where two suited men were gathered before the bench.

"Mr Blake, sir! Welcome to the island!" Mr Peabody was the senior magistrate on the Isle of Wight, and it seemed the Almighty had schemed to appoint Blake's polar opposite alongside him on the bench. He was an apple-cheeked,

6

energetic man of middle-age, with impressive but old-fashioned sideburns. His effusive manner contrasted the phlegmatic and clean-shaven Blake.

"I trust your journey was satisfactory? The crossing was not too rough, I hope?"

In truth, Blake had been green for most of the two hours on the lurching steam ferry from Portsmouth, but he considered such mild privations unworthy of complaint in view of the tragic subject of the inquest. "Yes, Mr Peabody, quite satisfactory, Now, to the matter at hand...?"

"Quite, sir, quite!" cried the magistrate. "It's a devilish affair, this one! There are a great many unknowns." He pursed his moistened lips and waited for the Coroner's polite agreement, which never came.

Undeterred, he introduced the other gentleman in the room. "May I introduce Mr Henry Rudd? He will be taking the third chair. Henry, I present Mr Frederick Blake, Her Majesty's Coroner for Hampshire County, presiding inquisitor."

Blake shook hands with Rudd, a younger but nevertheless distinguished-looking man, probably another lawyer or notary of the town. The man gave a courteous nod and Blake reciprocated.

The magistrate pressed on. "Now, Mr Blake, I have prepared the appropriate documents and the lists." He indicated the neat portfolios placed on a large polished table in front of the bench. There was one each for the three of them. Peabody picked out his and leafed through the meticulously prepared documents. "These are the survivors; here are the confirmed dead, and these are the missing. Here are the witnesses, both able-bodied and those still in hospital; and lastly the written statements submitted thus far."

Blake had already reviewed the case in the past week, but he now held the most complete record available.

Peabody was still animated. "Naturally I have already attended to the jury selection, and the key witnesses..."

As Peabody rattled on, Blake leafed through the pages of documents. The initial statements regarding the incident were quite disturbing, for the most part. Blake had been briefed on the case by the Solicitor General himself. Certain witness statements contained troubling testimony which had attracted the attention of the Crown. In the bland language of the civil servant, Blake had been asked to exercise the utmost discretion in his summarising.

Once Peabody had finished, Blake addressed them. "Gentlemen. Thank you for your service in this matter. It is not our task to wrangle with the causes and consequences of the tragedy; I am happy to leave that to the Board of Trade inquiry next month. Men have died. It is our duty to decide whether they died lawfully or unlawfully. My highest call is to the truth. And I promise you, we shall uncover the truth of how the Sailing Vessel *Irex* was brought to founder insofar as we are able with the facts laid before us. Let that be our watchword, gentlemen. Truth alone shall lead us to our conclusion, and nothing else will suffice."

The others nodded solemnly.

"We shall reconvene at half-past eight tomorrow morning. I wish to begin hearing testimony at nine o'clock sharp. Thank you, and good day, gentlemen."

He gathered his papers and took his leave.

PART ONE

I must go down to the seas again, for the call of the running tide
Is a wild call and a clear call that may not be denied;
And all I ask is a windy day with the white clouds flying,
And the flung spray and the blown spume, and the sea-gulls crying.

- John Masefield, Sea Fever

Chapter One

Near Glasgow
Monday, 9th December 1889

Captain William Hutton lay awake in bed as his wife stirred beside him. He always slept badly the night before a voyage, and this night seemed worse than most.

His heart had finally stopped pounding from the dream that had awoken him, another of the jittery phantoms that plagued him before every trip. He smoothed the hair behind his head with his hand and let out a deep breath.

He often dreamed of sailing, but his dreams always featured fantastic calamities like leaving port without charts, sextant or watch, or sailing into a tiny inlet from which there was no escape. Sometimes they were simply surreal or, like this night, a voyage beset by monsters.

This monster in particular sent a chill through his body; a dark, prowling beast loose aboard the ship. It was a relentless predator with only eyes, claws and teeth, terrorising his crew and closing on his cabin as he watched, terrified but powerless to stop it. He shook off the lingering chill of fear as he accustomed himself to the darkened surroundings of his bedroom.

Barely two months had passed since his last voyage and already he was restless ashore. Hutton had stepped ashore at Greenock after more than two hundred days at sea – days of relentless battles with weather, malnutrition, disease, and of course the sea herself.

Upon his return, Hutton had spent several days alone with his gentle Sarah, who had made the unenviable choice to wed a sailor. A seaman's wife needed to acquaint herself with long periods of uncertain separation. And even when reunited with her husband after a voyage, by no means a certainty, she had to rekindle her marriage to a hollow reflection of the man she had waved away months or even years before. He was likely to be malnourished, with sinew and bone pushing through skin as brown and dry as old leather, perhaps a few teeth short and sporting any number of cuts, scars, lesions and boils; sometimes missing a digit or even a limb. Beyond the physical ravages, there was something else – a perceptible trace in his eyes of the hardships which had scarred his soul. Life at sea was still prohibitively harsh, even in this modern age.

Hutton would placate Sarah's fears with tales of the wonders he had seen, once he adjusted to being the husband of a wife again. Their lives ran very different courses during their separation. Sarah's recounting of her life ashore was cathartic for her but Hutton found it tedious, and despised himself for it. He was unsettled by the frailty of Sarah's emotions and recoiled whenever she gave vent to them.

He kept his own feelings of grief and guilt deeply hidden. The strength of those dark emotions made him afraid. For there was nothing Hutton feared as much as losing his self-confidence; it was the beating heart of the sea captain within him, the unflappable confidence that informed his every thought at sea. Though he was ashamed to admit it, losing his command would forever separate him from his dark, brooding mistress, the sea herself; without her, he was doomed to be simply ordinary.

* * *

The Huttons avoided painful goodbyes at their parting before a voyage. There was no unresolved business; merely a final hug, kisses, a few privately shed tears, and the simplest of words. They prayed as they always did, then Hutton took his leave, with his sea trunk and navigational instruments packed into the company carriage sent from Greenock to fetch him.

The wind whipped around Sarah, who cut an upright but forlorn figure as she waved from the step. Hutton watched her waving figure recede, knowing she would wait until the coach was gone before retreating to her bedroom to sob out the powerful emotions she held back from public view.

Hutton tried to turn his mind to the forthcoming voyage. He had spent many days in port over the past few weeks with his reliable chief mate Andrew Mackie and the crotchety sailmaker Colquhoun, planning and cutting the sails for the first of these winter voyages. It was all the more important as this was a maiden voyage for their brand new ship, launched just two months ago.

The carriage jostled along the banks of the Clyde, rounding the hills to reveal the view that always quickened Hutton's heart – the man-made forest of masts and belching chimneys that signalled the port of Greenock.

He smelt the industrial centre of Greenock itself before he saw the giant foundries belching acrid fumes, the smoke whipped by the wind from tall chimneys as the steel for the next generation of ships was poured. Berths lay side by side as new keels were laid, while other hulls rose from the blocks and ways as hundreds of grimy figures toiled to bring them into being. It was an act of creation on a scale unseen in the whole of human history – Hephaestus himself never had a workshop like this.

Thoughts of home and Sarah faded as he drew closer to the heart of the docklands. Now, amid the brick and stone façades of the recent Victorian edifices and the humped, cobbled streets, there was a different hum of human activity; hundreds of people teemed in a constant blur of movement. Their clothing and faces were a vibrant reflection of the Empire, like a nest of exotic insects upturned and scattered.

Hutton's carriage negotiated the crush of people to reach the entrance gate to the Victoria Dock, where his new ship awaited. Free from the thronging crowds on the main street, the carriage clattered through the high gate and entered the dock.

As the carriage followed the tramlines along the dockside Hutton picked out the ship - *his* ship - from the rows of latticed masts, and his heart gave an involuntary leap.

The carriage pulled to a stop and Hutton stepped out into the sharp, blustery wind to take in the sight of Grubb and Co.'s newest and grandest addition – the full-rigged sailing ship *Irex*.

She was truly a modern leviathan. A steel-built, three-masted, square-rigged ship, with stout masts and yards, she was immense and very strong compared to the wooden ships

14

of previous generations. Every fixture was pristine and sturdy. He had to concede that Grubb had ordered a fine ship; moreover, they had not scrimped on its quality in any way. "Clydebuilt" was still the final word in ship construction.

He felt a surge of pride. Soon, he would take this fine ship out to the open sea, and sail to Rio de Janeiro, the burgeoning former Portuguese colony in Brazil. For the men it was considered one of the better destinations - rum was plentiful, as were the dusky and beautiful women; both were also ruinously cheap.

Hutton mounted the gangway and waved a greeting to Chief Mate Mackie and the abrasive old sailmaker Colquhoun, both of whom he knew from previous voyages. They were solid and experienced sailors.

He mounted the stairway from the main deck to the quarterdeck, noting the ever-increasing gusts of wind, and the whitecap waves in the estuary beyond the breakwaters. It was certain a storm front was approaching; the question was whether Hutton could reach open sea before it hit. He was keen to keep to his schedule. Other ships were departing Greenock and Glasgow for the same destination in the following weeks and competition among companies and captains was fierce.

Their cargo was already loaded – it had taken more than two weeks. Mackie had supervised the final preparations over the past three days. While not an exotic load, it would be comfortably profitable: over three thousand tons of iron drainage pipes and pig iron to meet the needs of an expanding and vibrant city.

Sailing time had been set for 4 p.m. – or eight bells by the afternoon watch – and it was already 11.45 as the crew arrived from their boarding and doss houses in singles and small groups.

Hutton descended to the main deck and entered the large space that occupied the entire stern area beneath the quarterdeck -the officers' and passengers' accommodation known as the cabin. Hutton took up office in his room. As captain, he earned a comfortable space, with the vital luxury of a private WC and bath.

There were six other rooms in the cabin, arranged in a horseshoe around a clear central space. Chief Mate Mackie had a room to himself. On the opposite side was a shared berth for the two other officers. There were three generous staterooms for passengers while the chart room for the navigation charts and papers occupied the rearmost space.

Beneath the cabin, accessed by an L-shaped, carpeted staircase was the saloon deck, an enclosed lounge and dining area for passengers and officers. *Irex* was no passenger liner, but nevertheless was built with some comfort in mind for the few passengers she would carry.

Hutton heard the heavy step of Mackie approaching his room; by voyage's end, Hutton would be able to identify every single member of the crew by his footfall or silhouette – even by his breathing.

The light knock at the door belied the huge man that stood beyond it Mackie stood over six feet high, thick through the chest and arms, with bulging thighs and huge hands. His head was large with meaty features, not handsome but more reminiscent of a Hereford bull.

At Hutton's bidding, Mackie folded himself into the room. His words rumbled like a Glasgow tram. "All crew aboard, Captain. The ship is ready for departure."

"Very good, Mr Mackie. I shall address the crew at noon, then I'm ready to embark the passengers. We'll sail on schedule as long as the weather holds."

"Very good, sir. I'll assemble the men at eight bells of the forenoon."

"Thank you, Andrew."

The mate touched his forelock and ducked out of the room.

* * *

Hutton waited on deck to welcome aboard his passengers. He was standing with his Third Mate, a spry and energetic twenty-one-year-old named John Reid. The young officer had bounced aboard full of vim and vigour, a hearty handshake and a twinkle in his eye. He had made a fine first impression on Hutton.

Hutton was pleased to see Reid had already tasked some of the apprentice boys to carry the passengers' baggage. The captain felt a fatherly protectiveness towards the apprentices, having been one himself. The boys were young - between fourteen and sixteen years old – and preparing for service as officers in the merchant fleet of the future. They inhabited the half-deck, a space below the galley used for dry-storage. They would suffer from bullying and homesickness along with the usual privations of the voyage, but in spite of this they were a tight-knit and mischievous bunch.

The first carriage to arrive was a standard taxi from the railway station which disgorged its two passengers at the foot of the gangway. Reid called up the apprentices, who scampered down to the dock and had the two trunks off the cab and ready to follow in seconds.

As the passengers mounted the gangway, Hutton noticed they were dressed in black uniforms with red trim. He realised they were Salvation Army soldiers. A thin, whiskered man and a trim, much younger woman, they shared a familial way with one another which made Hutton suspect they were a father and daughter, either off to the missions, or escaping the recent wave of persecution against their strident parades through cities around the country.

The middle-aged man, skinny and frail, laboured to the top of the gangway and addressed Hutton in a rasping voice.

"Major George Barstow, requesting to come aboard, sir!"

Hutton watched, alarmed, as he lurched heavily to the deck, just regaining his balance in time not to topple over. Hutton switched his gaze back to the gangway, and took a full view of the woman who followed close behind. He saw that she was quite beautiful, despite the garb and cape which whipped about her in the blustery wind. She was a fine, full-figured woman in her early twenties. She gave Hutton a cool but not unpleasant appraisal as she attained the top of the gangway, took his proffered hand, and stepped deftly to the deck in her heeled boots.

"I'm Mrs Barstow, thank you, Captain." She spoke in a low-pitched voice, smooth like silk. "Elizabeth. But you may call me Mrs Barstow, of course."

She gave a tight-lipped smile, and Hutton was momentarily lost for words. She had the most unusual pale-green eyes, and chestnut red hair, which was pulled back into a severe plait under her Salvation Army cap. She moved with a purpose and confidence that Hutton would have considered most unbecoming in a woman, were she not beautiful.

He realised he had stared a little too long, a fact not lost on the businesslike Mrs Barstow. She had already turned to assist her husband as Hutton blurted out his welcomes, catching sight of Reid's smirk as he scampered past them towards the cabin door.

The boys continued to manhandle the trunks up the gangway, in between lascivious glances and lustful commentary at Mrs Barstow's expense.

Hutton was still feeling flustered a quarter of an hour later when the second coach arrived. He almost missed its arrival as it pulled up near the foot of the gangway, but it was too gaudy an object to escape attention for long.

It was a wonderfully appointed private vehicle; he had only seen the like in the employ of wealthy businessmen or Corporation officials. It was drawn by two fine, dappled horses, wearing blinkers and headpieces, and the polished wood doors were imprinted with the arms of some distinguished family.

Reid and the boys clattered down the gangway, ready to receive this prominent passenger. As they reached the bottom, they were brought up sharply by one of the liveried footmen, who gestured in no uncertain terms for them to keep their distance. They formed a desultory group at the gangway, the wind still tugging at their clothes.

Hutton watched the carriage with interest. Not a soul had exited, as the footmen struggled to unload two enormous travelling chests, each at least three feet square, as well as a set of gentleman's luggage. Hutton signalled to Reid, who bounded back up the gangway like a monkey.

"Reid, fetch the steward and make ready the corner stateroom. I had no idea our gentleman passenger would be so distinguished."

Reid nodded in his efficient manner, and with a "Very good, sir," he made a loud whistle with his mouth, summoning his charges from the dock, and setting off to do the captain's bidding.

So it was that no-one but Will Hutton saw the two men emerge from the coach, remonstrating with one another, until the taller of the two turned towards the ship and regarded it, feet apart and hands on hips, as if it were his very own.

Hutton silently urged the remaining passenger to hurry up and board; he was sure they could get out before the storm hit. It was a race against time, but one which any captain worth his salt would consider profitable to win.

Hutton's remaining passenger mounted the gangway. As he drew closer, Hutton involuntarily took a pace backwards. This was a man who made a tremendous first impression. He was tall, almost as tall as Mackie, he might have guessed, but a different type altogether – this was a taut, slim man possessed of a vitality that lent him a formidable presence. He was young, perhaps no older than Reid, and wore no hat, preferring to show his thick, dark hair, worn so long that it fell in a curtain of locks over each ear. Yet even in this wind, it didn't make him seem unkempt, but suggested a refined and self-contained wildness. Even so, his beard was trimmed in the London fashion, cut close and shaped into neat lines, with a well-shaped moustache meeting it either side of his full mouth. He was wore a fine suit and topcoat with double rows of buttons like Hutton's own, and his bearing was upright and supremely confident, like an officer of the Guards.

His boots rang up the gangway as he strode upwards to the deck in front of Hutton. He stood again, hands on hips, and seemed to regard Hutton with the same attitude he had exhibited from the dock – ownership.

Hutton had never felt so immediately intimidated as he did before the mysterious traveller on his deck.

They locked eyes for the moment. Hutton forced himself to keep his gaze on the man's despite an irresistible urge to look away. The passenger's eyes were large, almond-shaped and pale blue, with a piercing intensity that belied his amused expression as they held each other's gaze. The man laughed, the lines around his eyes making the only breaks in his unblemished skin.

"Captain Hutton, I presume!" He had a voice that commanded attention, much as everything else about him. His entire demeanour exuded privilege and authority. "I must say, this is a fine ship!" He seized Hutton's hand in a firm grip and shook it vigorously.

The captain wondered why such a man would make his berth in a Greenock cargo vessel, rather than one of the luxurious steam liners that ran from Bristol and Southampton. "I'm Captain Will Hutton. You are very welcome on board, Mr...?"

"Clarence!" boomed the man. "Eddy Clarence! Do call me Eddy, Captain."

Hutton had never heard the clipped, affected tones of the English upper classes before. He didn't quite know how to respond to the man's entreaty. It seemed wrong, as if it were forcing the man to demean himself. He elected to play safe.

"Your baggage, Mr Clarence?" He indicated the large trunks still at the foot of the gangway.

Clarence's eyes lingered on the struggling footmen as they manhandled the enormous trunks. "Oh, yes! Have them brought to my room, Captain."

He surveyed the deck of the ship, his hands still on his hips. His studied gaze took in the raised platforms for the boats and the deckhouses for the galley and steam engines. He then raised his head to examine the huge masts and yards, buffeted but unmoved by the winds. Hutton couldn't tell if his interest was that of the layman or the professional – his bearing reflected the ramrod arrogance of the military officer.

Hutton looked back down the gangway, and noticed the other coach passenger watching, his concerned gaze fixed on Clarence. This companion was no flunkey, of that Hutton was certain; the gentleman seemed conflicted, even anxious. It was as if he was making certain his associate boarded the ship and stayed there.

The spell was broken by the arrival of Mr Reid, now accompanied by all six of the apprentices. They broke off their raucous chatter as they angled past the tall, well-dressed man on the deck amidships, each stealing a glance at the impressive figure; yet they all departed the scene hunched with suppressed laughter.

Hutton wondered why he had felt intimidated when the others clearly saw Clarence as ridiculous. In this environment he certainly looked out of place, all London fashions, long hair and fancy boots, staring around the ship like a simpleton. Hutton felt himself relax, but Clarence swivelled round to face him.

"There's going to be a blow, Captain. Nasty one. I expect you'll want to get going, what?"

"We'll be going as soon as I'm satisfied, Mr Clarence, you may be sure of that!" Hutton retorted, and immediately regretted his petulance. As the sailing master, Hutton had no reason to assert himself. It irritated him that he had let the man get under his skin.

He tried to temper his remark with a more amiable approach. "The boys will have your baggage in your room presently, Mr Clarence. Please go down to the saloon, we will dine at six p.m. by the bells."

Clarence was not affronted in any way. "Yes, Captain, quite...might I have a word with the cook? I have a few things of my own I'd quite like him to prepare. After all, forty days without a decent meal is quite enough for any gentleman!"

Hutton bristled again, but this time he contained himself. "You'll find the galley in the midships deckhouse," he pointed it out to the man. "The cook is called Mr. Campbell. Let him know I approved it."

Clarence looked amused. "Oh I am sure I will, Captain!" He turned and marched off in his silly boots, long coat flapping behind him in the wind.

Hutton bristled with indignation at the man's manner. He hoped Mr Clarence would spend his forty day voyage out of sight.

Above the wind, now whistling through the lines and cables aloft, Hutton heard boots on the gangway once again. The apprentice boys were struggling one of Clarence's enormous trunks up the way, and cursing every faltering footstep. Their language was salty enough, even if they were novices at sea.

"There's something bloody heavy in here!"

"P'raps it's full of gold," gasped one.

"You silly bugger, if it was, you'd need a bleedin' crane to lift it!" retorted another.

Hutton let them struggle past him towards the cabin door. He fretted about rumours of treasure circulating among the roughnecks of the crew – ships had been taken for less than a couple of trunks of gold. He made a note to inspect the customs forms – he would prefer such valuables to be locked in a cargo hold, far from desperate hands and avaricious eyes.

By the time the last of the baggage was squared away, the wind was whipping up more strongly than ever. Heavy steel-grey clouds menaced the western horizon above the hills.

It was now 3.45 p.m. by the ship's clock and the first sea watch was on deck and ready. Mackie, God bless him, was already out in front barking orders. The bosun stood at the forecastle, echoing Mackie's orders and relaying them to the steam tug, which wallowed on a light swell.

Mackie reported the ship's readiness to Hutton, who gave his approval for the lines to be let away. The belch of smoke over the bowsprit told him that the steam tug was ready, and he took his position on the quarterdeck with the helmsman as the great ship *Irex* eased from her berth on her maiden voyage.

Chapter Two

Isle of Wight
Tuesday, 4th February 1890

Mr Blake and his two colleagues took their places at the bench. Blake explained the purpose and scope of the inquest and proceeded to brief the jury.

He had no sooner finished when a clerk entered by the double doors at the back. The constable, stationed outside to prevent uninvited gawkers from entering the court in session, followed behind. A buzz of interest spread among the dozen or so onlookers gathered in the courtroom.

The clerk passed a sealed letter to Blake. He read it, frowning, and his mouth twisted in displeasure. The coroner beckoned the Clerk to the Court. At a few low words from Blake, he moved front and centre and announced, "Clear the Court!"

The jury bailiff began to usher the jury through their side door, while the two attendants did the same for the small group of newspapermen, visitors and interested parties. The constable closed the door.

Mr Blake addressed the remaining members present. "I should like to record that by request of the Lord Chancellor, this inquest shall henceforth be conducted in closed proceedings. Mr Clerk, the jury is dismissed; only witnesses, advocates and officers of the Court shall be admitted as long as the court is in session. Are my instructions clear?"

The Clerk bowed. "Perfectly clear sir."

"Very well. In view of this change, we shall adjourn until nine o'clock tomorrow morning."

The court reporter finished picking at the new stenograph machine and presented the roll to the Clerk. An attendant went out into the corridor and his words were lost as the door closed behind him. The raised voices of protest from the newspapermen were still audible through the oak.

"As I said, Mr Blake, a devilish affair indeed." murmured Peabody. "Why should The Lord Chancellor, of all people, not only take an interest in our provincial shipwreck, but seek to influence the proceedings? I have never heard of such manoeuvring."

Henry Rudd actually looked stricken, agitated and wide-eyed. Blake noticed his odd reaction.

The coroner stood, shuffled his papers into order and retrieved his portmanteau from the floor to receive them. "Gentlemen, I entrust this matter to your discretion. We shall reconvene at nine o'clock sharp tomorrow."

He dismissed the court staff and stepped down to the floor. It had been a most inauspicious start.

* * *

Blake pushed open the Orchard Hotel's reception door to a welcome wave of raw, dry heat created by the well-stocked fire crackling in the hearth of the lounge.

The receptionist was also the landlady, Mrs Orchard, a vivacious, well-preserved woman in middle age. She offered a cheerful greeting and retrieved his key.

Blake had tried to converse politely with her when he arrived the previous day but she swept aside his pleasantries with an overpowering familiarity that was disconcerting, even brazen. He was prepared to endure another bout before escaping to his room.

"How are we, Mr Blake? You're looking a mite troubled, if I may say! I can offer you a nice cup of tea and a cuddle by the fire if it would help?"

Mrs Orchard's coquettish affectations were wearing – she projected her middle-aged beauty with immodesty, rendering her overt flirtation more tedious than alluring.

Thirty years before, she had probably been the local beauty, pursued by the worthy men of the parish as a trophy wife. Blake had seen the like many times - a young provincial woman endowed with uncommon beauty, married off to a worthy but much older husband, widowed young by his early death, but then kept in a comfortable living from the proceeds of his legacy.

Mrs Orchard, to her great credit, had done well for herself. She had used whatever wealth she had accrued from the arrangement to make herself a decent living. One might consider her best days as still before her, as a free woman of self-sufficient means. Yet she clung to her pretensions of outward beauty, probably because she had been judged by that sole criterion her entire life. Blake longed to tell her this, but feared opening the door to her prurient entreaties.

"No thank you, Mrs Orchard – most kind, but I have much work to do."

She folded her arms and pushed up her expansive bosom. "As you wish, Mr Blake. Lunch is at noon, and I'll be serving tea at three o'clock sharp."

"Thank you very kindly, Mrs Orchard." Blake left quickly for the stairs.

* * *

He was at the desk in his room at around three in the afternoon when he heard heavy footfalls in the corridor outside. They stopped at his door, and he was already rising from the desk when three rapid knocks rattled it on its hinges. He opened to find a red-faced Mr Peabody.

"Mr Blake, I have some terrible news," Peabody announced without preamble. "Mr Rudd has met with a most unfortunate accident. I am afraid to tell you that he is quite dead. I'm sorry, sir."

Blake absorbed this information and opened the door wide. "Please, come inside. What happened, Mr Peabody?"

Peabody stepped into the room trembling, whether from the cold or the shock, Blake couldn't tell. The men took seats around the fire – Blake taking the time to light his pipe as Mr Peabody seemed to collect his thoughts.

"It was a horse! A cab horse, as I believe. It bolted down Main Street as the unfortunate man was leaving the main telegraph office. He was struck hard and his neck was broken. A most unfortunate accident. He was taken to the hospital but they were quite unable to revive him."

"Indeed?"

"A constable attended shortly afterwards, but there appeared no reason why the horse should bolt like that."

Blake remembered the placid horse that had drawn his cab from the station the previous morning: a skinny mare that endured the weather and cold with a stoic calm. Evidently, they were not altogether predictable.

"Mr Peabody," he spoke at last. "It has been a day of remarkable events. However, in my experience, a multiplicity of such remarkable events is never to be taken lightly. How did you travel here?"

Peabody's bushy eyebrows shot up at this unexpected tack. "Why, I came in my carriage, Mr Blake. It occurred to me that speed was of the essence."

"Very well. If I may request your transport this afternoon, I should quite like to know what Mr Rudd was doing at the telegraph office today."

* * *

Within the hour, Blake and Peabody were in the main telegraph office in Newport, a humbler annexe of the much grander post office next door. They had passed a pair of dishevelled-looking street sweepers on the way in, the only outward sign that their erstwhile colleague had died at this very spot that morning. They now stood in the administrative office with the postmaster.

Postmaster Rogers was a paragon of obstructive Victorian bureaucracy. Peabody was in the process of being dutifully obstructed as Blake watched.

"Sirs, as you well know, the Telegraph Service is part of the Royal Mail, and as such I may not divulge any information as to the content of any—"

"Yes, yes, of course!" Peabody's face was redder than ever, whether from the cold outside or the mental strain of maintaining his patience with Her Majesty's postal service. "We are enquiring as to the nature of the communication, rather than its content!"

"Sirs, I could only divulge such a thing if you were able to provide a court order to that effect?"

Blake leaned forward and held the postmaster with his level gaze. "What could you tell us in the absence of such an injunction, Mr Rogers?"

The man slumped slightly in deference, and reached for a flip-fronted clipboard to one side of his desk. He adjusted his spectacles and scanned the front page. "Sir, I can tell you that Mr Rudd came in just after eleven-thirty. He sent a communication that ran to thirty words, which was sent to an exchange in London. That's all I'm permitted to divulge. I'm sorry, sir."

Blake considered thirty words to be a long telegram to send to London, and must have cost Mr Rudd a considerable sum. It had to be related to the events of the morning. He concluded with some annoyance that Mr Rudd may have been working at cross-purposes to his inquest.

Then another thought struck him. "Did anyone else send a telegram from here this morning?"

Rogers consulted his clipboard again. "Sir, as it happens, yes. A gentleman cabled ten words to an exchange in Glasgow at ten seventeen. North Country accent, I believe."

In this industrial age, men could be so precise with their timings. Blake considered this would be a reasonable time for a newspaperman from Glasgow to pass the news to his employers.

30

Rogers added his final verdict. "That was all the traffic of the morning, apart from our regular customers."

"Thank you. We are in your debt, Postmaster. We shall not need to bother you again, unless our inquest into Mr Rudd's unfortunate death should require a subpoena of your records." He noted the flicker of fear across the Postmaster's features. "I assume you keep copies of all correspondence for the record?"

Peabody also spotted the postmaster's discomfort. To Blake's surprise he pounced on it.

"Would you like to reconsider if there was another telegram, Mr Rogers? Perhaps one was received?"

"Well, sirs, you did not ask me about—"

"Mr Rogers!"

The postmaster looked uncomfortable; lying was not something to which he was accustomed. He licked his lips and began to stammer, but Peabody cut him short.

"Are you going to stand there and brazen it out when our distinguished colleague was killed outside this very office? Speak, man!"

Postmaster Rogers looked dazed, and in a thin voice stripped of its earlier efficient tone, the story came out. "At eleven sharp, another gentleman cabled London, and received a reply at eleven twenty-three."

A request, and very probably an answer, or instructions, Blake surmised.

Peabody smiled, triumphant. Blake regarded this entire exchange with interest. It seemed Peabody was more than just a provincial bumbler – a perceptive mind was evident. Perhaps his verbose jollity was all part of his act, the very thing that made him a successful lawyer and magistrate.

"Where is the copy of the correspondence, Mr Rogers?" Blake asked in a conversational tone.

The hapless postmaster squirmed, clearly upset with the line of questioning. "Well, yes, sir, naturally I would make such records available if you had the proper authorisation—"

Blake had heard enough. Leaning in, he hissed through clenched teeth. "Who was it, Rogers? Ten minutes after this mysterious visitor received his reply, our associate was killed outside this very office. Does that not strike you as unusual?"

Rogers looked ashen. "I – I wouldn't have thought..."

"Did he threaten you? Or perhaps he paid you off?" Blake saw the flicker of fear in the man's face once again. "Yes, that's it. You took his money to keep quiet. Bribe-taking is a serious offence for an official of the Royal Mail, Mr Rogers."

The postmaster wilted, unable to maintain his pretence any longer. "Sir, I am sorry! It was an Officer of the Crown! He ordered me to destroy the facsimiles of the message and the reply. I swear this is true!"

"What manner of Crown Officer would do such a thing?" Blake persisted.

"God help me, sir, I don't know! I know he was a man of influence, as he bore a commission with the Royal Warrant. Since he told me to keep quiet, I fear I have already betrayed his confidence!" cried the wretched postman.

Blake leaned into the space occupied by the trembling man, whose chair was crammed against the wall. "You betrayed more than this man's confidence, Mr Rogers. I need to see Rudd's telegram, if you haven't done the devil's work with it too? Fetch it immediately."

Rogers squirmed. "I'm afraid our man took the copy with him."

32

Blake bristled. "You will hear more of this, Postmaster Rogers."

Peabody touched Blake's arm. "Mr Blake, there is one other possibility."

Blake realised it too. "Rudd. He must have had a copy of his own correspondence!" They turned to leave.

The postmaster looked stricken. "What shall I do if he returns? This Crown Officer?"

Peabody answered. "You will tell one of us, young fellow. Send word to us at the court house immediately. And do not tell another soul. Understand?"

Blake looked back at his colleague, where a fresh eagerness seemed to glint in eyes. *The thrill of the chase*, thought Blake, and he felt it too. They moved up to the front door, taking extra care to check up and down the road before stepping out.

* * *

Rudd's body lay in a small private sanatorium in Newport. It was a far cry from the larger institutions on the island where the *Irex* survivors and victims had ended up.

Blake tried to be sensitive to the weeping Mrs Rudd and her two young children who sat outside the morgue after attending the tragic loss of Henry, their husband and father.

"I offer my deepest condolences for your loss, Mrs Rudd. A terrible tragedy."

The woman was inconsolable. She was strikingly young, perhaps in her early twenties. Her face was twisted with grief. The children clung to her arms and she let the tears fall freely, unable to wipe them away.

Blake offered his fresh handkerchief but the distraught woman was almost insensible.

"Madam, I regret to ask at such a time, but we urgently need to examine your husband's personal effects. He may have been carrying some sealed court documents at the time of his…his misfortune."

Mrs Rudd's red, tear-filled eyes rolled upward. She said nothing but managed to nod. Blake left his handkerchief on her lap and proceeded inside the morgue.

The room was very small, with just one table, a sluice and various cabinets around the edges. Blake and Peabody crowded the mortuary attendant and a doctor who was finishing the paperwork on the covered body on the table.

The doctor looked up. He too was only a young man and wore his hair cut short with his spectacles pushed back to the crown of his head. "May I help you, gentlemen?"

"Good afternoon, Doctor. I am Blake, Coroner of Hampshire County."

"Oh, good Lord! Of course!" the doctor stood up and offered his hand, which Blake shook without thinking. "Dr Manning. Mr Rudd was your associate, was he not?"

"Indeed he was, Dr Manning. I was concerned he may have had some confidential court documents on his person when he was killed."

The doctor pointed to a tray beneath the table. "His belongings are in there. Everything has been inventoried – if you want to reclaim anything you will need to do it via the registrar's office."

Blake pulled the long tray out from under the table, which still held poor Rudd's body under a sheet. As Peabody tried to clear a space on the row of cabinets to examine it, Blake asked the doctor about his findings.

"Mr Blake, I'm sure you appreciate, we will need to move the body to one of the main hospitals for a post mortem. But I can't imagine there was any foul play involved. I would say Mr Rudd appeared to die instantly of a broken neck. They say he was hit by a horse."

Blake just nodded. He picked out Rudd's coat from the pile in the tray and began to go through the pockets. Peabody took the trousers. The doctor watched them curiously.

"Mr Blake." Peabody pulled a piece of telegraph paper from a pocket. Blake leant in as Peabody unfolded it.

Peabody let out a small cry of exultation as he saw what it was. It was Rudd's original handwritten text which was transmitted by telegraph that morning. The post office stamp and charge were appended, presumably by Rogers. Five shillings and twopence was a hefty charge for a telegram to London.

Blake read with anticipation.

URGENT DR FOSTER
INQST PRCDINGS NOW CLSD BY ORDER LCHLLR
WTNSS STMTS UNEQVCL
CONFM CLARENCE RPT CLARENCE NAMED IN RPRTS
BENCH NOT CMPRMISED
AM BEING OBSVD
RPLY WTH CARE
RUDD

"It's not in code exactly, but he has tried to cover his tracks," mused Peabody. "This reads 'Inquest proceedings closed by order of Lord Chancellor'...good Lord, he's leaking the details of the inquest! 'Witness statements

35

unequivocal'…'Clarence named in reports' – wasn't he one of the passengers? 'Bench not compromised' - what does he mean by that? 'Am being observed'…this all sounds exceedingly suspicious, Mr Blake! We should find out who exactly this Dr Foster of London is, and why he's involved!"

Blake initially read the words with a sense of mild alarm at Rudd's perceived treachery, but by the end he came to a different conclusion. He committed the words to memory before placing the sheet back in Rudd's trouser pocket. "Mr Peabody, I think that might be counter-productive. Perhaps we should first establish why Rudd was so interested in this Mr Clarence."

Peabody frowned. "Mr Blake, please. This is an egregious breach of trust! This Foster is surely corrupt."

"Patience, Mr Peabody." Blake turned to the curious doctor. "Thank you, Dr Manning. You've been most helpful." He replaced the tray, taking care not to get too close to the cadaver under the sheet.

Back in the anteroom, Mrs Rudd was no more composed than when they arrived. They left awkwardly without another word to the grieving widow.

Blake resolved to find out what was so important about Mr Clarence, that her late husband should have died so conveniently after mentioning him in his telegram.

Chapter Three

As the steam tugboat pulling the *Irex* breasted the dock entrance, the first swells from the Firth of Clyde estuary began rocking both vessels.

Hutton's tension returned when the unwelcome figure of Clarence emerged from the cabin, gave him a jaunty wave, and settled at the rail to observe the proceedings. Absurdly, Hutton felt he was being evaluated.

Third Mate Reid reported they were making four knots into wind. Hutton estimated it would take about three hours to clear into Bute Sound, after which they would be in deeper water. There were still hazards beyond, including The Isle of Arran and the rocky barrier of Ailsa Craig.

Clarence's presence made Hutton ready to second-guess himself to a degree he hadn't experienced as a captain. If he was honest with himself, he would have recognised the barb of intimidation. He silently prayed for peace and strength, and for the wind and waves to hold off until he had cleared the tugboat and was master of their destiny once again.

* * *

It seemed at least one of Hutton's prayers had been favourably received. As the channel narrowed, the gusting south-westerly wind had to break over the large hump of the Bute peninsula and didn't pummel them as severely in the lee of the mountains.

The tug laboured against the rising and falling swells, the cable held tight, and the huge ship made its way down the Firth of Clyde. Darkness had fallen, and the rain spattered in cold bursts, promising worse to come.

At the change of the watch, the comparatively reedy voice of Second Mate Robert Durrick replaced the stentorian boom of Mackie's. Durrick, though senior in rank and experience to Reid, was more of a disappointment. A rather dour young fellow of twenty-three, he seemed as lively as a slug, and Hutton feared the young apprentices he was supervising would give him the runaround. He seemed to be coping now as he urged the apprentices to climb aloft where the heavy piles of canvas were lashed to the Irex's immense yards. The rope lattices that led to the mast tops above were lit by hurricane lanterns.

Hutton hoped to God none of the youngsters fell. 'One hand for the ship, and one for you' was the motto of any sailor aloft – a loose grip would send the careless unfortunate on a two-hundred-foot drop to the ocean or the deck, providing he didn't hit anything else on the way down.

He watched the complex co-ordination of the men, like a ballet by candlelight performed by rough, heavily-clad men rather than elegant ballerinas. Hutton felt a surge of pride, the presence of Clarence forgotten, as he saw the crew making their ship ready to weather her first storm by herself.

* * *

The hours plodded as the *Irex* was towed down the Firth. The tide was helping to carry them out, and as bells rang for the end of the first dog watch, Hutton watched gratefully as Clarence abandoned his post at the rail and moved towards the cabin door, where supper would be served.

As if on cue, there were three short blasts from the steam whistle on the tugboat. The bosun waved it off and signalled to Mackie the ship was ready to make way.

The men stood poised in the masts, gripping the release lines on the sails, ready to unfurl them for the first time. At the call of "Let fall!" the hands let the sails fly while others on the deck far below took up the strain on the stiff ropes that hoisted the sails. The sails filled with a thunderous crack and seemed to glow in the reflected lights of the lanterns, the acres of white canvas now catching the strong winds. Hutton watched, fascinated, and noticed how sailmaker Colquhoun's face softened from its usual grimace as his handiwork flapped free for the first time.

Once through the channel the sea was more boisterous; heavy swells began to hit the ship, and it began to roll. It took careful handling – the sail was set with a strong crossing wind and the added swell—

There was a shout, the sound drifting from the bow direction towards Hutton's position, faint but urgent. He saw Mackie's big frame suddenly sprint forward into the darkness.

Hutton felt a deep rumble vibrating from the bowels of the ship, as if the sea had entered the holds and was roaring from inside. The *Irex* shuddered, and Hutton saw the masts swing away from the vertical, the entire ship plunging away from the wind.

He found his voice as these events overlapped each other within a few seconds, yelling at the helm to bring the ship into wind.

Mackie was invisible forward, probably wrestling the lines from the flapping sails together with the bosun. The ship still leaned to port, the men high above grappling with the canvas as others on the deck scrambled through the sea washing around their boots to pull on the heavy cables attached to the yardarms, trying to tack into wind.

Hutton saw the steam tug heave into view down his starboard bow. He called for more sail, and they began to outpace the tug on a northerly course. With the wind now on her port side, the ship in a half-hearted tack before the southwesterly gusts, Hutton expected it to heel back to leeward, but it stubbornly remained heeled into wind as the sails strained her the other way.

At that moment, Third Mate Reid clattered up the companionway from the lower decks, spying Hutton on the quarterdeck with helmsman Morgan, whose white knuckles gripped the wheel. Reid sloshed through the water on the inundated deck as the following sea began to rise over the stern, soaking the two men at the wheel. Shouting to be heard, he put his mouth near Hutton's ear.

"The cargo shifted, sir! I heard it go in the midships hold. A big fall to the port side. It must have been the sewer pipes; it sounded like the whole load went at once."

"Thank you Mr Reid!" Hutton shouted back. He turned his voice aloft, yelling for corrections to the sailing rig. He heard the high voice of Durrick the second mate ringing through the darkness, repeating his orders.

The piercing whistles of the steam tug sounded close aboard, and with a sinking heart, Hutton realised that the *Irex* would need to be towed back to Greenock to restow the load. He had lost this round to the sea.

Once the ship was under control and safely under tow, Durrick took Hutton's place by the helm. The captain splashed down the dripping steps to the main deck. The sea still intervened as tendrils of water reached across the decks.

He waited until the men were occupied with work or had gone below before going back to his room feeling something akin to humiliation at the turn of events, with Clarence foremost in his mind.

Only when he had composed himself did he summon Mackie to his cabin. The big mate knocked and entered, his expression speaking for itself.

"What happened, Andrew? How could the load have shifted in such a mild sea?"

Mackie shuffled his feet and rumbled, "Captain, I am sorry."

Hutton considered himself a reasonable man but he was smarting from the turnaround - his proud new ship was coming back into port under tow, listing like a wounded animal; his chief mate, whom he had trusted implicitly, had overseen a loading blunder that was the cause.

"I need more than that, Mr Mackie!" he snapped.

"Captain, one row of sewer pipes was loaded fore and aft instead of athwartships, and wasn't shored up." Any cargo that could shift easily, was never loaded so it could roll with the ship, but stacked across the axis of the hull. Stout timbers were used to shore it against the walls of the hold so that it couldn't, in theory, shift from its position. Mackie was suggesting that this simple exercise had gone wrong.

"How can you be sure? You didn't see it happen, did you?"

Mackie looked hurt at this; his large head dropped before lifting back to look Hutton in the eye. "No sir. But it fits what happened."

Hutton immediately felt ashamed. He was looking for a scapegoat, he realised, when the responsibility for the problem lay only with him. "Thank you Andrew. We will return to Greenock. Make our preparations and inform the bosun, please."

Mackie nodded "Aye sir." Looking somewhat crestfallen, he sidled from the cabin, closing the door.

Hutton listened to the wind and waves assaulting his ship, and quietly thanked God that despite the setback, no-one had been hurt. It was a blessing worth counting.

*   *   *

The wind chased them all the way back to Greenock. By the time they took their berth in the Victoria Dock, it was past one a.m. and the storm was buffeting the ship. She remained moored with the gangway up.

Hutton made his closing log entry, which made depressing reading; an official record of a heroic failure. He wrote reports to the company and port authorities – the passengers would remain aboard tonight, and he would give them the choice in the morning whether to stay aboard or take passage on another ship. It would take a week or more to restow the cargo, then perhaps another week until the tidal conditions favoured another departure.

Hutton decided to dine alone in his room that night, around three a.m. The cook must have smuggled some fresh meat aboard, for it was a splendid meal which he would have enjoyed had he not been trying to fend off the cloud of depression that dogged him like the storm.

Chapter Four

Isle of Wight
Wednesday, 5th February 1890

"I'm sorry; I must begin these proceedings today."

Blake attempted to dismiss the earnest young barrister who had presented himself holding yet another infernal telegram, *damn the things*, requesting he take the place of the deceased Mr Rudd on the Coroner's panel.

"Mr...Thornthwaite, is it?"

"That's correct, sir, Matthew Thornthwaite, Esquire."

"Well, Mr Thornthwaite, it is not in the public interest, nor the Crown's, that we delay further. I must begin hearing testimony today."

Thornthwaite, a well-groomed young barrister clearly of London, smoothly rebutted the coroner's challenge.

"Naturally, Mr Blake, but it is also in the Crown's interest to present a complete opinion. I'm sure you agree that three heads are better than two. We wouldn't want any impasse—"

"There will be no impasse," Blake pushed back gruffly. "I remind you this is an inquest, not a hearing. It will be my opinion, and I can assure you, I will not form an impasse with myself."

Thornthwaite appeared surprised by Blake's stubbornness. He lifted the telegram. "Sirs, the Solicitor-General—"

"No, Mr Thornthwaite. I have had enough intervention in my inquest thus far. Mr Peabody and I shall proceed alone."

Blake considered for a moment, and glanced at Peabody before looking back at Thornthwaite. The suspicious arrival of the bright young lawyer from London suggested more uninvited interest in his inquest. He decided to offer an olive branch in case some higher authority decided to force the newcomer onto the bench.

"I will allow you access to the proceedings, but you are not a participant. You must retain for my inspection any notes or communications you intend to share with whichever office has dispatched you. Those are my conditions."

Thornthwaite was pleased to accept. "Thank you, sir. I humbly accept your terms."

It was already 8.30 a.m. The court house was beginning to look busy. The Glasgow newspaperman was still in the reception area, and had been joined by a few others. Blake didn't like reporters, and recoiled as the man accosted him, his breath redolent of cheap cigarettes and a whiff of Scotch.

"Judge Blake!" exclaimed the man. "Gordon Rennie, Glasgow Herald. What's going on with this damned inquest? Why did you close it down?" Rennie's words spat out of him at machine gun tempo. Though his Glaswegian accent was strong, his diction was impressive.

Blake remained impassive. "Mr Rennie, you know the proceedings of the inquest are closed. Why are you still here?"

"Look, Mr Blake," Rennie shot back. "I've got a job to do, and as long as my editor wants me down here, I'll be hanging round here until I get something."

Blake considered this. He knew from experience that pressmen were among the least scrupled but most tenacious human beings alive.

"Your presence therefore suggests you have nothing, Mr Rennie."

"Blake, I promise you on my dear mother's life, God rest her, if there's something to find, I'll find it. People may not know me down here, but I tell you this, Gordon Rennie digs until he finds the truth. I am the terror of Scotland and the Northern realms!" He spread his hands theatrically, with his toothy grin not quite underpinned by the keenness of his piercing pale-blue eyes.

Blake smiled a thin smile. Rennie was certainly a character. "Very well, Mr Rennie. I cannot divulge anything about the inquest, since the proceedings are closed by order of the Lord Chancellor himself."

Rennie's eyes bulged at this morsel of inside knowledge. "Is that so, Mr Blake?"

"However, if your concern is genuinely for the truth and not sensation, I would be prepared to confirm or deny anything you might find out in your own investigations."

Rennie grinned again, but his eyes looked sharply into Blake's. "Well, could you confirm what happened to your associate Mr Rudd yesterday? I heard he was knocked down by a runaway horse."

Blake nodded. "That is correct, Mr Rennie."

Rennie looked at Blake through hooded eyes. "Did you know that was the first fatal traffic accident in Newport for almost seven months? And the first where the victim wasn't blind drunk in over three years?"

Blake was impressed, in spite of himself. "You appear to be remarkably well-informed, Mr Rennie."

Rennie gave a wink. "Aye, I have my sources, Your Honour. Are you going to replace him?"

Blake remained impassive, but glanced in the direction of Thornthwaite. "I imagine Mr Peabody and I will be able to cope."

Rennie hadn't finished. "So, what do you think about the telegrams he was sending?"

Blake actually blinked in surprise. "What would you know of such matters, Mr Rennie?"

"As I said, I have my sources, Mr Blake."

"I trust you haven't been interfering with Her Majesty's postmaster?" Blake was not going to tiptoe around the issue.

"God, no! But since you mention it, I might go and have a little chat with him."

Blake nodded slightly, his eyes searching Rennie as if reassessing him. He closed the distance between them, and spoke softly. "You should do that, Mr Rennie. I believe Mr Rudd may have been expecting a reply to his telegram of yesterday. It would be most unfortunate if anyone were to tamper with it before it fell into official hands."

Rennie grasped the hint and gave a conspiratorial wink. "Thank you, Your Honour. I tell you what – I'm staying at the Osborne Hotel right here in Newport. Room Fifteen. You be sure to take tea there, won't you?" He nodded his leave, and strode towards the court house door, whistling.

Blake watched him leave, satisfied. *Better a newsman in your hand than snapping at your heels.*

He turned back to the colonnade doors and noted the cool eyes of young Mr Thornthwaite studying him before they resumed their lazy but deliberate casing of the many faces in the hall. Blake thought it odd that such a capable, smooth barrister should present himself at the court house, letter of authority in his hand, barely eighteen hours after Mr Rudd's unfortunate demise. Another remarkable event to add to his unease. Blake instead turned his mind to the day's business and stepped through the oak double doors.

* * *

The short, grey-haired man sat at the large table in front of the bench. He was wearing clothes that clearly did not belong to him – the collar of his shirt hung loose around a chicken neck, and the sleeves were rolled up twice to clear his cuffs. He was unconsciously pulling at his waistband, indicating that the trousers were also those of a larger man. Those survivors of the wreck released from hospital had been taken in as waifs, and their clothes were the results of charity. Beggars, it seemed, really could not be choosers.

Peabody addressed him first. "You are Charles Campbell, ship's cook of the vessel *Irex*?"

"Yes, sir." Campbell's voice sounded papery and thin, barely able to overcome the ticking of the clock.

Mr Peabody continued, his tone avuncular. "Now Mr Campbell, this is not a trial. This is an inquest. We are not here to accuse or apportion blame, but to establish certain facts. That said, you are under oath, and when you are questioned by Mr Blake and myself, you must answer truthfully, to the best of your knowledge. Do you understand?"

Campbell nodded, "Yes, sir."

"Very well then. Please tell us, in your own words, what you know of the circumstances leading up to the loss of the *Irex* on 25th January 1890."

Campbell took his time and told a rambling story that was not very illuminating. Blake found it amazing that someone who had been present for such a tragedy knew so little about the event – he was the third man to be rescued, and appeared to have missed most of the drama altogether.

Blake avoided looking at the clock while witnesses were testifying, considering it rude, but he noticed that the cook had barely detailed the wreck at all and it was already nearly ten. He caught Peabody's eye, and the magistrate raised one eyebrow as the cook droned on in his raspy voice.

"One moment please, Mr Campbell…would you excuse us? We need to confer."

The two men conversed in murmurs with their heads together.

"I wonder if he didn't sleep through the whole thing, Mr Blake!"

Blake pressed his lips together. "He is the cook. He would have had the run of the ship. Try to get some background; it might help us along later?"

Peabody nodded his agreement and resumed the testimony. "Thank you Mr Campbell. Could you tell us about the dining arrangements on board the *Irex*?"

Campbell brightened at once. "Yes sirs, I'm on duty all the time, cooking meals for both watches and the cabin. The galley isn't much, but I can make hot food as long as the weather is all right. When it's stormy, everyone just gets salt beef and cold potatoes. Most of the rations are tinned and preserves, which the steward tends."

"Thank you. In your statement, you said that after you put to sea again, you did not make many hot meals. Was that due to weather?"

"That's right sir. We had a nice period after New Year, but storms for the rest of the journey, right up till she wrecked. That one was fearsome, sir. Worst storm I've ever seen." He crossed himself. Campbell bore the scars of what must have been terrible final days aboard the *Irex;* the skin across patches of his face was red raw, scoured by the wind and spray, still daubed with ointment from his time at the hospital. And he was one of the luckier ones.

Blake had noted Thornthwaite's diligent shorthand throughout this last questioning. He decided to play his hand a little. "Mr Campbell, did you talk to any of your passengers on this voyage?"

"As a matter of fact, sir, I did. The lady Mrs Barstow, a very fine lady, sir, thanked me for providing a 'welcoming table', she called it. I tried my best," he added shyly. "I only talked to her a couple times myself; it was the steward who told me." Campbell was actually blushing.

"I see. And what of the others?"

Campbell hesitated. "I, err..."

Blake saw Thornthwaite actually lean forward, pen poised.

"I shouldn't ought to be sayin' this, but it is God's honest truth. The very first night of the voyage, Mr Clarence came to speak to me. He was a very fine gentleman, sir, and he said, no offence intended, that he brought a supply of fresh meat for me to cook. Now, I know regulations afloat say we can only use ship's rations for food, but he was a fine gentleman, as I said, and I agreed that he couldn't just eat salt beef and tack biscuits. It turned out he had quite a stock of fresh produce and I got to cooking it when we were back in port. For several nights he kept bringing fresh pork fillets for the officers and passengers, and some lamb's liver, heart and kidneys which I made into stew for the crew. Everyone was mighty glad of that, what with us having to return to port and all!"

"Did Mr Clarence happen to say how he brought these aboard, Mr Campbell?"

Campbell had begun to nod even before the question was finished – Blake knew this eagerness to unburden himself was a good indicator that a man was telling the truth.

"Sir, there was some wild rumours flying around to do with Mr Clarence's travelling trunks. Some said they was full of gold, 'cause they were big and heavy. But now I know he was keeping the meat in one of them. Maybe it had ice in it that was making it so heavy? That's all I know about it, sir."

Blake saw Thornthwaite scribbling furiously. "Thank you Mr Campbell. Do you have anything else to say to this inquest?"

Campbell again looked conflicted. "Am I allowed to say anything? I mean, will anyone know I said it?"

Mr Peabody turned on his solicitous charm again. "Mr Campbell, these are closed proceedings. Nothing you say will be published or made known to other witnesses."

Blake shot a look at Thornthwaite who sat unmoving, his intense gaze boring through the back of Campbell's head.

"Sir, if I may, I never saw anyone die. But I know that none of those people would have died if it weren't for the captain. Captain went completely mad."

Blake interrupted. "As Mr Peabody said, we are here to establish facts. Since you state you did not see anyone's death, it is beyond the scope of your statement to make assumptions about their cause. Is that fair?"

Campbell, though somewhat bewildered, thought for a few moments and then seemed to collect himself. The pug-nosed seaman in him refused to be suppressed. "Sirs, I solemnly believe that the captain of the *Irex* was not in his right mind."

Blake listened. "Can you elaborate, Mr Campbell?"

Campbell hesitated, testing the water. "I know that he didn't sleep a good night for maybe two weeks, because I was in the cabin every day, making whatever I could put together. He refused to speak to any of the officers while we were running from the storm, and refused to go into port. Mr Reid told me that much. And he sat outside the lady's room night after night. I saw this with my own eyes."

Peabody interrupted. "The lady? Do you mean—" he shuffled his notes "—Mrs Elizabeth Barstow?"

"That's right sir." He reddened. "Some said Captain was...carrying on with the lady, sir."

Blake seized on this. "You know this? Did someone say it to you? Or was it hearsay?"

Campbell looked more uncomfortable. "No, sir, I just heard the steward say so a few times." He stopped to draw breath. As the pause lengthened, Blake decided that Campbell had probably said his piece.

"Thank you Mr Campbell. You have been most helpful, and your part in these proceedings is now complete. You are excused, with our thanks."

Campbell stood and was led from the desk by the Clerk. Mr Blake called an adjournment until noon.

As the courtroom emptied, he looked askance at Peabody and jutted his chin in the direction of Thornthwaite, who hadn't moved. The lawyer continued his shorthand as the men on the bench watched. Eventually the Clerk stood over him, and he reluctantly put away his pen. He sidestepped out of his seat, and turned to leave when Blake called his name.

"Mr Thornthwaite!"

The younger man turned back. "Sir?"

"Will you approach the bench, please?"

Thornthwaite stepped smartly across the space in front of the desk and stood expectantly, looking directly into Blake's eyes.

"Mr Thornthwaite, when did you receive instructions to attend this inquest?"

The younger man didn't miss a beat. "I was in chambers on Monday when I received a telegram from the Solicitor General's office. It said that there was an inquest on the Isle of Wight which might require the services of an expert in maritime law." The boast fell naturally from his lips.

"Mr Thornthwaite, I am concerned. I have elected to hear testimony in closed proceedings, at the request of the Lord Chancellor."

Thornthwaite didn't flinch at this portentous news. Blake considered that if it could move a hard-bitten reporter like Rennie, it should have had some impression on this louche young barrister. He could only conclude that Thornthwaite already knew.

Blake continued, "I am concerned that information is being leaked outside these proceedings."

To his credit, Thornthwaite expressed concern. "Disgraceful, sir. Do you know the source?"

Blake was unmoved by his unblinking eyes and convincing innocence. "No, Mr Thornthwaite, but I could use an attentive pair of eyes both inside and outside the courtroom. Where are you staying?"

Thornthwaite showed the first stumble in his otherwise smooth performance. His eyes flicked away and back again, a split second too long for a genuine truth. "Sir, I am staying with my aunt – she lives in Sandown. You see, I have an ailing uncle. They moved here three years ago to aid his convalescence."

"I see. Well, Mr Thornthwaite, I would appreciate your vigilance – particularly if you see anyone you recognise from around the court house frequenting the telegraph office on Main Street here in Newport."

Thornthwaite smiled blandly. "Of course, sir. I will provide any assistance I can."

"Very good. We shall reconvene presently." Blake watched the younger man pace from the courtroom.

"Quite the actor, our young barrister," Mr Peabody ventured. "I'm a poorer man if I can't spot a spy when I see one. We need to tread carefully, Mr Blake."

But of course, Blake had already come to this conclusion. "We have an hour, Mr Peabody. Perhaps another visit to the telegraph office is in order."

* * *

Postmaster Rogers' shoulders sagged when he recognised Mr Blake entering the door. He made to hide in his office, but decided to stand his ground as the two visitors crossed the reception area.

Rogers opened the counter to allow the men to pass through, and led them into his small back office. As they closed the door behind them, the postmaster slumped into the chair behind his desk.

"Sirs, your interventions have caused me grave distress," he began, rubbing the bridge of his nose. "It seems there are now three people desirous of subverting Her Majesty's mail from this office. A certain Mr Rennie claims he had your permission to collect a telegram for Mr Rudd. Though I assured him I could not do such a thing, he claimed to be an official of your employ."

The man looked miserable, and Blake could hardly contain his smile as Peabody began to explode with indignation.

"You didn't give it to him, surely! A complete stranger!"

Rogers looked utterly defeated. "After your last visit I had no idea what to think!"

Peabody was gathering himself for another attack when Blake spoke up in his measured tone.

"Thank you Mr Rogers – I believe you acted in good faith and we shall receive the note presently from Mr Rennie, I'm sure."

Peabody looked at him quizzically, but said nothing.

"There is just one thing, and I am sure we shall trouble you no more." This news seemed to both deflate and encourage Rogers at the same time.

Blake dropped his voice, so that the clacking of the telegraph machines outside almost covered it. "The crown servant you mentioned. Can you describe him?"

Mr Rogers, not for the first time, looked torn; he squirmed forward in his seat and let his fingers slide up over his eyes, displacing his spectacles as he sighed deeply. When he straightened he appeared resolved. "Can you promise me sir, that this will be the end of the matter?"

Blake hesitated, letting the tension build. When Rogers began to twitch, he gave a stiff smile. "Yes, Mr Rogers. You have my word."

The postmaster sank back in his seat, and proceeded to give a fairly passable description of Mr Thornthwaite, by Blake's reckoning.

"Thank you, Mr Rogers!" called Peabody over his shoulder as they crossed the reception to the front door. Neither man noticed the wintry chill that assailed them as Blake flung the door open, and they looked up and down the street. A carriage door slammed closed opposite, and the curtain was pulled, concealing whoever was in it. Peabody made to cross the road, but the coach pulled away in some haste, the driver wrapped against the cold with his hat pulled down and a scarf across his face.

Blake coaxed the magistrate back, satisfied that there was nothing more to learn.

"Now, Mr Blake, what on earth was that all about? Who is this Rennie?" Peabody's bluster was fuelled by suppressed indignation.

Blake gave a rare smile, and Peabody couldn't conceal his astonishment as the coroner let a small chuckle escape, his breath misting across his face. "Mr Peabody. Always keep your adversary on the back foot. Never let him find comfort."

Peabody was shaking his head. "What adversary? This Rennie character?"

Blake chuckled again. "We do indeed have an adversary, and I believe it has everything to do with the mysterious Mr Clarence, latterly of the sailing vessel *Irex.*" He looked across at Peabody. "Regarding Mr Rennie, at the close of our business today, I would like it very much if you could join me for tea at the Osborne Hotel."

*   *   *

The Osborne Hotel was one of the better establishments on the island. Blake was impressed that Rennie was afforded the luxury of such accommodations. Perhaps his self-aggrandisement was well-founded.

The wily newspaperman sat opposite them as they enjoyed a very sweet cup of Darjeeling and some daintily-cut sandwiches, accompanied by the ejected clouds from Rennie's cigarettes.

Rennie quickly steered them to the matter at hand without any preamble. "I had a wee chat with our mutual friend the postmaster," he rapped out, the salubrious surroundings doing nothing to temper his quick-fire delivery. "He was surprisingly co-operative!"

Rennie smiled his gap-toothed grin, and reached inside his tweed jacket. He produced the envelope containing the late Mr Rudd's reply from London. "I haven't opened it yet. I thought you gentlemen might like to share in the honour of that?"

Peabody's eyes were flicking from Rennie to Blake and back again, clearly aware he had missed something fundamental between the two men. "What the devil's going on here, Mr Blake? Have you two been designing some sort of conspiracy?"

Blake nodded slightly. "After a fashion, Mr Peabody."

Rennie gave Peabody a wink, then glanced furtively around the restaurant before handing over the thin manila envelope, simply marked "Rudd" in neat handwritten script.

Blake examined the envelope front and back, then took his silver-plated bread knife from the table and slit the envelope open. He took the folded telegram from inside and read it slowly.

++ RUDD STOP ++ MESSAGE RECD STOP ++ PROCEED WITH CARE STOP ++ CHECK HOSPITALS STOP ++ FOSTER STOP ++

He read it again and passed it back to Peabody, who was practically bursting to see it.

"'Check Hospitals'?" the magistrate blurted. "What can he mean by that?"

"I'd say, Mr Blake, your inquest is being fixed, at least as far as Mr Rudd was concerned." Rennie took another puff of his cigarette. "I mean, what was he doing on the bench of this inquiry in the first place?"

Peabody was quick to jump to Rudd's defence. "Mr Rennie, Mr Rudd was a respected member of our Chamber of Commerce and a non-stipendiary magistrate. He was the natural choice to co-chair the enquiry along with myself and the coroner. Not only that, but he was available immediately;

as you know the inquest had some degree of urgency in view of the circumstances."

"Aye, but why him? I'd say it was clear he wasn't working just one angle of the inquiry!"

Blake replied. "It's true, Mr Rennie, that Henry Rudd appeared to have divided loyalties in this inquest, but I'm sure he was not working against us."

"How so?"

"An opportunity presented itself to see the first half of a conversation, the other half of which you hold in your hand."

Rennie's shrewd eyes flicked between Blake and Peabody, though Blake kept his expression neutral.

"Therefore, we can be reasonably certain that Henry Rudd was not seeking to subvert our inquest. He may have been acting to protect it."

Rennie smelt a strong whiff of a story. "Are you gentlemen implying that somebody else is trying to sabotage the inquest?"

Blake removed his glasses, laying them deliberately on the small table next to his fine china saucer. "Yes. I believe that is the case."

Mr Peabody breathed out heavily. He exchanged a look with Blake which Rennie noticed.

"Listen, Mr Blake," the Scot said, "I appreciate the information. But I'm on borrowed time here. Perhaps we can help each other, if you understand what I'm saying." This time, no wink, no grin. Rennie was a newshound, and he had caught a trail.

Blake thought for a few seconds. Then he turned to Peabody. "Mr Peabody, have the Clerk bring our three witnesses to the court house tomorrow at nine o'clock. We will also need two coaches. I should like to conduct a visit to the scene of the wreck and make some further enquiries." He reached out and replaced his glasses. "Also, Mr Rennie, it would be fortuitous if you were to find yourself on the cliffs above Scratchell's Bay around half past ten tomorrow, wouldn't you say? In the meantime, you should take this Dr Foster's advice and check the hospitals. We three shall reconvene here the day after tomorrow."

* * *

That evening, Mr Blake stepped down from Peabody's carriage outside the Orchard Hotel shortly before half-past seven, long after nightfall. The darkness was thick, the air freezing, and above them the whole heaven of stars was visible. A beautiful night threatened a brutal frost the next morning.

Blake paused before walking into the hotel and instead leaned back inside the carriage, where Peabody was wrapping their shared blanket over his knees.

"Stanley." Peabody looked up, having never heard the coroner use his first name before. "Tread carefully. There is more to this affair than we know. Mr Rudd knew it, and his unfortunate accident is something that worries me greatly."

Peabody nodded, a grim set to his mouth. "Yes, Mr Blake. In fact, I entirely agree."

"Mr Peabody, from now on I want you to record everything. I feel certain that something will reveal itself. I also have the feeling that Thornthwaite is connected in some way to the passenger on the *Irex*, this Mr Clarence."

Mr Peabody merely nodded his agreement. Blake backed out into the freezing night, gathered his coat around him, and turned back towards the hotel. He heard Peabody's order to his driver, and the shout to the horse, which slipped once on the icy thoroughfare before finding its traction and drawing the carriage away.

Chapter Five

Greenock
Saturday, 21st December 1889

Thick snow fell. The deck, masts and yards and even the steel cables supported thick mantles of white powder. The glass at the helm station read thirty degrees Fahrenheit, while a chill wind whirled the snow in sudden flurries across the dockside. The water within the depressing confines of the dock slopped greasily against edges of the basin, forming rimes of ice.

Hutton remained in his room, waiting for a window of weather to restart his aborted voyage. For ten days, the ship's company had toiled alongside the Greenock stevedores inside their freezing steel container, restowing the heavy iron piping that had curtailed their maiden voyage.

The steam donkeys, coal-fired engines located forward and amidships, had been run throughout the night to provide some comfort and hot water for the men and passengers. Otherwise, their huddled forms were rarely seen outside the confines of their quarters.

Mackie had continued to post the watches according to the clock and bell. He seemed anxious to regain the trust of his beleaguered captain.

Hutton himself had endured a difficult reception at the Grubb offices after their undignified return to port. It could have been worse, for at least he still held his command of the *Irex*. But his report on the incident was forced to censure Chief Mate Mackie for the loading error. Notifying the man of the negative report was just another painful point on the cheerless voyage so far.

The passengers, to Hutton's astonishment, had elected to stay aboard. They rarely ventured from their cabins, which in the case of Clarence was a blessing. Hutton had seen nothing of the man, whose door remained closed and locked.

One of the man's huge travelling chests had been moved up to the deck, nestled under the quarterdeck companionway, now covered with a generous layer of snow. The trunk remained securely locked with two double-hasps and sturdy padlocks. Through discreet conversation, Hutton had divined that the crew's main rumour about the chest had switched from treasure to fine food.

He had to admit the cook had produced some exceptional meals in the first few days – clearly there was fresh meat from somewhere, and Hutton was inclined to believe that Clarence was the benefactor.

Hutton had seen little of his passengers in the past week; he suspected the unfettered admiration expressed by any of the crew who saw Mrs Barstow had encouraged her reticence. For the first week, Hutton had dined with the passengers in the saloon. Their conversations varied, but Clarence had been determined to regale them with his opinions about the 'new science'. After one such lecture, he earned a forthright rebuke from Mrs Barstow, who declared the God-given sanctity of life in such uncompromising terms that even Clarence backed off, bemused. The exchange suggested she possessed a formidable character, and would make short work of any lecherous seaman's ill-advised attention.

In the meantime, Major Barstow had contracted a heavy cold, so the husband and wife continued to take meals in their room. Hutton elected to eat with the other officers rather than share the table with Clarence alone.

Hutton had made several late night patrols of the cabin deck, mostly from idle curiosity. He found himself hovering outside the stateroom doors, and heard occasional racking coughs from the Barstows (Major Barstow, of course) and Mrs Barstow's soft, low voice offering soothing words of comfort; occasionally through the day there came the silky sound of her singing, accompanied by an accordion of some sort.

But from Clarence's quarters, there had been nothing at all. His lamp appeared to be lit for most of the night, and once Hutton heard what sounded like drunken humming. He satisfied himself with the belief that Clarence was a broken drunk, expelled from a prestigious regimental position somewhere and sent in disgrace to the Tropics to either dry out or succumb to his weaknesses. This thought gave him comfort.

He longed for a touch of good fortune, but despite his heartfelt prayers, and those he knew Sarah was offering at home, God was not easily bent to the will of man.

Hutton was a man of "good Christian character" – that highly valued middle-class combination of status, charity and sober reserve. He and Sarah shared a much greater commitment to the Christian religion than the conventional piety of the times; Hutton had been ordained as a lay minister in the Baptist tradition for several years, while his wife believed in the Almighty God and her Saviour with a special, personal fervour.

He tried to mark Greenwich Time midnight each day on his travels. He knew it was when Sarah would be praying for his safe passage and courage in the face of challenge. This was difficult in practice, as midnight in Glasgow was six a.m. in Bombay, four p.m. in San Francisco and midday in Sydney. Yet here he was, barely six miles from home, while Sarah probably imagined him well on his way to Rio.

More than once, he had considered leaving Mackie in charge so he could jump on a train and receive the comfort he needed in Sarah's arms within the hour. However, he felt it was his duty to be available for his crew and passengers until the *Irex* was ready to sail.

The midnight bells sounded, and the footsteps of listless men clumped across the snow-covered deck. Hutton emerged from his room, and stood outside the cabin door, the cold finding every tiny gap in his clothing. He watched as the muffled forms moved to meet their counterparts emerging from the forecastle hatch, their breath puffing from them like steam engines, while indistinct conversations exchanged relevant information. He spotted the erect figure of Bosun Hanson, with his characteristic jutting chin and rough hands thrust in his pockets, conferring with the slight form of Durrick as the smaller man pointed at various parts of the ship and rigging. They stood out starkly as black silhouettes against the luminescent cover of snow. Hutton watched until the last figures retreated down the forecastle steps before quietly closing the door, and retreating to his bunk.

* * *

Hutton awoke to the ringing of the four o'clock bells as the morning watch stood to. It had stopped snowing, and a light breeze lifted small wisps of the stuff where it had settled on the tops of the deckhouses and the covered helm station. Occasional clumps dropped from the yards high above, creating a new, unwelcome hazard.

It was midwinter on the Clyde, so it wouldn't get light before eight a.m. As he emerged from his cabin pulling his greatcoat tight Hutton noticed, for the first time in almost a month, the pinpricks of stars.

He quickly located Mackie in the helm station, arching his bulk under the covering. Mackie gave a small wave with his ham-like hand, and Hutton climbed the snow-covered steps, careful not to touch his bare palm on the icy railing.

"Morning, Captain!" Mackie's rumbled his greeting with his deep voice and clipped Glasgow vowels.

"Morning, Andrew. I dare believe we may have a chance to escape today."

Mackie had also marked the break in the overcast, and was keen to agree. "Aye, Captain. We're ready, sir."

"Very well. When the men assemble for the lime-juice ration at eight bells, I'll let them know."

Mackie nodded, the movement obscured by his layers of clothing and thick scarf.

Hutton went to see if Campbell the cook had fetched tea. As he approached the galley deckhouse, he could already smell the hot beverage in the galley – coffee, or what passed for it on board ship. Campbell was preparing Sunday breakfast for the officers and the passengers.

A few hours later, the sky was beginning to lighten as the men began to assemble for their lime juice ration. The entire crew received the traditional mandated measure of dilute lime juice, toted as proof against scurvy but inferior in all respects to lemon juice. As it was cheaper than lemon juice, it was acceptable to the shipping lines. In ports like Boston and New York, the tall ships from England were nicknamed 'lime-juicers' owing to this quaint regulation – their sailors were consequently dubbed 'limeys'.

It was Durrick's job to administer the ration. It was an egalitarian exercise, with the men receiving theirs before the officers, a tradition picked up from the Navy during those days when the ration was rum. Hutton was last to take his draught of sour juice, and nodded to Mackie in preparation to address the crew.

As he mounted the steps to the quarterdeck, the grey dawn began to break into a watery sunlight and the miraculous occurred – the sun's rays penetrated the wispy cloud cover for the first time in weeks and Hutton felt the warmth of its presence.

The snow covered deck came alive, brightly reflecting the blinding radiance the men had not seen for so long. Everyone squinted in surprise while the sun turned their steam breath into glowing clouds. The captain faced them from the quarterdeck, a silhouette limned by the diffusion of light behind him like a bearded Madonna from a defaced medieval fresco.

Hutton seized the moment with a genuine chuckle. "Men!"

Heads craned toward him with hands shielding their eyes and their caps pulled forward.

"It's about time we sailed for Rio!"

There was a hearty cheer from the three dozen grinning faces arrayed before him.

"If God smiles on us in the matter of a tug and dock crew by four bells, we'll sail on the falling tide this day!"

This time caps were raised in their acclamation; even the sullen bosun cracked a smile. John Reid clapped his hands, beaming as Durrick's pale face shared his grin. Tension seemed to rise off the gathered men like the steaming condensation of the snow from the ship, wherever it was touched by the kiss of sunlight.

"To Rio, boys!" repeated Hutton, spreading his arms to further cheering.

Mackie leaned over to Hutton and quietly reminded him it was a Sunday. Hutton thanked him.

"Men, I will lead a service of devotion at ten o'clock. There will be thanksgiving for this stroke of mercy. We will gather in the saloon, and I request our musicians to join me in leading the hymns." Unlike many captains, Hutton did not enforce religious observance; he had learned to choose his faith for himself, and believed that forcible compulsion bred only contempt. He was not surprised there were no cheers to greet this news, but the mood had tangibly brightened.

The bosun stepped forward at this point. Bosun Frank Hanson was a gruff man who more than once had tested Hutton's patience with his second-guessing and unsolicited opinions during their planning of the past two weeks. Worse, he gave off the unmistakeable aura of the sea-bully – short on patience and a little too quick to raise his hands when berating an errant seaman.

He was about to make an address of his own when a hefty snowball impacted the side of his neck. There was stunned silence for a second, before uproarious laughter engulfed the assembly.

Hutton knew immediately one of the apprentices was responsible; the youngsters were the butt of all the bullying and ribaldry among the roughnecks of the forecastle, but they were not afraid of striking back wherever they could.

The bosun looked up towards the assembled officers, and Hutton unexpectedly saw a flash of genuine anger, even hatred, in his eyes. Hanson was unpopular among the men, as bullies often are. The vicarious revenge of a solitary snowball seemed to serve a justice of its own for the whole company.

"Carry on, Bosun!" called Mackie in his granite voice, and Hutton could hear the smile in his voice.

It was a cue for the entire ship's company to erupt into a full snowball battle. Snow flew, while shouts, cat-calls and the choicest sailors' language traded with the thumps of snow hitting ship and person alike.

The officers enjoyed the spectacle from above, until a few balls began landing around the quarterdeck area. Hutton stepped back as one flew past his chest and hit Mackie on his meaty shoulder. The mate brushed it off before scooping an armful of snow from the roof over the helm position and mashing it into a formidable projectile, which he hefted in his huge right hand. Picking his moment, he launched it like a catapult, just as the miscreant apprentice peeped from behind the mizzen mast. The giant snowball met the lad with a muffled smack full in the face, snapping his head back and causing him to fall to the deck in a pile of gangling arms and legs.

Hutton roared with laughter. "A fine shot Mr Mackie!" He gripped the mate's huge forearm and squeezed it, smiling.

Mackie grinned broadly, his gappy teeth prominent in the sunlight. "Thank you Captain!"

The battered apprentice pulled himself up off the now sodden deck, breath heaving in billowing clouds in the sunshine. Elsewhere on deck, the men were wrestling, chasing each other down and stuffing snow and icy water down one another's necks and waistbands.

Thank God, thought Hutton. The malaise had been broken.

As if on cue, a loud whistle blast cut across the mayhem as Second Mate Durrick called the deck to order. The men, still laughing and jostling one another, began to gather again, their watch leaders mingling among them to assign duties in preparation for departure. The reminders went out for the ten o'clock service, and the sun continued to climb into a clearing blue sky, the breeze adequate for sailing but threatening no more than the occasional gust. Hutton felt his heart lift at last.

* * *

The clear conditions brought a convulsion of activity across the entire dockside. Several ships around them were beginning their preparations, and Hutton saw many men aloft among the high-slung yards of the ships filling the Victoria Dock. High above him he saw Colquhoun, the sailmaker, edging along the *Irex*'s vast lower yards with several of the men, among them the apprentice brained by Mackie's cannonball.

As he stepped across the deck, he saw the gangway was already set on the dockside. He assumed Hanson had done this. Hutton felt a new pang of unease, as the ship could have been left insecure.

As soon as his gaze fell to the dock, he found himself face-to-face with their esteemed passenger, Mr Clarence. He was standing on the dockside waiting to board the ship, smoking with an air of nonchalance as if he hadn't a care in the world.

"Mr Clarence! What on earth are you doing ashore?" Hutton's indignation bristled as he marched down the gangway toward the waiting gentleman.

"Ah, Captain!" boomed the taller man. "Life was getting a little tedious, so I decided to avail myself of some of the local hospitality!" He winked theatrically.

"Mr Clarence! You may not disembark the ship without my permission. We are still under customs restrictions. When did you leave?"

Clarence looked down at Hutton with his large almond eyes, their pale blue irises almost alight in the sunshine.

"My dear Captain. I simply asked Mr Hanson there last night, and he had the gangway lowered for me." He explained this as though he had asked for nothing more than a light for his cigarette.

Hutton was astounded. "Hanson just did it? He has no authority—"

"Captain Hutton." Clarence interrupted, fumbling at his trouser pocket to retrieve something. "Believe me, I have no more need of a Boatswain's permission than I have fear of a customs agent."

He brought forward a small postcard, printed on an expensive weave with an embossed crest and some tight, copperplate print. Hutton took it and held the card up to read.

"To Whom it may Concern,
The bearer of this card, Mr Ed. Clarence, is Our Most
Trusted Friend and Worthy Citizen of the Empire of Great
Britain.
Please afford the Bearer every Courtesy, allowing Him to
pass freely and without Hindrance, Malice or Restriction, at
the pleasure of Her Britannic Majesty Queen Victoria.
Signed
Edward, Prince of Wales"

Hutton almost dropped the card in astonishment. The power of the great institutions of the British Empire crushed him to impotence. He could only imagine how Hanson had felt.

After a few moments of silence he noticed Clarence's sympathetic gaze upon him. "I assume then, Mr Clarence, that you instructed Mr Hanson not to disturb me in making such a request."

Clarence beamed. "There you are, Captain!" He added in a stage whisper. "Can't have too many people making a fuss, can we?"

The blatant undermining of his authority injured him. "Mr Clarence, I must ask you never to do such a thing again. These men are my crew. This is my ship. You must not ask them to break the chain of authority aboard this vessel. Our lives, including yours, depend on it."

This protest sounded lame to Hutton, even as he said it. The man before him had a carte blanche from the bloody *Prince of Wales* to conduct himself exactly as he pleased.

Clarence's smile grew more pronounced. "Well, Captain, now we've had this little chat, I should be more circumspect in my dealings with the common men." He sniffed, and looked up the gangway once more.

By such a trifling gesture, Hutton realised, crestfallen, that he had been dismissed. "Thank you for your understanding, Mr Clarence."

As the man strode sure-footedly up the gangway, Hutton felt something akin to shame; and realised he had been subtly usurped as master of the voyage. The dangerous question now was Hanson. Hutton had mistaken the bosun's sullen demeanour as aloofness; he now realised, possibly too late, that it was disdain.

* * *

The fifteen men gathering for the church service in the saloon provided a constant buzz of light conversation that accompanied the scrape and creak of saloon chairs arranged beneath the large skylight roof. A generous dose of sunlight penetrated the only part of the ship that was furnished for guests.

Mackie and Durrick sat to one side; one a convinced Presbyterian, the other a staunch Catholic. Had it not been for their profession, neither would have found themselves sitting in a church together, according to the sectarian divisions in their native Glasgow. Hutton, himself of the Baptist persuasion, remained bemused by the deep and vitriolic rivalries of his adopted city; however, he was keen to tread only the common ground held by the various sects.

He prepared his page in a well-worn bible to read from a psalm, which he hoped would buoy up the rising mood of those gathered. Behind Hutton, the *Irex*'s trio of musicians

73

tried to tune fiddle, mouth organ and accordion into some rendition of well-known hymns; the three men were better known for their ribald shanties and popular songs in the forecastle and half-deck.

As the minutes ticked up to ten o'clock, Hutton heard laboured steps and heavy breathing coming from the saloon companionway. He was both astonished and heartened in quick succession to see George Barstow coming down the steps.

The major leaned heavily on the arm of his wife, who showed signs of weariness. She supported him as they laboured around the bend in the staircase; Hutton noted that she also carried a heavy piano accordion strapped backwards across her shoulders. He instinctively moved towards the couple to help, but Mrs Barstow gave him one of her tight smiles, and with a simple "We can manage, Captain," ushered her wheezing husband into one of the nearby chairs next to the two officers. She greeted the men with a politeness they didn't earn as they ogled her surreptitiously or, in some cases, brazenly.

The Barstows' arrival quietened the room and every eye watched as Mrs Barstow sidled up to the three musicians, and requested to join them in leading the music. Dick Stearne, the lively and affable fiddle player, immediately agreed, while the other two remained coy.

Mrs Barstow arched her back as she hefted the accordion from her shoulders with practiced ease, then strapped it back across her bosom almost in one movement, bringing delight to the watchers. So much for the *Irex*'s men of good Christian character, thought Hutton, who was as transfixed as the others.

He couldn't help being drawn to the striking woman in the Salvation Army uniform. He recalled the general frumpiness of most women's Sunday attire - the sartorial objective of the churchgoing classes seemed to be to present as little of themselves as possible to public scrutiny - but this wild, new sect of Christianity seemed to be oblivious. Mrs Barstow's uniform nipped tightly to her waist, and the skirts stopped daringly short below her knees. The tunic was also very snug around her upper body and shoulders, accentuating the generous curves, and stayed close-fitting all the way to her cuffs. She wore no gloves, and her small, fine-fingered hands were exposed to better reach the keys on her piano accordion. Hutton noticed long, well-tended nails which danced expertly across the maze of keys as she bellowed the instrument. Even her hair was combed high into a fashionable bun, revealing ears studded with small gold earrings.

Hutton realised he could feel the colour rising in his cheeks, so he tore his gaze back to the gathering, only to find that not a single eye was looking anywhere but at the tight cluster of musicians to his left. He cleared his throat, stepping forward, and the meeting settled down apart from the shifting of a few chairs and the occasional coughs of the overlooked Mr Barstow.

Hutton asked for a few hymns to begin the service, and the musicians obliged, all but led by the animated Mrs Barstow. The men, whom the previous Sunday had sung in desultory fashion, seemed to have found a new voice, and began to belt out the words at a lustier volume. The singing swelled with each successive hymn, the words flowing from memory, helped in part by Mrs Barstow's strong contralto voice. As he sang with them, Hutton's spirits soared, and he considered the extraordinary turnaround of their fortunes.

As the last chord ended, Hutton rose to read an uplifting passage about triumphing over enemies who would put the righteous to shame. He found within himself a strong voice, and noted with satisfaction that at least ten more men of the crew had descended from the deck and stood at the periphery of the assembly. He looked across the faces and held their eyes. He felt his own vigour returning, and led a prayer of thanksgiving before the meeting ended with another rousing hymn led by the mesmerising Mrs Barstow.

As the men thanked her and the other musicians, Hutton went and sat in the now vacant seat next to Major Barstow. The man had aged in the ten days Hutton had known him. Before the captain had even opened his mouth, the man Barstow spoke in a dry but clear voice.

"She is as noble as she is beautiful, you know."

Hutton was stumped for an answer, unsure whether to agree for fear of betraying his own feelings.

Barstow turned his watery eyes towards Hutton. "I know, you're wondering how we met. Well, everyone does, lad! We've been married but three years, and I still have to convince people she is my wife and not my daughter. Ha! Yes, I'm familiar with that look, Captain. There are only sixteen years between us, you know. Truth be told, I am not a well man. I convinced this fine young woman that we should travel to the southern climes for my own convalescence. But she would not hear of India, for it is a place of desperate injustice against the indigent people. So we shall join our brothers and sisters in the South American continent."

He paused to cough again, holding a very weathered handkerchief in front of his mouth. "We met in the missions of Liverpool. Elizabeth is from a fine family, and a great Christian heart beats inside her. She is a marvellous nurse, and could have worked in the greatest hospitals of London, but instead she has poured out her life to help those in need, the very dregs of society. If there is an outcast, Elizabeth will draw them in.

"Yet she rejected many wealthy suitors, and her family, God bless them, have never put burdens of responsibility or duty upon her. Ever since she joined the Movement, she has been embraced as a gifted leader and teacher, filled with the fire of the Holy Spirit!"

Hutton had involuntarily retreated a few inches as Barstow reached this crescendo. This fervency was of an order he had not experienced. He was glad that his other officers had not borne witness to this extremism. Even the most hard-bitten sea dogs were tolerant of the religious, but fanatical proselytes were given no quarter.

"Ha! I've scared you off, haven't I?" Despite the battery of deep coughs this diatribe had induced, Barstow recovered to catch Hutton with a mischievous look, a genuine twinkle in his eye. The coughing had attracted the attention of his wife, who broke away from her small crowd of admirers, heaving the piano accordion over to the seats. She took her husband's hand in hers and asked if he was all right.

"Thank you my darling. Yes, I'm fine; I was satisfying the Captain's curiosity about our presence here."

The lady took the seat on the other side of Hutton, who sat back in his chair to better accommodate conversation.

"Captain, did George tell you about our work?" she asked brightly. Her pale green eyes rested on Hutton's, while her smile revealed fine, even teeth in a wide, sensual mouth. Her face seemed to radiate light.

Major Barstow chuckled, precipitating another bout of coughing. "No, dear, I didn't regale the captain with any such thing, other than your own selfless work among the poor and downtrodden."

His wife pulled a face, "Oh, come, Captain, I am merely exercising the gift I have been given. I can take no credit for how I was created to be. I can only give glory to God that he caused me to realise my purpose in life." She paused, looking intensely at Hutton, who was fascinated by her confident delivery. He wasn't sure he had ever heard a woman speaking like this: open, heartfelt and with a strength and confidence of opinion which was the equal of any man.

"Captain, God has given each of us a role to play. We are not set adrift in life to seek out our own way." She pointed up through the broad skylight at the extraordinary weave of lines and masts that crisscrossed above their heads. "Look at your ship, Captain." Hutton warmed inside at the way she referred to it. "To most people it looks like a mess of ropes and masts. Yet I know not one strand of rope has been placed without purpose, and I would wager if any one of them were missing, it would put an unacceptable strain on its neighbour. Am I right?" She arched her fine brows, and a network of lines spread across her forehead.

Hutton found himself staring again. "Indeed. You have a firm grasp of seamanship, madam!"

"Thank you. Well, Captain, we are all like those ropes. We are all called and appointed with gifts that we use for one another, so that the whole may benefit. But then" – she smoothed her skirt across her lap and stood up – "not everyone accepts their part in the grand play. That is why some of us must work a little harder." She looked across at her husband. "This sunshine might do you some good, George! Shall I see you again outside?"

The man nodded. "If it's all right with the captain?"

Hutton was expansive in his approval. "By all means, Mr Barstow! Never mind the men, they'll be preparing for sail but you will be fine if you remain in the vicinity of the quarterdeck. I'm very pleased that we will finally be on our way, as I'm sure you are."

Mrs Barstow had retrieved her piano accordion once more and was heaving it upon her shoulders again. This time she let Hutton take the weight as she shuffled on the straps, and with a brief "Thank you, Captain," strode off in her high boots towards the saloon steps, through the bright squares of sunlight that poured through the skylight windows. As she passed through each one, she left a fine spray of particles in her wake that swirled in the sunbeams. The men watched her ascend the steps until she disappeared out of sight.

Barstow turned his yellowed eyes back to Hutton. "She speaks for herself, Captain. In the Salvation Army, our women are as respected and valued as our men. They lead, they speak, they debate and, God knows, they are as bright and dependable as any man alive. In Elizabeth's case, more so. You should listen to her; she will tell you things you need to know. She has that gift, too."

Hutton considered the flutter in his chest he felt at that moment, and resolved that he would do himself and his marriage a good turn if he avoided further opportunities to listen to the fiery Salvation Army woman.

"Mr Barstow, I am indebted to you both for attending this morning. You brought something new that lifted us all."

Barstow gave him a serious look. "That, sir, is what our Movement is all about. It is the presence of the Holy Spirit." He fell quiet, staring at his hands which he clasped together on his lap.

Hutton looked away, uncomfortable again with these strident declarations.

When Barstow looked up again, his eyes brimmed with tears. His voice this time was almost inaudible, barely a whisper. "Do you know, Captain, I thank God every day that among all the fine men in the world she could have had, she chose a poor old wretch like me."

Hutton squirmed with internal conflict. He felt compassion and even warmth for this humble and agreeable man, but beneath rumbled a restless envy.

Barstow's whisper almost trailed off. "If that is not the living embodiment of God's grace, then there is none left in this world. None at all."

As Hutton made his excuses and left the man to muse alone, he felt uncomfortable once more. Despite the positive effect on his humour and self-confidence the end result of his conversations had been a creeping feeling of guilt. He was afraid of becoming enamoured of Mrs Barstow, and knew he needed to bury those feelings. He prayed forgiveness for his masculine weakness, hoping the distraction would be short-lived; he had pressing matters of sailing to contend with, and absence of mind was one thing he could not afford.

Chapter Six

North Channel
Sunday, 22nd December 1889

The departure was an anti-climax. With the luxury of two steam tugs to depart the dock, the *Irex* came smartly away, and was released four hours later, well clear of the Cumbrae islands with a cheery "Godspeed!" from the lead tugboat.

Earlier, Clarence had been an irritating presence throughout their departure, just as he had been two weeks before. To Hutton's relief, the man had returned to his room without a word. He hoped Clarence would skulk at the bottom of a bottle for the duration.

With full sail set, the *Irex* stretched before a freshening north-westerly breeze, cutting her prow through the choppy waves which broke over the deck. The sun had set, the last crimson fires of its passing cut through by the long slashes of cloud at the horizon that heralded the approach of another weather front.

Hutton stood by the helmsman Morgan under cover of the helm position, feeling at last the roll of the ship before the wind at last. The thermometer peaked that afternoon at a relatively balmy 42 degrees.

In the lull his thoughts crept back towards Mrs Barstow. He recalled his conversation that morning: *some of us must work a little harder*. He again banished her from his mind, having noticed a tendency to linger when she surfaced in his thoughts. He tried instead to think of his wife, comfortable in their tidy, warm home, before chasing her away in turn as he tried to concentrate on the voyage to come

.

* * *

The *Irex* ploughed on, her prow cleaving the seas ahead, sending twin plumes of spray to each side at every plunge. The wind took up the spray and showered it in gusty deluges across the deck. She was doing her Clydebuilt heritage proud; the main cargo hatch was firmly sealed, the cargo was secure, and the sea was being kept out of the accommodations so far. It cheered Hutton to know his ship was showing good character so far.

Approaching midnight the winds increased further. The sea was rough, the spray hissing through the air at every crash of the waves – the wind came from north of west and waves were breaking over the quarterdeck and drenching the steering crew.

Hutton had remained on deck, keen to weather his ship's first storm and get a firm grasp on her handling characteristics.

Durrick was the watch officer and tucked himself inside the open-sided helm position. Helmsman Morgan had been relieved by George Brown from the other watch. Brown was another hearty, able-bodied Scot with saltwater in his veins.

He had helmed other ships, but was cursing in his choicest sailor's tongue at the effort required to hold the *Irex* in trim.

"She's wallowing like a bloody whale, Captain!" he yelled over the rush of waves and the wind that whistled through the lines with each gust. His sou'wester had slipped to a comical angle, so that only half his red-bearded face and one eye were visible to Hutton. "If we're going to keep running ahead of this wind, the waves are going to be pooping us soon!" In their exposed position, the waves breaching over the stern would submerge the hapless helmsman and anyone unlucky enough to be near him. The sea respected no man.

Hutton remembered an old adage of the sea: never take anything aboard a ship you can't afford to lose. He had once served as second mate aboard a clipper that had run into a fearsome storm rounding the Cape of Good Hope; the entire crew and all eleven passengers had ended up taking refuge in the rigging high above the deck, watching as the raging waves completely cleaned out the cabins, forecastle and saloon of everything they owned.

This memory jogged another thought for Hutton – Clarence's enormous trunk had been stowed loose on the deck under the quarterdeck companionway. He left the deluge which was now spewing over the transom and leaned forward to peer over the edge of the quarterdeck rail. The trunk was still tucked into the corner, but was shifting as the waves breaching over the deck buffeted it.

Hutton needed to gather a work party to deal with this problem. The bosun had put in eight hours of hard sailing since they left Greenock, and was getting his rest before picking up the watch again at four in the morning. His deputy,

Bosun's Mate James Murray, should have been filling in, but Hutton hadn't seen him.

He leaned in towards Durrick, shouting to be heard above the rushing of the waves and keening winds. "Bob, where is Mr Murray?"

Durrick frowned at the question. He called back loudly, though he was just two feet away. "Sir, I sent him forward to strike the jibs. He's probably still there."

"Very good, Bob. Wait here. I need to fetch him."

Hutton descended to the main deck, sloshing through the spreading pools of water. He ducked inside the cabin and lit a kerosene lamp, which he took out into the gale. The door slammed tight behind him, and his immediate surroundings were bathed in the ghostly white light from the lantern. Only now could he see the fine mist of spray that was constantly blowing around him, and the showers of droplets that glinted in their passage across the light's beam.

He kept one hand on the lifeline that ran along the full length of the deck and squinted through the spray and rain for a sight of the men still wrestling with the jib sails. The ship pitched and heaved, the wind now whistling through the wires and stays overhead like a tuneless pipe organ.

As he pressed forward he could make out the pinpricks of two more kerosene lamps far ahead, occasionally obscured by the mountains of spume that arched up at each pitch of the bow. He could feel the shock of each impact under his feet. With each step he received another generous soaking in salt water as the wind ripped it back from the bow and flung it into his face. He thanked God the lamp was still burning brightly; half-blinded by spray he could easily have fallen or even pitched over the side.

As he came closer to the bow, the water running over the deck was washing up to his knees at times, while his booted feet were completely submerged. He saw the lights ahead moving and swinging, occasionally masked by the bodies holding them as they tried to provide light for the men heaving on the lines. The men were trying to strike two of the jibs down while tightening the one furthest forward.

Hutton identified the busy figure of Bosun's Mate Murray urging the men on. They were almost finished.

Hutton was surprised to make out the sailmaker, crusty old Colquhoun, admonishing the men to fold the sail to his satisfaction. With the sailmaker present, Hutton felt he could take the bosun's mate from the scene, especially for such a trivial matter as an unstowed travelling chest.

He had to get within a foot of the man to be heard. The wind and waves were rising in ferocity, and here at the front the pitching of the ship was setting off great roars of spray as it ploughed head first into the waves. Overhead, the sails clapped with a papery crackling as the men folded them, battling with the wind for control.

"How goes it Mr Murray?" Hutton's voice was a shouted monotone.

Murray turned, his face white and stark in the kerosene lamp's brightness. He was soaked to the bone and the pupils of his watery blue eyes shrank to pinpoints as he faced Hutton's lamp.

"Aye, we're almost finished, Cap'n," he yelled back. Murray's cheekbones dripped with spray, the gaunt cheeks beneath them peppered with greying stubble. He must have been almost Hutton's age, an old hand from the tea clipper days, but the purplish-hued network of fine veins that stood

85

out on his nose and cheeks in the unforgiving light told their own story of a man who had battled drink for too many years. Still, it would be hard to imagine a better seaman.

Hutton put his mouth close to Murray's face to shout again. "I need you to come aft with one of the apprentices, Jim. There's a loose crate on deck that should have been stowed."

Murray looked puzzled, but turned to tap one of the smaller figures still holding the jib halliard as two other shapeless men tied it off to a belay. "Hey, laddie!"

He grabbed and shook the boy's shoulder. The apprentice turned to present as miserable a face as Hutton had ever seen, such a hangdog look that he burst into laughter in spite of himself.

Murray joined in and ruffled the boy's sou'wester-clad head. "C'mon lad, Captain has a nice light duty for ye. Might even get you back below before end of watch, eh?"

He turned round to Colquhoun and bellowed. "Billy! I'm headed aft with the Cap'n. Get the boys in when you're done."

Colquhoun nodded, barely a dip of his sou'wester, and Murray grabbed the boy's arm and placed his hand firmly on the lifeline. "One for the ship and one for me, right lad?"

The boy dumbly complied, and remained mute, stumbling all the way back to the aft end.

The walk was slow, the ship shifting and heaving as waves broke fully side on against the beam of the ship, falling across the three men like a cold, wet blanket at every roll. By the time they had staggered through the gauntlet of pile-driven water, they were deaf and blind from the pummelling.

They stood dripping in the sheltered corner of the quarterdeck rise next to the large chest. Hutton remembered how it took the efforts of four boys to heft it aboard two weeks ago. He suspected the riddle of its contents had resolved itself – no-one had eaten fresh meat for a good five or six days, so Clarence's largesse must have run its course.

He then lit upon a mischievous idea – it would be a legitimate excuse to disturb the smug man with the Royal Appointment card, as his wretched trunk posed a genuine seamanship problem which Hutton was required to solve tonight.

"Jim, wait here with...." He looked at the boy, who took several seconds to realise he was being addressed.

"Bonner, sir."

"Very good. Bonner, wait here with the Bosun's Mate – I will speak to Mr Clarence to make sure he is ready to take delivery of his property." He smiled, a gesture received in good humour by the bosun's mate but completely lost on the shivering boy.

Hutton entered the cabin to find it deserted. It was dimly lit by orange-tinted oil lamps that had been turned down by the night watch. The carpet-covered linoleum floor was wet but not soaked through. Hutton marvelled at the relative quiet inside. The wind was just an occasional whine, the waves merely rolling thuds like distant thunder. The rain still rattled at the skylight above his head, but the shelter was a great comfort.

The rooms were quiet. He paused, as he usually did, when he passed the Barstows' cabin on the left. This time there was silence, save the dull thumping of the waves on the steel sides of the ship. There was no light from beneath the door.

Hutton's feet squished across the carpet to the corner door, where Clarence had his double-size stateroom, the mirror of his own. Hutton felt aggrieved that the man had obtained such a favour, even before he had flashed the Royal calling card. He cursed the way he had allowed Clarence to so easily assert his superiority. Perhaps Hutton now had a chance to do some asserting of his own.

He stepped to the door and raised his knuckles to knock, but the light escaping beneath the door was blocked by a large shadow and he heard the bolt draw.

Clarence cracked open the door, recognised Hutton and opened it wide. Hutton couldn't see whole room but did notice it was strewn with clothing. There was a journal of some kind open on the table with a single lamp. But Hutton's attention was frozen on the man in front of him.

Clarence stood in the doorway and made no indication of inviting Hutton inside. He was stripped to the waist, with only his underclothing below.

Hutton was stunned by the man's physical appearance – he looked like an anatomist's model. His torso was perfectly delineated with symmetrical curves and ridges of muscle. His stout neck merged with strong collarbones into a tightly-muscled chest. His broad shoulders were well-defined and his muscular upper arms seemed to slot into them like those of a wooden mannequin. Hutton was staring again, and tried to rest his gaze on the man's pale-blue eyes.

"Well, well, Captain Hutton. To what do I owe this rather untimely visit?" His lips parted slightly with impatience, before clamping together, his jaw muscles working causing his neat beard to ripple like dark gills along his jawline.

"Mr Clarence, I'm sorry to disturb you at this hour. You can see we've hit some rough weather, and we need to strike your sea chest below as it is unsecured on deck."

Clarence stood a few seconds, unblinking. "Captain, I'd rather hoped it would have already washed overboard. I don't need, it and you can throw it over the side for all I care."

Hutton couldn't mask his surprise. "But what about the customs declaration—"

"I have already demonstrated, Captain, that such things are of no consequence to me. Now, if you would kindly dispose of it, we shall hear no more of the matter."

"Mr Clarence, I must insist – I need to know the contents for the voyage log. Maritime Law requires me to make declarations for all losses, especially if they are on the customs declaration..."

Clarence actually bristled. "Listen to me, *Captain* Hutton. There is nothing left in that trunk, and you and the others have had some very useful supplements to your plain fare from my own pocket. Consider it a favour. Now please see to the matter, and try to leave me alone."

As Clarence closed and locked the door, Hutton lingered for a few moments. It wasn't until Clarence's curt "Good day, Captain!" from behind the door that he trudged away.

He forced the deck door open against the wind, and sheets of spray assaulted him once more. It was still dark but he saw Third Mate Reid emerge from the other door from the cabin, bracing himself against the whirling gusts that whipped around him. The bosun was back up on deck, conferring with Murray, as the wretched lad Bonner still stood shivering, looking frail and insubstantial in oversized oilskins.

Murray looked up and the bosun turned to face Hutton, his usual flat line of a mouth the closest he ever came to smiling.

"Morning, Captain."

The man came across as sardonic even when he was trying to be civil. In any case, the words were whipped out of his mouth by the stinging wind and Hutton heard only the rattle of the spray against his sou'wester.

Hanson was yelling again. "The mercury's been rising since three o'clock; we should be out of this one by morning with any luck."

Hutton was leaning in close enough to hear the last part. "Very good, Bosun," he yelled back. "Mr Hanson, I need to know if there any men who are good with locks."

The bosun looked back, puzzled.

Hutton exasperated, pressed on. "Padlocks! Or at least, good with a crowbar!"

Hanson shrugged. "Andersson's bloody good with an axe, Captain!"

Hutton knew he meant Tor Andersson, the ship's Norwegian carpenter. "Then fetch him aft. I need to know what's in that chest." He indicated the large square chest with the double hasps under the quarterdeck companionway.

Hanson looked alarmed when he spun back to face Hutton. "Captain, that's—"

"I know whose it is! I also know I'm not going to have it sent overboard without knowing what's in it."

The bosun seemed to measure this as the wind buffeted the small group huddled in the lee of the quarterdeck. "Did Mr Clarence say we could jettison it?"

Oh, Mr Clarence to you is he, Bosun? Good friends already, it seems. Hutton remembered the incident of Clarence's unauthorised trip ashore. He wondered how many other favours Clarence had bought through his charm, influence and further largesse.

"Yes, though that is none of your concern, Mr Hanson."

The bosun seemed to relax at this. "Aye, Captain. I'll fetch him back here now." He pulled his sou'wester straight and marched off into the darkness, grasping the lifeline hand over hand like he was taking a stroll in the park in May, rather than wading the treacherous, heaving deck of a storm-tossed ship.

Hutton turned back to the bosun's mate and the shivering boy. "Let's get this chest into some space. With me, lads!"

They slid the chest over the waterlogged deck into the space by the cabin door. Hutton examined the locks by the light of his lamp and realised there were several holes drilled into the sides of the chest around the upper faces. Each hole was about half an inch in diameter and concealed by the same red fabric that covered the rest of the trunk. They would be invisible from all but the closest inspection. He elected not to point this out to his two companions, but wondered what possibilities it suggested.

Hutton hung his lamp on one of the hooks on the quarterdeck wall. The three men stood over the trunk without speaking, the lad still shivering. The wind still felt keen, and as he waited, Hutton began to register that he was feeling cold. His toes already felt numbed, insensitive to movement inside the felt lined boots; his fingers too were retracting, claw-like, into his fists when he wasn't actively using them. No wonder the slight youngster was shivering.

"Not long now, lad," Hutton encouraged. "We'll get this thing open and over the side, and you can get yourself below." The boy merely nodded, oblivious to the thick dribble of moisture running from his nose.

Presently he spotted the bobbing of a lamp moving towards them from the darkness amidships – Hutton recognised the indistinct silhouette of Third Mate Reid with a taller, broad-shouldered man close behind. They laboured through the rushing water, and Hutton saw the third mate's ruddy face in the light as they reached the quarterdeck.

"Home Help, at your service, sir!" grinned the ever-jocular third mate. His kerosene lamp combined with the light from Hutton's on the wall to make a gaudy brightness in their dark corner of the quarterdeck.

Reid's companion was the Norwegian carpenter, Andersson. An expert lumberman, he was a magician with axe and adze, and could produce anything from shoring timbers to fine piecework with uncanny skill and speed. Like most seamen, he was lean but strong, with broad shoulders and a mess of white-blond hair; his beard and eyebrows were the same white blond colour, and in the harsh light of the kerosene lamps he looked like a painting of the Son of God himself, had the Son of God had ever been portrayed in seaman's duds and brandishing a giant axe. Hutton decided it might be more appropriate to consider Andersson the embodiment of his namesake, the Norse god Thor.

Hutton showed him the hasps and locks on the trunk, and made it clear what he needed Andersson to do. It needed no translation, for Andersson's English was probably better than most of the native-born crew. The other men stood back, and Andersson was left in the glow of the kerosene, hefting the axe and taking aim. With unerring skill, he smashed the axe twice into the wood each side of the hasps, easily riding the rolls of the ship as he balanced each swing; with a final flourish he buried the axe head obliquely beneath the cuts he had made and wrenched it out again. The whole exercise took less than thirty seconds. His work done, Andersson took his leave, holding the neck of the axe in his left hand and sliding the other up the lifeline as he dissolved into the darkness.

Hutton leaned in and hooked his fingers under the broken hasps. The bolts crackled, caught on lumps of splintered wood as Hutton pulled them clear of the broken mounts. He slipped his fingers underneath the recessed lip of the lid, and began to lift. The hinges were oiled, so the lid swung up easily, falling back over the trunk until it thumped against the stops. Hutton took Reid's lamp and moved it over the top of the trunk, holding his breath. The two men looked in. Hutton's breath released. It was indeed empty.

Chapter Seven

Isle of Wight
Thursday, 6th February 1890

By ten-thirty the next morning, Blake stood next to the well-padded figure of Mr Peabody, freezing in his greatcoat and scarf. Both men clutched their hats in front of them as the wind rushed up the cliff-face beneath their feet. They stood as close as they dared, wary of the four hundred foot drop to the rocks and seething surf far below.

About three hundred yards offshore lay the wreck of the *Irex*, aground on an even keel, her bow pointing towards shore. The heavy surf still rolled over her from astern, crashing over the ruined decks and up over the bow in an endless series of lazy breakers. She still had swatches of sail set, a testimony to the skill of the sailmaker Colquhoun, who presently lay in the Ventnor Hospital, fighting for his life.

Despite the clear conditions overnight, the February dawn heralded the return of the clouds and high winds that had buffeted the island for weeks. This winter had seen particularly harsh weather, with low temperatures and gales throughout the whole of January, a relentless assault on the few hardy souls who dared to venture out on the water.

Among them were the crew of the Totland lifeboat, eight of the bravest souls who had ever walked the earth, if Blake was any judge. In the shrieking storm that had forced the *Irex* ashore, the men had launched their rowing boat, a tiny speck compared to the mighty ship they were trying to help. Three times they had attempted a rescue, only to be thrown back by the force of the waves.

There would be further opportunities to hear testimony from these men during the course of the inquest; Blake had also written to the nearby artillery battery commander whose men had performed amazing feats during the rescue that terrible night.

Blake believed in a providential presence; however, he was loath to call it "God" or any of the other anthropomorphisms of a force which fascinated him. There were many philosophical challenges in this case, not least the miraculous escape for so many who should have been dashed to pieces along with their ship but for the fortuitous appearance of so many capable volunteers.

Whatever drove Blake to question and investigate came from an inbuilt thirst to know the truth in its entirety. He was unwilling to compromise or be palmed off by indifferent authorities. Yet in doing so he knew he risked provoking others, men with influence who would not hesitate to take extreme measures to keep certain secrets hidden from public knowledge.

Blake remembered Rudd, of course, but his thoughts focused on Rennie. Although the man was blameless, he was a terrier. The little that Blake had shared with him was likely to put the tenacious newsman on a collision course with Thornthwaite and the men behind him.

It was almost eleven o'clock, and there was still no sign of the Scots reporter. Blake wondered if he might already have met with a nasty accident like Henry Rudd – a fall from these treacherous cliffs would be a simple thing to arrange, and no-one would ever think more of it, any more than they would question a simple traffic accident—

Peabody was talking to him. "I said, when would you like to begin, Mr Blake?"

Blake shook himself from his distraction, and for the next two freezing hours they moved to and fro along the windswept clifftop. They followed Murray, the bosun's mate, along with two of the other lucky souls to escape the wreck more or less unscathed.

By the time the men had finished their descriptions of the event using the stricken ship as a canvas upon which to project their vivid memories, Blake was already satisfied beyond doubt that the three deaths they had witnessed were accidental. But the most striking agreement in their descriptions of that final night was how each man testified to the captain's loss of reason.

Blake perceived the direction of the testimony singling out the captain as the cause of the disaster. But it did not explain the involvement of Clarence, nor the activities of the furtive young attorney who methodically scratched details of the testimonies into his own legal pad – Thornthwaite.

Blake watched the young lawyer, who seemed consumed by his writing, knuckles white with cold as he scribbled. Occasionally the man looked up, and his gaze flitted from face to face; he seemed very aware of his surroundings.

Blake's unease with Thornthwaite's prompted him to prod at the young barrister once again. "Mr Thornthwaite! May we confer?"

Thornthwaite gave a tight smile and approached.

"Mr Thornthwaite, are you acting as a representative of any of the deceased in this case?"

Thornthwaite almost smirked as he gave his reply. "Certainly not, sir! I should surely have declared my interest, were that so."

Peabody interjected. "What about any other interested party? Are you acting for anyone else?"

Thornthwaite smoothly sidestepped the question. "Sir, I was engaged by the Solicitor-General to assist in the conduct of the inquest. If I am here in any capacity, it is to act at the pleasure of the coroner."

Blake decided to call his bluff. "Of course, Mr Thornthwaite. In fact, we would like to ask for your assistance in some research."

Thornthwaite shifted on his feet slightly, but didn't falter. "Name it, sirs!"

"This Mr Clarence seems to be a key figure in the narrative. Would you be kind enough to enquire as to the reason for his presence on board the *Irex*? I will ask the witnesses, of course, but it would be very valuable to have some background on this Mr Clarence in view of his pivotal role in the inquest."

Blake had to give Thornthwaite credit for his admirable self-control. He betrayed just a flicker of alarm at the question which he quickly quashed.

"Surely sirs, such a matter is left to the process of the inquest? It would be prejudicial to your verdict were it to rely on evidence not obtained by testimony?"

"There is no verdict here, Mr Thornthwaite. My inquest is not restricted to evidence given under oath. There is no burden of proof, and since the Lord Chancellor's interference, not even a jury! We are to establish findings as to whether there has been an unlawful death. Since Mr Clarence is a missing person, and thus unable to present himself at this inquest, it would be wise to follow all lines of inquiry, would it not?"

Thornthwaite was about to continue his protestations, but closed his mouth. His eyes focused on the horizon beyond Blake's shoulder as he considered. "I shall see what I can find, Mr Blake."

Blake turned to Peabody, ensuring that Thornthwaite would know the conversation was over. The younger man moved back towards the throng of people and began to engage the crewman Murray in low conversational tones.

"That should keep him on his toes, Mr Blake," murmured Peabody. "I should imagine that our young expert is up to his scrawny neck in the affairs of this Mr Clarence. Still, it would be interesting to see if he produces anything of note."

Blake agreed, entirely convinced that anything Thornthwaite turned up for them would be worthless, if not outright misinformation.

Rennie still hadn't shown up, which was unusual for a reporter. That discomfited Blake again.

"Come, Mr Peabody, let us get back. We have a few hours after lunch to go through some of what we have learned today." He turned towards the wreck one last time. "Poor devils".

* * *

The wind wrestled the corners of the carriage as they pulled up outside the court house. Peabody was roused from his dozing, and the two men marched up the steps and were let in by the doorman again. The heat inside the court house was a most welcome tonic to the two men, still aching from the cold.

"Mr Blake, sir!" The reception clerk beckoned the coroner to the desk. "Sir, a telegram arrived for you, about an hour ago."

Telegrams again, thought Blake. *Was there anywhere a man could be free from the insistent stalking of modern communication?*

"Thank you, Jeremy." Blake took the envelope from the young man. Peabody hovered, careful not to read the lines of teletype pasted on the page within until invited.

++ BLAKE URGENT STOP++ ++MEET ME HOTEL SOONEST STOP++ ++RENNIE STOP++

"It's Rennie." Blake passed the page to Peabody. "He's found something. I think we shall take lunch at the Osborne, Mr Peabody. The work can wait!"

Blake was animated, the cold forgotten. He turned back to the reception clerk. "I need a cab, Jeremy. Fast as you can."

The young clerk gave the doorman a hand signal. The men were on the street and climbing into a cab a minute later.

"Sixpence if you can make the Osborne in twenty minutes, driver!" called Peabody to the cabby, who took to his task with gusto. Eighteen minutes later they pulled up outside the Osborne. The cabby grinned his appreciation as Peabody remained good to his word.

The two men hastened into the hotel lobby, where another blast of warm air embraced them from the grand fireplace. Stacked with crackling logs, it was belching heat like a foundry.

Blake's eyes darted around the lobby, and locked on those of Rennie across the room, sitting with a newspaper folded on his lap and a cold cup of half-drunk tea at his small round table. Rennie raised his paper in greeting, dispelling the cloud of smoke around his head. Blake flushed with relief at the sight of the Glaswegian alive and well.

Rennie had prepared two elegant dining chairs at his table, and the two men took their places as a waiter gathered their coats. The fire's heat soothed their chilled limbs, stiff with cold.

Rennie flapped the folded newspaper down on the table like a dead fish. "I can't believe this is what passes for a paper down here," he growled. "Aye, sure it's not Glasgow, but God help them!"

He looked back up at the expectant faces before him, cracking another toothsome grin, which faded as quickly into a more serious turn as he prepared to speak. "Look, I'm sorry I missed your little party earlier. I took our mystery correspondent's advice and went looking for hospitals. A few discreet enquiries led me to find that the survivors were taken to one hospital, but the dead were placed in another. Is that right?"

Peabody concurred. "Yes, the survivors were taken to the National Hospital in Ventnor. Four bodies were retrieved from the water since the wreck, and they were all taken to the mortuary at the Workhouse Infirmary."

Rennie stubbed out the remains of his cigarette. "Aye, that's what I heard. So this morning while you were having fun outside on the cliffs, I went to snoop around the hospitals. I told them I was from the shipping company's insurance."

Peabody's mouth formed an outraged O at this affront. Blake only gave an ironic twist in one corner of his mouth. *I expected nothing less*.

"Anyway, I got a quick look at the survivors and took some names, but I couldn't get near enough to speak to them. I'll try to get back there for you tomorrow and see what I can dig up." Rennie lit another cigarette, loosing an odorous cloud.

"Then I hopped in a cab and took the coast road to the Infirmary." He paused. "How many dead did you say were taken there?"

Peabody reiterated. "Four. We are still waiting to identify one of them, and Mr Blake released the bodies for post-mortem as of yesterday."

Rennie tapped out his cigarette into the brass ashtray on the table. "Aye, that's exactly what the administrator said. But here's the thing – when I went down to the morgue there were only three. It looks like one of your bodies just got up and walked out of there."

Chapter Eight

Irish Sea
Monday, 23rd December 1889

Hutton stood on the lurching deck, clinging for his life. The storm was the worst he had known in his thirty-seven years of sailing. He was by the mainmast, in the very centre of the deck, braced with one arm against the line of belays, the other gripping white-knuckled to the rope stays on the mast.

The wind ripped at his clothes, trying to strip his sou'wester from the back of his head. Its chinstay was almost throttling him. He could barely open his eyes as the spray hammered into them like grapeshot.

He was completely alone. There was not another soul within sight, not that he could have hailed anyone through the bedlam of shrieks. He watched through his fluttering eyelids as another enormous wave, fully thirty feet high, came rolling out of the darkness to assault the helpless ship. It reared up before him, black and marbled with foam, the crest forming high above his head.

He could do nothing but watch. As the wall of water reached the gunwale of the ship, he saw a white shape rolling in the translucent face of the wave; something that looked alive, like a dolphin or shark. Then the wave broke over him, its unbearable weight pushing him to his face. The wash lifted him from the deck, and he prepared for the final ignominy of being swept off his own ship by the indifferent sea.

But instead of throwing him over the side, the wave deposited him against the far gunwale. He choked up salt water, and the wash dragged at him as he struggled on all fours to stay upright.

As the waters receded, he saw the object left behind on the deck. At first it appeared to be a flour sack but as the water fell back, Hutton felt a rush of bile to his throat as it resolved into the body of a woman. The bone-white limbs were askew, her long black hair plastered to her body by the sea. Her head was unnaturally posed. The face looked directly back over her shoulder but her eyes stared, wide open.

He believed for a second it might be Mrs Barstow but it was obvious this was someone else. As another ripple gathered the body, it flopped over towards him. It wasn't her nakedness that drew Hutton's eye at that moment, but the gaping wound in her stomach. Her entire belly had been cut open, and the eviscerated remains lay open to the sea.

He felt the vomit rise in his throat, but his revulsion died in the grip of a primeval fear when he realised she was still alive. Her eyes moved to look at him, and her lips began to move, though Hutton could hear nothing over the wind.

Help me.

Fear gripped his throat and spasms zigzagged up his spine. He took a ragged breath and screamed in terror.

Hutton snapped upright in his bunk, the scream still in his throat. He was fully dressed, having crashed onto his bed after taking off his sodden oilskins. They lay where he had left them. He was safe in his cabin, and the storm overnight had subsided to a fresh northerly breeze.

The clock on the wall, dimly illuminated but legible, said ten before seven o'clock. He had slept barely two hours, and it was still dark outside. Despite the fatigue, the disturbing dream dismissed any possibility of falling back to sleep so he sat upright, feeling the easy rolling of the ship on the swell.

He could still hear the rattle of spray on his window, so he retrieved his oilskins and shrugged them on, pulling the sou'wester's chinstrap over his beard as he closed the door behind him.

Emerging from the cabin, Hutton felt the wind to be a little warmer than he recalled. He looked out over the rail into the darkness, and saw no enormous waves – nor were there any torn, naked women on the main deck. He shook off the lingering sense of fear at the dream, and instead concentrated on what was before him.

Visibility was much better, and when he looked up, he was impressed to see full sail set. The acres of white canvas stretching into the darkness above him produced a dizzying effect, inducing a sense of vertigo as the ship pitched and rolled in the swells. He felt a vibration through the companionway steps, and looked round to see Reid descending the companionway at speed, his usual smiling face visible under the turned up brow of his sou'wester.

"Morning, Captain! Mr Mackie did a fine job catching the wind when the storm eased off," he beamed.

"Where is Mr Mackie now?"

"He's up with Morgan; they're putting on a cracking pace now, sir."

Hutton pursed his lips. "What happened to the chest? The one belonging to Clarence?"

Reid held his gaze; if he was wondering about Hutton's obsession with the chest, he didn't mention it. "Andersson finished the job on it, Captain. It's firewood now. God knows we put it to good use – the men are getting their first hot meal since we left Greenock!"

Hutton smiled back at the grinning third mate. No cook could keep hot pans fixed to the stove when the ship was lurching through stormy seas; the easy rolling in the milder breeze now gave Campbell the chance to put on a decent stew and some hot brews.

"Very good, Mr Reid! And thank you. It may not seem like much, but it's actually a weight off my mind." He yawned and stretched, trying to shrug off the fatigue of successive nights with little sleep.

While the third mate busied himself with the men further up the deck, Hutton excused himself. He mounted the steps up to the quarterdeck, where Mackie stood with Hanson and Morgan the helmsman were riding the easy movements of the ship.

"Morning, Captain." Mackie gave his usual greeting without inflection. If the man was tired by the night's exertions, he gave no sign. His deep-set eyes peered out, impassive, from his upturned collar and sou'wester. "Fine morning it is, too!"

"Thank you Mr Mackie, that it is," agreed Hutton. "You made sail, I see." There was no implicit rebuke; a good captain allowed his watch officers to make their own decisions, applying corrections later if needed.

"Aye, Captain, we're making good speed. Should get a good fix by sunrise, I think."

Hutton felt that the man was doing his utmost to recapture the captain's good graces, so he nodded his approval.

Despite the tiredness which reached to the backs of his eyes, Hutton began to relax. The *Irex* had weathered the storm well, and the crew had worked efficiently. He had resolved one of his problems with the arrogant Mr Clarence, and it promised plain sailing, at least for now.

A faint glimmer of dawn brightened the eastern sky behind them. As the ship ploughed on, the winds felt milder; Hutton was surprised to see the mercury up at a dizzy 49 degrees. While it felt better for the body, it was not a good sign; a warm spell in late December generally promised trouble.

At least Hutton felt he could concentrate on the business of navigation; Clarence and, to a lesser extent, Mrs Barstow had been a distraction out of all proportion to the matters at hand.

He wondered how he had let himself be so rattled by Clarence. Hutton knew the upper-class gentleman threatened him. No seaman would have dared challenge him, but Clarence seemed to revel in his assumed superiority, protected by his own arrogance and sense of entitlement.

As Hutton passed his time ensconced in his own thoughts, the steward, Thomas Eustace, stepped from the galley door into the pool of light beyond. His usual domain was the storeroom under the galley, which he guarded with zeal and, if necessary, violence; its proximity to the half-deck quarters of the apprentices was too tempting a target for the young lads. They would have run a lesser man ragged, employing any variety of deception and decoy to filch valued items from the ship's store. But Eustace, despite his mild demeanour, had a hard edge like any old sailor – he was polite enough to the passengers when they enquired of him, but happy to clout any apprentice or even the old salts if he suspected any designs on his meticulously accounted wares.

"Bloody hell, is that Tom Eustace?" Morgan exclaimed.

Hanson, still attending the helmsman, nodded. "What's he doing above decks? I thought he dissolved in contact with water!"

The two men roared with laughter at this. Though Hutton and Mackie maintained a discreet silence, the observation may well have been true – the sight of the steward above decks was indeed noteworthy. Along with the cook and the ship's doctor, he was one of only three men not given to the watches; they kept their own time as they pleased. That luxury did not mean that they shirked – if anything, they were more likely to put in extra hours of work, if only to dismiss any notion of inequality.

In this regard, Eustace was beyond reproach, keeping hours long into the night to ensure that crew and passengers were furnished with the next day's sustenance. As a further duty, which he carried off with professional efficiency, Eustace was tasked with cleaning the passengers' rooms twice a week. He was probably the one man most intimately acquainted with the passengers.

Eustace had a rangy figure, all arms and legs, and he moved with a spindly gait towards the quarterdeck.

"Begging your pardon, Captain Hutton sir, I need to discuss a matter with you, if you please."

Hutton nodded, and beckoned Eustace into the cabin. He led the steward to his own room and closed the door.

"What is it, Mr Eustace?" Hutton enquired, once he had taken his seat at the table.

"Sir, pardon me if I'm speaking above my station, but I think the doctor should see Mr Barstow. He hasn't been out of his room since the morning we left, and Lord, if his pot is anything to go by, I'd swear he was not a well man."

Hutton considered this report; he had learned by long experience that a seaman's hunch was no small indicator of trouble ahead. "Did you speak with the Barstows at all? Since yesterday?"

"No, sir. I'm cleaning the room tomorrow, but I have noticed that Mrs Barstow hasn't been out of the room either. She has been by every day she's been aboard..." Eustace paused, abruptly turning a little pink. "Well, sir, I've been a bit soft on her and been giving her cakes which Campbell's been making for them." He looked embarrassed at this indiscretion, but Hutton simply smiled.

"Tom, you wouldn't be a man if you thought otherwise! I think every man on board is a bit soft on our fair Mrs Barstow!" He immediately regretted such a declaration, unveiling his own vulnerability, and reawakening the knot in his stomach whenever he thought about the woman.

Eustace regarded Hutton with increased scrutiny, searching his eyes for a possible joke. "Anyway sir, if the doctor knew about it...that's all I'm really saying."

"Very good Mr Eustace. If you see Mr Carroll, you may tell him to visit the Barstows with my permission." Hutton was about to stand up, but then couldn't resist. "While we're talking about passengers, how is Mr Clarence?"

Eustace's face flickered, a shadow of something unpleasant. "Mr Clarence, sir?" he swallowed.

Hutton felt a familiar clench in his gut whenever he sensed Clarence's involvement. It displaced the similar but more pleasurable clench he already harboured at the mention of Mrs Barstow. "Yes, Tom, has he been involved with the crew at all?"

Eustace ducked the question. "Sir, I'm happy for him to stay in his room for the whole voyage if it pleases him." He shifted his feet and looked down, a picture of discomfort. "If you'll excuse me saying it, Captain, I don't like being within a mile of the man."

"Why ever not, Eustace?"

"Sir, I have never been in his room. Now, I swear I haven't been derelict, but he just won't let me in, day or night. He locks it even if he's only walking up on deck for air. If I knock, he tells me to go away. But then sometimes I'm in the store late on, and he'll just appear at my shoulder. He knows it gives me a fright, but he does it anyway. Then he'll ask me for towels, or bedding – and I've never had any of it back, like he's hoarding it. I just get the feeling he's up to something, and I don't like it."

Hutton was intrigued. "What do you think he is up to?"

Eustace actually looked over his shoulder before he continued in a quiet voice. "Captain, I think I know what was in that trunk. The one he threw away."

Here it comes, thought Hutton. *Forecastle rumour of the day.*

Eustace checked over his shoulder again. "I think it was a lady."

Hutton's jaw actually dropped. He felt a rushing in his ears and an electric shock through his chest. An image of the woman from his dream flashed through his mind, unbidden. *Help me.*

"Why – Why would you say that, Tom?"

The steward shrugged. "I've heard things."

Hutton looked mildly shocked at this.

"No, I mean, from the crew. Some things about Mr Hanson and Mr Clarence. Just rumours. I wouldn't want to speak out of turn—"

"Good heavens, man, you're talking about a crew member aiding a stowaway! It's hardly a matter for discretion, Tom!"

Eustace shifted his feet again. "Captain, I don't want to be telling you rumours that might just be forecastle gossip. As God is my witness; we all thought Mr Clarence had trunks full of gold on the first day! But I reckon after two weeks in port he'd have put them ashore. Then we had the fresh meat the first couple days. That came from Mr Clarence himself – he gave it to me in muslin wraps. Fresh pork fillets and lamb's offal, he said. I swear it came straight from his hand, and Captain, I wasn't going to turn it down, believe me!

"When the meat ran out, he left one trunk standing empty on deck, so I suppose that settles the question. But I have a story to tell about the other one."

"Go on, Tom." Hutton was rapt.

"Captain, Mr Clarence is a most insistent gentleman. And he has Hanson eating out of his hand. I saw them the last night we were in port." Eustace again turned and peeked over his shoulder, his voice dropping lower. "I was in the stores, for I thought I heard rats. Anyway, I was sure I felt the ship moving; it must have been about three a.m., so I peeked out."

He paused again, his eyes flicking sideways once or twice, looking to Hutton as though he was wrestling with what he should or shouldn't say.

"I was right, Captain! They were shortening the lines to bring us close aboard the dock. I saw some of the bosun's men putting down the gangway, and the next thing four of them were carrying Mr Clarence's trunk off the ship, and he was with them."

"Who was? Hanson?"

"No, Mr Clarence led them off, and Hanson was watching from the top of the gangway."

Hutton was deeply dismayed at this flagrant disregard for regulations, not to mention his authority. His emotions ran high for the few moments it took Eustace to finish his story.

"I couldn't see over the gunwale, but I definitely heard a carriage. The men came back, but Clarence wasn't with them, and nor was the trunk."

"So how do you know what was in the trunk, Tom?"

Eustace looked embarrassed. "The men were miming something. It was quite easy to guess what they meant." Eustace thrust his hips in and out for the captain's benefit.

Hutton waved his arm to stop the charade. "Yes, Tom, I assure you I understand. It's just...did you see Clarence come back aboard?"

"No sir. I believe he came back that morning."

Hutton remembered his surprise at seeing the man sauntering back from the town after the Sunday celebration. *I should never have let him back aboard*, thought the captain. Once again, he rued how comprehensively he was being played by their gentleman passenger.

"Tom, do you think Clarence still has the lady in his room? Is that why he's not letting you in?"

"That's what I thought sir, but when you found the other chest empty, I don't know how she could have come back aboard. I swear it never moved the whole time it was out on the deck."

Hutton was having trouble focusing on the problem. His fatigue hampered his ability to reason. Clarence must have intended to bring the woman on the voyage, for who could have foreseen the shift in cargo that first night? If he decided to cut his losses and offload her the night before they sailed, it was difficult to see what profit it was to him at all. Another puzzle, and one which Hutton wanted to solve.

"Very well, Tom. Thank you for your candour, and well done."

The steward bowed and dismissed himself.

Hutton rubbed his eyes again. They pricked from lack of sleep. A headache was forming in the left side of his brain, while his innards felt disturbed by the apprehension he felt towards Clarence and his confused romantic feelings towards Mrs Barstow.

He tried to shake both feelings off by a few words of prayer, and turned his thoughts to Sarah at home; two weeks had gone by and he was barely two hundred miles from her. He knew another midnight rendezvous had gone by while he chased shadows during the storm the previous night; the sense of shame this provoked intensified as he also remembered the intimidating figure of Clarence looking on him with disdain.

The sounding of the bell above brought him back to his senses; eight bells was the signal for breakfast, and Campbell had wrought the impossible by providing a hot meal. Hutton pulled himself wearily to his feet, his knees cracking and back protesting, while the headache pressed at a point deep inside his brain. He prayed for a clear run this day, and hoped it would bring a few hours more sleep by the afternoon.

He checked inside the chart room next door, noting the dead reckoning course and the log slate showing the sightings and observations from the night watches. Mackie had been over-productive: good sightings from Ailsa Craig and Sanda lights had given a solid position fix about six miles south of Kintyre at 6.18 a.m.; distance logged at 140 miles in the past 24 hours. Not a great day's run, but at least they were moving.

Moving helped Hutton too; he emerged from the quarterdeck doorway into a grey half-daylight, and the fresh air helped to chase away the cobwebs.

The wind seemed to be picking up again – its gusts brought loud cracks from the canvas stretched in great expanse above him. Beyond the deck, the sea still rolled in six-foot, white-streaked waves across the ship's path. The visibility was much better; Hutton could make out the dim outlines of mountains on the far western horizon.

As he studied the environment, a warm waft of broth or stew from the galley amidships went straight to Hutton's stomach, producing an instant gurgle from his innards. It made his mind up to head straight for the deckhouse.

Mackie approached as the captain closed the distance to the galley. "Captain, I am preparing to tack. The glass is dropping again. I anticipate a swing round to the south-west, which would put the winds at our head if we maintain our present course."

Hutton, pleased, backed up the mate's assessment. "Very good Mr Mackie."

"Aye, sir."

The mate was about to return but Hutton stopped him with a hand on the big man's hefty arm. "Andrew. Good work."

The mate's lugubrious aspect seemed to brighten a little, barely more than a flicker across his eyebrows.

Hutton took his leave and walked down the deck towards the galley. He marvelled at how quickly the weather changed; this walk took scant minutes, when it had taken almost half an hour the previous night.

The smells grew ever more tantalising as he drew alongside the deckhouse – a small queue of men waited to receive their first hot meal since port. Inside, Durrick and the cook ladled broth and lime juice into the men's outstretched tin plates and enamelled mugs. The men downed the juice, and moved immediately to the side counter to refill with either the strong, sweet tea or bitter coffee from the fixed metal urns against the interior wall. Powdered milk completed the ensemble before the men proceeded to the fixed benches and tables to wolf down the welcome meal. Thus fortified, the men dropped their flatware into the deep metal sinks of hot water, and filed out of the door on the opposite side. It was no coincidence the unassuming Campbell was one of the most popular men aboard ship.

"Morning, Mr Campbell."

"Morning, Captain." The cook wiped his forehead with his arm; the temperature was agreeable for the men who had just walked in off the deck; for those who remained inside, it was oppressive.

114

Durrick also nodded his greetings in the formal way reserved between officers; in the strangely stilted social connections between ranks, even on a merchant ship, etiquette was observed.

Hutton addressed the second mate. "Has the doctor been through yet?"

Durrick answered in his characteristic nasal tone. "Yes, Captain, about twenty minutes ago. I believe he was going to head back to the cabin."

Eustace must have caught up with him first, decided Hutton. "Thank you, gentlemen. Carry on."

Hutton's stomach growled again as he left the deckhouse – he would have to wait until the officers were served their food from the aft galley. In the meantime, he would slaver quietly and try to keep his stomach growls out of earshot.

He continued down the deck towards the quarterdeck and cabin while the men toiled off their breakfast setting the sails to tack the ship to westward.

His hunger pangs began to subside as he felt the now familiar gut feeling as he approached the Barstows' room. *What am I, some love-struck lad? Grow up Hutton!*

He reminded himself that this was just emotion, nothing more. Thirty-seven years he had sailed the oceans, and for nearly twenty-four of those he had been married to Sarah. Not once had he compromised his marriage vows, and he could swear with a clear conscience before God to that fact. He had no doubt that a woman such as Mrs Barstow was equally solid in the defence of her honour. Hutton supposed she would have had infinitely more practice at defending hers than he had his. He couldn't imagine a woman like Elizabeth Barstow going anywhere without attracting the ardent attention of some man or other. It was likely a burden she had become accustomed to bearing.

Presently he arrived in the saloon area, and noticed movement shadowing the light beneath the gap under the Barstows' door. He knocked lightly and announced himself.

The handle turned slowly, and the door opened to reveal the face of Mrs Barstow. Hutton was briefly stunned. She looked older, careworn and tired. Her hair was askew; her face showed lines he hadn't seen in the sunlight of two days previously. Dark, maroon shadows marred the smooth skin below her eyes, and her full lips looked cracked and dry. But still, it was her eyes that held Hutton's awestruck attention; those beautiful, sparkling pale-green eyes from Sunday morning looked bloodshot and lifeless, red-rimmed from tears; it stripped her of the vigour that had captivated him since she first stepped aboard.

"Captain." Her firm voice had grown small, tired. Hutton guessed she had also slept little, if at all.

"Mrs Barstow. Ah – has the doctor called by?"

"He's here now. Though, as a nurse myself, I can't attest to his skills."

Hutton felt guilty – Grubb's crews, like many other firms down the pecking order, rarely carried fully qualified medical doctors; the best they could expect were second year medical students building up experience. The *Irex* was probably more fortunate than most, having the services of former Sergeant Major Stephen Carroll, who had served in the Army Hospital Corps before going to sea. He had a working knowledge of wounds and fevers which served him well at sea; from his military experience, he was also adept at spotting the onset of syphilis, a vital skill in stopping the spread of the disease aboard ship.

Mrs Barstow opened the door, and Hutton squeezed into the small room. Carroll knelt beside the bed, and Hutton saw the ghost-like face of George Barstow, wrapped in bedclothes like a mummy, with the same purple hollows around his eyes, his skin pallid as curdled milk. His face was the only part exposed; the rest of him hid beneath the covering, shivering violently, his limbs frail where the bedclothes draped over them, sharp points where his knees poked up. The temperature in the room was elevated, and the fever left the man drenched in sweat. His eyes rolled towards Hutton, yellowed and bloodshot. In spite of the discomfort, he tried to smile, and it rent Hutton's heart. *This is a good man*.

Mrs Barstow let out a loud sob, and Hutton looked back at her over his shoulder. Her face was contorted with sorrow, and the tears fell freely. She held her left arm tightly round herself, her right hand stuffed tightly beneath her chin, clenching a large fistful of her hanging chestnut locks up to her throat. Hutton noticed for the first time she was still only wearing her nightdress. He took off his greatcoat and offered it to her. She instead pushed forward and clutched him round the chest, sobbing into his tunic. He awkwardly put his hands around her, drawing the coat across her shoulders and patting her back gently, trying to ignore the confusing proximity of her body.

He looked back towards the bed, and George looked on, his breath shallow and ragged at each exhalation. Occasionally he erupted into wet, racking coughs, and flecks of blood stained the bedclothes in the aftermath.

Carroll hadn't moved throughout; he used a trumpet-like stethoscope to listen to Barstow's chest, monitoring intently. Hutton was not sure which battles he had attended during his army career, but the man was a rock when it came to concentration.

He tried to divert his attention from the sobbing, thinly clad woman crushing her chest against. He prayed for a resolution – it was clear Barstow was very ill, but was it a fever that might spread among the passengers and crew? Fever aboard a ship could amount to a death sentence; even home ports would insist on quarantine procedures, and the confinement usually meant a high proportion of the crew would succumb.

He looked down at the top of Elizabeth Barstow's head, and smelled her hair – it was unwashed and damp with sweat. He could feel her back still heaving as the sobs came out, and felt her squirm against his chest as she turned her head towards her ailing husband. He moved his hands to her shoulders, and she stood back a little, straightening up and trying to smooth her tear-streaked hair from her face. She still gulped back the sobs, but some of the tension had come out of her face.

"I'm sorry, Captain." she blurted between the small convulsions. "Sorry. We've been so seasick, and George—" She gave a huge sniff, chased by another sob. Hutton felt awkward once again, letting his hands fall from her shoulders.

"It's all right, Mrs Barstow," was all he could come up with.

The moment was interrupted by another eruption of coughs from the wretched Mr Barstow. This time Carroll got to his feet. He was a heavyset man, broad across the hips, and the type with thick black hairs across practically every part of his body. He looked at Hutton, and back to the woman, who quickly took Carroll's place at the bedside, clutching her husband's clammy hand between her own.

"Well, Captain. I can't rightly say for sure, but I think it's pneumonia."

Hutton flushed with relief for a second, but managed to restrain himself for the Barstows' sake; pneumonia wasn't contagious, so the ship was safe.

"I don't think it's consumption. I can't hear the rattling, although he has water in his lungs. I think the blood is just from coughing."

They both looked at Elizabeth Barstow who sat silently rubbing at George's hand.

Hutton motioned Carroll to step outside. "Mr and Mrs Barstow, excuse us for a moment."

When the door was closed, Hutton took Carroll down to the saloon and they sat on one of the bench seats.

Carroll was patting his breast pockets, feeling for pipe and tobacco. "Captain, he's had this for days, since before he boarded. I would expect him to last another week, perhaps less. There's very little I can do for him except keep him comfortable."

Hutton sighed, deeply. Deaths on board were not uncommon in seafaring.

Carroll puffed on his pipe, the aromatic cloud enveloping both men. "I have some laudanum in the lazarette; but I don't think she'll let me near him with that. She already cut me off when I tried to draw some blood."

"Can't you treat him down in the lazarette?" This was the name of the plainly-equipped infirmary aboard the *Irex* – little more than a standard-sized room containing a sink and sluice, pharmaceutical cupboard, bunk and flat operating table. It lay directly beneath them, and was Carroll's official space on board the ship.

Carroll shook his head. "I already asked her, but she doesn't want him below. She says he needs to see the daylight. They were both wretchedly sick during the storm."

"Thank you, Stephen. I'll send for you if you need to administer anything."

Carroll rose from the table and departed towards the door down to the lazarette. Hutton got up and mounted the L-shaped staircase to the cabin.

As he reached the top he was surprised to see Mr Clarence standing in the open cabin area.

"Captain!"

He seemed genuinely pleased to see Hutton, a feeling not reciprocated.

"Now, I've heard what's going on. The poor man! And his poor wife!" Clarence's eyes glittered, or so it seemed to Hutton. The man leaned in, conspiratorially. "Captain, I have brought a suite of medicaments for my personal use; I would be honoured to donate some to ease the poor gentleman's suffering."

"Thank you Mr Clarence. I am about to enquire of Mrs Barstow whether that will be something—"

"Of course!" boomed the big man. "Allow me!"

Before Hutton could voice the mighty objection he felt at that instant, Clarence whirled aside to the Barstows' door and knocked confidently. "Good morning, Madam! It is Eddy Clarence and the Captain to see you, if we may."

The handle turned slowly, and Mrs Barstow appeared, clutching Hutton's greatcoat to herself, covering her whole body from throat to ankles. Only her bare feet and tear-ravaged face were visible.

Clarence was all smiles and concern. "My dear lady, I am quite beside myself. I would like to offer any help I can to your husband."

She looked frail, vulnerable before the big man. Yet she did not bow to his offer, but stood impassive, as if daring him to go on.

"Now, I have a selection of remedies from the finest Harley Street surgeons—"

Elizabeth Barstow cut him off.

"Mr Clarence, thank you for your concern, but my husband is under my care now. I assure you he will not require your help."

She still had some of her fire burning; she was bowed by sorrow and discomfort but not broken. She shot a glance at Hutton which made him squirm. "Captain, if we require further assistance, you can be sure we will ask for it. Could you please arrange for fresh bedding, and we would like some drinking water. Thank you."

She switched her eyes back to Clarence. "Thank you, and good day to you, Mr Clarence. And to you, Captain." Without waiting to hear their replies, she closed the door firmly, but without malice.

Clarence looked across at Hutton and pulled a face, but Hutton felt stricken. Her assumption that he had gone to Clarence for help burned his soul.

Chapter Nine

Clarence seemed unmoved by Mrs Barstow's dismissal. He turned to leave towards the deck. Hutton followed, catching him up at the door.

"Well, I'm sure she's probably going to pray for him – that should do the trick, eh, Hutton?" Clarence rolled his eyes.

Hutton felt a strong defensive rebuke rise within him, but managed to take a breath, choosing other words. "What, you would begrudge her prayers for her own dying husband?"

Clarence looked perplexed. "Are you serious, Hutton? Or are you a believer as well?"

Hutton realised that the moment had come, as it always did – the point where all his relationships changed, the point where he openly declared the nature of his faith. The modern age had spawned a very modern backlash against the Christian gospel. The faithful had once been respected and admired, but increasingly were viewed as backward simpletons; unworldly, hidebound and wilfully ignorant. Hutton had little doubt that Clarence would view him as such; but the fire of indignation and his desire to distance himself emboldened him to stand up to this arrogant man at last.

He didn't get the chance. Before he could deliver his declaration, Clarence chuckled.

"Of course, you're one of them! Ha! I should have seen it long ago. There is something soft about you, Hutton,

122

something I have never observed in other captains. You think you can appeal to a man's better nature, don't you? Well, I can't commend that. Men are scoundrels, and the sooner you absorb that, the better."

Clarence guffawed at this again, but then motioned Hutton to sit in the saloon with him. Hutton felt his cheeks burning from shame more than anger; he was only glad none of the men had witnessed this little exchange.

The gentleman took a place at the long saloon table, and invited Hutton to join him. Hutton sat across the table and they regarded one another like chess players about to make their opening moves.

"Sir, you took that very well. I like that, Hutton. I freely admit I always try to poke and twist a man to get the measure of him. But I must ask myself, was it because you are a man of self-control and conviction? Or is it perhaps that you agreed with what I said?"

Clarence gave him a furtive smile which piqued Hutton even more. When Hutton didn't immediately reply, Clarence rooted around in his tunic pocket and retrieved a silver case. He snapped it open, took out a black ebony cigarette holder and inserted a slim and expensive-looking cigarette into the end. He took one of the matches from the fixed wooden box at the head of the table and lit it. He puffed out a small cloud of smoke, which drifted lazily between them.

Hutton eyed the neatly trimmed beard around that pouting mouth as it sucked the cigarette. This was clearly not the accustomed seaman's brand, but something far more expensive. To avoid a pitched battle with the man, Hutton opted to ask a question of his own.

"I'm intrigued, Mr Clarence. What are you doing here? How does a gentleman like yourself end up on a humble cargo ship, under sail, heading for the backwaters of South America?"

Clarence regarded him for a few seconds before asking a question of his own. "Hutton, wouldn't you rather like to know what makes me disdain your religion so?"

Hutton didn't, as he preferred not to explore that particular question while he was tired and facing the loss of one of his passengers; but it seemed he was condemned to have to speak to the man, so he hoped the discussion would lead to a disagreement that would put him out of Hutton's hair for the voyage.

"If it has any significance regarding your present circumstances, then yes, I would."

Clarence smiled again, another smirk. "I like you, Hutton. You keep your end up, that's for sure." He took another draw on the cigarette, and let a lazy cloud slide from his lips. "Captain, I believe the Christian religion is one of the most heinous visitations on the human race in its entire history."

Hutton stared. This was heresy he had not expected. He had heard many accusations against the faith – do-gooding, proselytising for monetary gain, control and manipulation for power and influence; but to be labelled an intrinsic evil was a new and baffling angle. His chuckle provoked a reaction from Clarence.

"You laugh, Hutton? Then listen well. We know that humans are nothing more than evolved primates. We have adapted and mutated by virtue of an inbred drive for change and improvement that has lasted hundreds of thousands, if not millions of years. These improvements have been hard

124

won, through struggle for primacy, the rise and fall of many populations, the survival of the most beneficial traits through selective breeding. Mankind did not arrive by the benign will of a superior Being; we struggled and fought to gain our place in the world, and had to displace others to get there."

He pulled at his cigarette again, holding it delicately by its elegant holder, a parlour room gesture strangely incongruent with the spartan lodgings of a rolling cargo ship.

"Then consider, Captain, how this struggle will end if we embrace a philosophy that limits our further development by committing us to subservience! Moreover, subservience to a higher Being that we can neither see nor hear nor touch. This would be one of the most ludicrous conceptions of the human brain, were it not so dangerous."

Hutton struggled to shape these unfamiliar ideas in his own sleep-deprived mind. He certainly hadn't expected a philosophical discussion to be a feature of his day.

Clarence hardly paused. "You see, Hutton, the spread of this idea, the relentless proselytising to the entire world through the colonisation of the lesser races; it will doom the human being to regress rather than progress; to become subservient, rather than self-fulfilling. That is why I sponsor and applaud the men of new thinking who are trying to roll back this tide of ignorance. They are pioneering a new science, one that will enable mankind to shake off the regression of superstition and be ready to step forward into a new age of enlightenment."

Hutton was not ignorant of the ideas that Clarence propounded, but he had never heard them stated with such passion. He remembered how Mrs Barstow had shuttered such discussion on their first night. Clarence must have been irked not to complete his discourse, so he had picked this moment to regale Hutton with his theories.

He had chosen his moment well - Hutton was weakened. Not just dog-tired and hungry but alone, without Mrs Barstow's reassuring conviction to defend his own beliefs. Hutton could only fall back on what he knew.

"I see then, that you are a Darwinist, Mr Clarence."

"Hardly so, Will!" laughed Clarence.

Hutton bristled at this over-familiar use of his name, but kept silent.

Clarence entered full flow. "Darwin was weak! He never appreciated the significance of his original theory. He remained a country parson in his thinking. He believed his theories could co-exist with religion. No, Hutton, I stand on the words of real men of science, modern thinkers like Spencer and Huxley, Lyell and Nietzsche, men of integrity and forthright character who refuse to pander to the dogma of the religious."

Hutton would never have credited Clarence with such passion. He had seemed a vacuous and shallow dandy of a man. "Mr Clarence, I'm sure this is an interesting field for you—"

"Listen to me, Will!" Clarence almost hissed, and pointed up the stairs behind him. "Just above our heads, a strong, intelligent woman is content to let her husband die at sea on a bloody cargo ship, because she doesn't understand the effects of modern medicaments and treatments. Instead, she would rather speak supplicatory thoughts to a non-existent Being, in the hope that he will bestow benign favour upon her husband!" He took another draw on the cigarette, blowing the smoke out impatiently. "Were such a Being to exist, he should never warrant nor deserve such devotion from a beautiful and forthright woman such as Elizabeth! He would garner only contempt from any right-thinking, rational person!"

He stared at the smoke rising from his cigarette, as if digesting his own words. "She could be so much more, given the right form of encouragement..."

Hutton panicked at this unexpected tack. The thought that Clarence might take an interest in Elizabeth Barstow was unconscionable "Mister Clarence! People like us have witnessed at first hand the intervention of God."

Clarence huffed and began to butt in, but Hutton was emphatic.

"You have no right to criticise her choices, or to pronounce upon her chosen faith. If she believes in God's mercy and compassion, then let her! Whether you believe in God or not doesn't dictate whether he exists or intervenes in our world. Who are we to judge the Almighty? What do we know about the past, present and future of humanity? How can we hope to understand the one who made all? It is simply not our place to judge."

Clarence placed his palms flat on the table. It was an assertive gesture which stopped Hutton in his tracks.

"Hutton," he said softly. "You have just described the very essence of subservience. You say we should not judge God? If not we, then who? Man created God, not the other way round! We should judge our creation if we begin to outgrow him. If the religious institutions will not allow their god to evolve, why should we let the outmoded idea of God disqualify ourselves?"

He finished his cigarette and stubbed it out in the ash bowl fixed to the table. "Hutton, allow me the indulgence of a story."

The captain would have very much preferred to sleep, but he felt Clarence was in the mood to talk, and it could work in his favour if he let the man finish his piece. "Of course."

"Hutton, you may have guessed, but I have spent several years in the Royal Navy."

Hutton nodded. He had suspected as much.

"About five years ago, I was a midshipman aboard a cruiser, the *Bacchante*. We were on a round-the-world cruise in squadron, perhaps ten ships-of-the-line. Off Singapore, the flotilla commander decided to perform a series of evolutions – ha! There's that word again! - in naval parlance, these are complex manoeuvres which steamships can perform at will, with a precision that sailing ships can only dream of."

He took some matches from the box at the head of the table and began to arrange them for Hutton's benefit. "You see, here we have the two lines of ships, port and starboard." He made two parallel lines of five matches on the table top, arranged in line astern.

"The plan was to turn in two lines away from each other, reform in line abreast, then enter harbour in line astern." He motioned with the matches, moving them precisely with his large, slim hands by way of demonstration. He quickly rearranged them again. "The two leading ships in each line carried the Admiral and Flotilla Commodore. I was here." He indicated the fourth ship in the starboard line.

"We began the evolution. A fine sight; ten great ships churning along at speed, White Ensigns flying. At the signal, the commodore turns smartly to starboard, expecting the admiral to turn to port. But he doesn't."

Clarence moved the matches, and Hutton watched, engrossed in spite of himself.

"No, you see, the admiral *also* turns to starboard. As his line of ships follow him, he cuts across the front of the next ship in the commodore's line. But the commodore doesn't signal to break formation. And so the ship right behind the admiral's ploughs on and hits his opposite number square in its side, sinking her." He smashed the matches together in a final flourish. "Four hundred men dead, and one of Her Majesty's finest battleships at the bottom of the Malacca Strait."

Hutton was impressed, in spite of himself.

"The point is, Will, there was not a single person in that flotilla who did not know exactly what was going to happen when the ships turned the wrong way. The only person who was surprised was that idiot of an Admiral. But here's the rub – no-one would break formation and risk court-martial even to save their ship. That is the lunacy of subservience, Hutton, and that is what drives me.

"Every man should be the master of himself, and should exercise his freedom to think and act. Not only for his own sense of identity and destiny, but as a sign for others. Your god is a barrier to that awakening. To be the servant of man is one thing; to be a servant of an imaginary god is quite another. Therefore it is a wretched man indeed who is servant of both! And yet that is what your bible teaches – to be the servant of both God and man. Do you know what happens to the man who believes this and does it?" Clarence paused, so Hutton shook his head.

129

"He becomes the slave of the church. Clergy, pope, ministers and archbishops – the worst charlatans in the world. They, of course, live as free men; free to enslave others to do their will, to obey their wishes, and to pander to their needs. They live in palaces, abbeys, and fine houses, exercising power over kings and queens! How? Because they have used the myth of God to gain privilege and power over men! They abuse their privilege to lord it over those poor souls who still believe in their fables.

"It proves but one thing – it is Man who is almighty, Hutton. The religions of the world are simply a means of control and manipulation. Their fear is that men will break free of their petty moral judgements, their double standards and lies. That men will evolve, and overthrow their laughable system for a new one, based on sound, scientific principles that will benefit the strong, regardless of their social status. A new world order, as it were."

Clarence regarded Hutton expectantly. Perhaps he expected Hutton to throw off his hard-earned faith in a moment of epiphany. Instead the captain merely smiled. "A fine discourse, Mr Clarence. But in my early years I have been a wastrel; a womaniser, a drunk and a prodigal. When I discovered the true Person at the heart of the religion you despise, it made me a different man. I too have...evolved, as you call it. I could never say I was a better man before choosing Christ."

Clarence looked at Hutton with disdain. "Captain, I thought you were an intelligent if misguided man. I now see that you are indeed soft."

He sniffed, once, his hands still flat on the table, his eyes boring into Hutton's, who struggled to hold the younger man's intense gaze.

"There are so-called men of faith, Hutton, who would rather see their flock die and be ravaged by disease and predation than admit they are helpless know-nothings. Sometimes they are clergymen, but usually they are admirals, or aldermen, or even Prime Ministers. Their adherence to this faith gives them a veneer of trust, as if they are better men by their adoption of these so-called Christian principles. In reality, it is a sham of respectability, a covering blanket for their arrogance. For they seek power, Hutton. Control is the height of man's greed and lust for power. Control of the sea brings guaranteed trade. Control of the land brings order and stability. Control of the food supply brings acquiescence. Control of the people brings a steady state of slave labour and subservience. Religion is simply an efficient method of controlling people, because it promises that subservience today will bring reward tomorrow. But since the reward lies in the afterlife, no-one ever comes back from the dead to reveal the fraud! It is a tidy trick, Hutton; and it brooks no argument save that of logic, knowledge and the new science, which will make all claims to mysticism, miracles and supernatural powers sound like the pernicious nonsense it is."

Hutton was tired of these patronising ideas. "So what do you propose in its stead, Mr Clarence? What will your New World Order offer that the greatest religion of the world does not?"

Clarence laughed again. "My dear Hutton, first we must offer only chaos. Chaos and disorder must increase, so that

131

people finally realise that their so-called Almighty God cannot rescue them. There must be an end to this charade."

He studied Hutton, perhaps looking for a sign that he understood.

"There are men who desire to exercise their will and their power over the masses. They will become more powerful. They will exercise the raw power born of our suppressed nature – hatred, anger and violence." He grew more animated, his hands scything the air as he continued. "Despotism shall rise. Wars will be fought and people will perish from starvation and disorder as the competition for resources becomes more and more desperate."

Hutton shook his head in disgust. "How is that better? This is preposterous, Mr Clarence!"

"Oh, no, Will! This is simply the first step. The religions of the world will degenerate as their impotence becomes plain to even the most ardent believer. No, once the greedy overlords have weakened themselves with their short-sighted lusts, those of us who wait shall strike! With one blow we shall sweep aside these petty warlords and become masters of the world. All humanity will look to us as the true saviours of mankind!

"We can build a new world, based on international brotherhood and co-operation. There will be no waste; the fittest and best equipped shall survive; the weak shall serve or perish, as it was always meant to be. We shall build a perfect society, built on reason and science, not some false hope of life after death. And from there, we shall evolve to become ever more masters of our destiny." Clarence finished stabbing the air as he emphasised his grand plan.

Hutton sat appalled by the prospective future Clarence was suggesting. "And who are these people you belong to? Who has the wherewithal to accomplish such fantastic plans?"

Clarence's mouth set hard, his eyes unwavering. It resolved into a grim smile. "Captain, we are *already* in control. We just await our time. It may not be in my lifetime, for we have a long plan, one which far outlives any of our people. But mark my words, Hutton; it will happen."

His passion soared once more, his eyes reflecting his visionary excitement. "We stand on the threshold of a great leap forward in human achievement. Our learning and understanding is far greater than any epoch before us. Right now there are men who stand ready to conquer all diseases, now that we have isolated the cause of illness with germ theory. Mr Freud of Vienna is unlocking the secret world of the human mind, the conscious and the unconscious, the seat of so many of our delusions and phobias. Engineers are developing turbines which will propel steel ships at over thirty knots. Man will soon be able to fly in adaptable machines. The horse will no longer be required for land transport. Already we have machines that power all production; the discovery of electricity means we will have machines that can run entire cities within decades."

His visionary zeal was actually infectious. Hutton knew about many of these developments already, and could feel Clarence's excitement. But the man was determined to bury Hutton's faith.

"There simply isn't room in such a world for your god fantasies, Hutton! When people see the true miracles wrought by human ingenuity, they will no longer need the

133

imaginations of the church. They will see that we can direct our own destiny. We need not hope for divine intervention when we have electric machines that can heal and sustain the human body, prolonging the human lifespan to centuries! Our own desire to better ourselves will outstrip our need to help the failing and weak in the name of some god. Surely you see this, Hutton?"

Hutton was feeling groggy from this onslaught. His headache was worse, and hunger still gnawed at his stomach. He was no longer in the mood for these lectures.

"Who was the man who dropped you at the docks?" The question came from nowhere, or at least somewhere unknown, deep inside Hutton's sleep-deprived mind.

Clarence, for once, was stopped in his tracks. "What on earth does that have to do with it?"

Hutton's mind stirred. This was a line of questioning Clarence didn't like. *All the more reason to press on.* "On the dockside, when you arrived. There was a gentleman with you. You seemed to have some sort of disagreement."

Clarence bristled, sitting up and folding his arms so that his biceps bulged through his shirtsleeves. "Oh, you think so, do you?"

Hutton felt the threat of the man; it seemed to gather around him like storm clouds. *Watch your step, Will.* "How did you come to be aboard my ship?"

Clarence tensed. Hutton wondered if perhaps he had stepped too far. The bigger man studied him with a hostile glare, his jaw clenching and setting his close-trimmed beard into ripples.

But then he seemed to deflate. "All right," he muttered. "All right."

He looked up the stairs towards the cabin area. There was no sound. He then lifted himself up and over the back of the bench seat and ran up the stairs. He looked around the deck and checked a couple of doors, pausing especially outside the Barstows'. Then he came back and checked the galley and steward's pantry before finally rattling the door that led to the lazarette. Satisfied, he returned to his seat.

"Hutton." He leaned in, beckoning the captain closer. Hutton complied, bending close to the table to hear.

"I believe everything I've told you today. Everything. I am not alone. All over the European and American continents, there are men like myself, awakening to possibilities for a new future. We agree that our vision will never happen as long as there are structures like your religion. So, we decided that some of us would begin to act. We have purposely begun to undermine your fairy tales with realities of our own. It is grim work, Hutton. But it holds an unshakeable morality of its own. We are not beholden to the ancient trappings of a Bronze Age manuscript. Already our actions have caused the common people to question their god and his acolytes in the church."

Clarence looked around again, before leaning closer. He clasped his hands on the table top, leaning his chest on them as he bent forward. His voice dropped to a murmur.

"That man you saw on the quayside – he is my...patron. Unfortunately he is as great a buffoon as ever walked the earth. Naturally he is also a clergyman."

They regarded each other across the table, barely six inches apart. Clarence edged his hands closer to Hutton as he leaned in further.

"I've never really been a Christian man, Hutton. Not even when it was forced down my throat as a child. In the navy and within my family, I had to feign adherence to it for the sake of decorum. But in recent years I have awakened to my own desires. I have thrown off the shackles of family and duty. The liberation I have felt, Hutton, is indescribable. I have become a new man. More than that. I have realised that I have become the *Übermensch* described by Friedrich Nietzsche." He spoke the last with a perfect German inflection.

"I can do and be whatever I please. People are my playthings, and my playground is the entire world."

There it is, thought Hutton. *That look I saw on the dock, and every day since. He believes he owns us.*

Clarence's pale blue eyes shone, his fingers touching Hutton's, the sensation joining with the scent of his pomade to draw all of Hutton's senses into this, his climactic account.

"There is no such thing as good and evil, Captain. There is only the will of man. A man can do whatever he pleases, and the degree to which he is willing to act cannot be judged by the mores of a slack-minded majority."

His hand crept up to clutch Hutton's sleeve. "But I *have* been judged, Hutton!"

Clarence's grip was uncomfortably tight, and the intensity of his gaze was reflected in his whole face. A flicker of a tiny muscle throbbed just beneath his eye. "The hierarchy of fools has judged me! They have despatched me to the New World to pursue my ambitions alone. The family have told their friends and sycophants that I am India-bound, even as they packed me aboard a common cargo ship to the Americas! But I can promise you this Hutton – I shall return. And when I do, it will be with the full intention of regaining the place my country has stripped from me."

Hutton's mind reeled. *He is on the run? A fugitive?* Another disconnected thought floated into his fatigued mind. Like a man without chips gambles everything on his last hand, Hutton gambled on his only coherent thought.

"What did you do? Did – was it anything to do with the woman you brought aboard?"

Hutton felt the man's breath on his cheek. They weren't even eye to eye any more. Clarence's other hand gripped Hutton's tunic at his chest and he had pulled him so close that his mouth was next to Hutton's ear, his words a sibilant hiss.

"You are a clever chap, Captain. Yes, Will. It is exactly why. That is why I killed her, too."

Hutton reflexively wrenched himself back. The dream vision rushed back into his head, joining the shock of Clarence's words. He struggled against the iron grip of Clarence, but the man was immensely strong and wrestled Hutton back to the table and held him close again. Hutton almost whimpered, as he pulled ineffectually at the hands fastened to his chest and arm.

"I was angry, Will! I brought her along for fun, just a girl from the town. It was our little secret. A dreamy, trusting young girl looking for adventure. But then you had to turn back, and I was trapped! It made me angry." His grip did not falter. "So I used her, and when I tired of her, I ripped her like a Whitechapel whore."

Hutton froze at these words. *Whitechapel?* His mind reeled back to the sensationalised events of the previous year.

But Clarence had moved on. "Oh yes, she's one of many, Will. You know what I mean, don't you?"

Hutton refused to believe what he was hearing. "No. No, not that...it can't be—"

Clarence kept his iron grip on the shattered captain. "Will, you must understand. I have done certain things that you consider monstrous, but I am no monster! Think of the good that has come about because of our decisive, unblinking actions! Whitechapel, Spitalfields, Bethnal Green - they were wretched, squalid places, filled with the dregs of society; the men all pitiful, broken drunks, while the women would sell themselves for a farthing! But since the murders, these people are no longer regarded as the idle poor; no, now they are helpless victims! Only now do the worthy and religious idlers take note. The police have turned the place into a detectives' jamboree; they're trying in vain to catch Jack the Ripper, but in the process they are turning out some of the worst gangs and whore-runners in England! Others, the wealthy and privileged, have taken note of the squalor and are trying to restore dignity and order to these wretched people's lives. The religious have been stung into action, helping relieve the poor of their vile privations. You have to see this, Hutton! The violence was so extreme, so random – it struck terror into an entire city, Will! It has created the conditions for men and women to act, to change wasted lives into something better. Something no religion ever did."

Clarence's eyes were shining with zeal, the conviction of noble ideas from which Hutton could only recoil in horror. He spoke the only words he could assemble from his reeling mind.

"You are the Whitechapel Murderer?" He could hardly bring himself to say the words. "Jack the Ripper?"

Clarence sighed. "Well, not just me, Will. We worked as a group. But I would say I was the most committed."

"But this last woman? You killed her on my ship! What possible purpose could that fulfil?"

Clarence smiled ruefully. "It's like this, Will – you begin a foul work born of necessity, but through repetition and familiarity, in the end you find it's easy. An efficient solution to an awkward problem."

Hutton felt faint, his mouth working as he tried to articulate the thoughts that were fluttering through his overwhelmed consciousness like flights of bats. Clarence's face hovered very close to his own, barely in the focus of Hutton's wavering eyes.

"I couldn't take her with me, Will, especially while you seemed so keen to stay in Greenock. I told you, I work to spread chaos for the good that it will bring! Your crew are quiescent exactly because of what I have promised them. By the time they realise it, we'll be snug in Rio. I'm actually helping you."

He relaxed his hold on Hutton and sank back into his seat. "See, Will – even if your god were real, he could not in good conscience stop me. For this reason you can give up praying him to help you put me down for the rest of this voyage."

Hutton hadn't thought beyond this one terrible moment; but at these words, his tortured thoughts began turning to God. Clarence's next pronouncement cut him short.

"Listen, Will. I already know how we are going to work this to a beneficial conclusion. You are going to read my little postcard again and do what it says. And if you breathe a single word of this to anyone – if you lift a finger against me – perhaps I will turn my attentions on *her*."

Hutton wilted at these words, fully aware of whom he meant.

"Yes, Captain Hutton. I could use her and rip her like the others. You wouldn't like that, Will. It would break you, wouldn't it? Don't think I haven't seen the way you look at her. You follow her around with your eyes like a lovestruck debutant. And you, a married man too, I'll wager! Well, I can't argue that you'd do well for yourself to keep a pretty young thing like that happy – perhaps when you've seen the back of her husband, eh? Won't be long, by my reckoning."

Hutton straightened up, filled with righteous anger but cowed by fear of the man sitting opposite, muscular arms now folded, having demonstrated his supremacy beyond any doubt.

The captain's disgust somehow found a voice, tinged with reproach. "For all your high ideals, you are simply evil, Mr Clarence. The very embodiment of the devil's pride. You sin grievously against men and women, and treat it as sport."

Clarence gave an encouraging smile. "Yes, be angry, Hutton. That might just be the beginning of your own freedom." He paused, and a look of what might have passed for concern crossed his face. "Look here, Will. I told you this before: I like you. I never wanted to bring you in on this, but you wanted to know. And I, above all men, appreciate what it feels like not to get what I want. Therefore, I had to tell you. I wanted us to get along. But I allowed you to choose."

He remained seated, still hunched forward, elbows on the table, smoothing his thick hair back with one hand, while staring into the middle distance, as if pondering the wisdom of his confession.

He is not merely evil, but insane. Hutton had no other means of measuring this terrifying revelation. *Is it even true? Perhaps he is just trying to intimidate me.*

He decided, in defiance of every instinct within, to dig a little more. His hunger was forgotten. He wrestled with the desire to clap Clarence in irons immediately, set against the terrifying thought that he might carry out his threat against Elizabeth; it would take time for Hutton to round up some loyal crew, ample time for Clarence to take Mrs Barstow's life. The thought of him violating the perfect skin of the woman's neck with a knife...Hutton convulsed inside.

He considered his own position. *What if I have already lost the crew?* He thought of Hanson's treachery, already reported by the steward. How else could Clarence enforce such a threat if he wasn't already expecting help? Hutton felt utterly trapped. He had sat down to eat with the devil, and was choking on it.

"Who was the woman? What happened to her?" He almost whispered. Clarence looked up lazily, continuing to smooth his long hair down the back of his neck.

"Don't worry, Hutton, no-one's going to find her, even if anyone came looking. She went off the ship in my sea chest along with the blankets, towels and everything else. In the care of my mentor, as it were. I left her as a message to them that banishing me has a steep price."

Hutton remembered the dream, vivid in its detail, as the monstrous wave brought the girl back from the dead. He shuddered. "When? When did this happen?"

"Ah, Hutton, is it worth worrying about? Really, man, what's done is done. The dead sleep and the living live on."

"But you used my crew to help you! You've made them your accomplices!"

"Now, Will, I use whatever I have available to achieve my goals. Your poor men are willing dupes, strung along on the promise of something they won't get!" Clarence chuckled at his own duplicity, evidently considering it a virtue.

Something else surfaced in Hutton's tired mind, rent to the point of exhaustion by the morning's events. A terrible thought.

"The meat? The meals we ate? Was it her?" he asked in a small voice.

Clarence stared at him for a moment before guffawing loudly, throwing his head back in peals of laughter that left him wiping tears from his eyes.

"Good god, *no*, Captain! What kind of man do you think I am?" He laughed all the more heartily, his broad shoulders shaking at the idea that Hutton should have turned the merely grotesque into the macabre.

"This is why I like you, Will. Really, your persistence is commendable. But come now, you should get some sleep, man. You look like you've had a rough night."

He rose from the table and stretched his long arms. He paused when he noticed Hutton staring, uncomprehending, a man set adrift on unfamiliar tides.

"Come on, Will. You just get me to Rio, and you can all go your merry way. Even the fair Mrs Barstow. As long as you keep our little chat quiet, we can get along as if nothing happened, what?"

He cracked his knuckles and set off up the stairs towards his cabin, giving Hutton's shoulder a manly squeeze as he passed.

Hutton rubbed the area he touched, as if trying to find the point of reality where the conversation had happened. He stood dazed, rocking slightly, the headache now hammering at his forehead between temple and eyebrow. Running out of resolve, he slumped back into the seat.

He was still there an hour later when the Barstows' door burst open and the distraught woman began calling for the doctor. George Barstow was dead.

PART TWO

Still treads the shadow of his foe,
And forward bends his head,
The Ship drove fast,
Loud roared the blast,
And Southward aye we fled.

- Samuel Taylor Coleridge, *The Rime of the Ancient Mariner*

Chapter Ten

Blake stood in the sparse, clinical space of the Workhouse Infirmary mortuary. His nostrils were assaulted by the sharp tang of carbolic and formaldehyde, a new chemical preservative being used for bodies, according to the hospital administrator, Dr Dean.

The doctor was occupied, fussing with the men from the Island Constabulary who were holding their lamps close to the walls, examining the entrances and windows of the tiled room.

Blake stood with Peabody, while they quietly digested the latest piece of information.

The missing body was unidentified, but it was a man, that much was certain; it was also the last body to be retrieved from the sea, two days after the wreck. The initial admission report, signed by Dean himself, stated that the person had probably died prior to the accident, as it was found wrapped in a sailcloth shroud, the usual preparation for burial at sea.

According to Dean, the man had been pronounced dead by the first doctor to examine him on its arrival at the National Hospital in Ventnor, where all the survivors were initially brought. He was later moved to this place – one of the remotest buildings on the island but the second-largest hospital.

Once the two policemen had examined the likely exits, a theory was proposed; the only plausible explanation was foul play. The sergeant, a slightly rotund, red-faced man with a bristly moustache by the name of Trevannion, helpfully suggested that the body had been removed by person or persons unknown, for reasons as yet unknown.

"Well, sirs, it seems to me that body snatchers would take advantage of an unexpected prize like some well-preserved and unidentified bodies. Theft for gain is not unusual in this day and age."

He put away his notebook and continued his theorising. "It would be worthwhile putting a notice out to the hospitals on the island to beware of attempts to pass bodies on for medical use or post mortem training."

Blake tapped his fingers on the brim of his hat impatiently. "You may pursue that idea, Sergeant, but we need to find out the identity of the body."

Peabody agreed. "Quite. As you know, we have an accounting of all but five of the people on board the *Irex*, and four of those are men. It would not be a stretch to say it was one of them, all things considered."

Blake pressed his lips together. "I rather fancy I know exactly which of the four it is." He turned to the sergeant, who was shifting impatiently himself, itching to leave the unfamiliar smells of the morgue. "Sergeant, I would like a constable to assist me. We have an investigation which cannot wait."

The sergeant, predictably, began to object. "Sir, with respect, as the coroner, you already have a case to hear; I really don't think—"

Blake interrupted him. "You've finally said something that makes sense, Sergeant. You really *don't* think." His abruptness caused Peabody to look up in alarm.

Blake followed up with another blunt rebuke. "I am coroner in this case, and a material investigation has arisen in direct connection to it. Therefore, Sergeant Trevannion, you will assign me a constable for the purposes of this investigation, and I shall discharge it in my capacity as coroner, and you shall respect my granted powers."

The sergeant gaped. Peabody stared, as if he expected the sergeant to vanish in a puff of smoke before his eyes.

Trevannion inevitably cracked. "Very good, sir. I will assign you Constable Hollis. He's bright enough, for a young lad. And, er, I'm sure we may offer you the resources of the Island Constabulary if you need them."

Blake nodded his appreciation, and followed the policemen out of the mortuary, shaking hands with the fussing Dr Dean as he went. Dean seemed to be more worried about the reputation of his hospital than any genuine concern about the theft of a body from a locked room. But Blake already knew that the likely body snatchers were not hospital employees, and their goal was to ensure that the body concerned never surfaced again.

* * *

The next day, Mr Blake arrived with Mr Peabody at the court house just before eight a.m. A fine drizzle fell as the men once

149

again mounted the steps. They had spent the better part of the previous evening piecing together the written testimonies and comparing them to the knowledge they had gained over the past two days.

Rennie had spent his day at the Ventnor National Hospital, trying to interview the frail survivors of the wreck. There were still too many gaps, not least the controversy of the mysterious Mr Clarence; Blake was keen to find out what the reporter had turned up.

The assistant at the door unlocked it to let them in; Blake breathed in the same dry, musty air as he had on the first day of his arrival. They went through to Court Room No.1 and settled themselves at the bench. The requirement for a closed session had resulted in a lonely courtroom for the inquest; there was no buzz of expectation among the visitors, no reporters and no jury. Blake glanced at his pocket watch and wondered when Rennie and Thornthwaite would be making an appearance.

As if on cue, on the dot of eight-thirty, the door at the back of the courtroom banged open, and the dishevelled figure of Rennie stumbled through the doorway.

"Mr Rennie!" exclaimed Peabody. "What on earth happened?"

The man was limping as he moved towards the bench, and Blake made out a livid red mark on his cheek, a split lip, and another contusion on the centre of his forehead.

"Good lord, Rennie!" Blake stood and made to move round the bench to the battered newsman, but the Glaswegian waved him to sit. The reporter slumped into a seat next to the table in front of the bench, and began rubbing at his knee.

"Bloody hell, Mr Blake! What have you gotten me into?" He opened his mouth and pulled at a couple of his teeth, satisfied that none came away in his hand. He shook his head and grimaced, rubbing gently at the angry lump on his forehead. Then he began to pat his pockets for a cigarette.

Blake was appalled. "What happened to you, Mr Rennie?"

He lit the cigarette and took a long draw. It seemed to calm him down. "I was downstairs at the Osborne getting my breakfast. I remembered I'd left my notes upstairs – the interviews with the patients from the hospital yesterday. When I ran back up to get them, I found two clowns in my room, stealing my notes!"

Blake's heart sank - Rennie succeeded at the hospital, but the conspirators had foiled them again.

But Rennie's story wasn't over. "The sons of bitches tried to lamp me but I wasn't born yesterday. So by my reckoning, one left a few teeth behind"– at these words, he held up his hand, showing a set of skinned knuckles- "and the other tried to grab me round the neck, so I guess he ran off needing a new nose!"

He pointed with the butt end of his cigarette to the lump on his forehead, the point of contact; Rennie was a brawler all right.

The terror of Scotland, recalled Blake. He marvelled at the man, but was genuinely concerned. Rennie was right; Blake had got the newsman involved, though he realised with some satisfaction that his hunch had been correct. Someone was trying to subvert the investigation.

"You'll be pleased to know I'm fine, Mr Blake. And in the end, they got away with precisely nothing." He held the cigarette in his mouth as he rummaged in his portmanteau;

151

his knuckles were wrapped in a bloodied handkerchief. He pulled out his notepad, which looked in scarcely better condition than the man himself. "And there are some things here which you need to see."

Blake was still concerned. "Very well, but I must know – did you recognise either man?"

Rennie shrugged. "One looked familiar, but I don't know from where. Perhaps from the telegraph office. Or maybe the court house. But if I saw them again, I'd know. Believe me, I have a perfect memory for faces once I've had a good look at one."

Blake called the Clerk over; the man had not batted an eyelid at the preceding exchange. "Mr Clerk, I would like to adjourn until I have reviewed Mr Rennie's report. We will delay the start of proceedings until further notice. In the meantime, inform the constable that a crime has been committed, a burglary and battery against our friend Mr Rennie."

The Clerk nodded again, "Very good, sir," and took off to make the necessary arrangements, despite Rennie's protestations.

"Mr Rennie, we'll review your evidence shortly; first I have some communications to arrange. This has finally gone out of hand." Blake stood up and walked out of the courtroom. He walked briskly to the main reception, where he attracted the attention of the ever-attentive Jeremy.

"I have to arrange a telegram, on court business. Direct to the Lord Chancellor's office. Immediately." The young man snapped to his work, disappearing once again into the back office, and reappearing presently to escort Mr Blake to the telegraph office inside the court house.

Blake dictated his message, watched as it was passed to the transmitter operator, and listened as the young man rattled out the transmission in a rapid series of clicks. While the message was being sent, he watched the other staff, looking for any sign that they may be especially attentive to his message; his paranoia was growing by the minute. If the main post office telegraph had been compromised, he should be equally careful of the one on his very doorstep.

"If you would, Jeremy, I need to make another enquiry." They repeated the telegraph process, but this time Blake's communication went to a different London address.

"And Jeremy? I shall require immediate delivery of any reply direct to the courtroom. This is a very urgent matter."

Blake thanked the young receptionist before making his way back to the courtroom. He took his place at the bench, and beckoned Rennie up. The Scot painfully negotiated the three steps up to the bench and took the spare seat formerly occupied by Mr Rudd.

Blake found himself liking the scrappy Glaswegian in spite of his deeply held opinions about news reporters. Rennie seemed to be cut from very different cloth to the despicable vultures of Fleet Street and Wapping with whom Blake was familiar.

"Right, sirs. I found a very interesting chap in the hospital by the name of Reid. As far as we know he is the senior ranking officer to make it. He swallowed a lot of water, and he is suffering from exposure; the doctors said he should pull through – he's a tough young lad by the looks of it."

"What did he say?"

"I'm getting there, Mr Blake." Rennie's quick blue eyes flicked up to Blake's own. He grinned from habit, and Blake saw the flicker of pain pass across his face as his cracked lips protested.

Just then, the door at the back of the courtroom opened, and the young constable, Hollis, walked in.

"Excuse me, sirs, but I've had a report of a burglary and assault."

Rennie waved a dismissive hand. "It's nothing, young fellow. They never stole anything, and as far as assault is concerned, you should see the other two!"

Blake realised what he had missed. "Wait, gentlemen! Of course! Constable, get on to your colleagues at Ryde. Tell them to be on the lookout for two men. Both would appear to be injured; one is likely to have a recent and obvious wound to the face. They may be boarding a ferry to the mainland. Have them detain the men and notify me when they are secured. Understand?"

Hollis nodded and read back Blake's words with perfect recall.

"Good boy. Don't delay!"

The constable touched his forelock and set off for the door.

Peabody clasped his hand on Blake's upper arm. "Well done, sir! I hope they can get the word in time. The ferry leaves at ten-thirty."

"We shall see, Mr Peabody. Now, please, let us get back to business."

Rennie continued. "Now, this Reid was Third Mate. He said the captain took him off his watch and assigned him to the Second Mate's position."

Peabody interjected. "The second mate is still among the missing, Mr Blake."

154

Blake nodded and motioned Rennie to continue.

"He says Captain Hutton took the second mate off his watch to look after the woman passenger, Elizabeth Barstow. Originally she was travelling with her husband, but he died on the voyage. Natural causes, Reid says. In any case, no woman is permitted to go about the ship alone, so the second mate was acting as chaperone."

Blake frowned. "Seems a little excessive."

"Aye, so Reid says; he was obsessed with the woman – he barely let her out of his sight."

"Reid was obsessed with the woman?"

Rennie paused to take a final draw on his spent cigarette. "Sorry, I meant – it was the captain. Reid said the captain was hovering around her cabin and even stood by outside when she was bathing. Captain Hutton watched over her at night while the second mate watched her during the day.

"Reid said throughout the entire week the storm was blowing, Hutton didn't sleep. He also said he believed the captain was – these are his words – 'greatly impaired by his attentions towards the passengers.'"

Blake raised his eyebrows, keeping his face still. "What did Reid say about the other passenger?"

Rennie gave another grin, and winced again. "Aye, he had some things to say. It doesn't sound good." He consulted his notebook again. "Aye... well – here is what he said: the first mate told Reid around the beginning of the storm that the captain had begun to deface the ship's log. Reid says the mate believed the captain was losing his mind, and the mate considered relieving him of his command."

The other two men gaped. Mutiny was an entirely new angle.

155

"Reid also thinks that the passenger Clarence was blackmailing the captain in some way. He said that the woman was involved."

Peabody shifted further forward. "Did he say why?"

Rennie shook his head. "He didn't know, but he felt there was some romantic triangle between the captain, this Clarence, and the girl. But listen to this. He said, and I quote, 'It ended badly.' So I pressed him for the rest, but he just started crying. That's the last bit of sense I could get out of him."

Blake steepled his fingers and closed his eyes. *A devilish matter indeed.* "I need some time to digest this before we hear the next group of testimonies. Thank you very much again, Mr Rennie, you have behaved with great integrity." He paused, regarding the newsman who laboured to his feet, nursing his right knee. "And Mr Rennie, I think another visit to the hospital on your own account might be advisable."

Rennie touched his forehead, close to the bruise which was already changing colour to a reddish purple. "That I might, Mr Blake."

"Take care, Mr Rennie. Please send word when you are back at your hotel."

"That I will, Your Honour." He let himself gingerly down the steps and limped with as much dignity as he could muster to the oak doors at the back of the courtroom.

* * *

By ten-thirty, Blake was ready to hear testimony. Unusually, he noted, the ever-present Thornthwaite had neglected to attend. He considered for a moment whether perhaps

Thornthwaite had been one of Rennie's assailants; but dismissed the idea as quickly. If the Glaswegian had as good a recall of faces as he claimed, then surely he would have been able to identify Thornthwaite from his presence at the inquest. He nodded towards the Clerk to summon the first witness of the day.

James Murray the bosun's mate was in relatively good shape. He had made no previous written statement, by virtue of being illiterate. Apart from the raw redness on his prominent cheekbones, the man bore fewer scars of their ordeal; he had been kicking his heels in a Ventnor boarding house awaiting his call to the stand for over a week.

Peabody was asking the questions at this point. "Mr Murray, the inquest thanks you for your assistance at the cliffs yesterday. For the record, did you personally witness any of the passengers or crew perish on the *Irex*?"

"Aye, I'm sorry to say I saw old Harry Grayson and Dick Stearne go. They had badly broken legs and couldn't climb up the mast. I saw them up by the boat deck when a fearsome roller came and swept them all away. I know someone else was with them – I couldn't say for sure, but I thought it was the doctor. And I definitely saw one of the apprentice boys – I think it was Ogilvie – falling from the mainstays as we tried to get to the foremast."

Blake understood. The three bodies so far recovered had been tentatively identified as the three men Murray had mentioned. "Mr Murray, did you speak to any of the officers in the days before the wreck?"

"Not really, sir. But I did notice the captain was acting strange."

"In what way?"

157

"Well, we all knew he was holding a candle for the lady we had on board —"

Blake cut him off. "Please limit your evidence to what you personally witnessed, Mr Murray."

"I'm sorry, sir. Well, the captain spent most of his time with the lady. The bosun was saying—"

"Mr Murray; if you are going to quote hearsay you need to make clear the bosun spoke directly to you."

Murray thrust his calloused hands forward on the table in a show of frustration. "All right, sir. The bosun told me straight that the captain was going mad with jealousy over this girl, and it was because Mr Clarence had got in with her."

Blake glanced across at Peabody, who raised his bushy eyebrows in his customary fashion. "Did the bosun say how he knew this?"

"Aye sir, he was quarantined in the cabin before the big storm, and he heard Clarence with the lady in his room – err...well, they were...together, you might say."

Peabody pulled a face, and Blake decided to move on. "Do you know where the officers were at the time of the wreck?"

"No sir. I was forward in the forecastle – I'd just come off watch at bells. The first thing I knew was hitting the shore; an almighty crash it was, everything in the forecastle that was still standing got knocked down, and then the waves started breaking right through our quarters. I just grabbed my boots and made for the rigging with everybody else."

Blake conferred quietly with Peabody before turning his attention back to Murray. "Mr Murray, do you have anything else you wish to say to this inquest?"

Murray thought genuinely at some length before answering. "Sir, I have one thing. I was with the bosun, must have been the third or fourth night of the hurricane, and I saw something I ain't ever seen in thirty years at sea."

Blake looked up. "Please, go on."

Murray swallowed. "It was the change of watch at four in the morning. The storm was running fierce. I was with the bosun, and was watching Mr Reid and Mr Mackie, closer than you are now, sir. They were saying straight to Captain's face that we should run for port. I thought it was bordering on mutiny. I remember exactly what Captain said."

Peabody had stopped scribbling. The stenographer paused. The air in the room seemed to stop moving; the only sounds were the clock and the faint hiss of the heating pipes.

Blake broke the momentary silence, wanting to be clear. "What did you hear him say, Mr Murray?"

Murray swallowed, and with an incredulous shake of his head, he spoke. "Captain Hutton said, 'I'll sink her before we put into port.'"

Chapter Eleven

Atlantic Ocean, 130 miles west of Bishop Rock
Monday, 30th December 1889

Hutton watched the young widow Elizabeth Barstow as she stared out over the ocean. She stood facing the setting sun, her head high with her long, loose hair flying behind her. She clasped her arms about her as if hugging herself in comfort.

Second Mate Durrick stood off nearby, vigilant for any prurient crewman who might let his lusts get the better of him.

Hutton had given Durrick strict instructions to keep Mrs Barstow almost a prisoner, chaperoned day and night, for fear she might be accosted or violated in some way. Though Durrick may have lacked some of the manly qualities of the other officers, Hutton felt he held sufficient authority to dissuade any crewman. As a last resort, the loaded revolver he carried would have done the job.

Mrs Barstow herself appeared oblivious to her vulnerability. Hutton twice tried to sit down and speak with the grieving woman but both times was soundly rebuffed. He noted with a great deal of shame how she remained under the impression he and Clarence were in some sort of convivial partnership; she blamed him for bringing Clarence to her door the day her husband died, though Hutton couldn't have wished for anything less.

Hutton couldn't conceive of telling her the truth without putting her life in danger. True to his devil's bargain with Clarence, he had told no-one of their conversation. He toyed with the suspicion that Clarence had fabricated the whole story, but instinct told him it was the truth. Most compelling were the dreams. The prowling beast he'd dreamt in Greenock and the dead woman on the ship inclined Hutton to believe Clarence was telling the truth. Would God have given him such prophetic dreams to warn him if Clarence were not whom he claimed to be?

It left him deeply disturbed at the presence of a notorious and unrepentant murderer on board his ship. If Clarence was the infamous Jack the Ripper, those murders were heinous indeed. And the perpetrator had proved a dangerous and so far untouchable man. Hutton couldn't afford to take Clarence's threats lightly.

Elizabeth hadn't moved for about a quarter of an hour. She came up on deck periodically, but had long ceased her visits to the saloon, preferring instead to take all her meals in her room. Tom Eustace had dutifully reported to Hutton that the lady was eating well, seemed to bathe regularly and was living a tidy if limited existence in the small cabin she'd shared with her husband until Christmas Eve.

The crew also felt for the young widow left with the ignominious task of finishing her solo journey to Rio, from where she would likely seek an immediate repatriation to England. Hutton resolved to personally find her a berth aboard a passenger steamer to take her speedily back to

Southampton or London – as soon as the odious Clarence was gone.

He ached from his head to his innards – concern for Elizabeth Barstow, fear of the predations of Clarence, and his own emotional turmoil conspired so he rarely took more than three or four hours of sleep.

The toll on his alertness was frightening. His eyes ached constantly – even the orange glow of sunset caused them to water. The emotional burdens he carried affected his appetite as acutely as his sleep; the dull cramps he felt in the pit of his stomach when he considered the situation chased hunger away, even when he was barely eating one meal a day.

He also carried the burden of the decisions he avoided. He tried to delegate contact with the passengers to Eustace the steward and Reid or Durrick; in the days since George Barstow's funeral he'd made little contact with the passengers at any rate. It was just as well, for Hutton no longer felt he could confront Clarence in the matter of his deeds past or present.

As Mrs Barstow left with Durrick trailing her, Hutton watched her go with a sense of lost love. He tried to discipline his feelings for her with greater resolve. He kept his midnight vigils for Sarah; he knew she would have kept hers from night to night, while he toyed with her affections by keeping one eye on another. His feelings of lovelorn butterflies had stopped overnight as the import of Clarence's threat took hold. Those agreeable clenchings had been replaced by a gnawing anxiety whenever he remembered Clarence's vile words. *I could rip her like the others.*

Once Mrs Barstow had gone back to her room, the men of the forecastle re-emerged. They appreciated the extended

162

twilight as the ship moved southwards; sunset was now at the civilised time of five o'clock.

Hutton actually drew some comfort from the behaviour of the crew so far. For the most part the men had worked hard and remained in high spirits, despite their false start and the death of a passenger. The musical abilities of Dick Stearne and his companions meant there were always snatches of music and laughter to be heard drifting up from the forecastle to soothe Hutton's frayed nerves. Only when the bosun appeared and barked his rough, expletive-laden maledictions did the mood falter.

The men's sustained high morale would have been testimony to their own good character were it not for Clarence's claims to have promised them something extra. Worse still, the gentleman seemed entirely prepared to renege, leaving Hutton with an even bigger problem at some point.

As he considered, Hutton felt a strong urge to speak to the ordinary seamen, as if their remoteness from his situation might somehow offer him comfort. He thought about visiting the men in their forecastle accommodation, but decided instead to honour tradition and wait to be invited.

His thoughts turned instead to the young apprentices, some of whom would be climbing the greasy pole toward a command of their own one day. The half-deck companionway was just behind the main deckhouse, and there were no barriers of etiquette to prevent Hutton from walking in unannounced.

As Hutton descended the steps, he began to hear another musical sound – a mouth organ accompanied by enthusiastic clapping. He stepped out from the companionway into the

163

low-ceilinged half-deck, and there before him, spread over a space about twelve feet square, were the lads' donkeys' breakfast mattresses, each with a neat stowage consisting of their sea crates and assorted belongings.

The lights burned brightly, which enabled Hutton to stand unnoticed in the shadow of the steps, aghast at what unfolded before him.

The lads lolled around the edge of their enclosed space, clapping as one of their number danced outrageously with a full-size mannequin of what Hutton could only assume was Mrs Barstow. They had made her from bedstraw and painted a face on a pillow cloth that covered the head of the doll. As it whirled in the inappropriately-placed hands of the dancer, he saw the resemblance in the full lips and large eyes – the horsehair stuffing of a pillow a passable facsimile of the passenger's chestnut hair which whipped from side to side with every fling of the dummy. The doll's chest was stuffed to an enormously exaggerated degree, far eclipsing the already generous proportions of the original.

More alarming for Hutton was the woman's dress and hat that the mannequin wore; he bristled with protective indignation that the lady's trust had been violated. He stepped from the shadows and within two paces was in the midst of the merriment.

"What the blazes is this?"

The music stopped abruptly, the lad dropping the doll in shock. All six apprentices leapt to their feet in a reflexive but sloppy attention.

Hutton was in no mood for a simple inspection. The pent-up tension of the past five days came out in a torrent of angry

164

remonstration. "What the hell is this? Have you no shame at all?"

Six crestfallen faces looked back at him with expressions betraying their emotions, a spectrum of discomfort ranging from bewilderment to outright fear.

"I want to know who did this."

If Hutton expected the miscreant responsible to break down and confess, he was to be disappointed. He looked into each set of saucer eyes and saw only loyalty among friends – no-one would be tattling; neither would anyone admit culpability.

"That's how it is, is it?" Hutton was actually shaking as the rage, not anxiety, came boiling out of him. *Don't any of you say a word*, he thought. *I don't think I'd be able to stop myself thrashing the life out of you.*

To the lads' good fortune, none spoke. Hutton promised reprisal, and barked a few home truths to the young men about life on board ship. He realised the rage was his own impotence, and here at last he had found a place to vent it.

The boys stood rigid, young Bonner in particular looking as wretched as he had the night of the storm. Hutton went round the eyes again, and decided that the oldest apprentice was also the boldest. He went and stood right in the young man's face. Hutton knew him as one of the lads who carried Clarence's chest, on the first day he'd had the misfortune of clapping eyes on the accursed man.

"Ogilvie?"

The lad nodded. "Aye, sir."

Not afraid, thought Hutton. *But he doesn't know what's coming.* "Ogilvie, where did you get these ladies' clothes?"

The lad's eyes squirmed to the sides, trying to catch a companion's eye, but Hutton's bearded face filled his field of vision.

"I will ask once more, and only once. If you decide not to answer, I will have you on the main royal yardarm on every watch through the night." It was a wild threat – to put a boy to work on the highest point of the main mast at night was practically a death sentence.

But the boy knew it was by no means an idle one. His Adam's apple plunged and rose as he considered his options.

"Last time. Where did the clothes come from, Ogilvie?" Hutton stood back so there was again a foot of space between their chests.

Ogilvie's eyes flicked again, before he made up his mind. "Sir. They were a gift."

Hutton wound himself up to explode again, but the lad quickly added, "The passenger gave them to us."

Hutton's eyebrows shot up in disbelief. "Mrs Barstow gave you one of her outfits?"

The lad again corrected himself. "I mean, the gentleman, Mr Clarence, sir. He said they were a gift from him and we could do what we wanted with them."

Hutton held his eyes for a moment longer, before he spun around to see the other lads against the opposite wall. Their shoulders had slumped when Ogilvie caved in, but now they stood up straight again under the captain's eye.

Hutton was about to begin a lecture, when the truth dawned on him. His sleep-deprived mind had tortured him for days, and this lapse was merely a symptom of the tension. His mind, usually sharp and focused, seemed to slither to the solution with all the urgency of molasses.

Why would Clarence have a woman's dress? It could only have belonged to his erstwhile victim, redundant and no longer part of his world, just as the chest had been. Hutton reeled again.

The boys noticed this sudden change as their captain once again seemed to deflate. He took a couple of deep breaths and then spoke, much more quietly, so the lads craned in to hear.

"You will destroy this...thing. Then you, Mr Ogilvie, shall report to the galley and instruct Mr Howes the donkeyman to burn these clothes in the steam furnace, and you will do this tonight. Do you understand me, you cretinous little vermin?"

The boys' faces expressed only horrified awe; none had ever heard the usually mild-spoken captain use such language. Six heads nodded in complete agreement, and their muted "Yessirs" overlapped one another in their eagerness to bend to Hutton's will.

The captain clasped his trembling hands behind his back and stalked out of the lit space, ducking back into the darkness of the stairway until he emerged on deck, where the lamps had been lit and the sun had vanished below the horizon.

Hutton stared at the darkened sea as he tried to fight the emotions that threatened to engulf him. *Why would God do this?* He was on a ship with two passengers who threatened to tear him apart. He guessed it was some kind of test.

He realised he needed to lie down. The rage that poured out of him eased the dead feeling in his stomach but drained him physically and emotionally; he knew that sleep would come easily.

Pausing for no-one, he walked half the length of the ship and let himself into the quarterdeck cabin. Without a single thought for Mrs Barstow, he locked his door behind him, threw off his clothes and lay on his bed. As soon as he closed his eyes, a wave of heaviness rolled over him; within ten seconds he had fallen into a black, dreamless sleep.

*   *   *

Hutton awoke suddenly, his heart pounding hard, though he had no idea why. The side of his face was mired in the saliva collected on his pillow, his eyes filmed with sleep. In the darkness of his room he had no idea what time it was, nor how much, or how little, sleep he had managed. Then he heard the soft knocking at his door that had startled him into wakefulness.

He flung back the blankets and stepped across the room, feeling the chill of the air on his body; only as he reached for the door handle did he realise he was completely exposed.

"Who is it?"

"Eustace, sir" came the muted reply. Hutton let out a sigh; he quickly located his trousers and pulled them on, grabbing his tunic and reaching for the door. It swung halfway open, and the angular face of the steward peered at Hutton's, with a look of concern.

"What is it, Mr Eustace?"

If Eustace was bothered, he didn't betray his feelings. "Sir, we missed you at four bells – I wondered if you wanted your supper."

Four bells? "Four bells of the morning?" Hutton was confused, still clearing sleep from his mind.

"Sir, it's ten o'clock in the evening now."

Hutton gulped – it meant he had been asleep for just four hours. "Very well, Eustace. I shall bathe first, and take supper in the saloon." He paused. "How is Mrs Barstow?"

Eustace's shoulders fell at this – an almost imperceptible gesture which conveyed his weariness at his captain's obsession with the woman.

"She took supper in her room at four bells of the first dog. She appears to be in good health, sir."

Hutton nodded, his eyes looking elsewhere. "Very good, Tom. I'll be downstairs in twenty minutes."

It was the steward's turn to nod, and he padded out of sight, long arms swinging, as Hutton closed the door.

The baths provided for passengers and officers aboard the *Irex* were luxurious by the standards of previous generations. The steam engines on the ship provided an abundance of clean, hot water for bathing, though it was warm at best by the time it had negotiated the byzantine plumbing. Hutton ran his to the most satisfying depth he could manage and lowered himself into the water, letting the warmth flood into the cracks of his skin and felt the weariness in his mind and body seem to float off him like the detritus of clothes fluff and skin that lifted from his body. He let his eyes close.

The image of the leering face of Clarence leapt unbidden to his mind's eye. He shook his head to rid himself of it. He tried to think of home, and Sarah, but instead the image of the weeping Mrs Barstow, her chest pressed against his, displaced these more honourable thoughts.

He slid downward in the tub and let his head sink into the water. He pondered the twin poles of attraction and revulsion represented by his two passengers. It stung that his strong

169

attraction to Mrs Barstow was met only by her coolness; and yet Hutton's own deep antipathy towards Clarence was undermined by the genuine fondness the monstrous man showed him in return.

Hutton prayed. He reached out to the Saviour who had been a source of comfort, peace and reassurance throughout his darkest hours; but today, as on every day of this miserable voyage, the Lord was silent.

He broke the surface of the water, his lungs filling with cool air as the water shook from his face. He wiped the water from his eyes then gripped the edges of the tub to haul himself upright.

He stood for a moment, feeling the chill on his body as the water dripped off him. He reached for the towel and pressed it to his face, the rough cotton pricking his skin. As he lifted his head and opened his eyes, a new thought entered his mind; like a dawn break, it brought immediate relief, a sense of breakthrough in his mental impasse.

Stop fighting this, Will. He toyed with the thought for long moments as he dried and rubbed himself with the rough towel. *I am trapped, but not imprisoned.* He was still captain of the *Irex*, and by God, he would take her to Rio, conclude his business with Clarence, return Mrs Barstow to England, and continue his voyage unmolested.

The simplicity of the answer stunned him. He had been trying to fix the situation, but in fact the answer lay in running before the storm, not ploughing through it.

His pact with Clarence remained intact. Mrs Barstow was safe, or as safe as she would be in any case, as long as he maintained his silence. Clarence had no reason to molest her, and his misdeeds of the past would remain unpunished only

170

until Hutton was able to seize the chance to report it to the Brazilian authorities. As soon as Hutton was sure Mrs Barstow was beyond Clarence's reach, he would do so.

The pure joy this conclusion awakened in Hutton's heart was visceral. It brought a new vitality to his movements.

He dressed fully, putting on shoes, uniform tunic and grabbing his hat from the floor. He paused in front of the small mirror on his modest dresser and inspected himself in the mirror for the first time in days. Sleep had darkened his eyes, but he could see a spark within them again. He combed his salt and pepper hair before carefully placing the hat. *Captain Hutton*. For the first time since he had left his own home, he actually saw himself smiling.

He unlocked and opened the door, and almost walked straight into Mrs Barstow.

"Oh, Captain!" she blurted, startled. Hutton stood, half in and half out of the door, still holding the handle. Without thinking, he smiled broadly at the sight of her.

"Good evening, Ma'am. Ah... do you need anything at all?"

She nodded, looking up into his face with the same direct manner he found so disconcerting. He was some inches taller than her, but in his mind she was always eye-to-eye. She was wearing a full length green dress of a modern cut, with shoulder puffs and a lace-covered, low back, while her long, chestnut-coloured hair had been tucked neatly into another high bun, with some strands falling to frame her face. He hadn't seen her in Salvation Army garb since George had died. She had fashioned a black armband from a stocking, which remained the only outward sign of mourning. Otherwise Hutton couldn't help but notice that she looked in better shape than him.

171

His unusually sanguine greeting left her looking puzzled. It didn't occur to him to ask why she was waiting outside his door.

"Captain, I... well, I wonder if you would care to accompany me to the saloon?"

Hutton must have looked startled, as she smiled, open-handed. "I meant, I was going to spend a little time in the saloon, and I wondered if you might be able to accompany me."

Hutton was grinning like a schoolboy. He realised this was their most intimate moment since she stepped aboard, her grieved clutching notwithstanding. "Of course!" he beamed. "I was just on my own way there. Would you excuse me if I eat? I haven't had a chance all day."

"Not at all, Captain! One must eat, of course." The formality was becoming strained as they both felt their way down this unfamiliar course. They stood awkwardly for a moment, before Mrs Barstow stepped back and let Hutton out of his room. He locked the door, and gestured for her to walk ahead of him down the stairs.

At the bottom, he motioned for her to sit at the same bench and table where he had confronted Clarence and heard his terrible confession. Hutton didn't appreciate the memory.

They didn't say a word until Eustace had placed Hutton's meal and silverware and retreated back upstairs.

Hutton tucked into his corned beef hash like a starving prisoner. He tried for the sake of decorum to eat slowly, but the hunger got the better of him.

Mrs Barstow regarded him with what he felt was a sympathetic eye rather than a scornful one. "Captain, you must take better care of yourself. We all depend on you."

172

When he met her eye, his mouth full, she added, "In some way or other. You are our captain, after all." She gave one of her tight smiles.

Hutton mumbled that he did indeed look after himself. Mrs Barstow studied him for a few moments, looked up over her shoulder at the cabin deck, and then leaned slightly forward. Her dress rustled as she moved her hands from her lap to the table. Once again, Hutton noticed, she wore no gloves so her bare arms and painted nails were placed in front of her on the table top.

"Captain, I have misjudged you. I feel obliged to apologise." Her earnest look and the unexpected words almost made him choke. He actually paused taking his next mouthful, and felt a low-intensity murmur in his gut as he looked back at her.

"When you came to my cabin the day George passed," – she paused momentarily to collect her emotions – "when Clarence came, I thought you had sent for him. I thought you a lesser man for bringing him to our door." She looked up and behind again. "I realise now that was a misjudgement on my part."

Hutton breathed out. It was a long time since he had enjoyed any words a woman had spoken to him quite as much. If he had left his bathroom in a state of renewed hope, this absolution made him euphoric. "Yes, that's true. Of course I never wanted him to approach you at such a difficult time." His appetite was waning. "May I ask – what caused you to change your mind?"

She looked behind her again. Hutton hadn't heard the tell-tale click of the door handle from Clarence's room; but Mrs Barstow clearly did not want the man to hear her speak.

"I've been watching how you behave around Mr Clarence." She spoke in a straight, no-nonsense tone, without condescension but not deferentially or demurely either. Hutton wondered if she might be one of the Suffragists, an infamous group of troublemakers demanding votes for women.

"You don't like him. I would go as far as to say you are repulsed by him. Yet he treats you like a friend, and you make no complaint. Would you say that was a fair judgement?" She glanced up again, then back to Hutton, who stared back at her in awe.

"Ma'am... I would say you were entirely correct."

She responded with one of her tight little smiles, and a slight nod. "Good."

Hutton's heart began to beat faster. Mrs Barstow broke eye contact to look at her hands on the table in front of her, linked her fingers and bent the tips of her thumbs together.

"Then I am sorry, Captain Hutton. I have judged you unfairly, and request your forgiveness."

Hutton swallowed. "Of course, ma'am, you have it. Unreservedly."

She smiled back, revealing her even teeth and the wide curve of her lips. "Thank you very much, Captain. Now please, finish your dinner. Though there are a few matters I would like to discuss with you."

Hutton tried to be polite and forced down the last of the hash; somehow his throat seemed to have constricted in the past few minutes. Having finished his mug of water, he mirrored Mrs Barstow's posture, clasping his own hands on the table before him. "Please, ma'am, what would you like to discuss? If there is anything I can do to improve your accommodations—"

"Nothing of the sort, Captain. It concerns my own welfare." She once again glanced up and behind towards the cabin deck. "I have become desperately lonely." Her lip trembled, and tears sprang into her eyes. Hutton saw her frustration as her emotions overcame her resolve.

"I needed someone to talk to, and I had to know if my conclusions about you are true." She sobbed once, as she reached quickly to retrieve a white handkerchief from the pocket somewhere in the folds of her dress. She dabbed quickly at each eye, and then quietly composed herself.

Hutton began to reach his hand across the table but thought better of it. He managed to fumble his hands back together and hoped she hadn't noticed.

She continued to speak, pausing every now and again to swallow as her words began to tremble. "George... was a good man. I don't know why the Lord took him. He has left me to continue alone, and the Lord has shown me that this will be a difficult voyage."

Hutton couldn't stop himself nodding in agreement.

"But I see that you are a good man too, Will Hutton. I didn't want to believe it, because I thought you were a friend of the man whom you brought to my door. But the Lord convinced me. And you convinced me by your dignified actions."

Hutton shifted awkwardly; a week ago he would have begged to hear such words drop from the lips of Elizabeth Barstow, yet now he felt uncomfortable.

"I need someone to talk to. I mean no impropriety, of course. But I want to trust you, Captain Hutton. And I need you to trust me."

Hutton felt this an odd request, and he looked at her as she dabbed again at her eyes; he wondered if he weren't perhaps walking into another confidence that might bind him, as he had with Clarence. The thought flashed across his mind that perhaps she had been the woman in the other trunk, colluding with Clarence to murder her husband and elope; perhaps they had been plotters together for many months. They would have made a formidable and handsome couple; he would have readily paired the composed and beautiful Elizabeth with the dashing and charismatic Clarence, were it not for their polarised beliefs.

If that is truly the case. Suspicion clawed away at his trust.

As he pondered, looking at her earnest, fine features, he decided that she was simply in need; a bereaved woman set adrift on the ocean without a single reason to be there anymore.

"Of course you can trust me, Mrs Barstow."

"Thank you, Captain Hutton."

They held another tense silence, during which both of them checked the top of the stairs and searched the quiet of the cabin deck with their hearing. Then Elizabeth leaned forward and spoke in a low murmur. "God showed me something else."

Hutton looked back at her. *I wonder if she had a dream?*

"Beware of Mr Clarence. Do not enter his confidence. He is not a good man, as you are, Will." He was surprised to hear her use his informal Christian name, as Clarence had. But in Clarence's booming tones it carried an assertion of ownership

176

and intimidation. In the soft voice of Mrs Barstow, it carried a frisson of intimate confidence.

Hutton suddenly ached to unburden himself to her; like an inverse of Scheherazade, he wanted to keep her near and spin his own tales until he was completely freed from the crushing burden he was hiding.

"Mrs Barstow—"

But she put a finger to her lips. "Captain, guard your words and your heart. We will speak again, and soon."

She held out her hand. Hutton took it uncertainly, and she brought the other up to clasp his rough, seaman's hand between her own, delicate and soft by comparison. "Thank you. And may God bless you. You will need all your strength for what lies ahead, I have no doubt." She released his hand. "Would you be able to take dinner with me each evening? Here, I mean?"

"I would be delighted to, ma'am, my other duties allowing, of course."

"Very well, Captain." "We shall meet here again." With another chorus of rustling, she edged herself out of the bench seat and smoothed down her dress front and back. "Until tomorrow, Captain."

Hutton melted before the full beam of her smile but betrayed nothing to the lady herself. The ache was back in the pit of his stomach as he watched her, flowing towards the stairs and dancing up them, holding up her skirts. The motion of the ship seemed to have no dampening effect on her progress, and he remained where he was until he heard the click of her door, feeling the familiar cocktail of conflicting emotions once again.

Then he remembered the words of poor, good, dead George Barstow: *You should listen to her; she will tell you things you need to know.* He resolved to do right by George, and Sarah, and God. But in reality all he had resolved was to listen to his Scheherazade, in the hope all their lives might be spared.

Chapter Twelve

"Come!" Mr Blake called in response to the knock at his hotel door. He'd just returned after a hearty breakfast downstairs in the Orchard Hotel. He rose to his feet as the door opened to admit the battered figure of Gordon Rennie.

The Scot was using a stick to walk, and he hobbled towards the chair by the fire opposite Blake's. The coroner felt another pang of guilt as he watched Rennie settle, grimacing, into the seat.

"Are you all right, Mr Rennie? What could have brought you all this way so early?" *In your condition*, he wanted to add, but thought better of it. The man's face was a blotchy mess of red cuts and healing grazes, haloed by bruises which varied from deep purple through a spectrum of blues and greens to a sickly yellow. The palette was completed by the stains of iodine applied by the hospital, and he carried with him a distinct medicinal whiff.

Rennie's reply was to wave his copy of the Sunday edition of the *Island Courier* and slap it down on his lap.

"Have you seen this bloody thing?" he exclaimed. "They've only blown my whole story! You mind telling me how they

179

knew so much, after being unable to tell their arses from their elbows for the past three weeks?"

Blake glanced at the paper lying accusingly on his desk. He cocked his head, one eyebrow raised in question.

"They know *everything*! They couldn't tell you the time on Wednesday! Now, suddenly they know about the ship, the crew, the rescue, and even the names of the dead and missing! *You* don't even know that for sure, and you're the bloody coroner!"

He took a breath to light another of his cigarettes. Pursing his lips made him wince in pain, so he took just one puff before throwing it angrily into the fire. "It's a small-time rag, Mr Blake! They can't even get the winners of the Island Flower Show right. Yet somehow overnight they've become Nellie bloody Bly! Investigative journalism of the highest calibre. Well, I'm not buying it!"

His stream of invective over; Rennie collected himself, feeling the bruises inside his cheek with his tongue. He paused to nurse his flamboyantly-coloured face – in his vexed state he looked like a peeved mandrill. "Someone blabbed, Blake, and I've got a good mind who."

Blake pursed his lips as he did when considering. He still awaited the replies to his telegrams, sent on Friday. "Who do you have in mind, Mr Rennie?"

Rennie shrugged. "How well do you know Peabody?"

Blake immediately shook his head. "No, Mr Rennie. Peabody cannot be the source."

"Come on! He's local, and he's the senior magistrate on the island! He knows this is getting big, he knows it's making the police look bad, and he wants to wrap this up. He threw the case to the local rag to cut off your investigation. Who else could it have been?"

Blake held up a hand, wearily. "Mr Rennie, I am sure it wasn't him." He reached back to the desk for the paper.

"HEROIC RESCUE BY ISLAND MEN OFF SCRATCHELL'S BAY

Island coastguards, R.A. garrison and lifeboatmen made miraculous rescue from the foundered ship *Irex*

32 people, to wit 26 men, five boys and their passenger were rescued off Scratchell's Bay during the night of January 25th to 26th. The heroic feat was undertaken using a Boxer rocket apparatus which reached the ship, stuck fast on the rocks 300 yards offshore. For more than 12 hours, these survivors were winched one at a time up to the safety of the cliffs, while the Totland lifeboat, *Charles Luckombe*, made three gallant attempts to come alongside.

Not a soul on the island will soon forget the violent tempest that swept in on the night of Saturday 25th. That this gallant rescue was undertaken in such treacherous conditions is all the more commendable.

According to survivors, the ship encountered hurricane force winds in the Atlantic for more than ten days. An attempted landfall on 24th January at Falmouth was thwarted, and the ship drifted until its misfortune at Scratchell's Bay.

The survivors' reports claim that the Captain had difficulty accepting the extent of the problems facing the *Irex*, driving her ashore in error. It was only the swift action of the officers that prevented the ship from being lost with all hands.

The survivors were taken to the National Hospital at Ventnor, where more than 20 continue to recuperate. The dead were laid to rest at the Workhouse Hospital. Three died and three more are said to be missing. The dead have been identified as Mr Grayson, Mr Stearne, and apprentice Mr Ogilvie, all of Glasgow. Missing are the ship's master, Captain Hutton, Mate Mr Mackie, and Boatswain Mr Hanson. Islanders are asked to report any flotsam found in the area to the police.

The ship was also carrying a single passenger, Mrs E Barstow, who was rescued but has since gone missing. Any member of the public with information as to her whereabouts should contact the police immediately.

A full account of the rescue can be found on page 7 and 8."

Blake didn't bother to read on. "I can safely say that this had nothing to do with Mr Peabody."

"What makes you so sure?" Rennie seemed utterly sold on his personal theory.

"One thing alone. Mr Peabody and I already knew Henry Rudd was leaking details of the case."

Rennie remained unconvinced. "Peabody could have been involved. He might have been two-timing us from the beginning!"

Blake noticed the "us". It gave him no small pleasure. "No. We already knew it was Rudd. And he died, conveniently." Blake paused to let Rennie have another chance to interject, but he didn't. "But the clearest reason is that whoever fed this news to the paper omitted one rather obvious fact."

Blake paused, noting the reporter's puzzlement. "There were two passengers, Mr Rennie, a man and a woman. And Mr Peabody has been trying, as I have, to pin them down. And in one case alone, namely the man, somebody has been trying to prevent us from doing so." He smiled. "But this time, they have actually helped us."

Rennie's agreement was hampered by the strength of his earlier conviction. "How so?"

"They have played their hand, Mr Rennie. They named the dead and missing. But only three dead. Yet we know that four came ashore."

Blake let the sharp-minded Scot ruminate for a second more, until the grin of realisation spread painfully across his damaged face. "He's our dead man walking!"

"Precisely. If neither dead nor missing, he's somewhere on the island, and possibly in better health than we were led to believe."

Rennie was shaking his head again, more in wonder than doubt. "Do you know what we're getting into here? Someone out there has some very good friends. Powerful friends, I'll bet."

Blake fixed his gaze on the battered reporter. "Mr Rennie. If I tell you something, I need your word that you will not publish it without my permission."

Rennie's eyes popped, as they had on that first morning just four days ago, as he anticipated the import of Blake's information. "All right. On my word."

"The man we are looking for is a Mr Clarence." Blake paused to see if anything registered.

Rennie merely raised his eyebrows and jutted his chin. "I've heard mention a couple of times. So?"

"He is the missing passenger, most likely the missing body, and I have no doubt he is the reason my inquest was sequestered, and the reason for your own misfortune."

Rennie cocked his head, intrigued. "What's the problem, then? Who is he?"

Blake pursed his lips again before answering. "I don't know for certain. Someone has been trying very hard to keep his name out of the public record. I believe that our erstwhile colleague Mr Rudd came by his accident precisely because he was attempting to do exactly that."

Rennie stared. "Are you going to tell me that wasn't an accident, Mr Blake?"

Blake didn't answer. "I've enlisted the help of an old colleague who could help us identify Clarence. I've heard that name before but it seems too much of a coincidence. And there are frightening implications if it is the same person."

"Who's the 'old colleague'? A copper?" Rennie's cheek bulged after this question, his tongue running over the unseen contusion.

"Yes, he was a detective."

Rennie couldn't help himself. "Were you a detective yourself, Mr Blake?"

Blake paused before answering. "I'm a lawyer."

"Of course you are."

184

The men held their gaze for a few moments more, until Rennie let out his breath in a wheezy laugh. "Well, Mr Blake, I'd be honoured if you would take me along. You never know when an insurance agent could come in useful."

Blake smiled. "It would be my pleasure."

Rennie rose from his seat, struggling to manage the stick, still very unfamiliar to him. "See you soon, Mr Blake."

Blake rose to get the door. "I look forward to it, Mr Rennie."

Rennie paused as he limped out. "Don't forget now, will you Mr Blake? My editor wants to recall me – it's only getting beaten up that's keeping me here!"

"I won't forget Mr Rennie. You have my word."

"That's good enough for me, Your Honour!" Rennie touched his forelock, avoiding the worst of the bruises, and set off down the hall.

As Blake took his seat again by the fire, he heard the unmistakeable voice of Peabody meeting Rennie in the corridor. Though he couldn't hear the words, Rennie's voice sounded cordial enough. He rose again, and managed to get the door as the ruddy face of his associate appeared, chilled from the cold wind. His coat and hat were wet, as was the stout Gladstone portmanteau held in one hand.

"Goodness, Mr Blake! It's like Piccadilly Circus! May I?"

Blake beckoned Peabody in; Rennie's seat was probably still warm. With the door closed again, the two men sat while Blake filled his pipe. Peabody abstained.

"What did Mr Rennie want at this hour? My goodness, the sight of the man!"

Blake lit the pipe and puffed as the tobacco in the bowl caught, flicking the match into the fire. "I told him about Clarence."

Peabody turned purple. "Mr Blake! Really! Nobody knows about this outside the inquest!"

Blake held up his hand. "I wish that were true. Thornthwaite knows, which suggests others. Dr Foster of London knows, and whoever he may be working for." He took another puff on his pipe as Peabody accepted this. "Rennie's also a very useful investigator. He has provided some excellent information." He reached behind to the desk and produced the newspaper which had so vexed Rennie. "Have you read this?"

"It's the reason I'm here, Mr Blake. You don't think Rennie might have betrayed us?"

Blake couldn't stop himself laughing.

Peabody looked offended. "Well he is a reporter, Mr Blake! Hardly known for their discretion."

"Mr Peabody, I've just spent considerable time convincing Mr Rennie that it wasn't you."

Peabody's mouth formed the outraged O that betrayed his disgust. "He never did!"

"He's also helped me believe that our friend Mr Clarence is probably alive and still on the island."

Peabody looked offended again. "Well, I was about to suggest the same thing. The newspaper only lists three dead and three missing, yet we've known since last week that four dead were recovered. It can only be our missing passenger."

Blake took the pipe from his mouth. "Quite, Mr Peabody. Do you remember the hospital where the body was originally taken?"

186

Peabody opened his portmanteau and produced a sheaf of well-organised notes. He flicked through the leaves until he alighted on the one he was looking for. "Let me see…. according to the record, the body was received at the National Hospital in Ventnor at ten-fifteen on the morning of 27th January. He was declared dead at that time, and the body was transported to the mortuary at the Workhouse Hospital the same evening. It was discovered missing five days later when required for autopsy. However nobody can say when it was removed during the intervening time."

Blake reconsidered. "I think then, it's possible he was actually dead, and the body was removed to prevent identification."

Peabody read it again. "I think not, Mr Blake. The body was recovered two days after the wreck. There was already a standing instruction that the dead were to be taken to the Workhouse, while survivors should be taken to the National Hospital. Whoever brought Clarence in certainly believed him to be alive."

Blake pointed his pipe stem at his counterpart in approval. "An excellent point, Mr Peabody." He bent forward to tap out the bowl against the hearth. "A *most* excellent point."

Peabody shuffled through his notes, modestly occupied before the unexpected fulsomeness of his colleague.

Blake straightened. "We need to find out who brought the body in. And perhaps more importantly, who declared him dead. We're already a week behind."

Peabody concurred. "A week…they're always one step ahead. We need a stroke of luck, never mind a good detective."

"Well, we have Rennie."

Before the magistrate could answer, both of them were distracted by the sound of heavy footfalls ascending the stairs at the end of the corridor. The steps continued to approach until there came a jingling of keys and the sound of heavy breathing which preceded three brisk knocks on the door. Blake was already there to open the door.

Constable Hollis stood at the threshold, his rain cape and uniform dripping from the rain outside. "Pardon me, sir, but I have some urgent news. We've picked up someone at Ryde matching the description of your burglars. Are you able to accompany me there, sir?"

"Of course! Where are they?"

"They're holding him at the main police station on the Esplanade, sir."

Blake beckoned Peabody, who hastened to pack up his bag, carefully handling the pages so as not to disorder them. Blake grabbed his black greatcoat and hat, and followed the constable out into the corridor. As they set off briskly toward the stairs, Blake leaned in to Peabody to speak softly in his ear.

"I'll go with Hollis. You come in your own carriage, and make sure you fetch Rennie. We'll meet at the railway station."

Hollis' police carriage was now drawn up directly at the end of the drive, while Peabody had to leave them to retrieve his own from the stableyard behind. He gave Blake a brief wave before hurrying away.

Blake got into the carriage with Hollis, noting it lean alarmingly on its springs as the two large men got in. Hollis was almost as tall as Blake, but a lot sturdier – he had yellow-blond hair over reddish, freckled skin, with thick hands and arms. Hollis leaned out and called the destination to the driver, who spurred the long-suffering mare into ponderous action.

"Can you tell me about the man your colleagues have caught, Constable?" Blake had removed his spectacles and was trying to rub away the raindrops.

"Sir, I received the telegram less than an hour ago. It just said, 'Further to your enquiries, etcetera, we have taken a man with facial injuries into custody for questioning.' Travelling alone, they said, sir."

Blake considered this. It would be too much to hope for Clarence himself, he supposed. Still, one of Rennie's assailants would make a valuable witness for interview.

* * *

Ryde was a veritable metropolis by comparison to Newport. As the largest town on the island, even on a dreary Sunday morning it was busier. It lay in an untidy sprawl along the northeast coast of the island, and affected a grubby grandeur. The Victorian buildings that formed the rise of houses and institutions that built from the shoreline were some of the finest on the island.

The busy railway lines sprouted from the shoreside station, with branch lines coming from the pier head where stately paddle-steamer ferries collected and deposited the visitors and workers from the mainland.

The Esplanade was a mile of flat, clear promenade that ran along the entire seafront. Couples attempted their Sunday stroll, sharing umbrellas that folded and flipped in the wind, trying to ward off the persistent rain. Church bells rang, their monotonous chimes carrying through the damp air; far from bringing glad tidings, their tolling lent to the dismal aspect of the day.

The smell of railway coal and chimney smoke mingled under the low overcast as curtains of fine droplets drifted across Blake's view. He was mounting the slight incline from the railway station to the Ryde Police Station, a functional Victorian structure of crenellated white limestone blocks set in plain red bricks, punctuated by severe, rectangular sash windows.

He and Peabody ascended the front steps trying to accommodate Rennie, still struggling with his stick. For such a vital man, the reporter seemed to be fighting his enforced limitation, refusing to submit. It fed Blake's increasing admiration for him.

The men entered the police station which had the same musty, papery smell as the Newport law courts. The sanitary tang of cleaning chemicals and carbolic also hung in the air, creating an amalgam of the court house and hospitals that had occupied much of their investigation.

An L-shaped desk faced the entrance, with a heavy door to its left that led to cells and offices. Hollis introduced them to the heavily moustachioed sergeant at the desk, who led them to the side door. He allowed the four of them through, peering curiously at the bruised face of Rennie, but did not offer any other observation.

The men were led by another Ryde constable, with Hollis in their lead, down a short corridor with several locked doors on each side. The constable stopped in front of one of the doors and examined the notes on a clipboard hanging from a hook outside. He replaced the clipboard and jangled a set of hefty keys on a ring attached to his belt. The locks turned with oily clicks and he swung the door open.

Hollis led Blake and Peabody into the tiled room, while Rennie manfully manoeuvred around the tight corner. Blake couldn't help but let a chuckle escape as he regarded the suited man who sat before him on a standard iron-frame bunk. Despite the two black eyes and bandaged nose, it was undoubtedly the face of Matthew Thornthwaite who looked sullenly back at him.

"Well, well. Mr Thornthwaite, I believe."

Rennie laughed out loud. Peabody maintained a satisfied smile.

"'E says his name's Marston, sir," interjected the constable. "We picked 'im up at the Pier. Said 'e got kicked by an 'orse."

Blake glanced at Rennie. The Scot's grim smile faded as he fixed his erstwhile assailant in his sights. "Is that so? Didn't kick the bastard half hard enough, if you ask me."

Thornthwaite took this moment to speak. "Constable, who are these gentlemen?"

Peabody spluttered in disgust. "Come on, man. We've caught you cold. Did you try to deceive the police by telling them your name was Marston?"

The man's confident tones sounded comically dampened by the break in his nose. "My name *is* Marston. Thomas Marston. I was on my way to Portsmouth for the boat train to London. Fat chance of that now, the ferry's probably long gone." He still had his arrogant voice, despite the duck quack undertone it had developed. "Am I under arrest, Constable?"

The policemen looked slightly uncomfortable. It was Hollis who answered him.

"Sir, we need to establish your identity in order to eliminate you from our enquiries. Do you have any identification on your person?"

Thornthwaite didn't miss a beat. "Of course, Constable. Ask them to bring my bag, will you?"

The Ryde constable squeezed past them back through the door. Blake watched him go, then quickly shut the door behind him. He pointed at the prisoner. "Rennie, is this one of them?"

Rennie's gaze never wavered, fixed on the man still sitting on the bunk. "As sure as I'm standing here, Your Honour. That's the man who grabbed me round the neck, and if he got kicked by a horse, I'm a Chinaman." He lifted his fingers to the livid swelling on his forehead, rubbing it lightly. "It's him."

The man known to them as Thornthwaite stirred where he sat but did not utter a word.

"You said you didn't know him. Had you ever seen him before the burglary?" For Blake this was the question. If Rennie's self-professed recognition skills were in question, it would make it difficult to prove the story, however compelling the circumstantial evidence. But the Scot's gaze remained fixed on the other man's damaged face, his brow furrowed despite the swollen mass on his forehead.

"Aye, I do believe I saw him at the court house the day after you locked us out, Your Honour. Some smart arse lawyer, I think."

At this, Thornthwaite did look up. He shot one accusing look with his black eyes at Blake, but said nothing.

Blake turned to Hollis. "Constable, arrest this man. He is implicated in a serious assault, and tampering with the inquest of Her Majesty's Coroner."

Thornthwaite exploded. "You will do no such thing, Constable!"

Hollis glanced at Blake, who nodded in Thornthwaite's direction. The burly copper took a step towards the seated man, when Thornthwaite suddenly leapt from his place. He piled his shoulder straight into Hollis' solar plexus, knocking him into the cell wall. Hollis' breath left him with a sharp groan, and he slid to the floor. Thornthwaite continued his movement, swinging his elbow into the side of Peabody's head, snapping his head sideways and rendering him immediately senseless. He spun his other hand up and rammed the heel of his hand firmly in the centre of Blake's chest, a blow that knocked the breath out of him and sent the astonished coroner flying backwards into Rennie, piling them both on the floor in the other corner.

Thornthwaite leapt the prone men to wrest the door open, only to find that it had no handle on the inside. He barely paused, turning immediately to crouch by the floored Hollis, who was still struggling for breath and ineffectually clawing at Thornthwaite while he expertly turned the policeman's pockets out. The lawyer soon retrieved Hollis' heavy set of keys – the telltale jingle of the metal carried above the hoarse grunts of their erstwhile owner, to the ringing ears of Blake, still stunned.

Thornthwaite wasted not a second in rising from the weak clutches of the gasping Hollis. He spun on his heel and turned toward the door, already sifting the keys for the most likely candidate, when he took the full force of Rennie's stick right across the bridge of his already broken nose.

To Blake, the howl that burst from the would-be escapee cut through his stupor, and brought the cell interior into clarity. Rennie had scrambled from beneath him while Thornthwaite was rifling Hollis' pockets; by virtue of the runaway lawyer's swift movements, he had caught Thornthwaite right on the most injurious spot.

The reporter now tottered as Thornthwaite joined the others on the floor, clutching at his face and whimpering in considerable discomfort. A final, sharp jab with the end of the stick satisfied Rennie that his quarry had lost his stomach for the fight. He applied Hollis' dropped handcuffs to Thornthwaite's wrists while the dazed man still moaned in pain.

Thornthwaite had fallen straight on top of Peabody, who remained limp on the floor of the cell. Rennie lifted the broken fugitive and laid him flat on the bunk. Fresh blood now stained the dressing pad he had worn over the previous injury; by Blake's reckoning, it was giving the Scot tremendous satisfaction to see his assailant bloodied again by his hand.

He turned to survey the rest of the wreckage – his own chest burned where Thornthwaite had struck him, and although his breath had returned, he was given to an involuntary cough which sent spasms of pain radiating across his ribs from the sternum.

Peabody was the main concern – he still lay unconscious, though his breath sighed through his open mouth.

Hollis was breathing again with occasional coughs, as Blake was. The constable raised himself, one limb at a time and straightened his hat and tunic, embarrassed at being caught cold by the mystery man. He picked up his set of keys, remarking that a lot of good it would have done him, since none of them would have fit the door.

Blake gathered himself up with more care, first kneeling over Peabody to check him. The men all breathed heavily, shock and exertion making high demands on their circulation. Blake felt the blood gathering at the point on his sternum where Thornthwaite had struck; he also felt aggrieved at having been despatched so easily by the man on the bed. He felt his muscles and ribs throbbing as he moved Peabody into a more comfortable lying position.

All the while, Rennie was practically strutting in the meagre space he had available. His broken lips and multi-coloured face were beaming again, the gap-tooth visible for the first time since his beating.

"Aye well, I'd say you've caught your man, Your Honour! The little bastard thought he had us, too! Well, wee man, lightning doesn't strike twice. Unless you're Gordon Rennie!"

He brandished his stick with considerable glee, though his theatrics were lost on the man on the bed, who continued to groan, bruised eyes closed and breathing punctuated by the thick sounds of mucus and blood rattling through his clogged and swollen nose.

"God help me, this is the best story I've ever had! Aye, Mr Thornthwaite, or Marston, or whoever the hell you are, you might have fancied your chances against that horse after all!" Rennie guffawed, and Blake couldn't help but smile, though it was more of a grimace. Hollis looked on, bemused, while Peabody didn't stir.

The keys rattled loudly in the lock and the Ryde constable returned, carrying a smart leather portmanteau with Thornthwaite's belongings. He looked doubtfully at the three faces turned towards him then glanced down at the two prone men.

"Don't tell me – another 'orse?"

This provoked another fit of laughter from the irrepressible Rennie. His unfettered delight moved even Blake to laugh, although he immediately regretted it as he choked back another spasm of pain-filled coughing.

Hollis answered the Ryde man between short breaths. "We're taking this man —" he indicated the groaning Thornthwaite – "into custody at Newport. We're going to need a doctor for this one –" he motioned to Peabody, breathing on the floor – "as quickly as you can call one."

Blake tempered his satisfaction at Thornthwaite's capture with a grudging resentment that the smaller man possessed a punch like a mule's kick. He had greatly underestimated the lawyer, if indeed he was one.

Blake paused to cough again. "I would say our fact-finding trip to the hospital was cancelled in favour of more urgent requirements, more's the pity."

He cursed the luck that would put them another day behind, yet he enjoyed the feeling that Thornthwaite's capture would provide a trump card he should be pleased to play soon. "Then again, the hospital might be exactly where you need to head today. God knows, our man Peabody surely does."

Rennie seemed to have found a new store of vitality, and Blake saw him puffing away at his stinky cigarettes for the first time since his beating.

"Listen, Your Honour – let me get this wee fella back to Newport with the young constable. You make sure you get yourself an ambulance with Peabody. I'll meet you when I've found an appropriate hidey-hole for this bastard. We don't want his friends springing him from jail."

Blake considered this for a second, before he nodded his agreement. "Very well, Mr Rennie. And good work with the stick."

Rennie grinned through broken lips and a cloud of cigarette smoke, almost opening his wounds again. He mimed another swing of the stick. "Aye, sir. That it was. Bloody lucky shot too."

The men laughed – even Peabody stirred.

*   *   *

Blake was by Peabody's bed in the Workhouse Infirmary when the plucky magistrate came round. The gaslights were dimmed and it was dark outside; the rain hissed against the large windows in the ward, driven by more of the limitless supply of wind that persisted in its onslaught of the island.

Blake himself had a bruise like a hen's egg square on the middle of his sternum; no doubt his own skin would soon replicate Rennie's cavalcade of colour. He was pleased to note no ribs were broken.

Thornthwaite's violent turn had done for them all; if Blake hadn't closed the cell door the mysterious lawyer would have made a clean escape. Judging by the skills the man had demonstrated, he was no ordinary lawyer; Blake relished the forthcoming interrogation.

Peabody's eyes barely opened, but he sounded in good shape. "Dear God – what happened? I feel like I've been kicked by a horse."

Blake couldn't suppress a chuckle. To his surprise the laughter provoked tears and a heavy lump in his pained chest rose to his throat. He swallowed back the sobs that seemed about to overwhelm him, and wiped away the tears with his fingers. *Come on, man!*

He realised in that instant how deeply he was committed to this investigation, and more poignantly, to the men he had befriended. The Peabody he knew now was far from the bumptious man he had perceived in that warm courtroom barely a week before. He had misjudged everyone, he realised. Peabody, Rennie, Rudd...and Thornthwaite, of course.

He squeezed Peabody's hand as he couldn't trust himself to speak in an even voice. There was a squeeze back, before both men felt the awkwardness of the gesture and withdrew their hands in mutual embarrassment.

"I fear you've spent too much time around Rennie," murmured Peabody. They both chuckled – the Scot's exuberance was wildly eccentric compared to the Victorian reserve of the day.

"I'm very grateful you're feeling better, Stanley." Blake used his name generously.

"Well, there's better, and there's *better*, you know, Mr Blake?" Peabody turned his head painfully to look at Blake. "What did he hit me with? Hollis' truncheon?"

Blake shook his head. "It was his elbow, I think. A solid contact."

"Indeed." Peabody closed his eyes again.

198

"I don't know much more than that, he floored me straight after you."

"The devil! So he has escaped?"

Blake smiled. "He tried, but didn't get far. Rennie took quite a swing at him with his walking stick. Poor Thornthwaite."

Peabody closed his eyes and smiled to himself. "I would have liked to see that. Poor Thornthwaite, indeed!" He shifted his position, eyes scrunched in pain.

"The doctor saw you a while ago. He says you probably have a concussion. You might be here for a week."

Peabody grimaced again. "I'll see you tomorrow at the court house, Mr Blake. You can count on it."

Blake felt the rush of emotion again. He remained silent for a long while, swallowing back the lump and looking up at the ceiling.

"When you're ready, Mr Peabody," was all he could say in the end.

Chapter Thirteen

Eastern Atlantic Ocean, 82 miles WNW of Ushant
Monday, 6th January 1890

Hutton stared at the idle, flapping sails for hours on end. For two days and nights it had been flat calm. The days gave hours of unbroken sunshine while the nights had been bitterly cold but filled with the myriad stars of the northern sky. Orion and the Big Dipper stood out among the constellations, while the Milky Way formed a rippling band of fainter light behind them, dotted with innumerable pinpricks of shimmering light from remote stars.

With such benign conditions, Mackie and Hanson had been able to fix their position with pinpoint accuracy throughout, but it made depressing reading in the log; barely 21 miles travelled the whole of the 5th, while today was looking to be even worse, perhaps not even 15 miles for the whole day. Though the *Irex* had set her day's best run on the 3rd and surpassed it again on the 4th, the hundreds of miles travelled amounted to barely three degrees of southerly progress. Hutton had wondered and prayed again, enquiring of God himself if he was preventing them from straying too far.

Hutton counted almost a full calendar month since the voyage began and yet they were still barely out of the blocks. He continued to wrestle with thoughts that the voyage was somehow blighted, even though such things were unacceptable to the man who believed in a sovereign God.

He had continued his midnight prayer sessions, and comforted himself with the certainty that Sarah would be unstinting in her duty to meet with him at the appointed hour. To his great relief, he also had found that his nightly dinners with the widow Barstow were actually bringing his feelings for her into a much healthier perspective; the familiarity of her presence and the ease with which she conversed doused much of his ardour. He saw how much he had idealised her. He could appreciate her much better, admiring her without the lovesickness that had crippled their relations previously.

As his passion for her waned, he also began to perceive her faults – a tendency to dismiss others for perceived lack of faith, moral fibre or fervour. Durrick, chaperoning her by day, was finding it particularly wearing, being a Catholic from birth. She also displayed an irritating habit of speaking over others if their arguments did not appear robust enough for her exacting standards. Still, he felt privileged to have a staunch believer on board for Christian companionship, and to act as a foil against the odious Clarence.

To his shame, he also perceived that she was braver than him; she possessed a courage that spoke to him in a way that her beauty could not. He understood why Clarence had manipulated him and shunned her; she would never have dithered as shamefully as Hutton, had their roles been reversed.

It was indeed Clarence, Hutton's perpetual thorn in the side, who gave the captain the greatest grief. There seemed nothing Hutton could do to disabuse the man of the absurd idea that they were friends.

Clarence was still effuse in his greetings, pumping Hutton's hand at every morning meeting, sharing his every observation about any trivial matter of shipboard life he noticed. Whereas Hutton regarded the man's earlier revelations with abhorrence, Clarence treated the shared secret as a bond of companionship – something Hutton tried desperately to avoid. It was maddening.

For this reason Hutton stood out on deck at the twilight, until the dog watches drew to a close. Here at 49 degrees north, the days stretched to almost five o'clock, lending a reprieve from the dark nights of Scotland.

He shivered in his greatcoat as the last crescent of the sun dipped beneath the western horizon; the sudden chill fell over him like a shroud, nipping at his nose and ears, while his arms and legs eased into a protesting shiver. The horizon was black under a skyline ablaze with light and colour; deep crimson at the base, topped by a glowing layer of yellow and pale blue. The sky higher above remained a darkening blue; the first stars of the evening, the planets Venus and Jupiter, picked out sharply by their unwavering spots of white light against the falling curtain of night.

Hutton let his breath out in a billow of steam, which seemed to phosphoresce in the faint final rays of the sun; he made an audible sigh that caught the attention of helmsman Morgan, silently attending to his superfluous duty at the wheel.

"Needs to blow, Captain."

Hutton turned to see Morgan standing relaxed, one hand on the outer spoke of the wheel nearest to him. The laxity of his posture was a rare moment indeed for a helmsman, who needed a sturdy back to brace the shifting wheel when the ship was moving.

"Aye, Morgan, it does." Hutton was captivated by the appearance of his breath in the cold air, instantly coalescing into a tangible cloud, and as quickly dissipating into nothingness. He considered it a metaphor for their own existence, a brief bloom in a physical universe, before disappearing from sight forever. "It surely does."

Could there be a more wretched picture of an existence without purpose, he wondered. Here sat his enormous ship, freshly minted from the most advanced foundries on the face of the earth, her lines drawn by master shipbuilders and her interior the preserve of master craftsmen. Yet she was becalmed and immobile, thirty days behind schedule, filled with an uninspiring cargo of pig iron and sewage pipes, her only passengers a young widow on a now meaningless voyage, and a murderous social philosopher banished from the society he yearned to change. Even Hutton himself was master in name alone, incapable of changing a single feature of their bleak circumstances. He laughed out loud at this thought, to the bemusement of the helmsman.

As the clouds of moisture evaporated around him, Hutton had another thought. Steam was now the lifeblood of maritime commerce. As long as there was a ready supply of coal, a steamship would never find itself in their predicament.

"Morgan, have you considered going into steam?" It was the dilemma facing all modern seamen – whether to persevere in the tougher but more rewarding trade of sailing a ship, or to give in to the easier life aboard a steamship.

The helmsman's face dropped in surprise. "No, sir, I have not." He crossed himself in the Catholic manner before continuing. "Sir, them steamers are nothing but paddle boats for dilettantes. Every man jack on a ship knows his trade from cap to boots. Them steamers are full of Johnny-come-lately know-nothings. Why, a man aboard ship who knows no trade but shovelling coal? It's a foul shame!"

"Aye, Morgan, that it is." Hutton nodded with approval. He knew Morgan to be a union man whose passions were strong regarding the present economic squeeze on experienced sailors.

Sailors had become a commodity much like whale oil. Once greatly prized and produced by the hard graft of expertise, danger and dirty, bloody experience, nowadays you just had to dig into the ground to find the alternative. Whale oil was a curiosity, worth a fraction of its former value. Purists would swear that it was better in every respect than ground oil, but the stiff-necked men who ran enterprises would gladly settle for less as long as it was cheap and easy to obtain, and garnered greater profits. So it was with the modern seaman; the old, sacred knowledge of sail and sea was of scant worth in a ship that merely needed to be pointed rather than dressed, set and tended. No sailor in the world would argue that a steamer was a better education in seamanship than a full-rigged sailing vessel; but if it promised a steady income, comfortable accommodations and a better chance of returning alive, then seamanship would come second to a good living.

Against the darkness of the eastern sky, Hutton noticed the milky glow of the rising moon, a perfect half-circle of blue-white light. It cast a splendid reflection in the calm seas. The sails overhead seemed to radiate it back. The decks were better lit by this reflection than by the lamps glowing along the companionways.

It was by this illumination that Hutton caught sight of two sailors remonstrating near the main mast. Their gestures were clear – they leaned towards each other, their chopping hand movements and emphatic pointing betraying an argument in full swing.

Hutton recognised the distant figures as Second Mate Durrick and Bosun Hanson. Alarmed, he set off down the steps to the deck. As their raised voices began to carry towards him, he saw Hanson push Durrick away. The young officer tottered back but regained his footing and pushed Hanson straight back into the thick rope footings of the mainmast. The bosun scrambled to balance, but fell sideways. He leapt back to his feet and brandished his fists.

By now Hutton was running. He shouted Hanson's name, but he was too far away.

Durrick, of slighter build than the bosun, danced backward to avoid one scything swing of the enraged seaman's fist. Hutton roared his name again, and this time Hanson's head whipped round to see the captain, coat flying, barely ten yards away. He dropped his fists, but only for a second. Without another look at the captain, he drew back to swipe at Durrick again. Durrick stood with his feet apart, balanced and alert. The bosun feinted first with the left and followed up immediately with a right hook which caught the weaving second mate a glancing blow on the side of his head, knocking him to the floor.

As Hutton reached the scene, Hanson was winding up a powerful kick with his thick seaboot.

"HANSON!" The captain grabbed the man's coat shoulder and jerked him back. The kick missed the prone Durrick, who leapt up at this split-second reprieve like a scalded cat. Hanson began to overbalance again, and grabbed Hutton's coat. The two of them fell flat on the deck.

Hutton lay on his back, stunned for a second, before the granite features of Hanson heaved into view. With a shock, Hutton saw the man had pulled back his fist again. He tried to catch his breath to shout again, but a deafening shot arrested the entire scene.

"Stand fast, or I swear I'll shoot, Bosun!"

Durrick's voice, thin enough to begin with, was a shriek. But the smoking revolver he just fired overboard now poked into the back of Hanson's neck. It was enough to snap the bosun out of his rage. He stood back from Hutton, who clambered to his feet, panting with exertion.

A few of the crew emerged from the recesses of the foredeck, alerted by the shot.

Hutton collected himself. He glared at Hanson who stood rigid, clenching and unclenching his fists.

"Mr Hanson, report to the chart room, now. You are under charge. Mr Durrick, you are relieved by Mr Reid. Remain at the helm station." He managed to keep his voice even, despite shaking with shock.

Durrick lowered the gun with a trembling hand. He turned it butt-first to the captain, who placed it into his large greatcoat pocket.

Hanson glared at any curious sailors reckless enough to meet his gaze. Hutton dismissed the idlers with a barked order to resume their stations. He kept his hand on the gun in his pocket until Reid arrived. *What's next on this voyage*, he wondered.

Reid had the curious look of a newly-arrived bystander who knew he should have been there five minutes earlier. His quick eyes darted between Hutton and Hanson.

"Mr Reid, escort Mr Hanson to the chart room. I will meet you there presently. You will assume the watch until eight bells."

Reid didn't question his captain. "Very good, sir."

He beckoned the bosun to follow. Hanson dropped his shoulders and turned, scuffing his boots as he walked in the direction of the quarterdeck.

Hutton cast his eye around the deck, making sure that the sailors had assumed their stations. The tension bled from his body as he felt another wave of fatigue roll through him. He thrust his hands into his pockets, where his fingers met the cold metal of the revolver.

He walked back to the quarterdeck and mounted the steps to meet Durrick by the covered helm position. Morgan held the wheel with both hands, trying to lay low. Anyone who took the helm of a ship was known for sharp eyesight in any light, so he would be a key witness to the incident.

Durrick was still shivering from shock and cold. The second mate had impressed Hutton with his unexpected bravery and nimble feet. Hutton berated himself for misjudging the young officer as a callow, indolent youngster; he was made of sterner stuff.

"Bob. What happened?"

Durrick never hesitated. "Captain, I think Mr Hanson is a danger to Mrs Barstow."

Alarm gripped Hutton once more. "Explain!"

"Sir, you made me responsible for Mrs Barstow's safety. I took the second dog watch after supper, and left her in her cabin. Mr Hanson turned in for the watch and I heard him speaking to someone about her. I feel he is unable to contain his designs on her."

"Who was he speaking to?"

"I didn't see, sir. He was in shadow behind the galley house. I only heard Hanson's voice."

"What did he say?"

Durrick looked uncomfortable. "I heard him say he was going to have her tonight, that he'd been promised, or something. I warned him about his conduct, and said he'd better not try anything while I was watching her. That's when he pushed me. He threatened my life, sir!"

Their heads jerked around when they heard a faint scream from the cabin. A woman's shrill exclamation, which was cut off in mid cry. Hutton instinctively looked towards the salt-encrusted glass of the skylight and made out the struggle of shadows in the lamplit gloom beneath.

God, thought Hutton, *please, not this.* He grabbed Durrick's sleeve to follow him, and leapt towards the companionway. He rattled down the steps, jumping the last three, and raced around the companionway towards the door.

He reached the door and wrenched it open, having to arrest his forward flight to pull it toward him. In another split-second he was over the threshold and squinting into the light of the cabin.

He found he was late again. He saw Hanson fly sideways from the Barstows' door and land in a heap against the opposite side. Clarence appeared from Mrs Barstow's room; a second later the opposite door flew open as Mackie burst from his own room in his trousers and seaboots with shirt flapping, alerted by the commotion. Meanwhile Reid lay retching on the floor by the chart room.

There was no sign of Mrs Barstow. Hutton yelled to Mackie to secure Hanson, while his eyes sought out Clarence.

The passenger winked at Hutton and turned back to Mrs Barstow's room. Hutton immediately strode over to the open door, and peered in.

Elizabeth Barstow sat on the floor, bare-shouldered and semi-clad, her nightdress askew. Her hair was loose again, as Hutton had seen her on the day that George had died. As Clarence stood her up, her nightdress fell back into place, restoring her modesty, and she stared at her rescuer.

Hutton noted jealously that she regarded Clarence with mute curiosity, eyeing his muscled chest visible through his open-necked shirt.

"No harm done?" enquired her rescuer. He still held her by her bare shoulders.

"No. At least - your intervention was very timely, Mr Clarence." She squirmed slightly to shrug off his hands. "Thank you."

"I should bring you water, my lady!" he cried, turning quickly and passing through the struggling, prone figures back to his room as if oblivious of the chaos. In seconds he had retrieved a jug and glass from his own room, and in three strides was offering them to Elizabeth as she stood shivering, hugging her nightdress round her under the eyes of the men.

"Thank you, Mr Clarence, you have been most gallant."

For a change, added Hutton to himself, upset at the man's intervention in Mrs Barstow's plight.

Clarence turned and took one of Elizabeth's slim hands in his own. "A pleasure, m'lady." She didn't flinch as he kissed the hand and clasped it to his chest. "Always a pleasure to help out a beautiful lady."

At this she regained some of her composure and gently twisted her hand from his, thanking him again. Clarence hovered as Hutton called to her from the door.

"Madam, I am so sorry—"

"I'm fine, thank you Captain Hutton. I'm not sure what happened – I heard a scuffle outside, and when I opened the door, that man...attacked me."

She stepped up to the doorway and brushed past Hutton. He sidestepped to allow her to look at Hanson, now pinned beneath the considerable weight of the chief mate. Clarence moved up behind her and once again placed a proprietary hand on her bare shoulder.

"When I was struggling, he said that I owed him, and I had promised him, or something like that. Perhaps you can ask him what he meant." Her lip trembled slightly as she faced down her assailant. She again dipped her shoulder to remove Clarence's hand. She turned on the spot, waiting for him to move aside.

Instead he remained in the room, and topped up her glass on the dresser with the jug. "Please, madam, you must keep yourself in good health. Such a frightful mess! If there is anything else I can do for you, please, just ask". He again looked at Hutton over the top of her head, before sidling out of the room.

"I'm sure I shall, Mr Clarence." Her voice seemed to take on a slightly flat tone, and she fixed her gaze on Clarence with a searching look, blinking more rapidly than Hutton had noticed before. One thing Hutton had always noticed was her level, confident gaze, which seemed to bore through the subject of her interest. Now she seemed to regard Clarence with a more dreamy aspect.

"Do you need the doctor to see you?" offered Hutton, and immediately regretted asking, as the memories of Carroll's last visit rushed back to him a split-second too late.

Elizabeth, even in her shaken state, was tougher than his sensibilities. "No thank you, Captain. I've had quite enough attention from your men for one night. I feel quite spent, in fact."

Her glance flicked to Clarence and back to Hutton as she leaned on the door, still half open.

Hutton blushed, ashamed of his gender, and felt affronted. *Your men.* By omission, Clarence was absolved, though he had fluttered around her like a popinjay, crowing his triumph and maximising Elizabeth's approval for his act of manly valour.

Hutton instead stammered his regrets and apologies, while she nodded and bade him goodnight, closing and locking the door behind her. This time as Hutton turned back to the cabin floor, he was containing a rising anger.

Clarence still stood, cock of the walk, attracting the admiring approval of the other officers, including Reid, being helped to his feet by Durrick.

"What the devil do you think you're doing? Saving her one minute and trying to seduce her the next?" Hutton hissed. He kept his voice low, out of Elizabeth's earshot, but hoped she was still listening at the door.

Clarence looked hurt. "Why Captain, that's hardly fair, now, is it? Had you been keeping your vigil, this might never have happened!"

Hutton struggled to control his anger, not least because Clarence was right. He was aware the men in the cabin were watching him. "Mr Clarence, we may need to discuss this later. For now I must attend to my crew."

"As well you should, my dear Captain," Clarence said as he sauntered back to his room. He stopped beside the flattened bosun, still bulge-eyed, red-faced and squirming for purchase underneath Mackie, his muffled cursing underlying Clarence's speech. "It's a poor show indeed when a young woman can't sleep safely in her bed. I hope your ship remains a better locale than the likes of...Whitechapel."

He emphasised the last word before turning back towards his room with a final smirk over his shoulder. Only Hutton noticed it, as all other eyes in the room were on the captain, white-knuckled and trembling with impotent rage.

He whirled on the spot towards Hanson. The bosun had been struggling like the devil, only contained by the substantial weight of the chief mate, but suddenly he had become quiescent, perhaps depleted by his violent exertions – the fight in his stone hard eyes had subsided. Instead he seemed dazed, eyes rolling confusedly from man to man and, to Hutton at least, looked like he was in the throes of a stroke.

'Andrew, let him up. Reid, fetch the irons. Mr Hanson is to be confined to the spare stateroom for five days. Only the officers may attend him. Durrick, inform the steward that Mr Hanson has taken ill, and must receive his meals in the cabin, to be served by the watch officer for quarantine purposes. Gentlemen, it is important that the men are not informed of

212

our problem here. Mr Durrick, you shall resume your duties toward Mrs Barstow, and Mr Reid shall assume your watch. Mr Mackie, you are to assume responsibility for Mr Hanson. He is not to leave the stateroom in view of any of the hands, including the helmsman. Are these instructions clear, gentlemen?"

The chorus of Ayes was followed by the purposeful movement of men to their duties. Hutton stopped Reid as he moved past, still rubbing his stomach area.

"Are you all right, John? Do you need to see Mr Carroll?"

The third mate gave a tight-lipped smile. "I'm fine, sir. My pride is more dented than my breadbasket. He walloped me as I was unlocking the chart room. He's quite handy, is our bosun!"

"Good lad." Hutton smiled solicitously, but still fought the trembling caused by his lingering anger at Clarence. He turned to the bosun, back on his feet, held up by Mackie's huge hand on his collar.

"Bosun Hanson, start at the beginning. I want to know the reason for this complete desertion of both your duties and your senses." Hutton's tone brooked no argument.

Yet the bosun just looked on, his usual surliness replaced by vacant bemusement. "Begging your pardon sir, what happened? I feel like a spar fell on me. Was there an accident?"

Mackie shook the man's collar roughly. "Don't play silly. Answer the captain, man." His growl would have shaken any man in his right mind, but Hutton realised that Hanson was not one of those men. His genuine bewilderment was far from his usual surly intransigence.

"Andrew, leave it. I want him in leg irons and locked in the stateroom as soon as Reid returns. You alone shall retain the key. And call Mr Carroll once Bosun is pacified. I think he might be knocked silly."

"Very good, sir."

"And thank you, Andrew."

"Aye, sir."

The mate shuffled the listless bosun into the vacant stateroom which lay between Clarence's and that shared by Durrick and Reid. Hutton watched as Mackie sat him on the bed and stood back to block the door until Reid returned with leg irons. Hutton marvelled at the change. The bosun had become passive, staring at Mackie as if he were struggling to recognise him.

Reid walked back into the cabin ushering in a waft of cold air. The irons jangled in his hands, heavy iron cuffs linked by about a foot of chain. A key hung from a separate chain and brushed the heavy cuffs at each step.

Hutton stood in the door as the two officers secured and locked the irons just above Hanson's ankles. The bosun stamped his feet once they had finished then looked up. Concern deepened the many lines of his weather worn face.

"What have I done?"

The other three men looked quizzically at one another.

"Do you really not know? What do you remember?" Hutton was mildly alarmed at the bosun's passivity following his intense outbursts. The bosun appeared to give this serious thought, his eyes flitting up as he visibly searched his memory.

"Captain, I had supper tonight. Then someone called me over as I was leaving the galley." He paused; his hard face seemed pained, struggling to remember. "Then I felt this great weight on me, just now. Him." He gestured towards Mackie.

The mate harrumphed loudly "Sir, I say leave him be. Let him sleep it off," growled the mate. He sniffed at the bosun's face. "Have you been moonshining forward? I swear I'll tip every last drop from you before I'm done."

Hutton intervened. "Andrew, fetch the doctor. If Mr Hanson has any liquor in him, we'll find out. In the meantime, secure him. Mr Reid, you have the watch; you will keep the stateroom key until Mr Mackie takes over at first watch. We will turn over the key at the handing over of the watches." The other officers agreed and withdrew. The last thing Hutton saw as the door closed was the bosun's furrowed brow as he continued to stare into space.

* * *

Hutton had dozed on his bed for a few hours when he was roused by an unfamiliar sound. It was a well-known peculiarity aboard ship that a seaman could sleep through the watch changes, hourly bells, pounding seas and screaming wind, but the slightest sound out of place would jerk him awake like a cannon shot.

He listened again. The ship betrayed nothing, still barely moving on a calm sea. The sound came again, faint but unmistakeable. A woman's laughter.

He put on his jacket and trousers, and opened his door. He could now hear the low tones of a man's voice, and again the giggle.

Clarence has another woman?

He leaned over the stairwell and saw the table in the saloon. Reflected in its polished surface were the faces of Clarence and, incongruously, Elizabeth Barstow.

He carefully lowered himself to a crouch and descended the first few steps. He could now peep unnoticed beneath the balustrade and had an almost full view of the table and its bench seats. What he saw sent a spasm through the centre of his gut.

Mrs Barstow wore only her nightdress, open at the neck with the lace fasteners undone, her cleavage exposed brazenly for a lady in company, and criminally for a grieving Salvation Army widow.

The pair were well over halfway through what looked like their second bottle of wine, judging by the empty one adjacent to it. Clarence nestled snugly against her side, his arm draped across her bare shoulders. With the other hand, he was tipping her glass to her mouth, and she was taking copious gulps, the red liquid running down the sides of her mouth and dripping down her chin and neck, provoking bursts of giggling which sprayed wine over the table and her front. She shook her head and wiped her mouth, before gesturing him to repeat.

Hutton stared, unblinking, utterly skewered by this incomprehensible scene. He struggled to reconcile what he was seeing with the Elizabeth Barstow he knew. He was already well aware that the Salvationists were among the most uncompromising teetotallers in the whole of Christendom. Aghast, he watched her take several generous draughts again before pulling her mouth away, her lips and chin stained with the wine, giggling like a young girl. Her nightdress and chest were stained, in patches saturated with

216

wine, the thin fabric translucent where it clung to her breasts. Yet she didn't seem to care at all.

Clarence took the next draught from the glass, but this time held it in his mouth and beckoned her to drink from his lips.

Hutton considered making some sort of noisy interruption to disturb the scene, perhaps to snap the young widow out of the moment and prevent her from making such a terrible error of judgement. But he remained transfixed. He dreaded what might happen, yet he knew he would have to see it in order to believe it.

Elizabeth gazed into Clarence's eyes for a moment then leaned decisively into him, lifting her lips to his. As the wine flowed between them, she drank, but their intimate contact overcame them.

Hutton squeezed his eyes shut, refusing to believe them.

Why is she doing this?

Close on the heels of that thought came indignation. *She is supposed to be a woman of God. She is supposed to listen to Him. She knows this can't possibly be right.*

His final thought was pure judgement. *She is barely two weeks widowed! How dare she throw away her honour and dignity with this man? She knows what he is!*

He opened his eyes again, beseeching God that the scene might have changed, that the unthinkable hadn't happened. But the man and woman below, who Hutton once daydreamed would make a handsome couple, were now tightly entwined in each other's clutching arms, mouths locked together, the wine now forgotten in their escalating passion.

Hutton felt his innards churning with passion, anger, and ultimately loss. He shuffled backwards from the scene, and returned to his cabin, closing the door without a sound. He knew he would get no more sleep tonight.

Chapter Fourteen

Newport, Isle of Wight
Monday, 10th February 1890

When Blake walked into the court house at a quarter to eight the next morning, he was dripping. Heavy rain had descended on the island like a curtain, bringing dark, grey skies and an incessant drumming of droplets since the early hours. Although it lent a sheen of cleanliness to the landscape, its relentless assault on the residents of Newport had turned the town into a population of hunchbacks, cowering under umbrellas where possible, and enduring rivulets of water down every crevice where not. The heavens were in no mood to relent their assault upon the people below.

Blake placed his portmanteau at his feet and passed his dripping accoutrements to the clerk, taking care not to shower his carefully prepared registers and documents He waited to see if there had been any post. The pain in his chest, or possibly the events of the past week, had introduced an element of impatience into his manner, though he was a stoic man. He tapped irritably at the desk while the clerk went through the morning's post.

"Here you are, Mr Blake," the clerk noted brightly, handing him a telegram, received at the court house office that morning. Blake opened the sealed envelope and unfolded the contents. It was an encouragingly short message:

++BLAKE STOP++ ++CONFIRM YOUR CLARENCE WAS MY SUSPECT STOP++ ++REGRET AM UNABLE TO INVESTIGATE DUE BUSINESS STOP ++ TREAD CAREFULLY STOP ++WALTER STOP++

Blake smiled to himself; the pieces were coming together. 'Walter' was an old colleague of his from Scotland Yard days, now retired from the police and working for the legendary Pinkerton Detective Agency - so far he was their only London agent. Sadly he was unable to assist Blake, but he had provided an important piece of the jigsaw, and a warning that was borne out by recent events.

Blake needed more good luck than time to close the investigation and conclude his inquest. Only the *Irex's* missing people remained unexplained; in the disappearance of the woman, he could only clutch at shadows. But a clue to Clarence's identity was an important, if worrying, development.

He still awaited news from the hospital in Ventnor, hoping that more of the survivors would be able to respond to the inquest and fill the gaps.

Blake knew that today would be different; he would hear testimony at court alone. He knew it was mere bravado on the part of Peabody to expect to be present; the man was quite injured, and would need time to convalesce. Rennie had other matters to attend to; he and Hollis had secured Thornthwaite at the constable's family home in the village of Brading, a fact known only to the three of them. Though nominally under arrest and in the custody of the Newport station, Blake had decided it was prudent to keep him out of reach of the powerful friends who might conspire to release him. For the time being it was an adequate arrangement, but it kept Rennie fully occupied.

Blake continued to the courtroom. As he passed the usual figures sitting outside the other rooms, he felt exposed; without his trustworthy companions, he was alone and embroiled in a deadly controversy. It occurred to him that their present circumstances had left each of them alone – he had no recourse but hope their current separation would not give opportunity to an as yet unknown enemy.

Blake greeted the court staff took the steps to the bench, sensing the space on his left where Peabody had been sitting faithfully until today.

Blake opened his folios and reviewed the witnesses Peabody had prepared; only two would be testifying today, and another had submitted a written statement.

The coroner was interested to hear what the helmsman, Brown, would say – he may well have been privy to conversations among the officers that had so far remained opaque to the inquest.

As it was, Brown took his place at the table, announced himself and swore his oath at precisely 9.24. He presented a dishevelled appearance, as had the others; he did have the advantage of being of average height and build, and so his borrowed clothes fit him at least. Brown had a shock of gingery hair above a high forehead, and a very unkempt beard of the same colour, showing multiple strands of all shades from blond through red to grey. The red scouring of his face and hands was identical to the other men who had appeared so far.

Blake began. "Mr Brown. You have provided a written statement of the loss of the *Irex* from your point of view, and it is entered into record. However, I would like, if possible, to ask you about events that transpired before the wreck."

"Aye – yes, Your Honour," replied Brown in a broad Glasgow brogue. Another rough seaman on his best behaviour, decided Blake. They were certainly a breed apart.

"Mr Brown. In the days immediately preceding the wreck, did you hear any conversations between the officers that struck you as unusual?"

"Sir, the last days of the storm, they were bloody – I mean, they were very bad, sir. We were all exhausted. No man slept—"

"Mr Brown, please keep your testimony to events you actually witnessed or heard yourself."

"Aye? Sorry sir. I mean, I never slept a damn – I mean I never slept a wink. I didn't see Mr Durrick since the day before the wreck, and I never heard a thing about him until afterwards. But I did hear rumours, you know?"

"You may only repeat what was said to you for the purposes of the inquest."

"Aye, I hear that. Well, sir, the bloody – I mean the steward came to me at night, sir. It was blowing like you wouldn't believe! Captain had us running for port in Falmouth, I think. He said as much to the Mate the night before. I surely heard that, sir, he was standing closer than you are now, but, you know, the noise of the storm and everything...?" Brown seemed to lose his thread.

222

Blake looked sternly from his elevated position. It was hard to get coherence from the working man in the court environment. He knew many a conviction went wanting for lack of a convincing testimony. It was no coincidence that most successful convictions came about as a result of a positive identification of the culprit or fabrication of evidence, rather than any powers of recall or expression by the witnesses. Such was the modern justice system.

"The steward, Mr Brown?"

"Aye, the steward, Well, sir, he comes to me and says he swears that Bosun Hanson is being kept under lock and key in the cabin. I asks, 'why the hell –, I mean why would ye say that?' He just shrugs and says he knows, 'cause he's seen him in irons when the mate took him his supper, right? Now, we've been getting told all along that Bosun is sick and in quarantine, right? So we all thinks, that bastard – I mean that fella, he's probably got the syph, right? Now old Tom, he says—"

"Excuse me, Mr Brown, but who is 'old Tom?'"

"Aye, sorry sir, that's the steward. Tom Eustace, we call him old Tom, on account of him being, you know..."

Blake looked calmly back at the verbose Scot at the table. "Please continue, Mr Brown."

"Aye, of course, so, old Tom says to me Hanson is in irons on account of that he done for Durrick a while before."

"What did you think he meant by that?"

"Sir?"

"What did you think Mr Eustace meant by 'done for'?"

"Aye, I was coming to that sir. Old Tom says Hanson shot Durrick dead the last week, and the officers they'd been covering it up, on account of the bad luck we'd been having on the voyage, sir."

"Did you see any evidence yourself to cause you to believe Eustace?"

"Aye, I'm getting there, sir - I said as much to him. I says he's a damn fool and a liar, 'cause I seen Mr Durrick up and walking about alive and well not two days previous, and Hanson went in quarantine about four days back."

"Thank you Mr Brown. Did you hear any words among the other officers about this?"

"Aye, there was one thing. Morgan, he helms on the starboard watch ... each watch has a helmsman. I'm on Port watch, Morgan is on Starboard. Right, sir?"

"Thank you. Do you know each other well?"

"Well, no. Only on the ship. We hand over at the start of each watch. So this night when Hanson went sick, Morgan hands over to me at eight bells on the last dog watch and says he seen Durrick and Bosun going full at each other on the deck, and then Captain had to pull them apart and threatened to shoot them both. Next thing he sees Durrick and Bosun coming back to the cabin, and then he says Captain goes running in there and there's some more trouble."

Blake steepled his fingers and pursed his lips. This sounded like a significant event but the people he really needed to speak to were Morgan and Eustace. In Peabody's absence, he had to assume that they were among the twenty or so still recovering in hospital.

"Thank you, Mr Brown. One last question: did you personally witness any of the officers suffering accidents or injuries at any time after the ship was wrecked?"

Brown paused and ruffled his wayward beard as he thought. Blake had already begun to straighten his papers for the next testimony. The Clerk looked at the clock.

"You know, sir, I was one of the first off the ship. I wasn't at the helm when we hit the rocks, so the first sign of the sea coming into the forecastle, I grabbed my boots and took off up the rigging. So I was sitting right on the royal yardarm when the rocket hit it. Hell of a shot, that; a blind shot in the half light, and they snagged the rigging. First bit of good luck we had, sir. Right, so, we got the Indian lad Chowdury to carry it up to the skysail tops, he climbs like a goddamn – I mean, he's very quick up the ratlines. So he makes fast the line for the breeches buoy. We sends Niccolls over first on account of his size...if it can hold him, it can hold anyone. So it was taking about twenty minutes to draw the buoy, and we went one at a time. So when it's my turn, I reckon I'm maybe number six or seven off the ship. It's getting brighter, but still blowing a bloody – I mean, a right hooly. I was fearing for my life in that little buoy! So I looks down at the ship. God, she's in a terrible state, sir. On an even keel and in one piece, mind. Good ship. The waves are coming over from astern, and everything not safe in the rigging is just getting smashed to matchwood." Brown stopped and cleared his throat; the ravages of that night were clearly of great import to him even now.

"Aye, so I looks down at the ship, and I see Captain and the doctor trying to launch a boat! It was the only one left - the others were smashed, like I told you. I'm thinking they don't have both oars in the water, you know? That's sailor talk for crazy, Your Honour, before you ask. The sea was over the gunwales, almost up to the boat deck. But they were getting there, and I sees the mate, Mr Mackie in the boat! He

225

looked hurt. He's a big lad, but he was bent over and struggling. But they got the boat loose, and lowered away."

Despite the tortuous manner of Brown's delivery, Blake was hooked. This was the first hint as to what had happened to the officers since the inquest began. "Did you see what happened to them?"

"Now, Your Honour, I didn't see what happened to their little boat, on account of being pulled nigh to the cliffs. But I tell you what I did see. In that boat of theirs, I saw a body all wrapped up in sailcloth! So if you want to know what happened to Mr Durrick, I think you should start with that boat. I think he died on the ship. When I was in the hospital I heard one of the boys saying Mr Durrick went overboard in the night but I reckon he was right there. So perhaps Bosun got to him in the end."

Blake was unimpressed by Brown's theories, but pounced on one detail. "Mr Brown, did you say the body you saw in the boat was wrapped in sailcloth? Are you sure?"

"Aye, sir. I mean, I've seen enough of them in my time. I know what it was."

"Thank you Mr Brown. You are excused, with my thanks."

Blake was encouraged by the unexpected end to Brown's rambling testimony. The missing body from the morgue had been wrapped in sailcloth when it was found. Blake suspected the captain of the *Irex* was trying to launch a boat with Clarence on board, even if he was presumed dead.

Rennie's report of Third Mate Reid's testimony came to his mind. *It ended badly.* Blake had the first tantalising glimpse into what the man might have meant.

* * *

The next testimony was short. Another returnee from the hospital had been able to deliver his testimony at short notice, and was reading directly from the written testimony he had prepared the previous day. Blake was careful to let the man finish reading his tedious account of his rescue, before returning to his one salient point.

"Mr Howes, you say you saw the passenger Mrs Barstow on the day of the rescue?"

Jim Howes was that rare commodity on a sailing ship – a steam engineer, or donkeyman. A native of Jamaica, his Caribbean twang was a mellow counterpoint to the harsh staccato of the Glaswegian who preceded him.

"Yes sir, me seen her pulling herself up the lines from the deck, up to the main yardarm then all the way along to the foremast then up to the royal yardarms. That's a strong woman, sir. It take her nearly two hours, but she don't give up. And she been wearing Captain's coat, so me thinking she seen him before she gone up the mast."

"Did you see the Captain at any time after the wreck?"

"No, sir, me not seen him since maybe two days before. But when me seen him, Captain looked very tired. We all looked tired, but him look exhausted. Some sayin' because of the lady." Howes smiled slightly at this.

Blake ignored the innuendo. "Did you see Mrs Barstow leaving the ship?"

Howes shrugged. "Maybe two, three hours later? Me know she gone after me, 'cause the lady was still down the mast when me get my turn."

"Did you see her reach the clifftop?"

"Yes, sir, me seen her in Captain's coat, must be forenoon. The soldiers, they took her in, but the Major, he took her straight to their own place in the fort. Me never see her again, not even in hospital."

"Do you have any other information you would like to give the inquest?"

"Yes sir. Me been thinking there's another woman on the ship. A different woman – she come on board with Mr Clarence."

Blake looked up, surprised. "Why do you think that, Mr Howes?"

"The apprentice boy, Mr Ogilvie, God rest him, one night him bring me a woman's dress. Him say just burn it, no questions. Me ask him, if it's from the Captain's lady, but him say no, it belong to the other woman, who came with Mr Clarence. But I never seen no other woman, just the Captain's lady."

"Thank you, Mr Howes. Could you just explain what you meant by 'Captain's Lady'?"

"Captain's lady? Sure, the widow lady, she been with Captain since her husband died. So say the steward, Mr Eustace. So say everybody."

"Thank you Mr Howes. That will be all. Thank you for giving evidence – you are now excused from this inquest."

Blake ordered an adjournment, writing down the names of the witnesses he believed he most needed to see: Eustace was top of the list, followed by the helmsman, Morgan. In brackets he added Elizabeth Barstow, though she had been missing for some time.

Blake sat back in his chair and exhaled. This had been a difficult session, and he felt the absence of his friends. He had

228

known the two men for barely more than a week, yet he felt their kindred spirit, their fundamental decency, and it gave him no small pleasure to think of them as friends. He was surprised how affected he'd been by Peabody's loyalty, and reflected how much better things seemed whenever Rennie appeared with his gap-toothed grin and unquenchable energy.

Thinking of Rennie reminded him of his chest injury. The contusion had taken on hues worthy of anything Rennie carried on his face, but the only discomfort he now felt was if he touched it or breathed too deeply. Each stab of pain across his chest reminded him of Thornthwaite's treachery. Tonight, he would begin interrogation of the captured lawyer; in the meantime, he awaited the response to his enquiry of the previous week.

Blake gathered his documents and decided to use the time to eat the cheese and chutney sandwiches Mrs Orchard had provided for him. He had barely begun to chew when there came a knock and the reception clerk entered.

"Begging your pardon, sir, your telegrams."

For once, Blake was eager to receive them. "Thank you, Jeremy."

The first was from the Lord Chancellor's office.

++BLAKE STOP++ ++BARRISTER THORNTHWAITE EXPERT ON MARITIME LAW STOP++ ++INQUEST WOULD BENEFIT FROM HIS EXPERTISE STOP++ ++PLEASE EXTEND EVERY COURTESY STOP++ ++HALSBURY STOP++

The second was from his friend and former master, Sir George Mapperley, who held chambers in Lincoln's Inn Fields. Blake doubted there was a straighter man in the profession. Blake had asked him for background on Thornthwaite – if the lawyer were for real, Mapperley would certainly have known him.

++BLAKE STOP++ ++MATTHEW THORNTHWAITE BARRISTER MARITIME LAW SPECIALIST STOP++ ++CROWN EXPERT WITNESS STOP++ ++CREDENTIALS INDISPUTABLE STOP++

It looked like another dead end, but the telegram continued.

++SINCE FEB 3RD IN ANTWERP FOR SHIPPING LAW CASE RETURNS FEB 12TH STOP++ ++CAN OBTAIN FAVOURABLE RATES IF YOU NEED HIM STOP++ ++MAPPERLEY STOP++

Blake slapped the table in an uncharacteristic show of emotion. *That's it. I've got him.* He spoke the words in a murmur to himself, and felt a flush of triumph.

He remembered Rennie's beaten face; Peabody's insensible form on the cell floor; and the shock of losing Rudd. He felt a visceral surge of righteous wrath against Thornthwaite. *Oh, you treacherous, vile young man. Crown Officer or not, I am coming for you now.*

PART THREE

"Wouldst thou,"— so the helmsman answered,
"Learn the secret of the sea?
Only those who brave its dangers
Comprehend its mystery!"

   - Henry Wadsworth Longfellow, *The Secret of the Sea*

Chapter Fifteen

Atlantic Ocean, 49°08' North, 011°44' West
Wednesday, 8th January 1890

The *Irex* had broken free from the calm only to run into more unfavourable southerly breezes. Hutton turned the ship west, forced to take a more northerly course yet again. After a full twenty-four hours sailing, they put another 180 miles behind them, but once again lost ground regarding their destination.

The frustration among the officers was affecting the crew, and another minor fight had disrupted the forecastle late the previous evening. Third Mate Reid had been on hand to separate the miscreants with help from Bosun's Mate Murray; the latter had taken on the acting duties of the bosun while Hanson was still detained in the cabin. Durrick meanwhile resumed his duties as Second Mate without censure.

From the bosun himself, there was barely a peep. He seemed incapable of explaining himself. He still claimed to have no memory of his disgraceful behaviour. Mackie found no witnesses in any part of the ship to uphold his opinion that the bosun had been drinking. The big chief mate was sceptical, but the seamen's widespread dislike of the swaggering bosun gave Hutton the impression there would have been no shortage of volunteers to implicate him had he been guilty.

As far as the captain was concerned, the voyage had become an almost unbearable burden. He longed for something to divert him from the general fog of misery that had overtaken him since the other night. To his surprise, he had slept on the night he spied on the passengers' frolics; he awoke barely three hours later, before dawn, and wrestled with the idea that his consciousness had deceived him; that perhaps he just had another vivid dream that articulated his worst fears.

He took breakfast in the saloon, where he found no trace of what he had witnessed the previous night. Hutton acknowledged it may have been a delusion caused by the strain of what had happened earlier in the evening. However, any comfort Hutton he took was swept away by the steward's news that he had cleaned up any trace of the passengers' excesses before Hutton arrived.

"Someone had quite the party last night, sir," he scolded. "Several bottles of Burgundy, I'd say, though I'm no expert in such things. Just a shame they couldn't put more in the glass and less on the floor."

He gestured for Hutton to look, and the ruddy stains on the carpet lay exactly where Mrs Barstow had disgraced herself. His mind immediately filled with fresh images of the previous night; he tortured himself with them since, though he hadn't seen either passenger for the rest of the day. He had turned up for supper at their usual time, but Mrs Barstow did not emerge. Durrick asserted that he looked in periodically, but her door remained locked.

Hutton collared Eustace again, who merely smiled knowingly, and said that he had found the source of the wine while clearing out the bedding from Mr Clarence's room late in the afternoon.

"Was he there when you went in, Mr Eustace?" Hutton asked, trying to keep a neutral tone.

"Oh, yes, he was there." Eustace hadn't been able keep the smile from his voice.

Hutton knew he needed to ask his next question, but he had dreaded the answer. "Was he alone?"

Eustace actually looked sympathetic when answered. "Yes sir, but I saw the lady leaving his room just after two bells on the afternoon watch. She was still in her nightwear, and it looked generously stained with what I'd guess was last night's wine. She was quite brazen about it, sir. She didn't shy when she saw me – actually, she seemed pleased to see me, and greeted me quite politely."

God help her, Hutton thought. *She has completely lost her mind.* He had been so stunned, he didn't even finish the conversation; he had needed simply to disengage.

Without another word, he turned his back on the steward and went instead to the chart room to write up the log, before retiring to his room, where he remained for the duration of the night.

He heard the characteristic click of the Barstows' door late in the first watch, at maybe two a.m., followed by the soft footfalls of the woman as she crossed the cabin to Clarence's door across the hall. He definitely heard her open and then softly lock it behind her. Then Hutton had buried his head under the pillow, refusing to hear any more.

* * *

The captain now stood by the helm again, holding a glass to his eye and looking along the northern horizons for the tell-tale cloud formations that would signal the approach of a favourable front. The only trace he found was in the far southwest.

Morgan stood at the helm, while Mackie took sightings from the setting sun for the final position of the day. They expected a shorter total for the day's run, as Hutton had ordered to take in sail; what was the use of haring along at full tilt, when their course took them no nearer their destination?

Hutton once again felt impotent. He felt an overwhelming need to speak to Clarence; he feared for Mrs Barstow's safety even as he despised her carelessness. He needed to know if their present consorting had changed the nature of the threat to her life; or whether it was part of Clarence's perversity to seduce her simply to torture Hutton all the more.

In truth, he was desperate to know the nature of Mrs Barstow's sudden and complete reversal. He had taken supper with her in the saloon every night for days – her conversation had been almost exclusively about her love for God, her work with the poor, and other pious discussions that had bolstered Hutton's own grip on his faith even as the circumstances continued to undermine it. Hutton reciprocated with his own stories of past deeds and experiences, his wife and children, and the lady had seemed most approving. However, if their talk turned towards Clarence, as it had on several occasions, her animosity had almost matched his own. She reiterated her warnings to him, and seemed to take pains to keep Hutton from over-familiarity with the man. In his turn, he had been on the cusp of betraying his confidence; on three separate occasions, he had warned her in turn that the man might have amorous designs upon her; these she had dismissed with her customary forthrightness.

And yet – in the space of a day, the sum of her animosity and all her warnings had been discarded in favour of a reckless attraction which she had acted out brazenly and without shame or remorse. Hutton was truly appalled, and had to know why.

He was staring over the rail considering these things, when the bulk of Chief Mate Mackie drew alongside him.

"Captain, I need you to see the bosun. I have to say, I'm beaten."

"What is it? Is he all right?"

"That's just it, sir. He is fine. Gentle as a lamb. If I hadn't seen him the other night I'd have said he couldn't have done it. Could you come and look?"

Hutton followed the mate back into the cabin; he couldn't help himself steal a look at the Barstows' door, which remained closed. There was no light beneath the crack. He looked back over to Clarence's door, and saw his lights were on. He tore his attention away from the troublesome passengers, turning back to see Durrick standing outside the stateroom currently acting as the bosun's prison cell.

"Mackie – is that wise, letting him see Durrick?"

"Captain, this is what I want you to see." The mate took the key and turned it in the lock.

Hanson was lying on his side, his feet still manacled, and looked up, puzzled, as the captain and mate crowded into his room.

"Sir. Captain." Hanson had never been big on greetings. His face was still hard as flint, but his eyes bore no animosity.

Mackie, not taking his eyes from Hanson, called "Mr Durrick, please come in." The second mate entered cautiously, remaining physically alert to any moves by the bosun.

"Sir." Hanson's greeting was as neutral as the ones he had given the other officers.

They all stood puzzled. Mackie cocked his head slightly to look fully into the bosun's face.

"Do you know why you are detained here, Mr Bosun?" Hanson looked irritated by the question.

"Aye. I'm in quarantine. But God knows why. I feel fit as a butcher's dog. There's bugger all wrong with me, beyond a few knocks on the head."

The officers exchanged glances. Mackie continued to ask questions. "Do you remember arguing with Mr Durrick here?"

"Aye. Well, we've had a few disagreements about sail, but I don't remember what you might call arguing."

"Have you ever tried to strike Mr Durrick?"

"God, no! Who told you that? I'll admit I've lifted my hands on a few sailors, but I've been at sea long enough to know to keep my hands to myself around the gentlemen!"

Hutton broke in. "Mr Hanson, tell us about Mr Clarence."

The bosun practically jumped at the name. "Clarence?"

"Our passenger, whom you have befriended."

Hanson looked uncomfortable. "Aye, I've shared a wee dram a few times in his room, but never on watch."

"Tell me about the chest. Clarence's trunk."

238

The other officers exchanged glances. Their feelings about Hutton's obsessions with the passengers lay very near the surface.

Hanson sighed. "Sir, the night before we left port, I did help Mr Clarence to get off the ship. We carried off his sea chest."

"Did you know what was in it?"

Hanson seemed to glaze slightly. His mouth moved as if he wanted to speak, but no words came out. He just looked at them helplessly.

"Answer the question Mr Hanson!" Mackie's growl was not usually defied, but the bosun seemed incapable of answering. He mouthed like a fish, but no words came out.

Hutton decided. "Gentlemen, would you excuse us? I would like to speak to Mr Hanson alone."

"Sir, he might be faking—"

"Then lock the door. I'll call you if I need help."

The other two, with some reluctance, filed out of the door. Hutton waited until he heard the click and then sat down on the chair opposite Hanson, whom he motioned to sit on the bed.

"Hanson, listen to me. How did he get to you? What has he promised you to run the ship?"

This time Hanson stared for a few moments before speaking. "He said if we make a smooth crossing and made no trouble, he would give each of us a gold guinea."

Hutton breathed in and held it, if only to maintain his composure. He let the breath out and locked his hands together to stop the trembling. *How dare he*?

"Who, Hanson? To whom did he promise this?"

"Well, he's giving me thirty guineas to share between the watches. Not the officers and boys, obviously. Just the fellows."

Hutton fumed inwardly again. Then he remembered the words that Hanson had apparently said to Mrs Barstow on the night of the attack.

"What else were you promised? What else did he owe you?"

Hanson grew visibly agitated at this question. His manacled feet shuffled, jangling the chain. His knees pumped and his head twisted from side to side, one hand gripping the blankets, while the other scratched at the back of his neck.

"I – I – don't...something...I can't remember..."

"What does he owe you?"

Hanson shook like a dog. "It's...something. Yes...yes, I'm owed...what?"

Hutton stared, fascinated. *What witchcraft is this?* He realised he had this one last opportunity to find out.

"Was it her? Did he promise you Elizabeth Barstow?"

Hanson looked up as if slapped. His eyes rolled to the door. He still seemed to be wrestling with himself. His breath exhaled in puffs as he continued to be agitated. "Is it...? Yes! A...a promise. What I'm owed—"

"Hanson. It's time to collect what was promised. She owes you. She promised."

The bosun exploded from his bed, knocking Hutton back against the wall, chair and all. He pushed to the door and began pulling at the handle. Hutton heard the door lock turning and shouted a warning.

"He's free! Stand fast!"

Mackie must have unlocked the door, because the bosun snapped it open, piling onto the floor outside as he forgot his manacled legs. He tried to pull himself up, but Mackie was upon him again. Hanson fought like a tiger to get up, spitting curses, his eyes bulging and the veins standing from his red forehead and neck.

"She's mine! She owes me! She promised!"

Directly across from Hutton, Mrs Barstow's key turned in her lock and the door cautiously opened outward. She poked her head around the door, her eyes widening as she beheld the repeat of the previous night.

"Eddy!" she called, her voice ringing over the commotion.

Clarence's door opened, and the man stepped out. Bypassing Hanson and the struggling chief mate he moved towards Elizabeth, but stopped and stared across at Hutton before he reached her. He looked angry.

"What are you doing, Will?"

Hutton realised he held a new card. "No, Mr Clarence, I need to know what *you* are doing."

Clarence stepped over to him, avoiding the struggling men. "You had better be sure you want to do this, Will. I told you I was going to make it right."

This time it was Hutton who leaned closer. He didn't have to lower his voice, as the screams of the bosun were ongoing.

"What have you done to him? I know this is your doing. And whatever witchcraft this is, I know you've done the same to her. They are not in their right minds!" He clasped his head in exasperation. "What more do you want from me, Clarence? I've kept my word!"

To his surprise, Clarence smiled, his face brightening. "Oh, Will. Everything has to be mystic with you, doesn't it? Well

241

watch this. I give you my word, you shall know the truth by the end of this night."

He spun back to stand by the bosun – he was still screaming, but Mackie had firmly pinned him, and the leg irons were impeding his progress. Clarence dropped to his knees and spoke very close to Hanson's ear. Once again, Hutton observed the extraordinary quietude come over the bosun, just as it had the other night.

Mackie stared as Clarence rose to his feet, wiping his hands together. The bosun remained subdued. Mrs Barstow opened her door and skipped over to Clarence, taking his face in her hands and kissing him again, before cuddling into his chest, as she had with Hutton the day her husband had died. Unlike Hutton, Clarence took her in a full embrace, hands soothing her back. They stood back for a moment, and Mrs Barstow looked into his face with sincere gratitude.

"Thank you again, my darling."

Hutton looked on in fury –a look that did not go unnoticed by Durrick. Elizabeth touched Clarence's lips with a fingertip, and went back to her room, locking it behind her. Clarence looked at Hutton and shrugged. Hutton nearly blew a fuse.

"We will speak now, Mr Clarence. Please wait for me in the saloon."

Clarence held up his hands. "As you wish, Captain." He walked around the two men on the floor and made his way to the stairs.

"Durrick. Detain the bosun in the stateroom again. He is a danger to everyone aboard, Mrs Barstow in particular. Andrew, thank you once again. Without you, we may have had no recourse but to shoot him. You will continue to keep him safe. I believe he will have no memory of this episode. Keep him in quarantine, and ensure the men are told no more."

"Aye, sir." Once again Mackie led the bosun meekly into the stateroom, though both still breathed heavily from their exertions.

"Andrew, I will be with Clarence for the evening. Tell Eustace we will take dinner in the saloon at six bells."

He felt revitalised again. He now had a purpose, and that purpose was to break Clarence's hold on his ship, and on the widow he had entranced by whatever means he had captivated Hanson.

*　*　*

"Will, what is wrong with you?" Clarence sat in his usual wide-legged pose, taking up almost half of the bench seat along the table. He wore his open-necked shirt with sleeves rolled up to show his forearms, striated with muscle and bristling with fine hairs. He carried his usual superior smile.

Hutton struggled to maintain his temper, but knew he must. The last time they had spoken together he had been physically and emotionally weak but now he felt stronger in every way. Anger would dissipate the advantage he now held.

"Clarence. It's time you really came clean."

Clarence feigned hurt. "Now, come on, Will. You can't say I haven't been honest with you."

"No, this isn't about the past. This is about what you're doing right now. I want to know what you've done to Hanson and the woman."

"Oh, she's 'the woman', now? Very *sang froid*, Will. I suppose you're going to tell me you've gone back to your wife, now? Lost the battle but still won the war? Very wise."

Patience, Will! Hutton swallowed and opened his hands, letting the tension leave. He knew Clarence would be playing to get under his skin and into his head, make him doubt himself.

"Mrs Barstow."

Clarence snorted. "Do you know what her real name is? Elizabeth Alexandra Victoria Bayes-Montagu! That's quite a mouthful, isn't it? That also happens to be one of the finest families in England. They have a country patch in Buckinghamshire. Missenden House, it's called. Nice little pad, been there once myself. Marvellous grouse shooting, and a trout pond to see once and die. No, our Elizabeth is no commoner, Will. She's something of a runaway." He smiled the wolfish grin that Hutton had come to despise.

"At first, I admit I despised her, Will. Too big for her boots. But then I began to watch her. And I listened to you talking for several days."

"What?" Hutton was stunned. They always checked upstairs for listeners before they spoke, keeping hushed tones if they mentioned Clarence.

"Oh, come on Will, do you think I was going to pass up an opportunity like that? You two, coming down here every night on the dot of bells for your little chats?" Clarence wore his wolfish grin. He pointed at the pantry, barely six feet away behind a partition wall. "I just sat in there. All I had to do was pay Eustace a sixpence not to hang around."

Hutton fumed again at how easily he had been undermined.

"I know what you said, and it genuinely doesn't concern me. But as I listened to you speaking, Will, I realised that you mean every word you say. It's admirable. I might even say

244

you are the last honest man on earth and that's why I want you to prosper from this voyage. The world needs honest men, deluded as you are. But that's not the interesting part." He paused to pick an imaginary speck from his fingernail.

"What really caught my fancy is that Elizabeth is different. She says a lot of things, but she doesn't really mean them. Perhaps she wants to believe all the things she says, but she doesn't, Will. Not really."

Hutton was taken aback by this new approach by Clarence. "How can you possibly say that?" he spluttered. "You've seen how she is! Her dignity and grace, the way she conducts herself—"

"Will! Listen to me! It's all a show. She's been hounded all her life because she is a sensual delight! Men have tried to own her, trap her and possess her for themselves. She has adopted this religious fervour to facilitate her escape! What do you think she was doing bringing a sick, old man on a bloody sea voyage in winter, for god's sake? She married him to keep the wolves away, and now she has discarded him. Don't you see?"

Hutton began to ponder this but pulled himself back. "I rather fancy you're seeing what you want to see, Mr Clarence."

"And you think you're not doing the same?" retorted Clarence.

They sat quietly for a few seconds.

Hutton digested this information and tried to fit it into what he already knew. "Even if it were true, Clarence, how did you change her mind? Concerning you, I mean? She hated you from the moment you met."

Clarence shrugged. "I just waited for my chance. She didn't hate me. She just knew you did."

Hutton flushed. "Is it obvious, Mr Clarence?"

Clarence clapped him on the shoulder. "I still like *you*, Hutton. You see, I find I am despised by all lesser men. That's not just a boast, Will. It's a fact. Men of status don't like being upstaged. It's just nature. But it gives me the power to choose whomever I wish to like. It's a fine thing."

Hutton was extremely irritated to find himself once again the second fiddle in this orchestra. "I need to know, Clarence. How did you fix the bosun and Mrs Barstow? Did you mesmerise them?"

Clarence smiled again. "That's very good, Will. How did you come to that idea?"

Hutton bristled. "It doesn't matter. Did you, or not?"

The moment was interrupted by the opening of the main deck door as Eustace entered. He passed the two men without comment, other than a quiet greeting. He continued to the pantry, and began clattering dishes and cutlery in preparation for their meals. It took fifteen more minutes for Campbell to deliver the food and Eustace to serve it. When he had finished serving, the steward was about to go back to the pantry. Clarence gave him a quick whistle, accompanied by a flick of the head, and Eustace excused himself, vanishing up the stairs and through the door. Clarence sat down and began to load up his cigarette-holder.

"I know you won't like this, Will, but he just earned himself another sixpence."

Hutton just clenched his teeth and shook his head, looking down at the table. "I'll admit, when the bosun went spare, I suspected it was you. Every wayward act aboard this ship seems to involve you somewhere. But I thought you'd just bought him off, like so many others. But after that charade in the cabin, which I saw with my own eyes, I realised you had done something else to him. Something devilish."

"Well, I'd like to congratulate you Will, but you only got it the second time around."

"No, Clarence. I guessed the key word that brought on his frenzy. I just need to work out how you did it."

"In that case, I congratulate you. Bravo!" Clarence clapped his hands. "Yes, Will. I did use certain techniques on the bosun. But it's far simpler than you think. There's no witchcraft or sorcery or other bunkum involved. It's just about knowing how minds work."

Hutton looked sceptical. "It's one thing to trick a dupe in a stage show. It's quite another to do it to a sailor at sea."

Clarence shook his head. "No, it isn't. You just need a willing subject. You know, I had Hanson in my room several times. He is partial to fine Scotch, and I have some of the finest in my possession. I used our time to cultivate certain thoughts in our dull bosun's mind, things that he believed already. That he's undervalued by the men. Or that the officers are out to get him. And of course, that he is smitten by our Miss Elizabeth." Clarence drew on his cigarette, lazily letting the smoke out. He hadn't touched his food.

Hutton chewed at his own. Campbell had outdone himself again. He had managed to bake no small amount of bread during the calm, so the men and officers alike were eating like kings by seamen's standards. Despite Hutton's emotional discomfort, the food was too good to despise.

"You see, Will, I knew that Elizabeth's ploy was a clever fraud. No-one can be that clever and still consumed by

247

nonsense. And let me tell you, Will, she is very clever. Keen as a whip. It's taken me a few weeks to really figure her out. Now you know why I had to push her the day her dear George died. And she put on a hell of a show that day, did she not?"

Hutton's face fell a mile, his fork in mid journey from plate to mouth. Clarence laughed again, smoke popping from his mouth and nose to form a cloud that haloed his face. He reminded Hutton of Mephistopheles, laughing in the faces of the damned.

"But...no, that's nonsense!" Hutton remembered the grief of the woman, her face buried in his chest. "She was grieving!"

Clarence put on his patronising look again, part apology, part pity. "Ah, Will Hutton! You are as trusting as you are honest. She's been playing with us all. I haven't established what she intends to do in Rio, but I rather fancy she has made arrangements. But perhaps she can be yet persuaded to change them?"

He looked knowingly at Hutton, who abandoned his efforts at finishing his meal. "You see, Will, all it took was a touch of planning. Lately, I began to experiment on the bosun with hypnosis. You've heard of Mesmer, of course? But Freud's hypnosis is so much more effective, because he has defined the conscious and the unconscious. His hypnosis lays bare the unconscious mind, that part which lies hidden even from the man himself. Just as you can elicit truths from a person's unconscious under hypnosis, you can in turn plant ideas. The marvel of this, Hutton, is that these ideas are masked from the man's conscious mind – he doesn't remember what he knows!"

Hutton listened, trying to make sense of these mysterious ideas. He had seen the mesmerists of Calcutta many times, and dismissed them as the heathen spiritual practices of the Orient; to hear such practices raised to the level of science was hard for him to grasp.

"Will, he is burning with passion for our dear Elizabeth, but his conscious mind doesn't know it. In the conscious world, this trickles out of him, expressed as an unreconciled anger. But at the trigger word, all his boiling lust comes out in a rush. He will stop at nothing until he can take her. You see, even under hypnosis I can't make him do anything that truly grates against his will. After all, it is only an idea, and his will can reject it. But I have carefully placed these thoughts of Elizabeth in a constant and steady feed. What his unconscious believes, his conscious can easily accept."

Hutton was appalled. "So what have you done to him? Is it permanent? Will he carry this for life?"

Clarence shrugged. "Who knows? I imagine that, freed from her presence and the environs of this ship, the idea shall fade with time. But listen, Will; I alone know the trigger phrase, although you seem to have stumbled upon it – that was foolish. If your chief mate had not been at hand, Hanson would have been able to overpower Elizabeth when I wasn't at hand to save her."

Hutton realised the import of the man's words. "As long as only you know the trigger, you can control these outbursts. So you would always be perfectly positioned to play the saviour."

Clarence beamed. "You see it, Will! Well done. I had to gain Elizabeth's confidence when her guard was down. She's been able to control every situation since she came aboard. The perfect way to wrest control from her is to make her into a damsel in distress. She can out-think all of us, Will, but she is still of the frailer sex."

"Indeed. And what of the phrase you use to stop him? Is that also part of your trick?"

"As you guessed, Will. Though you wouldn't have, had you not interfered. I would ask you not to do that again."

Hutton shrugged off the warning. "If that is the only thing wrong with him, then how can I keep him locked up for another month? Tell me the password. He is still a valuable member of the crew, and despite his actions, he should be freed if he poses no further threat to my ship."

Clarence thought about it. "Very well, Will. Straight as ever, aren't you? The trick is very simple. At the utterance of a single word, the conscious man is re-established. He will forget everything that occurred between the two, except maybe in the dead of night in dreams." He gave a rueful smile. "Since you were never meant to hear it, you of all men may find this droll. The word is 'Whitechapel'."

Whitechapel, remembered Hutton. Clarence had said the word clearly on that first night. Hutton had considered it an embarrassing slur against his leadership and crew, but it was much more. A man placed in a trance and woken as easily by a specific word. He shook his head in wonder. "Why did you do all this, Clarence? All for one woman?"

There was a long pause. Clarence stubbed out his cigarette, and didn't look at Hutton for some time. He pushed his food around the plate with his fork, sniffing at it; he decided to eat the bread, dipping it into the cooling stew sauce and dabbing his napkin at the corners of his mouth.

Hutton persisted. "What designs do you have on her now? Will you continue to threaten her in exchange for my silence?"

Clarence's pale eyes fixed on the captain as his demeanour hardened. The threat was back. "Will, you are not my equal, but I'll grant that you are a man of some strength and no small cunning. I've been impressed how you have carried your burdens with dignity, if not much resolve."

He again glanced up at the stairwell, and Hutton drew close to catch Clarence's lowered voice, barely a murmur.

"You are right about our covenant, Will. I still need your silence." He hunched his meaty shoulders forward, ducking his gaze for a second or two; for the first time in Hutton's presence, Clarence actually looked uncomfortable.

"Our terms need to change. The things I told you, Will, I told you because you needed to keep clear of Elizabeth. Yet you have continued to try to gain her trust, and she has humoured you, like the good boy that you are. I commend your discretion so far; it seems that you have truly not told another soul. But now I must impress this on you, though it pains me to tell you; if you breathe a word of my former deeds to Elizabeth, none of your crew, not even yourself, are immune from my retribution. You now forfeit your own life for hers."

Hutton was surprised by the relief he felt at these words. Despite his threats – which Hutton had no doubt he would carry out if he wanted to – Clarence had betrayed a weakness: love. It was written in his discomfort at having to change his terms; the admission that a change of priorities had occurred because of his sudden romantic success with Mrs Barstow.

Hutton felt he had some leverage for the first time. "Really, Clarence? And what good would that do for your own plans?"

Clarence's eyes narrowed. "Don't cross me, Will." The words came as a warning hiss, the first rattle of the diamondback as the careless hiker came too close. "I guarantee it will end badly for you. And you may consider that the merry widow may well come to harm if things do not turn out in my favour by our voyage's end."

Hutton felt a chill again – Clarence was eminently used to getting exactly what wanted "And what has the lady herself to say about your arrangement?"

Before Clarence could answer, the Barstows' door clicked open and fell closed again. The familiar sounds of Mrs Barstow's footsteps and the swish of her clothing were audible over the creaks and groans of the ship, and both men turned to look as her booted feet appeared on the stairs, gradually revealing her elegant form as she descended into full view.

She was dressed in as close to finery as was possible aboard ship – a pale red gown with fine crepe trimmings, bare arms but puffed shoulders, her neck revealed all the way to a box-cut neckline that ended considerably lower than her Salvation Army uniform. Her hair had been gathered up in a piled cascade of chestnut red curls, held with a feather pin that let the errant locks spill down each side of her face. She seemed to glow beneath the orange-tinted lamps having transformed into a society lady overnight.

"Good evening, gentlemen!" Her voice was smooth as glass. She nodded at Hutton as she approached the table, then took her place close beside Clarence, offering her hand which he took in his and lightly kissed the knuckle, never taking his eyes from hers.

"I expect Eddy has been spinning you some tales about me, Captain; I thought it better to let you speak before I joined you. Eddy, would you be a darling and fetch Eustace for some tea? And take your time, for I would like to speak with Captain Hutton alone, if you would."

Clarence appeared surprised by such a request, but rose and excused himself. As he passed back behind the bench on his way to the stairs, he shot Hutton a warning look.

When Clarence had gone, Elizabeth turned to Hutton and pinned him with her intense, pale-green eyes.

"I imagine you're rather disappointed in me, Captain," she began.

Hutton was momentarily mute, unable to consider where to start.

She laughed lightly at his indecision. "Let me help you, Captain. I was born Lady Elizabeth Bayes-Montagu on the Montagu estate in Amersham. My godfather was the Duke of Cambridge. My parents received the congratulations of Her Majesty herself on my birth."

She paused, but Hutton remained silent. He sensed she was merely gathering herself.

"We lived an idyllic life. There were forty servants in our household, thirty acres of grounds, stables, hunts, an ornamental lake..." she trailed off, re-living her childhood in unseen images. "The summers were the best life that mortal men ever lived.

"I was fourteen when one of my father's friends tried to force himself on me. Naturally there were no repercussions, save that I was locked away for a whole summer." She pouted at the memory. "Thereafter others came, a constant and fearful menace until I was eighteen. I was to be betrothed to the Earl of somewhere or other, an aged noble who would keep me as a trophy wife and birthing mare in exchange for a vast fortune, no doubt. Well, Captain, that was the end of it for me.

"I left with a trunk of clothes, and a vow never to return until I would claim my share of the estate, either with the man of my choosing, or alone. From that day I have chosen my own path, Captain. I took a place in a hospital, where I used my name to my advantage. And yet within weeks I was once again set upon, this time by a young doctor, whose ardour far outweighed his capacity. I turned myself over to the missions as soon as I qualified. I was twenty-one, Captain Hutton. I should have been married off and living as a wealthy, kept woman. But I would not be beholden to the whims of any rich, old man, nor stifled by any young pup." She glanced up the stairs, but Clarence had not returned.

Hutton decided that he could finally interject. "And your mission service? Your faith? What about those?"

Elizabeth sighed. "Captain, I have served the poor. They are no more ennobled by their poverty than the rich are by their wealth. Their assaults upon me were brazen but clumsy. The poor are beset by the same lusts as the high-born but lack the conviction of entitlement. I would no more regard the desultory groping of a toothless vagrant than the buzzing of a fly." She sighed. "Oh, Captain, I have served, I have prayed, I have sought God's hand on so many occasions, yet he provided nothing more than an occasional sop to my despair."

She looked at her hands, and spread her fine fingers before them both. "I learned the piano, Captain. I was taught by a fellow of the Royal Academy. I could play Rachmaninov, Liszt and Chopin by heart. I ended up playing the accordion every Sunday in a Salvation Army hostel in Liverpool. Freedom demands a steep price from a woman."

She shifted in her seat to fully face him. Her large eyes seemed less inviting than he had previously supposed. "I met George in Liverpool. I chose George, Captain. I chose him because he was a good man. He believed what he believed, and lived true to it, like you. But we could never truly be partners. He lived in awe of me. He never sought to possess me, because he knew he never could. Even in our bed, he was afraid to touch me. But he gave me legitimacy, Captain. If a man wanted to molest me, I was a *married* woman. Pitiful as it sounds, as a married woman, I was another man's property. A man takes more caution before acting on his lust when the object of his desire belongs to someone else.

"I grant you, I played along for George's benefit, as I concede I played along for yours." She gave the first hint of a smile. "It's not personal, Will. I never set out to deceive you, but I have learned over time that it's easier to be acceptable than to be oneself."

Hutton was about to speak again but she silenced him with a gesture of her hand.

"With that, I confess to you that I am going to be with Eddy. I suspect we shall be wed, and he will return me to England once his business is concluded."

Hutton's jaw dropped. "But, Mrs Barstow…"

She snapped at him for the first time. "Will, you know little enough of me, beyond what I have confided. But you know even less of him!"

Hutton swallowed his indignation. He felt he was being drawn into the eye of a whirlpool, where he would be wrung and all his secrets would spill out. And yet the sting of humiliation made him more ready than ever to unburden himself. He imagined the look on *Lady Elizabeth*'s face when her new beau turned out to be either the world's most notorious murderer or its greatest charlatan.

But Elizabeth was already looking round again, and, seeing no-one, leaned forward to speak quietly. "He is not just any gentleman traveller, Captain. He is—"

Just then, the cabin door banged open and Clarence strode through, descending the stairs in twos. He looked quizzically at Hutton, who just looked back at Elizabeth.

"I trust you've had plenty to talk about, lady and good sir?"

Hutton's mouth seemed to have dried out. "Yes, Mr Clarence, some interesting conversations, it must be said."

Clarence sat down heavily, moving snugly up against Mrs Barstow and adopting his sprawl-legged attitude, one arm across the back of the bench encompassing her shoulders.

"Pray tell."

His hand dropped from the back of the seat to rest on her bare shoulder, thumb gently caressing the skin. Her hand moved up to take his fingers in her own. It was a curiously intimate gesture which added to Hutton's awkwardness. As so often in Clarence's presence, he felt inhibited. But his indignation had been growing by the minute, and this time he had no qualms over where he would go.

"Who are you really, Mr Clarence? It is a question that has vexed me for our entire voyage. You have answered me before. Please, humour my impertinence with an honest answer."

Elizabeth's eyes widened in surprise. Clarence was unperturbed, giving one of his strained laughs that sounded more like a cough, and moving his head to look up the stairs, before turning his gaze back to Hutton.

"Will, there are some things you can know about me, but then there are some that you cannot. You need only know that I am here, for the time being." His eyes narrowed, though Elizabeth remained unaware. "In the meantime you will allow a gentleman his discretion."

Elizabeth must have sensed the change in his tone, for his last utterance was as cold as the first had been cordial. She turned to look at him, and he merely smiled back and withdrew his hand from hers. He stood up and stretched again.

"Elizabeth, my dear, I shall retire to my room. Should you wish to join me, I shall be delighted to entertain you there."

The brazen statement appalled Hutton, but Elizabeth's eager acquiescence was, for him, even worse. Clarence ended with a wink at Hutton, and clumped up the stairs again. They both waited until the door clicked shut before Elizabeth spoke quietly again.

"You have misjudged me, Captain. I have been true to myself. I remain in my faith, for it has comforted me at times, though I am not as convinced as you, I would hazard. Nevertheless, I see in Eddy the man I have sought these past years. He doesn't seek to possess me, nor is he intimidated by me. Nor am I by him. He is a powerful man, Will. He commands respect and deserves nothing less. I had dismissed him as the type of upper-class bully and arrogant show-off who would undoubtedly try to take hold of me at some point. For that reason I played cool and out of reach, keeping him far from me. Captain, I always thought that I could make my own way without needing a man permanently by my side. But when he pulled your rabid sailor from me and hurled him across the deck...it was then that I finally saw the noble side of him – the protector."

Hutton almost choked, but held himself together. He wondered what she would make of Clarence's plan to deceive her. Then he pictured the 'noble man', slashing with a knife, shoving the unfortunate victim in a trunk and conning some simple sailors to carry away the evidence of his murder to a waiting accomplice. But Hutton voiced none of these thoughts.

"I am a woman, Captain. My strength may be found in every part of my being, but in my body alone, I am weak. Men covet me; they seek to take this body by force, with no regard for the woman within. They seek to seize, to possess and to own. Well, I am no man's mere property. Though I may need no partner for my being, in these corrupt times I have need of a man to protect my vulnerability."

Hutton felt a stab of shame that he had miserably failed in that duty. But then it dawned on him at last why they were having this meeting. This meeting was Mrs Elizabeth Barstow's valedictory. He would see the prim Salvationist no more; from now on there was only the society belle Lady Elizabeth, who would forever regard him as beneath her. He decided to throw caution to the wind.

"What makes him so different? That you would throw away all memory of your husband and, if I may venture, your virtue?"

She skipped the insult without a beat; her rapt attention did not waver. "It does not matter. He has asked me to come and I am going with him."

Hutton felt a wild force drive up through his innards, hot as the blood that rushed to his face. He took her soft hands in his own leather-lined palms.

"You could…well, you could come with me."

Her head cocked slightly, green eyes crinkled at the edges in amusement, her mouth widening in a smile. She squeezed his hands in return. "No, Will. You are a kind man. Go home to your wife. She deserves you, I am sure."

"Please, Mrs Barstow. Not him, I beg you."

She glanced up the stairs again, before speaking in a whisper. "He is a prince, Captain Hutton."

Hutton shook his head vigorously. "I suggest you are too quick to pedestal such a man—"

"No, Captain!" she hissed. "He is a *prince*. Prince Albert Victor. Second in line to the throne of England. And he *will* be my husband."

* * *

Towards midnight, Hutton stood on the heaving deck in his usual place next to the helm. In the darkness, Brown held tight to the wheel, cursing the ship and the weather with equal ferocity. There were now sizeable waves breaking from the port side, and the glass had fallen an impressive six points since the last watch. There was a warm, humid feel in the air, and the combination of the three was worrisome for the captain. The wind came in gusts from the south-south-west, so Hutton decided to turn the ship back toward the east.

For the first time he felt an emotional detachment from his troublesome passengers. Not just the numbness that had attended his first conversation with Clarence, but a genuine closure, akin to relief. Barely half an hour before, he had stood outside Clarence's door, the light still glowing from the slit beneath, and heard the unmistakeable sounds within. He remembered a casual moment, weeks before, when Clarence had observed *sotto voce* that he believed Mrs Barstow "had never drunk deeply from the well of love." The man appeared to be doing his best to compensate for her previous deficiencies. Their cries had been audible throughout the cabin; no doubt the bosun imprisoned in the stateroom next door had been privy to their exertions.

Yet here, standing on the wet deck with the wind and spray back in his face, he felt for the first time the absence of conflict. He was liberated from his own mixed feelings about Mrs Barstow, and his fear and antipathy toward Clarence. They had chosen one another; him for his nobility (ha!) and her for her beauty, if nothing else. He felt they deserved each other; if Elizabeth's duplicity was to be outdone by Eddy's, she would find out sooner or later. For now, Hutton at least felt freed from any obligation to either of them.

Even so, he grappled with the sudden shift in their identities: Elizabeth, the pious, newly-widowed Salvationist, now a titled aristocrat jumping between the sheets with a man she had shunned until this week; then there was Clarence, the well-bred gentleman who was a backstreet murderer on the run, and now apparently a prince of the Realm!

He questioned if any of it were true. Both had shown themselves to be secretive and deceptive; it would not have surprised Hutton if the two had pre-arranged their stories in order to elope.

Nevertheless, it gave him respite from the weeks of constant pressure – he felt able to devote his full attention to the job of sailing his ship.

Midnight was approaching, and he felt bound to pray with his wife, given his guilty slip at the table with Mrs Barstow. Though his weakness caused him shame, he realised he had made a final appeal to her virtue and godliness, to see if they were genuine and not the projected phantoms of his own desire. Yet she had turned him away with amusement and a mild rebuke, adding to his humiliation.

He wondered once more about the dreams he had experienced, and questioned the will of the Almighty as he saw his erstwhile ally and enemy entwined in his mind's eye, both lost to him. They cavorted together in his imagination before swirling into the heaving waves.

Chapter Sixteen

Ventnor National Hospital, Isle of Wight
Tuesday, 11th February 1890

The National Hospital at Ventnor was a modern, attractive building. Its corridors and wards bustled with nursing staff, commanded by haughty sisters and cajoled by a fearsome matron, a spiky, grey-haired woman whose default expression was an icy glare. She was openly hostile as she realised Blake had turned up to ruin her afternoon.

"None of these patients is in a fit state to discuss matters of such import. You may not interview them, Mr Blake."

Blake refused to wither, which just made her angrier. He couldn't help wondering how Rennie had managed to sweet talk his way past such a gatekeeper.

"Madam, I'm sorry, but time is of the essence! There are other lives depending on the outcome of this inquest."

"Then they shall have to wait. I shall not have you bothering these patients, the poor wretches can scarcely breathe, never mind speak!"

Blake sighed. "Then perhaps you could help me in another matter?"

The matron blew out a frustrated breath. "Mr Blake, this is a hospital. I cannot waste my valuable time with your guessing after the fact." But she didn't walk away.

"Please, madam, I have just one question to ask of you, regarding two people. A man and a woman both absconded from this place ten days ago. Do you know anything about this?"

The matron scowled. "Absconded? Sir, are you accusing us of foul play?"

"Not at all, madam. They are material witnesses to my inquest, and both are now missing. Both were last seen here. Though one was declared dead, we believe they are still alive."

"Nonsense! The gentleman was dead when he arrived. He had been in the sea for two days. He was sent immediately to the mortuary at the Workhouse." She practically spat the last word; it seemed her contempt for Blake was surpassed only by her contempt for the rival hospital. But it was clear she knew to whom Blake referred.

"And the woman?"

"There was no woman that I recall, Mr Blake. Now I must attend to my hospital!" She turned on her heel and marched towards the door. "And I require you to leave the hospital now. If you would like to interview the patients, please apply in writing to the Registrar. Good day, sir."

Blake was left facing an apologetic nurse and two orderlies, one of whom ushered him back towards the main entrance.

"Terribly sorry sir, she's like that sometimes." The orderly volunteered this as they approached the ornate vestibule.

On a whim, Blake asked, "Were you on duty the night of the storm? When the wreck survivors were brought in?"

"Oh, I was, sir. Terrible thing it was, but the heroes there were that night! So many saved. It makes you proud, sir."

"Did you see a man brought in two days later? He was alive, but pronounced dead later?"

Without missing a beat, the man replied. "Oh, yes I did, sir. We wheeled him out of here. They said he was dead, but he didn't look it – his lips were still red, you know. But we put him on the ambulance and they took him to the morgue."

Blake was delighted by this unexpected witness. "Who declared him dead? A hospital doctor?"

"That I wouldn't know, sir."

"Who took him to the Workhouse? Was it hospital staff?"

"No, they sent an ambulance for him. Probably from the Workhouse, I would have said." The orderly thought about it as Blake donned his coat and hat. "Now I think of it, that was queer. Why would they send an ambulance over here for a dead man? We would have taken him in ours if it was a delivery. Very queer, now I think of it."

Blake pushed the door open and the rush of cold sucked at the gap. "Indeed. You have been most helpful." He slid through, letting the door fall shut behind him, set his collar up and pressed into the wind, heading for the police carriage where Hollis was waiting.

"The Workhouse Infirmary, Hollis. Quickly!"

The constable called to the driver and they set off into the murky drizzle of another miserable afternoon on the island.

It took forty-five minutes to reach the Workhouse Infirmary, a forbidding-looking stone and glass structure that reflected in every inch its former purpose, a place of

264

relentless misery and servitude. Blake again left Hollis with the carriage while he continued his investigations.

He had barely walked five steps down the first corridor when his heart sprang at the sight of Peabody, fully clothed and walking towards him holding the arm of a homely woman in her forties.

"Mr Blake!" the magistrate exclaimed. "It appears I am in rude health once more."

Blake quickened his pace to reach Peabody and clutch his hand. "Wonderful, Mr Peabody, truly wonderful news!" Peabody and, Blake presumed his wife both looked surprised by Blake's effusive greeting. "But how are you? What is the news?"

Peabody looked frailer than before but the colour was back in his cheeks. "So-so, Mr Blake. But first you must meet my wife. Joyce, this is Mr Blake."

The woman graciously took his hand, and ventured a few kind words. Blake felt a flush of shame, since it was mainly his doing that Peabody should have found himself in hospital. "Ma'am, I am deeply sorry for your husband's injuries."

Peabody dismissed him. "Please, Mr Blake! Enough nonsense! I'm fine, and would have it no other way!"

They shuffled blame and apology in such fashion for another minute before Peabody cut to business.

"But, you haven't come to visit me this time, have you?"

Blake again felt a slight pique of shame, but realised Peabody was genuinely asking.

"Mr Peabody, it is good that you are leaving. I fear that my trailing of our mysterious corpse has led me back here with a purpose. I shouldn't wish for you to tangle with these men again so soon!"

Mrs Peabody looked baffled. Peabody glared at Blake, who realised he had spoken out of turn.

"Ah, Mr Blake, how you like to dramatise our work!"

Blake backpedalled awkwardly. "Indeed! So I do." He hoped Peabody would rescue the conversation.

"I'd sooner tangle with men than another horse, wouldn't you say, Mr Blake?" Peabody gave a desperate wink out of his wife's sightline.

Blake fought to maintain his straight face. "A horse? Yes, of course! Horses. I may never understand the creatures."

Mrs Peabody just nodded sagely and continued to lead her husband to the entrance.

"I shall call on you soon, Mr Blake," sang Peabody over his shoulder. "Take care!"

Blake watched them leave, smiling at the episode. He pitied the various imaginary horses that had been blamed for their misfortunes; then he remembered Rudd, and his stomach clenched. *These are powerful men. Do not underestimate them.* He resumed his passage up the corridor in search of Dr Dean, the hospital administrator.

* * *

The administrator's office was a small, oak-lined affair, neat and tidy without ostentation. It was a reflection of Dean himself, a fussy, irritating man with a bureaucratic attitude that Blake deplored.

"Really, Mr Blake, this is most irregular. I have already furnished Sergeant Trevannion with the details of your so-called missing person. I truly don't know what else I might offer. It was an oversight, and nothing more. I suggest you

266

take it up with the Constabulary." Dean affected disinterest as he fussed over the papers on his desk.

Blake sighed inwardly. He reached for the one thing he knew might unlock Dean's impassivity.

"Dr Dean, did you read Sunday's newspaper? The *Courier*?"

It provoked the hoped-for reaction. Dean abruptly stilled and looked at Blake intently. "I am afraid I did not, Mr Blake."

Blake did not reply, and waited to see if Dean would fill the silence, which he did.

"Why do you ask? What did it say?"

"Dr Dean, it was more interesting in what it did not say." Blake paused again.

"Sir, you speak in riddles! Come, what was in the paper that should concern me or this hospital?"

Blake felt enormous satisfaction at these words. He guessed from their time in the mortuary room that Dean's prime fear was compromising the hospital's reputation. The competition from the Ventnor National Hospital must have been intense.

"You see, Doctor, there was some very detailed information concerning my inquest. The reporter was quite well-informed. One might say extremely so."

"I hope you haven't come here to suggest any impropriety on the part of my staff here, Mr Blake!" Dean exclaimed.

Blake ignored the protest. "However, Dr Dean, there was one very important piece of information that had been deliberately changed. Something very few people know about. In fact, there may be only five people on this island who would know about it, and one of those people is you,

267

Doctor. You originally told my associate Mr Rennie there were four bodies in your morgue."

"An oversight, as I said, Mr Blake. A clerical error which led to a regrettable wild goose chase. Please accept my apologies for wasting your time. Sergeant Trevannion was most gracious—"

"Please, Dr Dean. I happen to know you were telling the truth. I imagine you mentioned it in the mistaken belief that Mr Rennie was an insurance agent. No doubt you expected to pocket the insurance money for yourself."

Dean rose from his seat, his face reddening. "Outrageous! You accuse me, sir?"

Blake pushed forward across the desk to meet him.

"Please, spare me your histrionics, Doctor! I need to know who took the body, and when."

Dean's eyes popped, his cheek trembled, a flush of red over each cheekbone. "Mister Blake, this is unconscionable! You must leave my office at once!"

Blake sat back down in his seat. "I have just come from the National Hospital in Ventnor. I know the man was alive when he arrived. I know he was brought here, and with your full consent and co-operation, certain gentlemen arranged for this man to be taken into their custody. I need to know who took him and when. Or tomorrow it will be your name in the paper. And not just in the *Courier*. Your corruption and this hospital's complicity in aiding body snatchers will be in the *Times* of London and every paper between. I shall wager that your patrons, whom I shall also name, will be less generous in the coming year."

Dean was a gaping fish, gasping for air. He finally spluttered a response. "Mr Blake! This is blackmail! I shall not bow to such pressure."

Blake's face hardened. "Why not? You already did it for money. But since I have none to offer, blackmail it is."

Dean trembled. "Get out! Get out of my office at once, you impertinent devil!"

"I will. When I have what I need." Blake folded his hands on his lap.

Dean puffed for a moment, before sinking back into his seat. "I shall write to your superiors! They shall learn of your brazen extortion!"

"Fine. It shall no doubt be appended to my inquest report detailing your corruption and dishonesty."

Dean clenched his fists. He reminded Blake of the hapless postmaster, dazzled by the Royal Warrant and the passing of a few banknotes.

"Let me help you, Dr Dean. Were the gentlemen by any chance Crown Officials?"

Dean looked shocked, but still he said nothing.

"I see. They told you the person was wanted for crimes against the Crown, or something similar? Swore you to secrecy? Yes?"

Dean blinked but didn't reply.

"What if I told you he was no more than a common murderer with powerful friends who have abused their position to protect him?"

Dean couldn't contain himself. "Then I should say you were a liar, sir! You have already proven yourself a duplicitous blackmailer, so it would be no far cry!"

"Thank you, Dr Dean. When did your conversations take place, and when was the man removed?"

"Damn you, sir!"

"Was it on 28th January? The Tuesday night?"

"It matters little to me." Dean's fire had gone out, replaced by a sulky rudeness.

"Where did they take him?"

"I do not know, and I do not care!"

"How did they remove him from the premises? In a casket? Think about it, Dr Dean. Body snatching is a serious offence."

Dean thought for a moment before answering. "Mr Blake, one could hardly be accused of body snatching if there were no corpse."

Blake held his breath. The greedy doctor had swallowed the bait.

"That's turned the tables hasn't it, sir?" Dean's truculence had returned. "I can tell you that he walked out of here supported by his friends. On his own feet. You may own that you can blackmail me, sir, but discharging a living patient to the appropriate authorities is no crime!"

Blake stood up, trying to contain his amusement. "Indeed not, sir. Thank you for your help, and I trust you have a good day."

Dean scrambled to stop him leaving. "What, sir? You will just walk away?"

"Of course. I have what I need. Enough, at any rate."

Dean's disgust was written all over his face – every feature looked folded toward the centre in a mess of angry wrinkles. "How dare you—"

Blake pushed back into the man's space. "No, Doctor, how dare *you!* Your accursed avarice has caused men to die. You have no idea whom you released, nor to whom you released him. All for a pat on the head and thirty pieces of silver to look the other way! How dare *you*, sir! Now, allow me to take my leave, or in God's name you shall hear more of this!"

Dean was affronted, but guilt drove him a step back.

Blake breathed heavily, driven by an anger that had surprised him. He threw open the door and stalked back up the corridor, eager to turn his attentions upon Thornthwaite.

Hollis was still in the carriage, shivering, when Blake returned. "I'd say you got what you came for, Mr Blake," he observed levelly.

Blake didn't answer. "Hollis, we are going to visit your mother and her house guest. Immediately."

Neither spoke again until they reached Brading, after the sun had dipped below the horizon, shrouding the piled clouds in the black folds of midwinter darkness. Blake ached from the hours he had spent in the carriage. The cold gnawed at the extremities of his limbs. It reminded him of the first day he'd arrived on the island, a week and a lifetime ago.

The coach dropped them in the centre of Brading to conceal their ultimate destination. The police driver took off back to Newport, another forty minutes away. Blake had no idea what arrangements he would make if he were to return to the Orchard Hotel that night.

Hollis's parental home was considerably grander than Blake expected. The young constable was not the working-class boy made good Blake had assumed. The house was set back from the darkness of the rural road and appeared to be a large, family home – two storeys with a high pitched roof,

271

housing another level of accommodation. It was stone-built, with thick slates for the roof and boasted an impressive array of chimney stacks in four rows along the peak. They had chosen their hiding place for Thornthwaite well – it was unassuming enough from the road, but solid enough to intern its new guest.

Blake's senses pricked in anticipation despite the stiffness in his limbs and the cold. He had seethed on the long journey until he was calm enough for the coming confrontation.

Hollis led them up to the stout, wooden door, and rapped the heavy iron knocker twice. Only seconds later there came a series of rattles as locks were turned, bolts withdrawn and chains unhitched, before it swung on its oiled hinges and a tall, striking blonde woman in her forties peered at their faces. She saw Blake first, eyeing him uncertainly for a second, before her gaze moved to Hollis, and her face broke into a warm smile.

"Christopher! Come in, quickly!" She swung the door wide, and the air that rolled out enveloped Blake in a most sensual way, almost overcoming him with warmth and the glorious smell of something delicious. "Shall I take your coat, Mr, er…?"

"Please, madam, call me Blake."

"Oh, *you're* Mr Blake! Very nice to meet you, sir. I've heard such wonderful things about you."

Blake actually flushed, though it may have been the transition to the marvellous heat of the house. "I'm flattered, ma'am!"

"Heavens, you'll join us for supper, surely?"

"If I am invited..?"

She cuffed him on the shoulder. "But *of course!* Don't be shy!" She took their coats herself, leaving the maid bemused as she hovered at her mistress's shoulder. Instead, Mrs Hollis took them into the cloakroom herself, emerging moments later as they were looking around the vestibule. "Christopher, do show Mr Blake into the parlour."

They moved into a pleasant space with sofas and chairs around a well-stocked log fire, the heat melting all memory of their uncomfortable journey along with their chilled limbs.

Blake sat in a yielding chintz armchair decorated in a floral pattern, and leaned into it, stretching his legs. It felt like an extension of his own home, although the energetic presence of Mrs Hollis was very different to the maid who was his only house companion.

The fire crackled, a clock ticked, and Blake began to feel drowsy. The sheer gratification of the last five minutes almost allowed him to forget the reason he had come.

He heard women's voices from the direction of the vestibule, and guessed that Mrs Hollis had kept the help on in anticipation of their guests. A few moments later, a young maid entered and curtseyed to them.

"Mistress Hollis would like to know if Sir will be staying tonight? We have a guest room available."

Blake had not planned for such an eventuality. "If there were any chance of returning to Newport after dinner, I shouldn't need to stay."

Hollis felt the need to interject at this point. "Mr Blake, sir, it would be worth your while to stay tonight. We have a driver who usually takes me to the court house each morning."

Blake felt uncomfortable about staying at such short notice but it was the most logical choice. Hollis nodded to the maid, who curtseyed again and left. Hollis followed her out the door, presumably to catch up with his mother.

Blake was left alone with the warmth of the fire and the comfort of the armchair. He let his breath out slowly and breathed in the dry air like a tonic, feeling his eyelids grow heavy.

He was dozing when a loud noise woke him. On the very edge of his consciousness, it resolved into a voice as he emerged from his sleep.

Rennie stood grinning from ear to ear, the gap in his teeth prominent. "I said, he does nothing for two days and I find him asleep on the job!"

The man's Glaswegian tones were like music to Blake, who hauled himself to his feet, meeting Rennie halfway across the rug. He gripped Rennie's hand in his own, bringing the other up to grasp his wrist and shake warmly. He then blinked frantically at the fire as he felt the tears rise again. He glanced back at Rennie as he cleared his eyes of the troublesome emotion, noting that Rennie looked in much better shape. The bruises had resolved into yellowish stains around his forehead and cheek, but the spark was back in his eyes; in walking, he moved more easily, with no stick in evidence.

"You look well." Blake awkwardly let go of his hand.

"Aye, I feel well. Better, in any case."

As if to underline the point he produced a pipe from his jacket and began the laborious process of filling it. He caught Blake's quizzical look and shrugged. "Aye, the lady of the house, God bless her, she doesn't like cigarettes. But she allowed me this."

Blake noted the change. He'd hardly seen Rennie without a cheap cigarette in his mouth since they met. Suddenly he had changed overnight to a pipe on the word of the redoubtable Mrs Hollis. He found the idea amusing. Rennie had a weakness after all.

The Scot puffed at the stem to get the pipe going, then gestured with it towards the stairs. "Now, I don't know when the delightful lady of the house is serving supper, so if you want to talk to our friend upstairs I would recommend a short visit."

Blake gave a terse nod. He glanced back at Hollis and gestured him to follow.

Rennie led them up the staircase, a wide wooden affair with impressive balustrades and a central carpet, secured with brass fixtures. It turned at a right angle about five steps from the top and opened to a wide landing area that undulated past three or four doors, becoming darker as the landing stretched away from the solitary lamp at the top of the stairs.

They reached the end room, where a dim light shone from the slit beneath illuminating the darkness of the corner. With a flourish Rennie produced a key and unlocked the door, pushing it wide to admit them.

Blake couldn't suppress a pang of concern when he saw the prone Thornthwaite. He lay blindfold and spread-eagled on his back on a bare mattress, his hands cuffed to the iron bedstead and his feet manacled through the brass fixtures at the foot of the bed. He was in a poor state. The dressings on his face were still crusted with dried blood, while his

275

underwear looked soiled. A rubber sheet lay beneath to protect the mattress. He smelled quite ripe, the sharp smell of urine vying to overpower the general body odour.

Rennie saw Blake's reaction, but merely shrugged. "Look, Mr Blake, it's not like I was going to let him loose to use the loo, now, was I? You saw what he did before. It's been the pot, or be damned."

Despite his animosity, Blake's dismay was evident. "Has Mrs Hollis seen him like this?"

Hollis answered. "No, sir. I told her he's a special prisoner and to avoid any contact. She's asked about him a few times but she's wise enough to know not to disturb him. The maid brings food up, and we bring it into the room. But to be honest, sir, he hasn't shown much interest."

Blake worried at this. "Could you remove the blindfold, at least?" He addressed the prisoner directly. "Mr Thornthwaite?"

"I can hear you, Mr Blake." His voice sounded thick and snotty, the result of his nose not having been set. Blake's guilt racked up a notch, knowing more pain lay ahead for the wretched man in the resetting of his nose.

Rennie pulled up the blindfold. Thornthwaite blinked as he focused on the room. He glanced briefly at Blake but then fixed his gaze on the ceiling.

Blake began. "I'm glad you finally admit you are the gentlemen known to us."

"Indeed I am, Mr Blake."

"So who is Thomas Marston? An alias?"

Thornthwaite sniffed. "He was just a means of leaving the island unnoticed."

Blake was astonished by the man's candour. "Well, I shall continue to address you as Mr Thornthwaite. Though I imagine it would be difficult for you to be in two places at once. Aren't you supposed to be advising on a case in Antwerp?"

Thornthwaite was silent for a moment, then gave a chuckle. "You should know, Mr Blake, I warned my superiors they should avoid you. I told them we should bypass you altogether and just concentrate on our job. But they honestly thought you were a country bumpkin out for a quick settlement. They insisted I try to steer the inquest away from all mention of our mutual friend."

Thornthwaite's openness was disconcerting to Blake. He wanted to drive at him with the anger he felt on behalf of his friends, but the man's calm explanation was unsettling. He pondered whether he should pull back from a potential trap, or just press home the advantage while Thornthwaite was in a talkative mood. Unable to contain his curiosity, he opted for the latter.

"Who are you really, Thornthwaite?"

Thornthwaite shifted his position on the mattress, letting Blake see the red weals across his wrists, and releasing a waft of his unwashed body to the gathered men.

"I represent Her Majesty's high interest, gentlemen. As you shall all soon stand accused of treason, it is of no import that I tell you this."

Rennie laughed at this, but Hollis looked conflicted. Blake shook his head. Thornthwaite hadn't finished.

"You have obstructed me from performing my duty in the name of the Crown, detained me as I went about my duties, and subjected me to unlawful imprisonment." He snorted, taking another breath. "It is my duty to inform you that upon my release, which is only a matter of time, I shall seek the highest penalties from you, and I am sure you know what that means."

"God, the man can talk," interjected Rennie. "If he could fight that well, he would have gotten clean away."

"No, Mr Rennie, I do not need to run. I'd rather remain to see you dancing on the end of a rope."

"Aye, but you'll be hanging right alongside on a rope of your own. One attempted murder, maybe at least one successful one too."

"Rennie, if I had wanted to kill you, you would be six feet under as we speak."

Blake put his arm up to stop the exchange. "Mr Thornthwaite, you have admitted your identity, as we know it. The person you claim to be is implicated in several crimes – burglary, assault and battery, extortion of a Royal Mail postmaster and interfering with the Royal Mail. You have admitted using an alias to gain transport and flee from your crimes. You have admitted trying to interfere with a coroner's inquest on orders from higher authority. I would say you had less chance of avoiding punishment than ourselves."

Thornthwaite snuffled. "No doubt, you will want to add bribery of public officials and body-snatching."

"I would want to add the alleged accident that killed Mr Rudd. Was that your doing as well?"

Thornthwaite left a long pause hanging after Blake's words.

"No, Mr Blake, I regret you are mistaken. A horse bolted. Mr Rudd didn't look where he was going. An unfortunate traffic accident occurred. Nothing more. It was frustrating for

278

us, in fact. We were following his correspondence with Dr Foster. It would have been advantageous to us had he been allowed to continue." He almost seemed apologetic. "I'm afraid there is no crime there, Mr Blake."

Blake felt a sudden chill. It had been a simple, blind accident after all? Could it be that such mere chance had started his whole investigation? Rudd's death had fuelled his hunch that sinister forces were at work. Now he felt the first uncertainty that perhaps he had come out on the wrong side of the law.

But the other facts spoke for themselves. "Just as there was no body-snatching, Mr Thornthwaite. Not a dead one, at any rate."

Thornthwaite rolled his eyed to focus on Blake for the first time. "True. It was a dead man walking, much as you are."

"Mr Clarence is alive? Is he still on the island?"

Thornthwaite snorted his laugh again. "Oh yes, he's very much alive. Right here on the island. Getting better by the day I hear. It takes more than a dunking in the ocean to snuff out a true gentleman."

Blake wrinkled his nose in distaste. "Where is he?"

Thornthwaite lifted his head, sneering. With his bruises, he looked like a defiant panda. "Let me assure you, Mr Blake, he is precisely where you will never be able to get to him. And when my patrons have discovered where you are keeping me, your last chance of finding him will be gone." He let his head fall back on the pillow, stained with his sweat and small blotches of blood. "Gentlemen, enjoy your last days of freedom. I promise you, they shall indeed be your last."

He closed his eyes. Blake knew the conversation had ended.

Rennie pulled the blindfold down over the quiescent prisoner's eyes and then checked the manacles and cuffs for security. He stayed behind to change Thornthwaite's pot, while Hollis and Blake left the room.

Blake was disappointed in the interrogation, which had gone quite differently to his expectations. Yet his discomfort was nothing compared to Hollis.

"Sir, that can't be true, can it? That stuff about treason?" The young constable was quite agitated.

Blake placated him. "Constable, you saw exactly how and why we placed Mr Thornthwaite under arrest. The only irregularity has been his temporary imprisonment here. But that was for our own protection. I guarantee you we are not at risk from his threats."

Though Hollis looked unconvinced, Blake remained committed. Tomorrow would be a long and difficult day, but he knew, for better or for worse, it would probably end with the fulfilment of his investigation.

Chapter Seventeen

Atlantic Ocean, 250 miles WNW of Ushant
Friday, 10th January 1890

It was the long-awaited blow, but once again it came from the wrong direction. Hutton had known better than to try to run their heavy ship close to the wind – now he tried to run before the storm until it blew through.

Hutton stood with Mackie again as the waves rose and fell around them, their booming collisions with the ship's hull cascading spray across the gunwales in salty sheets that made normal communication impossible.

The landscape presented a monochrome vista – only the explosions of spray and the pallid rolls of sail broke the shades of grey separating the perpetually-moving sea, the cloud-obscured sky and the nebulous horizon where they merged.

The men held the quarterdeck rail with leathery hands as the deck heaved under their feet. Movement was difficult as their floor tilted first leeward and back to windward, dropping away to create an exhilarating rise in their bellies before sharply propelling them upward again. For a sailor it was a pleasurable sensation.

Hutton's thoughts flitted to his two passengers ensconced below. It amused him for a moment to imagine what dampening effect such buffeting would have upon their ardour!

The sails stood solid against the wind as the lines that held them stretched taut as bowstrings. The ship was behaving well so far; it kept a steady ploughing motion as it rose from trough to crest and down again, burying its prow to the foot of the bowsprit, before riding clear again. They were still not going anywhere meaningful, but Hutton was thrilled that the *Irex* was sailing again.

Morgan gripped the wheel now, assisted by Mackie when adjustments needed to be made. His white face peered from beneath his sou'wester, eyes blinking away the spray that battered his face with the ship's every plunge.

The ship was heading east. With luck they would be driving south within two days, hoping to pick up the precious trade winds south of Spain within a week. At least that was Hutton's hope.

Even as he held on, Hutton was aware that the air seemed unseasonably mild, and the dousing of water he received every other second lacked the shocking chill he usually encountered in the middle months of winter. The glass was still falling; not with the precipitous drops of the previous day, but nevertheless it had not bottomed out.

Hutton signalled his departure from the helm position; Mackie returned the gesture, his huge bulk unmoving as his oilskins whipped around his solid frame, as flames dance in the wind though the coals do not stir. Morgan also nodded, only the dip of his sou'wester betraying the gesture. He maintained a steely grip on the wheel, placing his whole body weight into the effort.

Hutton struggled against the wind and the heaving deck to the companionway, and made his way down with steady steps. His body naturally swayed to maintain his equilibrium with each heave of the ship.

He wrenched the cabin door back against the wind. As he struggled with it, he saw the corner where Clarence's trunk had lain; it seemed so long ago, and yet they had barely moved since – all the movement had come from the human side of the endeavour. The door closed heavily behind him as he stepped into the relative calm of the cabin, even though the deck still lurched precipitously.

He gripped the banister as he descended to the saloon, and saw his irksome passengers sitting huddled at the table. Elizabeth looked pale and green as the room swayed around them. They held hands on top of the table, Clarence appearing to comfort her. He couldn't help the swell of satisfaction he felt at the sight; in this, at least, he was vastly their superior.

"Mrs Barstow and Mr Clarence! It's a fine morning for sailing!"

Their sudden elevation into the high aristocracy lent a strained aspect to his interactions which had been absent just days before. They were no longer guests but rivals for leadership. He swayed in front of them while they were rooted to their seat; he was under no illusion what the sensation would wring in their seasick state.

"Quite so, Captain." Mrs Barstow's pluck would not be defeated by her present condition. "And if you please, I wish to revert to my maiden title. You shall continue to address me as Lady Elizabeth." Clarence squeezed her pale hand in encouragement at this.

Hutton considered how his rank had now been shuffled down the pack. "Very well, Lady Elizabeth, as you please. Is Mr Eustace aware of your wishes in this regard?"

She looked across towards the pantry, but was seized by another bout of sickness, raising her handkerchief to her mouth and dry retching.

You were far more dignified when you were simply Mrs Barstow, thought Hutton with a cruelty he didn't realise he still possessed. He rebuked himself inwardly and sought to undo the unspoken slight. "I'm sorry, my lady, is there anything we can do to help?"

She collected herself, though her eyes remained watery, lacking the conviction of her usual gaze. "Eustace is fetching us water, Captain. Really, it would serve us best if you would find a route out of this storm!"

He knew she was joking, and it brought a smile to Clarence's face. He, the former Royal Navy officer, seemed to be bearing the storm a little better but, knowing the man, must have found his lover's incapacity frustrating.

"And Mr Clarence, sir? All is well?"

Clarence's smile dropped. "Fine, thank you, Captain. Though your manner leaves much to be desired."

Hutton felt the blood rise in his face. The pantry noises stopped as Eustace no doubt turned his well-attuned hearing once again to his captain's vexations with his passengers.

"I – I beg your pardon, sir?"

"Hutton. I know you have had romantic pretensions upon Lady Elizabeth since she boarded the ship. I am sorry you have felt this way, as it would have been an unthinkable outcome – though of course you weren't to know her true station." He paused to dab at his mouth with his own handkerchief. "I am telling you as a gentleman, Will, that you must let these fantasies go. Lady Elizabeth and I are betrothed."

For the first time Elizabeth took her eyes off Hutton, and turned to direct a beatific smile at Clarence, entwining her fingers in his.

Hutton stared, struggling to maintain his composure as the saloon still lurched around them. "Mr Clarence." He fought to find the words he should say in place of the ones that flew to his lips in the heat of humiliation. Courtesy of Eustace, this conversation would be all over the ship by the afternoon. "Far be it from me to question a gentleman's judgement, but I do not lie when I say I could not be more pleased at this good news. I would be delighted to celebrate your occasion in the saloon with my officers, should you so wish."

Clarence gave an ironic smile and nodded at his gracious riposte.

Elizabeth didn't change her level gaze, just gave a slight twist of her lips which may have been discomfort from her wretchedness. Nevertheless, it was she who spoke. "Captain, I forgive you freely for any impropriety you may have committed, however inadvertently. I would graciously accept your invitation, should the opportunity ever—"

She broke off again to retch into her handkerchief, her bosom heaving, while Clarence placed a consoling hand on her back. A string of saliva stretched from her mouth and snapped into the handkerchief as she lowered it from her mouth, her eyes filled with tears.

There was a click from the pantry door, and Eustace appeared, deftly balancing a tray with twin tankards of water upon it as the deck continued to tilt. He admonished them to maintain their hold on the vessels and keep them clear of the table.

They sipped the cloudy liquid, Elizabeth very gingerly, keeping her handkerchief clutched in one hand.

Hutton realised he had not been dismissed, but neither passenger appeared keen to continue speaking. He decided that he needed to take his leave.

"Ma'am, Sir. Thank you for your words, and for your pardon, Lady Elizabeth. I can assure you that there will be no such impropriety for the duration of our acquaintance."

Clarence nodded, while Elizabeth cuddled into him, a large tear rolling down one cheek.

Hutton gave a slight bow, and moved downhill towards the pantry, finding himself climbing uphill again by the time he reached the door.

Eustace was inside, busy strapping the contents of the cupboard in place before latching it closed. He looked up momentarily, but looked away quickly when he saw the expression on Hutton's face.

"Mr Eustace, I would imagine you know much about our passengers' current predicament. So hear me well. I shall dine now in my room. You shall attend me there, and I shall request a short conference with you. I shall give you the intervening time to prepare what you would like to say. I warrant that whatever you might divulge I shall keep in confidence. But equally, whatever you should speak out of turn, I shall revisit upon you with the full extent of my authority." Hutton felt the hotness of his anger radiating not just through his words but also from his face.

Eustace wobbled slightly as the pantry tilted but did not waver his gaze. Hutton, in his own heightened state, found it difficult to read the steward's features, but decided that fear was prominent among them.

He passed the couple at the table, nodding as he made the stairs. He gripped the banister, sliding his hand up as he climbed, the stairs becoming shallow and then prohibitively steep as he mounted them in the heaving sea. As he reached the top, he walked toward the chart room, passing Mrs Barstow's – *Lady Elizabeth's!* – room as he went. There was a commotion of sounds within, as if it were being ransacked. He realised she hadn't secured her personal articles before the storm on account of being shacked up with Clarence in his room.

He shook his head as he pondered the time that had passed since that first storm leaving Greenock. They were barely into the Atlantic and were now running back towards the British Isles, yet they had been aboard ship for a month. Sarah would be expecting an arrival signal from the company office in the next ten days or so! He knew how much it would worry her – though it was not uncommon, seafarers' wives had a sense of the unusual. Often Sarah claimed to have known exactly when her husband had faced peril, to the very hour, and had roused herself to pray fervently for his safety. He reasoned that she may have had as little sleep as himself on this voyage – the rug beside the bed was probably worn out by her knees!

Inside the chart room he inspected the log – it was strapped to the plinth on the table, the inkstand sealed

287

against spillage. He studied its anodyne entries. It spoke nothing of the burdens he had endured so far, merely detailing their progress without blandishment, saying nothing at all of the human dramas that had been enacted throughout. There was only one poignant note, the statement of the death of George Barstow. This had been a good man – Hutton himself had stated it at the ceremony; so had his grieving wife as they tipped his iron-weighted body, wrapped in Colquhoun's precious sailcloth, into the indifferent ocean. Even in recent days, his widow still spoke of him as a good man, though she had discarded his memory as easily as she had tossed his redundant cadaver into the sea.

But what use was a good name? Hutton hoped he wouldn't have spent his latter days in the self-discipline and self-sacrifice of Christian virtue, as George Barstow had, only to be so comprehensively forgotten within the space of mere weeks.

His Saviour remembers him.

The thought rose unbidden to Hutton's mind. The log does not record the humanity of the voyage. The common seaman does not long hold to sentimentality in the face of meagre pay and back-breaking work in servitude. The upper classes do not pass a thought for those who lie beneath their station. History forgets the men and women of no import; they are footnotes at best, and only where their humble existence intersects with those of greater stature. But their Saviour remembers them.

Hutton felt tears prick his own eyes. He realised again that he was alone. The anger he felt had subsided into melancholy, fed by solitude and the sting of loss. He mourned not just the friendship of his erstwhile ally Mrs Barstow, but the total loss of the person. Mrs Barstow, whom he had loved, had been nothing more than a phantom, a construct that fell away to be replaced by the haughty, class-conscious Lady Elizabeth.

In the uncomfortable exchange just now he realised they had usurped his position – he, as captain was now the second tier of society aboard his own ship. He clenched his teeth, feeling humiliated. Class was beyond authority. It came only from breeding, and it trumped knowledge, experience and expertise every time. He suddenly remembered Clarence's story of the naval manoeuvres; whether true or not, it didn't matter. Hundreds of lesser men died to spare the blushes of a *gentleman* Admiral!

Hutton turned back from the chart room into the open cabin area, as Lady Elizabeth's tossing belongings continued to destroy themselves in her room. She would surely be able to afford more and finer things as a wealthy heiress and Queen-in-waiting, if Clarence were to be believed.

He glanced over to the empty stateroom opposite. The bosun had been freed by a show of hands among the officers after he had been examined by Carroll and declared free of both disease and illicit liquor. Reid and Hutton had favoured releasing him, but Mackie and especially Durrick were resolutely against. In another victory for authority, Hutton's vote had carried the day.

For the past twenty-four hours, the bosun had been true as an arrow, and expressed some resentment at the harsh words Durrick had reserved for him. The second mate had shown a renewed grit since the incident, and the sailors of his watch found themselves under more insistent scrutiny than before. The second mate was reluctant to believe that the

289

bosun's change had been anything other than artifice – consequently he seemed equally reluctant to let the bosun forget they had unfinished business despite the man's professed ignorance.

His musings were interrupted by the sound of Eustace's footfalls and the clink of his tray as he mounted the pitching staircase. Hutton held his door open and Eustace expertly rode the ship's rolls and delivered his tray. He managed not to spill a drop of the coffee in the half-empty cup. The only other thing on the tray was a salt beef sandwich, the bread already dry and stale. The worst of the mould had been carefully sliced off.

Hutton sat on his bed, sandwich in one hand and coffee tankard in the other, balancing them as the room lurched. He ate quickly, motioning Eustace to sit in the chair fixed under the window. The spray and rain lashed against it on the windward side, a racket that meant they would have to raise their voices despite the nature of their conversation.

Hutton spoke between mouthfuls, chewing as Eustace spoke his replies.

"Mr Eustace. Since we will be speaking confidentially, I give you leave to speak frankly. You have been privy to all the cabin activities since arriving on board. You may speak freely, but our words must not carry beyond this room. Do you understand?"

"Yes, sir, perfectly, sir."

"Then please tell me what you know."

Eustace sighed. "Captain. Since I may speak freely, if you'll excuse me saying, I must say that all the problems you've had with the passengers are of your own making, sir."

Hutton simply took another savage bite of his sandwich, washing it down with a liberal draught of the coffee.

Eustace seemed emboldened by the neutral response. "Sir, Mr Clarence is right. Every man jack aboard knows you have had designs on the lady. No-one blames you mind, like you said, sir, every man went soft—"

Hutton cut the air threateningly with his half-sandwich, still chewing. He motioned Eustace to move on.

"Begging your pardon, sir. Well, the lads forward are calling her "The Captain's Lady" if you must know, sir. It's no secret what the men think."

Hutton forced a mouthful down. "I trust you have disabused them of that notion, Tom!"

Eustace looked uncomfortable. "Well, it would do no good, you see, sir. See, they think you've done quite well for yourself. It's making them look at you in a different way, sir. Better, in fact."

Hutton groaned inwardly. As an adulterer with a girl half his age, he was more palatable to the common seaman! "Very well. Go on."

Eustace continued. "In fact sir, the men don't really care much for Mr Clarence. You know he is tight with the bosun. Well, they don't much care for the bosun either, truth be told. So I felt it would be better if they thought it was you knocking boots with the lady every night instead of the gentleman, sir. Everyone knows something's going on, 'cause Brown heard them at it."

Hutton had finished his sandwich. The tankard, empty, lay on the bed. Hands thus freed, he clapped them to his face and hung there, elbows on his knees. *Lord, help me.* His sigh was audible above the racket at the window.

"So what exactly is going on across the cabin, Tom? Have you been in at all since we last spoke?"

Eustace shifted in his seat, whether from discomfort or to steady himself as the ship lurched was unclear. "Sir."

"And?"

"These four days, she hasn't left his side."

"So I've heard."

"The whole ship would have heard, I'd say, sir."

"That's not what I meant."

"Ah, Sorry, sir. But, ah, it's quite the scandal, though isn't it, sir? She being the grieving widow and all?"

"Tom, if what you say is true, you have hardly defended her honour, yet perversely, somehow defended mine."

"That would look to be the case, yes sir."

Hutton lifted his head to look at the steward. "The sooner I see the back of them both, the brighter my life will be, Tom."

"Aye, sir, affairs of the heart can be tricky—"

"No, Tom! They have been a constant distraction and drain on my reserve of patience and grace. I want nothing more than to see them *both* off my ship."

"Sir."

"Who knows about Clarence and the lady?"

"So far as I know, our present company and the officers. And obviously the bosun. He had nothing to do all day but listen to them carrying on."

Hutton finally realised why Mackie had objected to the bosun's release. He didn't want the bosun's version of events to destabilise the chain of command any further. "Send for him at once! I don't care where he is. And Eustace? I expect Lady Elizabeth will need some help with her room. And I expect you to notify me of any changes in the passengers' circumstances."

Eustace affirmed his instructions, and rose slowly to his feet, accommodating the heeling floor and making his way to the door. Hutton shook the empty tankard at him, and he took it before he exited, the door swinging shut behind him.

Hutton sat on the bed, using his arms to absorb the constant changes of attitude as the ship continued to corkscrew. He watched the water pulse over the window with each wave, and fall in droplets down the pane until the next lashing of spray covered it again. His voyage had been like this; one deluge of trouble after another, with scarcely enough time to settle before the next one rose over him. He thanked God that he had ridden his own storm through this far – he considered that he might have broken had he been a heathen.

He rose, grabbed his sou'wester from the hook on the door and plumped it on his head, pulling the chinstay tight. At least Hutton knew where he stood against the storm outside.

* * *

Back on deck, the noon bells had sounded, and Durrick was back on the quarterdeck, slouching inside the covered helm position. Brown now held the wheel, cursing the spray that took his breath with every wave. His wiry ginger beard dripped water like a sponge, accompanied by the spouts of ingested seawater spat from his mouth between curses. Hutton thought of him as an inelegant water feature from a stately garden, and the irreverent juxtaposition provoked laughter in spite of himself.

He abruptly remembered how good it felt to laugh. Even as he thought this, he erupted into such a fit of mirth that Durrick, deafened by the waves and wind, assumed he was choking and roused himself from his slouch to help. Hutton waved him off, ending his moment of riotous joy hiccoughing and spluttering as the buckets of spray combined with the laughter to leave him fighting for breath.

"Everything all right, sir?" yelled Durrick in his ear.

"Yes, Bob. I forgot how good it feels to laugh!"

"Beg pardon, sir?"

"I forgot – never mind, carry on, Mr Durrick!"

Durrick looked anxiously at his captain, just as another drenching shower of spray cut between them, ending the conversation. Brown let off a chain of expletives, which ended in garble as the next wave crashed against the gunwale, sending another prodigious cascade over them.

The last two waves had sent something of a shock through the hull. Hutton wiped his eyes to look at the barometer glass. He pulled Durrick's sleeve to alert him.

"When did you set the index, Mr Durrick?"

"Eight bells, top of the forenoon, sir!"

Hutton pointed. The mercury had fallen by two points in barely twenty minutes. "Batten the main hatch. Secure the galleys and alert the donkeyman. This one is going to blow."

He switched his gaze back to the deck, swaying crazily. Durrick had recalled the topsail lookouts, and the tops were describing loops and figure-of-eights in the air as the ship plunged and rose through the increasing waves.

Distracted by the storm, Hutton only noticed the figure of the bosun, edging hand over hand along the deck towards the quarterdeck when he was approaching the mizzenmast. Close

294

behind him was bosun's mate Murray. An apprentice named Barham followed nimbly in their wake. They held their footing as the deck repeatedly fell away from them, and great gouts of water crashed over the gunwale.

They had almost made it when a much larger wave rolled in from the starboard side. It topped the gunwale, fully twenty feet high, and the crest broke its full energy into the three figures. Two immediately lost their footing and were knocked to the floor. Murray appeared to hold on to the lifeline, but the lad was swept clear across the deck. By sheer chance or grace alone, the deck rolled back to starboard, lifting the gunwale clear of the water on his side. Had it remained submerged, the lad would have been lost. Instead, he scrambled to his feet, grabbing for the lifeline on the port side.

Hanson, who had kept his feet and his grip throughout, bellowed encouragement to the lad and told him to stand fast. He and Murray reached the companionway, and Hutton pointed them towards the cabin. Hanson turned himself around, and gave Murray a kick to get him to do the same.

Again, Hutton found himself in the relatively calm surroundings of the cabin, while the contents of Elizabeth's room still lurched around, sounding more like shattered rubble than objects. He leaned over the staircase and saw that the passengers were still huddled, the wretched Elizabeth still green and clutching her handkerchief. Clarence still held her, murmuring into her hair as she buried her head in his chest.

He pointed the dripping men towards the chart room. The floor slipped crazily from side to side, and they felt successively crushed and weightless as the treacherous deck rose and fell.

Here, in the aftermost part of the ship, the men found themselves almost squatting to absorb the violent rise of the deck to meet them; then their feet almost left the floor as it dropped away again.

Hanson and Hutton took the fixed chairs on each side of the chart table, while Murray just braced himself against one end. Hutton shooed him away as the drops from his oilskins began to encroach on the chart, so he knelt on the floor, gripping the back of Hanson's chair.

"How goes it, Bosun?" Hutton asked.

Hanson looked puzzled. "How do you mean, Captain?"

"Since your release from quarantine."

"Aye, sir, I feel fine." He looked nonplussed. "Sir, I hope you didn't haul us all the way here just to enquire of our health!"

Hutton bristled. It was a typically intemperate remark from the surly bosun, and put him in no doubt that the man was very much back to his original mind.

"No, Mr Hanson. I have another reason, of course. Since Mr Murray is here – though I did not invite him – Mr Murray, you are aware that Mr Hanson spent some time in quarantine here in the cabin?"

Murray nodded uncertainly, and the look that Hanson gave him was not missed by the captain. "Aye, sir."

"Has he mentioned any of the interactions with the passengers and officers since he returned to duties?"

Hanson broke in. "Now, begging your pardon, Captain—"

"I am addressing Mr Murray, Bosun!"

Hanson fell silent. His craggy face was cast in a hard stare fixed on Murray, as inviting as a stone wall set with broken glass.

"Mr Murray, if you please." Hutton was determined to press home his advantage.

Murray looked deeply uncomfortable. "Sir, if you please, I'm not sure I understand—"

"It's quite simple, Murray. Has the bosun spoken to you about the passengers' conduct?"

Murray's eyes flicked between Hutton and Hanson. They eventually fixed on Hanson, imploring him to help.

The bosun clicked his tongue impatiently, attracting Hutton's attention. "Aye, sir, very well. I told Jim that Mr Clarence was balling your fine lady, sir. For three whole days."

His face twitched, and Hutton mentally summoned the word 'Whitechapel' in anticipation; but the feared explosion never came. The men sat in silence as the room rose and fell again, a deep resounding boom greeting every fall of the stern as it crashed into the waves.

"Have you told anyone else about this?"

"No, sir, on my honour."

Hutton did not think this much of a guarantee, but he took it at face value. Murray also shook his head emphatically.

"Keep it that way. You too, Murray, or I'll find you both alternative accommodations for the duration."

"Sir." They chimed in unison.

Then the bosun added, "Captain. Are you angry about this?"

"That is none of your business, Mr Hanson. But in the interests of our agreement, the answer is no. In fact, it solves many of my problems."

The men exchanged a look which left Hutton in no doubt that they believed not a word.

"Thank you for coming, gentlemen. You may return to your duties. Don't forget to attend to young Barham on your way back."

Hanson nodded his leave, but Murray looked impressed at Hutton's recall. "Aye, sir."

Hutton watched them slide out of the chart room. He considered paying another visit to the happy couple in the saloon downstairs but found himself completely overcome with disgust towards them both. Shame and revulsion opened his eyes at last to what he had allowed to occur on his ship. The upper class pair had played them all for simpletons. The physical threat of Clarence had cowed him. The intimidation of their class and Elizabeth's self-assured superiority in particular had barracked him into subservience, just as Clarence had said.

He realised at last he had nothing to gain and everything to lose by keeping his counsel. Hanson believed him weakened, as did Mackie. He imagined Durrick felt no different, undermined by the release of his assailant without charge. And Reid? Surely he agreed with his brother officers?

What would Clarence do? Would he really kill Elizabeth? Would it matter even if he did? Hutton felt shocked by his thoughts but let them roll, fuelled by his burning indignation. *Let him kill her.* Then he would clap the man in irons and drop him off at the nearest English port to face justice!

Another thought came. *What if Clarence turned on another officer?* They all knew about his paramour. Hutton resolved he would do the same.

And if he were to turn on me?

Proof. If Clarence were to dispose of anybody, there would only be Hutton's word. Without Hutton himself, there would be no record…

Unless. There was only one legal document worth a fig in a maritime court, and it was his own voyage log.

Hutton shook out of his dripping oilskin jacket, letting it drop to the swaying floor and turned to the log. He steadied the inkwell and detached the fountain pen from its holder, using the lever embedded in its side to fill the reservoir.

With the table still rocking at every wild movement of the ship, he began to write a new entry in the log, pondering each thought before committing it to the permanent record of the voyage. He smiled as he realised some of the human drama would make it into the official record of the voyage after all.

Addendum 10th January 1890

Passenger Ed. Clarence announced his betrothal to the Passenger Lady Elizabeth Bays-Montague, formerly Barstow. Lady Elizabeth is the widow of George Barstow, d. 24th Dec. aboard this vessel. (Refers, 24th December 1889)

Clarence is reportedly the travelling name of Prince Albert Victor, second in line to the throne of England.

Passenger Clarence has admitted to me that he committed an act of murder aboard this vessel on or about 12th December 1889 at Greenock. The alleged victim was a female stowaway, identity unknown. The body was removed ashore and passed to persons unknown.

Clarence also confided in me that he is one of several men who committed the Whitechapel Murders under the alias 'Jack the Ripper' in 1888.

Passenger Clarence has also made threats against the lives of passengers, captain and officers if this confession should be made known. I hereby commit it to the legal and public record of the voyage.

Signed as a legal witness statement, this 10th January 1890 Captain William Hutton, Master

Hutton felt a palpable sense of relief, like a cleansing stream carrying away his anger. He felt exhausted, the fatigue falling over him. He sobbed, overcome, hot tears stinging his eyes. It was the catharsis he had sought since Greenock a lifetime ago. The deep sobs shook his body, and he whispered prayers of deep thanks as peace rose in him, stilling the anxiety that had gnawed at him for weeks.

Beneath the emotional release came the certainty of his return to command. He had shaken off his paralysis and committed to action. Clarence's fate was at last in Hutton's hands.

Chapter Eighteen

Newport, Isle of Wight
Wednesday, 12th February 1890

Blake sat beside Rennie in the Hollis family's plush carriage as they rattled along the road to Newport. They were complimentary about the accommodation they had enjoyed courtesy of Mrs Hollis. The Glaswegian in particular expounded his appreciation of both the accommodation and their hostess in unabashed terms.

Blake's curiosity about the affluent circumstances of the young policeman and his mother didn't overcome his discretion, preferring to respect their propriety. But Rennie had no such qualms.

"Well, I had to make my enquiries, Mr Blake – there's no Mr Hollis, you know? He was a Colonel in the Hussars. Spent years in the Orient. Got an unhealthy taste for local flavour, you might say. Died about three years ago of the black syph! Mrs Hollis now lives as a happy widow on an outrageous pension."

"Really, Mr Rennie. How do you find out these things?"

"Seriously, Mr Blake? You know I can't divulge my sources!" Rennie gave a wink.

Blake noticed how Rennie was very much revitalised since the capture of Thornthwaite. He wondered if the wily reporter might not have gained some vitality through other activities, perhaps at the house, judging from his lyrical praises of Mrs Hollis.

"She is a truly grand woman, Mr Blake. The finest! She knows what she wants in life, I must say. She's been very accommodating since my arrival. *Extremely* accommodating! It's been positively invigorating!" He smiled to himself, dreamily looking out of the window once more.

Blake swore he heard the man sigh. He shook his own head in wonder. "Rennie, you truly have a unique talent."

"Aye, I do. Thanks for noticing, Mr Blake. I don't get half enough credit."

"There is one thing I've wanted to ask you. When you spoke to the survivors at the hospital last week, however did you get past the matron?"

"What matron?"

"Never mind."

Blake watched the grey, rolling landscape, the drizzle now falling in lazy curtains, accompanied by a light breeze and a noticeable rise in temperature. Perhaps there was the merest taste of spring in the air, a hint to the end of this harsh and punishing winter?

The case of Thornthwaite gnawed at him; he was now concerned there was a problem with how he had handled the man. It was to be a busy day – the telegraph office and hotels needed to be visited before the court house. He hoped at least one of them would have received a communication from Thornthwaite's people regarding their missing man.

They remained silent in their individual reflections until the coach pulled up outside The Osborne. They alighted and entered the fancy lobby, where Rennie immediately received the attention of the receptionist.

It turned out to be the manager, whose comical appearance owed itself to anachronism – he was an obese, red-faced man with Dickensian whiskers, a smart suit that was too tight to be recently tailored, and a pocket watch chain from the fifties. But his complaint was very much of the modern age.

"I'm sorry sir, but your employer has refused to pay your bill since Monday. If you are unable to foot your bill, I regret you may no longer continue your stay." He presented Rennie with a sealed envelope from heavy paper marked with the hotel monogram and inscription. In the same hand was a telegram addressed directly to Rennie, care of the hotel.

"I'm sure it's just a misunderstanding, sir." Rennie kept calm as he opened the telegram first. He opened it up and read quickly, his eyes flicking across the page and narrowing with each line. "For Christ's sake! They've bloody fired me!"

The manager shushed him, looking around. "Sir, there are ladies and gentlemen present!"

"Bugger the lot of them! Look at this bloody nonsense, Blake!" Rennie passed the telegram and immediately set upon the bill as Blake read.

++URGENT   RENNIE   STOP++   ++RECEIVED
SCANDALOUS   REPORTS   FROM   POLICE   STOP++
++JUDGEMENT AND CONDUCT CONTEMPTIBLE STOP++
++YOU   ARE   NO   LONGER   IN   EMPLOY   STOP++

++RETURN SOONEST STOP++ ++MACPHERSON STOP++

Blake read it again, but was distracted by another torrent of expletives from Rennie as he consulted the bill.

"Eight pounds? For five bloody days? What the hell, Todd, is this the Savoy? I haven't even been here! I've been enjoying much better hospitality to be fair, and it didn't cost me my eye-teeth! I'll remind you that I was heinously attacked right here in this palace of yours!"

"Mister Rennie! Please keep your voice down!" Mr Todd was only too aware of the guests who were beginning to turn their haughty attention to the little scene in the corner of reception.

"Listen here, Todd. I'll pay you two pounds for my meals, but you can whistle for the rest."

"Then I shall have no option but to call the police."

"Excellent. Call the bloody police. Right now."

Blake intervened, trying to placate the manager and divert his focus from the incandescent Rennie. "Sir, please pardon Mr Rennie, he is still recovering from injuries he received from a break-in at this very hotel. He has just received some awful news at this moment, causing him distress. I can vouch for him – he is currently working with me. I am the coroner conducting the inquest into the wrecked ship *Irex* and Mr Rennie is assisting me in recording the case. Can we not come to some amicable arrangement?"

"Well, sir, I am sure you realise this is most irregular—"

"Of course, Mr Todd. It is just that Mr Rennie is of great importance to Her Majesty's inquest at this time?"

Todd sighed dramatically, rolled over by the wheels of service to the Crown, just as Rogers the Postmaster had been. At least this time the wheels turned in their favour.

"Very well, sir. Though I shall insist on payment within seven days. No more. But Mr Rennie cannot stay at the hotel from today." Rennie was re-reading the telegram. He looked up during the pause, nodded at Blake, and folded the thin paper into his breast pocket.

"Eight pounds?"

Todd licked his lips. "In the interests of our goodwill concerning your accident, we will deduct your meals. Six pounds."

"I've had to stay elsewhere due to my anxieties; I've been scared to stay here since the attack." Todd studied Rennie's face, still bearing the bruises of his fracas. He gave another laboured sigh.

"Very well, Mr Rennie. Please accept our compliments for two nights. Four pounds, payable within seven days."

Rennie looked huffy, but winked at Blake as the manager passed behind the reception desk to write up their new contract.

Ten minutes later, the newly-liberated Rennie was back in the coach with Blake.

"We'll make a reporter out of you yet, Mr Blake. Thanks for your help. I thought you would jump in sooner, I have to say. I was laying it on thick!"

Blake shrugged. *Nothing seems to dampen this man.* "What about your job?"

"Pish. Looks like someone's trying to stitch me up. Probably hoping I'll panic and cry and turn little Thorny-Boy over to the police without a fight." He chuckled. "Ah, I'll smooth it all out when this is over. Macpherson won't sell three papers without me holding his hand, and he knows it. He's just trying to get me to come back."

Blake considered this. "Then I thank you for remaining to assist me." Then he turned to look at Rennie, a smile playing at the corners of his eyes. "I suppose it has not all been bad, regarding your accommodation."

"Hell fire, you're right, Mr Blake! I hope Mrs Hollis will be welcoming to a waif and stray like me." He practically hugged himself. "When are we heading back?"

Blake smiled again. "First, to business, Mr Rennie."

* * *

They next entered The Orchard Hotel, finding the landlady leaning over the small reception desk. She leaned on her elbows, folding her arms beneath her bosom as they approached, eyeing Rennie with interest.

"Morning, Mr Blake! Who is your gentleman friend?"

"Good morning, Mrs Orchard. This is my friend and associate Mr Rennie."

"Charmed, ma'am." Rennie touched his forelock, and Mrs Orchard blushed. Blake half-expected her to offer him her hand.

"Been in the wars, dear?" Her lips pouted in concern, and she cocked her head in sympathy.

"Aye, ma'am. Well, I have, in a manner of speaking. Damned horse—"

"Mrs Orchard, is there any post for me?" Blake interrupted. Another shaggy horse story was not what he needed.

306

She tore her eyes from Rennie. "Indeed there is, Mr Blake. Just a moment." She swished her impressive bosom from the desk, and searched among the pigeonholes set in the wall behind.

Rennie pouted at Blake, fanning himself theatrically. Blake emphatically shook his head.

"Ah, here it is. Delivered by hand yesterday. By a soldier, no less! Very smart lad he was too." She handed over the letter. It was sealed with a military-style wax seal, no stamp or postmark. The envelope was written in a neat hand Blake immediately identified as a woman's.

"Thank you very much, Mrs Orchard. I have already taken tea, and by the way, I shan't require supper tonight."

"Well, absent friends again, are we? If you don't want to stay, you can always leave your friend if you like. He looks like he could do with some care and attention." She fluttered her eyelashes at Rennie.

Rennie pulled his most charming smile. "No thank you ma'am, duty calls, and all that."

"Thank you Mrs Orchard, we will retire upstairs for now. Could you please entertain our coachman for an hour?" He cringed as he realised what he had said.

"Well, I shall do my best, Mr Blake! An hour, you say?"

Blake nodded wearily. "I should say so." He hoped the coachman would understand.

They ascended the stairs to Blake's room again. This time Rennie tapped his arm as they reached the upper floor, and put a finger to his own lips. Blake nodded. They crept quietly to the door and listened before Blake unlocked the door. He opened it warily. Nothing.

They remained on high alert until they had made a cursory check of the wardrobe and desk. Empty.

Having set the fire, the solitary log smacking and popping as the flames licked around it, they shrugged off their coats.

Rennie sat back in the easy chair and waited for Blake to read the latest piece of evidence.

Blake set his glasses back on his face and tore open the envelope. Inside he found several folded sheets around an embossed postcard. The papers crackled as he folded them flat on the desk and held them in front of him to read.

'Sunday 9th February
Frederick Blake Esq, Coroner.

Dear Sir,

In the matter of the Irex, I must tell a disturbing story which I fear may not be supported by any other witness at your inquest. I must insist, it is of vital importance that you are aware—'

Blake stopped reading. This looked very much like witness testimony. He decided to establish whether it was in fact evidentiary testimony, and whether it was appropriate to read it. He put the letter down and turned over the postcard. Though damaged by water and much creased, it was beautifully embossed with the Royal Seal, and there at the bottom was the signature of Albert Edward, Prince of Wales and heir to Queen Victoria's throne.

"To Whom it may Concern,

The bearer of this card, Mr Ed. Clarence, is Our Most
Trusted Friend and Worthy Citizen of the Empire and
Nation of Great Britain..."

In a moment of startling clarity, Blake saw the pieces, past and present, fall together and realised exactly who Mr Clarence was. With a jolt through his chest, he saw for the first time where the real threat to his inquest lay. As he had said to Mr Peabody several days ago, a multiplicity of such remarkable events is never to be taken lightly.

He considered for a few moments, and then picked up and read the rest of the letter, spread over two crackling pages.

'...it is of vital importance that you are aware that many of the events that took place on that blighted voyage were witnessed only by a few, all of whom I fear are now lost, save I alone.

It is my desire that you know, from the outset, that three of the lost were murdered in cold blood, and that the murderer was the man known to us as "Clarence". The loss of the Irex may indeed be laid entirely at this man's feet, such was his influence over those who brought her to founder.

His sins must not be allowed to die with him. He was a monster, not a man; his high standing should not absolve him of this fact. He should not be permitted to slip silently from public scrutiny, his deeds unknown and his reputation unsullied.

Mr Blake, I write these words to you knowing I can never repeat them in court; nor shall I breathe them to another living soul, for I should never be believed. The shocks of that horrific journey were injurious to both my health and sanity. To repeat in court such things as occurred would without doubt invite censure, harassment or even confinement in an institution; even should my constitution last to bear the telling, for I am greatly weakened by these events. Withal, I confide these things to you, Mr Blake, in the hope that it will encourage you to uncover this truth: an Evil exists in our world; it stalks in the form of vile and wanton men who stop at nothing to satiate their cruel lusts. One such man was our travel companion aboard the Irex, and never such justice was done before God than that he perished with her.

For my part, I thank only the mercy of Almighty God that I did not also perish, though I am ashamed that I did not. For I surely deserved the fate that befell the brave man who saved our lives – his name is Captain William Hutton. Though I have lingered upon this Island these two weeks in the hope that he may yet have been plucked alive from the sea, it is my fear that not only did this good man perish, but that his good name shall be forever maligned by your inquest.

I beseech you, my dear Mr Blake, to bear in mind my testimony to his goodness; for it is the truth I declare before our God and Judge that what Captain Hutton carried within him for those terrible final weeks should not have been the preserve of any one man, but that he did
310

so in order to protect and deliver the souls aboard the Irex, even at the cost of his own life.

Furthermore, and worst of all – I in turn betrayed the trust of a good man, as surely as Judas betrayed his Lord. My sin was the more, because William Hutton at no point behaved shamefully, yet he chose not to judge me, but rather saved my life, giving up his own in my place. God may have forgiven me my wanton sins toward Clarence, but in the matter of William Hutton, it may take my ill-deserved eternity to forgive myself.

May God bless you and give you wisdom in the pursuit of your investigation.

Yours faithfully,

E.B.M.'

Blake was confident that he now held the sole piece of evidence that pointed to the survival, if not the whereabouts, of a key witness, Elizabeth Barstow. It wasn't difficult to join the dots – the letter was in a woman's hand, described events on board the *Irex*, and had been signed with the initials "E.B.M." He wasn't entirely sure what the "M" meant – perhaps an attempt to hide her identity – but he was sure she must know that anonymous or unsubstantiated evidence was inadmissible.

Still, it was compelling. Blake assumed that the Thornthwaite's people had discovered the woman at some point. She must have felt sufficiently threatened to cause her to run from the hospital to an unknown hiding place. The military connection narrowed the options – it seemed the Royal Artillery position at the Needles Battery and specifically the helpful major described by Mr Howes, would be useful to visit.

Blake read it through again, noting the specific details. Though she had not elaborated on the "sins" she mentioned, it was not difficult to work out what she meant from the guilt-ridden confessionals and words like "betrayal". It seemed that Clarence had assumed no little influence over the people on the ship. It struck Blake as odd that a widowed woman could jump into another man's arms barely two weeks after the death of her husband – in polite society, the minimum mourning period was at least a year – then again, affairs of the heart are never certain, and being the sole woman aboard a ship would have rearranged Mrs Barstow's priorities in the name of necessity.

Nevertheless, Blake mused, at least it was lucidly written. It pointed in the opposite direction to much of the testimony they had heard so far regarding the conduct of the captain, and suggested that he may have known more than the rest of the crew realised. But the truly frustrating part of this otherwise useful letter was that in her misplaced fervour to confess her own failings and clear Hutton's name, she neglected to actually name the three murder victims mentioned at the beginning.

Blake set the letter down and pondered what to do. He decided it was time to see Peabody, and commit to their final act in this investigation. Rennie, now unemployed, needed a vocation.

"Gordon Rennie. Raise your right hand."

Rennie raised his hand straight in front of him. Blake showed him what he meant, palm outwards and fingers straight. Rennie corrected himself.

"Repeat after me: I, Gordon Rennie..."

He swore Rennie in as an appointed officer of the Court.

"Congratulations, Mr Rennie. You now work for me. Your salary is four pounds, payable for this week only. That should cover the hotel bill." He smiled at Rennie's grin of delight.

Rennie clapped his hands and let out a hearty peal of laughter. "Much appreciated, Mr Blake, sir!"

Blake smiled broadly, an unfamiliar sensation for him. "You may now review this piece of evidence I have obtained. I don't know what you will make of this, but I believe it is from the missing passenger. The woman, Elizabeth Barstow." He handed Rennie the letter.

Rennie read it and laid it on the table. He also examined the postcard, then looked enquiringly at Blake.

"Who is this chap Clarence, Mr Blake? You know, don't you? It's written all over your face."

"I believe I do know, Mr Rennie. I received a telegram from my old friend. The detective. I believe this Clarence is the same man who was a suspect in the Whitechapel murders two years ago."

Rennie laughed out loud. "Not Jack the bloody Ripper! Come on, Mr Blake, every windy bugger who wants a few column inches claims to be him!"

"Please, Rennie, listen. He was a real suspect in the case. I worked the legal case alongside my friend, Walter Andrews, a senior detective. He was investigating the Ripper murders and firmly believed there were two or three men involved. He even tracked one to the United States, but was unable to secure an extradition. The other went missing, but he believed the third suspect, whom he held responsible for three of the murders, had been actively protected by members of the Establishment, even servants of the Crown.

"The reason Walter dropped the line of enquiry into Clarence, though I didn't know his name at the time, was because we were ordered to. By the highest legal authority in the land."

"The Lord Chancellor," murmured Rennie. He drummed his fingers on his chin.

"Walter confirmed the Whitechapel suspect's name was Clarence. Now we have the woman telling us that this Clarence was a multiple murderer. I now believe those poor wretches were trapped on a ship with the worst man in the world. And he will walk away scot free, not simply because he is a clever gentleman. He has the full organs of state at his disposal."

Rennie looked even more perplexed. "How so? Who is he?"

Blake leaned back in his chair, steepling his fingers in front of his mouth. "Gordon, listen to me. If I tell you this, you will never be safe again."

"God Almighty." Rennie exuded only excitement, not fear. "Go on. I'll die anyway, if I don't find out."

"Walter told me this in great confidence, but I dismissed it. If I am honest, I found it ridiculous and forgot until this week. According to Walter, Clarence is Prince Albert Victor. The Prince of Wales' eldest son, and second in line to the throne."

Rennie hardly breathed. His face paled, accentuating the vestiges of his yellow and purple hues. He just stared at Blake, his fingers still on his chin, not moving.

"Mr Blake, you are neither a joker nor a lunatic, I think."

Blake nodded. "I share your opinion, so far as I can tell."

Rennie puffed out his cheeks, letting the air whistle out. "I'm sorry Mr Blake, but it sounds impossible."

"Improbable, yes, but by no means impossible once one has assembled the circumstantial evidence."

Rennie looked through the window into the middle distance. "This is bigger than...well, anything. There is no law which could arraign him. No court will ever try him. God, no paper will even dare print it, even if he signed a confession in his own blood! The scandal would be too great, Blake. Worse, these people can make us vanish, Mr Blake. This investigation is finished. We need to drop Thornthwaite on the police's doorstep and run like hell."

Blake nodded grimly. "Rennie, we cannot turn back. We have taken their man. They have to deal. First we have to make sworn written statements and assemble our evidence. I shall post it all to my lawyer friend in London as our insurance. Then we shall meet with Thornthwaite's people and come to an agreement."

Rennie held his hand out again, this time to shake Blake's. Their eyes locked as they made their own agreement.

Rennie's grip was warm and firm. "I'm staying with you, Blake. All the way to the end."

Blake nodded. The tears pricked his eyes again, and he quickly turned away to retrieve his legal papers.

* * *

Two hours later, they were being driven by the Hollis family's coachman, who seemed to have more of a spring in his step. He'd not stopped his cheerful whistling and had even cracked a few smiles as he helped the men into the carriage. Rennie gave Blake a huge wink as they saw Mrs Orchard blowing their driver a kiss and a cheeky wink as she closed the door on them. Blake just shook his head in wonder.

Then again, it might just have been the change in the weather. The drizzle had stopped, and the weather felt milder, although the sky remained overcast and the chill breeze still had a cutting edge. They were on their way to the post office, a securely wrapped parcel in hand, daring to hope that the mail was uncompromised since the detention of Thornthwaite so their package would arrive unmolested with its intended recipient.

Blake was relieved that Postmaster Rogers was not there, possibly at his lunch. The clattering sounds of the telegraph and the distinctive electric smell immediately reminded Blake of the first day he had dared to turn his inquest into an investigation and considered the mixed feelings this evoked. *We are committed*, he realised. Then he realised they had been committed from the moment they had taken the train to Ryde to pick up Thornthwaite.

He hoped Peabody was fine, and resolved to see him next. Then there would be a trip to the fort at the Needles, and finally the court house by the afternoon session at three p.m.

Blake paid the fee and watched the postman place his parcel into a normal looking sack, one of eight suspended on hooks behind the counter. The man betrayed no special interest in the package. Blake hovered for a few moments more before Rennie cleared his throat and inclined his head towards the door.

Blake turned and left. *It's in the lap of the gods*, he thought. He didn't even bother to check the street before he stepped out. Rudd had just been unlucky after all.

They stopped by the court house to check messages. There were two, a telegram from Paddington Station, London, addressed to "Mr Blake, Coroner". The other was more intriguing: a handwritten note to "Frederick Blake, Esq" in a plain, sealed envelope of expensive vellum weave. It was unmistakeably a man's handwriting.

Blake decided to read them in the coach on the journey to Peabody's home. But as they descended the steps outside the court house he saw Peabody's familiar carriage pull up opposite. There was a shared bonhomie as the three men reacquainted themselves for the first time in days. Two of them still bore their scars, but the mood was entirely convivial.

Blake explained Rennie's new status as the third chair of the inquest. Peabody's response was muted but positive.

"Stanley. Will you ride with us? We are going to the Battery at the Needles. We could use your local knowledge."

Peabody eyed the coach, which boasted a better ride than his humbler carriage.

"Indeed I shall, Mr Blake!" He climbed into the roomy interior, helped by Rennie. Once aboard and on their way, Blake drew the curtains for privacy, letting enough light in to read his latest mail.

The telegram was the first he read.

++BLAKE CORONER STOP++ ++PAIGNTON GAZETTE REPORTS BODY FOUND ON BEACH 5TH FEB STOP++ ++CLOTHING IDENTIFIES R DURRICK GRUBB IREX STOP++ ++DEVON CORONER TREATING AS UNLAWFUL DEATH STOP++ ++FOSTER++

Blake almost dropped it in surprise. The elusive Dr Foster, Rudd's correspondent, had contacted him with a quite shocking report. If nothing else, it proved beyond doubt that the man in the sailcloth shroud seen by Helmsman Brown could not have been Durrick. The seamen's gossip about the second mate's overnight disappearance had likely been correct. If the Devon coroner had already ruled the death unlawful, there must have been obvious evidence of foul play.

He passed the telegram to Peabody while he opened the handwritten note. He noticed his hands were actually trembling as he tore apart the gummed flap of the expensive envelope. Here, probably, was the contact he had desired and dreaded in equal measure.

Frederick Blake Esq, HM Coroner for the County of Hampshire

Sir,

My Lord, being Representative of Her Majesty's Government, would be honoured by your presence at the Newport Court House at 2 o'clock p.m. this 12th day of February.

His Lordship has urgent business to discuss with regard to your Inquest. These are important matters of State and may not be postponed. His Lordship shall await your presence until 3.30 p.m., at which time, should you be unable to attend, he shall endeavour to engage you by other means.

Yours Faithfully,
Your humble servant,
LLOYD, for Lord Dunsfold, Home Office.

Despite his elation at this important contact, Blake felt only a dull ache in his belly. He needed to have everything in place for this meeting, for it felt unlikely there would be much future in his inquest after this meeting. If he were to have any kind of future at all.

The others looked at him expectantly, but he folded the letter into his suit pocket, and sat back in his seat.

The journey to very western tip of the island would take a good hour by coach. Blake hoped his unannounced arrival would still meet the approval of the well-meaning major and attract an audience. If not, it at least gave them time to bring Peabody up to date with their investigation.

Blake did the talking, describing in terse terms the letter from Barstow, the telegrams and the astonishing theory about Clarence.

Peabody struggled to believe it. "Good Lord, Mr Blake! You cannot be serious. This surely cannot be true!"

"I regret, Mr Peabody, it is all too true. The latest letter I received shall prove this fact beyond any doubt." He passed the letter round.

As they read it, Rennie's knee began to pump again, while Peabody simply looked bemused. "How could it have come to this, Mr Blake? What manner of men have we become, that a murderer should walk freely and without censure by virtue of his birth? It's unconscionable! We must see the matter through. Devilish as it is."

Blake remembered the first words he had heard Peabody say; they were practically the same words he had just uttered. What a stout-hearted friend he had turned out to be; very far from the bumptious provincial that Blake had first judged him.

"Gentlemen, I fear this may be our last day working together. I am sorry, but events have at last caught up with us."

The others nodded sombrely. They passed the rest of the hour in silence save for a few observations along the way.

It was nearly noon by the time they heard the boom and crash of the waves. The cliffs that fell away on both sides of the headland led to the extraordinary chalk formation known as The Needles. The wind was more pronounced here, piling up against the cliff faces and spilling up and over the headland, pulling tiny chips of chalk with it and spattering the sides of the coach. The coachman huddled, pulling his cape over his face. The drizzle had not returned and there was a yellowish quality about the overcast as if the sun, which had not made an appearance in weeks, was trying to break over the island at last.

Rennie puffed impatiently. "Mr Blake – why are we coming here? It's a pleasant little ride and all, but what do you think we'll find?"

Blake thought for a second. "I must admit, Mr Rennie, I think we shall find only memories again. We have fallen far behind our adversaries. Yet we must follow the trail to its end."

Rennie nodded, as if he understood.

Peabody then hailed them both to look out of the window: a solitary patch of sunlight played on the sea, maybe half a mile out while breaks in the cloud were visible further to the southwest. Blake took it as a good omen, or perhaps a final benediction.

*   *   *

Twenty minutes later they sat in a functional office cut into the rock of the cliffs. The entire artillery battery was dug from the chalk and limestone at the tip of the island. Thick stone and brick ramparts had been built above the ground level, while tunnels led to cavernous galleries carved in the stone deep underground. Storerooms and magazines held the stacks of enormous shells that fed the hulking steel guns lurking in their casemates, pointing seaward.

The office was part of the administrative section near the eastern end, a neat room about twenty feet square, set with wooden desks around the edges. The central area held display tables stacked with books and charts, a typewriter and other paraphernalia. The walls were plaster over chalk, and held pin boards with the various posters, orders and admonitions that festoon any military administration office. The battery also had that most wonderful of modern inventions – electric lighting. Blake couldn't help but glance up from time to time, fascinated by the glowing incandescent bulb that hung from the fixture.

The three men sat in rotating study chairs with castors for feet. Facing them was Major Owen of the Royal Artillery, a very correct and upright gentleman with a large, bushy moustache, waxed at the ends and sufficiently impressive that none of them could stop looking at it whenever he spoke. His one obvious vice seemed to be tobacco; but every soldier the men had seen since they arrived seemed to share in it.

Owen took a few puffs of his pipe. Clouds of aromatic smoke rose around him and collected around the dangling light bulb. "The Colonel sends his apologies, as he is currently engaged with business. I would be most happy to help you with your inquest in his stead, sir."

The three men, led by Blake, added their own thanks and greetings. "Thank you, Major. First I would like to pass on my hearty thanks and appreciation for the brave and gallant job your men performed on the night in question. You undoubtedly saved many lives at the risk of your own."

Major Owen bowed his head graciously. "Thank you, sir."

"I would like to ask, Major, if any of your men were responsible for finding any of the survivors or victims of the wreck in the days following the disaster."

Major Owen answered immediately. "Sir, I would have been notified immediately had that occurred. Unfortunately, I know of no such finding. In any case, I would have notified the local authorities had any of the men discovered any persons, whether living or dead." The major answered without guile but appeared not to be anticipating a long visit.

Blake sensed he was trying to help. "Major, may I ask – has there been any other investigation since the wreck?"

322

Owen considered for a second. "I believe the Colonel met with a police sergeant shortly after the wreck – it may have been the twenty-seventh or twenty-eighth. The weather was still atrocious, but I think he was more interested in commending the soldiers who assisted with the rescue." His eyes flicked down for a second.

Blake noticed. "Major, I too was very impressed by the conduct of your soldiers that night."

Owen modestly bowed his head once more. "Thank you, sir. It was a pleasure for me to see them rise to the call in such exemplary fashion."

However, Blake was far more intelligent than the bumbling Sergeant Trevannion. He had more juicy morsels of information to squeeze from the confident major. "Were any of your men injured in the rescue?"

Owen shook his head. "Nothing more than a few bumps and scrapes. Why do you ask?" He took another draw on his pipe and let the smoke out slowly, letting it whirl toward the ceiling.

"I was wondering – did any of your ambulances have cause to attend the Workhouse Infirmary on the night of the twenty-seventh?"

Owen pursed his lips for a second, then plopped his pipe into his mouth. He puffed slowly at it, his mouth working on the stem. Long seconds passed, and his brows furrowed as he considered the question, and his range of possible answers. "I wonder why you might ask that, Mr Blake?"

"It was just a possibility I had considered."

"As a matter of fact, we did have a request for an army ambulance on the twenty-seventh. A soldier was admitted to the hospital at Ventnor the previous week for acute appendicitis. On that particular date, we were asked to move him to the Workhouse due to the large number of admissions from the wreck." He puffed again. "Unfortunately, the fellow died last week. But the body was collected from the hospital in Ventnor, where it had been since his original admission."

"That is indeed strange."

"I hadn't thought of it until you mentioned it, Mr Blake."

"Tell me about the woman you rescued."

This time Owen reacted. He shot the draught of smoke he had just inhaled from his mouth and nose with a small cough. "I beg your pardon?"

"The woman. How long was she here?"

"I believe, Mr Blake, this meeting must now come to an end."

"Please, Major. This is of crucial importance to my investigation. I have to find her."

Owen shook his head. "I'm sorry, Mr Blake, but I will not discuss that matter."

"She came back, didn't she? After the rescue. She told you she was being pursued."

"Mr Blake, you and your associates must leave."

"I assure you, she was not running from us! We are trying to save her. She is in very real danger!"

"I know that, damn you!" hissed the major, turning hostile. He knew he had blundered.

Blake had to know how close he was to finding Elizabeth Barstow. "When did she leave, Major? We have to know!"

The major placed his pipe down on a rack at the corner of his desk. He locked his fingers together in front of him on the desk top. He seemed to wrestle with his conscience for a few moments. "I will tell you – but then you must leave. I will tell you no more, and shall forever deny we ever spoke of this matter."

"On my word, Major."

"All right. I took her in on the day of the rescue. That was the Saturday, the twenty-fifth. She was completely spent, but had been well-protected. Her head and face were covered and she wore a large naval greatcoat. She had no injuries save on her legs and feet, but she was in a state of complete physical and mental exhaustion. Delirious and freezing cold. I took her inside to our sick bay. We have very limited facilities, hence the need for our ambulances. But she was simply exhausted. I let her sleep here while I kept guard, personally. She must have slept for twelve straight hours. By the time she awoke, the rescue was complete – it was about midnight on the night of the twenty-fifth."

He groped for his pipe again. No-one dared interrupt the major – it seemed he might change his mind at any time.

"The survivors were being transferred to the hospital at Ventnor. Some of them were barely alive. The last few were in a particularly sorry state. I arranged for the lady to be taken to Ventnor in a hospital ambulance.

"It was a great surprise to me, therefore, when the guard at the gate sent word to me on Monday that a fine lady was asking for me by name! I went up to the gate and it was her – Elizabeth. She begged for my help. She claimed she was being pursued by ruthless men, powerful friends of her former husband who were seeking her life! She claimed only to need a spell of hiding and then she would leave the island – again, with my help. So I took her in."

He lit the pipe again, letting the lazy spirals of smoke rise towards the stained ceiling. He was momentarily lost in his memory.

"She was a pious woman. No nonsense with her at all. And a strong character. Very beautiful, but deeply unhappy, and scared with it. I fretted over keeping her here – it is completely against Queen's Regulations. I was able to conceal her presence from the officers, though I still had to feed her and keep her. My batman looked after her – he said he would find her praying as often as crying when he knocked. I slept on the floor while she took the bed. She slept badly – she seemed to have fretful dreams, but remembered nothing of them when I quizzed her.

"Sirs, for two weeks she remained here, until last Sunday, the ninth, when she read the newspaper and cried for about an hour. Then she told me she must take her leave, and begged me one last favour. She insisted that I should deliver a letter for her to the coroner investigating the wreck.

"After that, I gave her what I could – shillings and sixpences – and smuggled her out in a cape and coat. I put her on the road to Freshwater, where she could get a train to Ryde. I swear to you, that was the last I saw of her." He stuck the pipe in his mouth once more.

"Thank you most kindly, Major Owen. I assure you that your story shall go no further."

"If you ever do find her, please send a kind word from me."

"Of course. Goodbye, Major."

The other men touched their hats and mumbled thanks as they opened the door into flashes of bright sunshine through patchy clouds. The wind was still fresh, but the unexpected brightness was exhilarating. They pulled down the brims of their hats against the blinding moments of full sunlight as it reflected on the chalk-white cliffs, only to be masked moments later by the succession of clouds.

The gate guard let them through, and just a few minutes later they climbed back to the road where the coach sat awaiting their return.

"Mr Blake, I must have missed something else." Peabody mused once they were back on the road to Newport. "What was that business with the ambulance?"

Blake explained, "The army ambulance is how they got Clarence out of the National Hospital into the Workhouse, where they paid off Dr Dean to make the 'body' disappear."

"I see. And what's this girl done?"

Rennie put it succinctly, the copywriter's gift. "Ah, Mr Peabody, she had a dalliance with the esteemed Mr Clarence on the ship. It looks like he may have given away too much about himself in the throes of romance, and now they want to shut her up. That's how it looks to me."

Peabody passed his judgement. "You know, gentlemen, this woman sounds like a terrible strumpet. She's had them all running after her – the captain, a prince and now an army major. A floozy, but one with impeccable standards."

Rennie roared with laughter. Even Blake allowed himself a chuckle, though the bleak feeling soon returned. This final leg of the journey would lead to a date with destiny.

* * *

An hour or so later, they were mounting the familiar steps of the court house. The attendant saw them through the glass

327

door, and Blake saw him point at them, mouthing towards someone out of their view.

By the time he reached the top, the attendant opened the door and Blake was faced with a grave-looking man about his own age attended by another who looked like a carbon copy of Thornthwaite. He differed only in his sand-blond hair and grey twill overcoat with a velvet collar.

As Blake peered closer, he saw the younger man had a recent and significant cut to his lip. He exchanged glances with Rennie who gave a knowing nod.

Blake was beyond any doubt that the final reckoning had come. He felt a dull thump of nervous excitement deep in his innards, bringing him to peak alertness. He swallowed and prepared for the confrontation.

"Mr Blake?" the older man enquired. He was wearing a finely-fitting and very expensive silk suit. His associate eyed Rennie with barely disguised disdain.

"I am he, sir." Blake took the man's proffered hand. His glove must have been from the same couturier as the rest of his ensemble. Even in the brief contact Blake felt the fine leather sigh against his cold palm.

"My name is Playfair, Mr Blake. If you would be so kind as to accommodate my associate Mr Lloyd and I in your court room for a few moments, I should be much obliged, sir."

"I should be delighted, Mr Playfair, sir."

Playfair remained impassive. "If I may beg your pardon, Blake, we would like to speak with you alone; we would not wish our conversations to be recorded. You understand to whom I refer." He cast a baleful glance at Rennie.

Blake smiled, the picture of affability. "Naturally, sir; however, Mr Peabody here is the senior magistrate on the

328

island; Mr Rennie here is my associate in my inquest and as such, I shall require him to be privy to our discussions."

Playfair frowned. "Perhaps been misled – I was given to believe that Mr Rennie here was a gentleman of the Press."

Blake was all apologies. "I can understand why this impression may have been given, sir; it seems that certain aspersions were cast on the good character of Mr Rennie while he was indeed employed as a reporter. This has led to his release from that employ, and I was only too happy to engage his services in my own as an officer of the court. A quite fortuitous event for my part, as it happens!"

Rennie smiled and raised his eyebrows at Lloyd for added effect. The man scowled.

Playfair sighed in melodramatic regret. "I see, sir. Very well. There are certain things, then, that I shall not be able to discuss in front of your associate."

"That is your choice, of course, Mr Playfair. If I may venture, sir, I was given to understand that Lord Dunsfold of the Home Office was to attend our meeting?"

"I am he, Mr Blake, though not in my official capacity."

"I beg your pardon, my lord."

The sparring over, they stood awkwardly for a few seconds before Mr Playfair stepped aside and beckoned Blake to lead them.

Blake, Peabody and Rennie walked ahead of the pair, all men completely silent. Peabody tried to catch Blake's eye, but the coroner stared fixedly at the floor until they reached the door of Court Room No.1.

Inside the familiar courtroom again, Blake decided the jury room was the best location for a meeting. He slid the sign on the door to 'OCCUPIED' and closed it behind them. The

329

men hung their coats on the brass hooks and seated themselves on opposite sides of the table.

Blake waited for Playfair to begin. He felt he had just put his head in the lion's jaws. He had no idea whether the jaws would snap shut, or if he would get to live another day.

Lloyd opened a leather document satchel, and produced two bound files, which he passed to Playfair. The man took a small case from his inside suit pocket and produced a small pair of gold-rimmed spectacles. He made a show of polishing them, and Blake fought to resist the sense of rising tension.

Rennie sat with his hands together on the table in front of him, a picture of calm. But Blake could feel the slight vibration from his knee, which was nervously pumping up and down. Peabody remained passive, his hands folded on his lap. He didn't take his eyes off Playfair.

At length, Playfair clasped his own hands across his midriff and spoke. "Mr Blake, it appears you have overstepped your authority somewhat."

Blake paused before his rejoinder. "My lord, I assure you that I have acted within my implicit authority as Her Majesty's coroner of this inquest."

"Then I shall use the remainder of my time with you to convince you otherwise."

"I should like to see you try."

Rennie's head snapped round to stare at Blake in amazement. This was a bold opening indeed.

Playfair sighed. "Very well, Mr Blake. I shall begin with your decision to conduct an inquest in the form of an investigation. It is the purpose of an inquest to establish grounds for further investigation, not to conduct the investigation itself."

330

"My lord, I beg to differ. I am gathering evidentiary testimony and background to directly assist with the findings of the inquest. Such evidence was missing at the outset of the inquest due to certain key witnesses having died. Or gone missing." He let that one hang for a second.

Playfair's face betrayed spots of red on each cheek. He was not in the mood to be defied. "Nevertheless, sir, is it not true that you are conducting an active investigation into the whereabouts of certain missing persons, and have employed powers of arrest and detainment to secure testimony not directly related to your inquest?"

Blake trod carefully. "My lord, I have been granted powers of arrest and detainment in order to secure testimony and prevent key witnesses from absconding."

"But sir, come now, is it not true that such powers are to be exercised with the co-operation of the local constabulary and legal authorities?"

"I have acted only with the full co-operation of local authorities." Blake felt rather than saw Peabody turn to look at him. He had already decided not to name Hollis to protect the home where Thornthwaite lay manacled.

Lloyd raised a finger to attract Playfair's attention, and indicated something on the file in front of him.

"Mr Blake, we have reason to believe you have kidnapped a Crown Servant, who was assaulted and detained without cause. We believe he is being kept illegally in a private residence, at a place unknown to the local constabulary or magistrates? Is this true?"

"With the greatest respect, my lord, I believe you have been misinformed. I have asked the local constabulary to arrest and detain an unknown man suspected of attempted

331

murder, assault and battery, absconding, interfering with a Crown inquest, bribery of Crown officials, tampering with witness testimony and fraud by impersonation. He is being kept in a private residence for his own protection, as I believe his life may be at risk."

Playfair removed his glasses and looked evenly at Blake. "You choose to play this game, sir? I must venture that your hand is by no means strong."

"I still hold a few cards yet, my lord."

"Well, this is no game, sir. You have committed material breaches not only of your calling as a servant of the Crown, but also of the law. Indeed, I have come to turn you from a course that will end in charges of treason."

Peabody suddenly sat forward, his demeanour changing from passive to fearful.

"What change of course do you suggest, my lord?" Blake's apparent penitence seemed to encourage the dignitary opposite them.

"Firstly, you shall deliver our man to us unharmed by bringing him here tomorrow at noon."

Blake merely nodded. Peabody held his breath.

"Then, you shall complete your inquest based on the available evidence to date, and deliver your report to the County Registrar with your finding by Friday at the latest. I would expect that all recorded deaths shall be attributed to an unfortunate accident. Any blame resulting shall rest with the master of the ship."

"And what of those deaths of which we know nothing?"

"I imagine, though you are the best judge at present, such missing persons shall be declared lost in the accident."

Blake fired his last shot. "And what should I record of that one particular person whose absence is entirely due to the gentlemen working on behalf of my lord?"

Peabody gave a sharp intake of breath. Lloyd almost snapped the nib from his pen.

Playfair's temper exploded. "Damn you, man! Do you not see the hole you have dug for yourself? Do you wish to make it deeper?" His face was turning crimson as he turned on Blake's companions. "And what do you other men know of the matter? Has this loose-tongued coroner poisoned your minds as well as his own? You'll both follow him to the gallows if you avow anything of this matter between now and eternity!"

Even Rennie kept his mouth shut at this. Peabody's eyes bulged. Blake had never seen him express fear until now.

Still the coroner kept his course and spoke up. "I want to see him. Allow me speak to Clarence, and I will consent to whatever outcome my lord requires, I give you my word."

"Utterly preposterous! My conditions are clear. You shall carry out my wishes in exchange for avoiding the noose. Those are your only options, Mr Blake."

"Then it is my duty to inform you, my lord, that if anything untoward should happen to me or my associates here, sworn affidavits stating the name, true identity and detailed crimes of the man known as Clarence will be circulated to every leading newspaper office and dignitary in Europe before my body is cut down from the scaffold. I do believe that the newspaper editors of France and Germany will be less compliant than those of England. And certainly the details shall spread to America, where I am certain they will receive a fair hearing."

Peabody crumpled in shock. Rennie smacked his fist into his hand, grinning from ear to ear. Lloyd clapped his hand to the table, but Playfair froze in outrage, his fleshy features now turning purple.

Touché! Blake had dared, but it was his last throw of the dice. He hoped against hope that his gambit would work.

Finally Playfair's colour subsided, and he sighed heavily. "You, sir, are a fool. A stubborn, bloody fool. You are finished, Blake. Do you not understand? You can never speak to him. Never, you hear?"

"I merely propose a trade, my lord. We each appear to have a missing person in one another's custody. Allow me to meet and interview Mr. Clarence. I shall not seek to inconvenience either him or my lord any further. I merely seek to establish certain facts. His activities have gone uninhibited and unpunished for several years. If I am privy to certain facts, it may encourage our man and his household patrons to curb his future activities to protect the public safety. It is a justice, of sorts. In the event, you shall have your man returned. What say you, my lord?"

The lord's lips formed a sneer. "A poor gambit, Blake. I have already said that you shall never meet Clarence. But you are correct about the missing persons. Although you have already miscounted, sir. You shall deliver our man and drop your threat to the future of our monarchy. In return, we shall withdraw your prosecution for treason, and deliver the woman to your custody."

Blake's face fell, despite his efforts to control his expression. *They had Elizabeth Barstow!* He couldn't stop himself from glancing left and right at his companions, who returned his stricken look.

334

Playfair noted the change and continued triumphantly. "Should you forfeit, she goes to the gallows as a treasonous blackmailer. Then you too shall hang, Blake. Your reputation will be ruined and smeared – not only your own, but all of you gentlemen, so that no-one will heed a single preposterous word any of you may ever speak against Mr Clarence. Agree to our conditions, you have my word that you will save your own necks and hers. How is that for a trade?"

Blake was beaten. And everyone at the table knew it.

Chapter Nineteen

Western Atlantic, Exact Position Unknown.
Tuesday, 14th January 1890

The storm abated in the forenoon of Tuesday 14th. The *Irex* had been battered. The ship was hove to, the sails kept out of wind, wallowing and going nowhere.

They sat in a stiff wind, the waves still buffeting the ship, but the furious gales of the past days had subsided. The momentary respite gave the exhausted men a chance to gather the remnants of parted lines and damaged rigging to attempt to secure the replacement sail and fit the ship for the remaining journey. It was testimony to the ship's excellent design and quality that the main yards and all masts were as sturdy as the day she sailed.

Aloft, the men gripped the lines, white-knuckled as they furled and tied the remnants of the upper sails that had failed in the hurricane force winds. The sailmaker snarled his instructions at the men two hundred feet above, while others swarmed around the sail locker stretching new sails to replace the lost.

Hutton swayed on the heaving quarterdeck, alongside helmsman Morgan and Chief Mate Mackie, his eyes stinging, his face raw and drawn from the crushing exhaustion that sapped his attention. He had slept barely six hours in the last four days, one of which he swore happened as he stood upright next to the helm. He was too tired even to feel hungry; his body had decided to starve rather than continue distracting him with hunger pangs.

It seemed clear from the increasing gusts that another blast was coming, but the direction eluded him. He maintained an easterly course, though their exact position was a mystery – neither light nor star had been visible for days. He studied the glass again, noting that the pressure had risen by eleven points in a matter of hours, as the worst of the winds had blown through. Now it was falling at a similarly precipitous rate.

The decks looked scoured – small lakes of spillwater still eddied around the planked surface, carrying torn lengths of rope, loose fixtures and wood splinters from the starboard boat. The boat deck trestle was bent like a pipe cleaner. Most of the boat it once held had been lost overboard, the remnant smashed to matchwood. The *Irex* had taken a beating.

Hutton looked across at Mackie – the mate had red-hued eyes, bloodshot and constantly watering from the wind. Morgan also looked spent, holding the wheel steady despite their lack of way, his knees knocking as they held each other upright. For much of the past two days, the wheel had been lashed to prevent the forces overpowering the helmsman and watch officer who worked together to keep it trimmed; Morgan had fallen into his hammock after the previous night at the height of the storm's fury. At the forenoon watch it had proved so difficult to wake him that Reid had resorted to tipping him out; he had barely roused himself even now.

Tired men speak little, and so it was aboard the *Irex*. Hutton had attempted to hold a Sunday devotion before the gales took hold. This time there had been no music, only a desultory group of men in the saloon, holding on to the benches, tables and one another as the ship rolled. Hutton risked just fifteen minutes of devotional reading, prayer for their safe passage and an *a cappella* rendition of 'Eternal Father'.

He was surprised to see Mrs Barstow attend the meeting. He had gathered from recent events that she was no longer an adherent.

She sat on the floor, wedged inside one corner of the saloon, hands folded on her lap and her legs tucked up in front of her. Remaining in this self-contained pose, she still clutched her handkerchief, appearing as drawn and tired as the rest of the crew. Hutton watched her mouthing the words of the prayers and spending time with her head bowed, despite the constant motion of the waves. Even some of the more seasoned sailors had been sick during the last blow – he could only feel pity for Mrs Barstow, probably the least experienced sailor on the ship.

She hadn't remained behind after the devotions; her watering eyes and the beads of sweat on her brow told the story of her wretched condition. Handkerchief clutched and retching again, she fought her way up the stairs, stumbling back to her own room. Eustace had cleared it and set it straight while she frolicked in Clarence's room, before the storm made any such activity too difficult.

Hutton had seen nothing of Clarence himself for days. The gentleman had respected the captain's orders not to go above decks, but it seemed he had no desire to leave his room, even when Mrs Barstow was not there.

Two more days had passed, during which the storm increased in ferocity so that Hutton's last log entry had been just three words, *Estimate Force 10*, the most he could scrawl while the ship was bucking like a horse trying to unseat its crew of hapless riders. There seemed little else he could do but remain on deck.

Hutton turned to Mackie, who was staring back at him, his sou'wester pouring water down his back in small rivers as the waves continued to bat spray at them, mocking their condition. The sail changing operation was likely to last the remaining daylight hours, so they had little to do but plan for the next onslaught.

"Captain." Mackie called him.

Hutton moved to him in slow motion, feeling the inertia of being underwater. "Yes, Andrew?"

"Captain, would you like to go below? I can keep the helm." His voice, which rumbled out of him at the best of times, sounded gravelly with fatigue.

Hutton looked back up the ship. The operation was in good hands, with Reid forward and Mackie aft.

"Thank you Andrew. I shall check on the passengers, but please fetch me if you need anything."

"Aye-aye, sir" He nodded.

Once, Hutton might have argued with the mate but realised he must look even worse than he felt.

Only in the confines of the cabin did the fatigue roll over him again. It caused his eyelids to close involuntarily. He considered going to his room to drop his foul weather gear, but knew if he went anywhere near his bed, he would simply

339

collapse on it and never return. Instead, he half-staggered across the cabin to Clarence's door, and knocked.

"What is it?"

"Mr Clarence, it is the captain."

"Come!"

Hutton tried the handle, and it opened. He was greeted by a strange clash of smells. The most dominant was vomit and stale sheets, but there was a medicinal tang which almost masked a strong bodily smell. After days of the fresh sea blast, it was a potent nosegay.

"Are you all right, Mr Clarence?"

Clarence was lying on his cot dressed only in his underwear. The blankets were pulled back revealing his taut skin which was covered in a sheen of sweat. He held his pot next to him on the bed. "God, Hutton, what kind of tossing tub is this? I've never felt the blight of the sea so badly."

He struggled upright, his face paler than Hutton had ever seen him. His hair was unkempt for the first time in the voyage – it hung in loose, greasy strands across the man's face, and he smoothed them out of the way and back over the top of his head. His muscular torso glistened as another attack of sickness struck him, and he dry-retched into the pot.

"Shall I send for some water?"

"Heavens, yes, Will. For pity's sake. I'm drying out here." He sat up, swinging his feet to the floor. He sat for a moment, his head in his hands. He grunted a couple of times, then hawked into the pot beside him. He finally stood up, swaying with the ship.

"Will, I need to get up top. So does Elizabeth. Can you give us permission?"

Hutton was astonished by the sudden humility that Clarence showed in his discomfort. All the arrogance and entitlement seemed to have dissolved into a proper respect for his position.

"I will allow it. Just for an hour or two. You must return below at four bells by the afternoon watch."

"Four bells. All right, Will."

"I'll have some water brought for you."

"Good. Thank you, Will."

Hutton was taken aback. "I'm going to check on Mrs – Lady Elizabeth now."

"That's good, Will." Clarence was tottering around, trying to release the straps on the drawers to fish some clothes out.

"Good day to you – I may see you on deck?"

Clarence just nodded.

Hutton closed the door, and made his way across to Mrs Barstow's room, and again gave a light knock. There was no answer. He knocked again. "Mrs, er – Lady Elizabeth?"

He was met only with silence from inside the room. He tried the door handle, and it clicked open. He slowly opened it and called again. "Lady Elizabeth, it's the captain. Are you in here?"

He looked around. She had drawn the curtains, so there was only gloom. He saw that once again she had not strapped the drawers – two of them had slid free of the chest, spilling their contents on the floor. The same smell of vomit was the dominant vapour in the room. He felt her presence in the room, although she remained undetectable to his senses.

"Lady Elizabeth?"

He tried to make out the shape on the bed, but it was too dark. The darkness fuelled his fatigue, so that his eyelids pulled closer together. He fought to keep them open.

His eyes adjusted to the darkness, and he saw her lying on her side on the bed, facing the wall. She had shaken her nightgown off her arm so that her entire form was exposed. Like Clarence, the skin glistened all over, and her curled, chestnut coloured hair had matted into rats' tails with sweat. He heard a quiet sob.

"Lady Elizabeth! Are you all right? It's Will Hutton."

She gave a loud sniff. "Oh Captain. You can't see me like this." She laboured to pull the loose gown over herself, but she seemed drained of all strength.

"Shall I fetch Mr Clarence?"

She snorted, a bitter sound. "No. Please help me, but be a gentleman."

His heart began pounding, and he suddenly felt wide awake. He approached the bed, and gently gathered the loose gown and passed it over her shoulder and legs. She slid her feeble arm into the sleeve and gathered the rest over herself.

Standing over her, he couldn't help but look upon her, like a masterful sculpture and as pale. He both thrilled and cursed himself at the same time. The lady was an exquisite woman. He stepped quickly back and let her adjust herself.

"Ma'am, I just wanted to see that you were all right."

"I just need water, Captain."

"Of course, I will see to it as soon as I can."

She turned her head toward him, so he saw her face in profile. She looked very pale, paler than her usual flawless complexion.

"Is the storm over?"

Hutton pondered how he might explain the momentary lull, but his hesitation was answer enough.

She turned back to the wall. Her shoulder shook again, and another sob escaped.

"Ma'am, I—"

She lifted her hand and beckoned him over. He went over to the bed where she was mercifully covered up. In a voice thick with emotion she bade him sit on the bed.

"Ma'am, I'm soaking wet."

"Please, Will."

As he sat, she rose and hugged him tightly around the neck, though he was still in his thick oilskins. He whipped off his sou'wester and let his hands settle on her shoulders, finally clasping her head and shoulder to his neck, squeezing her back as tightly. She cried, her body shaking with the exertion.

For maybe a full minute she remained there. He remembered George Barstow's deathbed, and the episode they had shared then, but this felt very different.

She eventually drew back from him, her hair tangled and face still contorted in sadness. Her wide, green eyes were filled with immense tears that welled and fell in larger drops than those still falling from Hutton's oilskin coat.

She wiped at her face with the backs of her hands, still fighting the sobs that seemed to shake her whole body. She let herself fall back slowly to the bed, holding Hutton's rough hand in one of hers, while the other arm drew back across her eyes. She lay for a few moments as the sobs subsided, but gradually focused, remembering herself, and wrapped her gown tightly back closed again. She stared at the ceiling for a little while more, while Hutton sat mute as a statue, trembling with his own emotions.

"Seasickness is probably one of the worst conditions known to mankind." he ventured.

"No, Will. It is love. The most awful, treacherous disease."

Hutton actually recoiled. He was in no way fit to act as her romantic advisor after the shenanigans of the past week. "Ma'am, I should fetch your water. You may wish to be, er, more presentable for the steward." He shuffled to get up, but her hand stopped him.

She sighed, wearily. "I had resolved to live without a man at all, and yet this body craves to be loved. Worse, it carries the mind with it!" Elizabeth seemed to have recovered since the outpouring of her emotion. She plumped up her pillow and sat up; leaning her back to the pillow, she drew up her knees, hugging them.

Hutton tried his hardest not to look beneath the tent of the gown formed by her knees, and eventually shuffled himself sideways so he was no longer facing her but the door.

"Will, I am in love with Eddy. God knows, every part of me desires him, to be with him, to be united with him. Every minute I am away, my senses scream for his touch, his form, his breath. The very sight of him excites me in a way that I cannot bear."

Hutton gulped. He still could not speak.

"And yet my soul loathes him! I lose myself with him in every way, drinking deep of every pleasure; but at the parting, when he sleeps, I lie awake and feel wretched within. My heart is rent with bitterness and I despise him with my whole soul. I cry out to God for forgiveness, I receive his peace that my sin is released, and I sleep, vowing to part from

Eddy by morning. And yet morning brings only the glorious touch of his love, and I am lost in him all over again." She sniffed loudly. "What shall I do, Will? I am lost. I feel guilt. I feel joy. I feel pain. I feel relief. He says we are to be betrothed. The thought excites me like no other. Yet after our indulgences, I want to run and throw myself in the sea to escape him. Then the next day begins and brings the same cycles of joy and shame. I am wretched with sickness, and have been parted from him for two days. I have desired him and been repulsed by him in equal measure. Since the storm, he has not come to me, yet I have lacked the strength to go to him."

"Say something, Will. For goodness' sake, anything!"

He felt the confusion of his fatigue. He wanted nothing more than to lie down beside her and sleep, nuzzled to her bare back, cuddling her incomparable form to himself. In his befuddled imagination, he actually did it. As she turned to embrace him within the pleasurable dream, her soft, full lips pressed upon his own. He abruptly nodded with a start to find himself still sat on her bed with her expectant eyes upon him.

"I'm sorry Will. You are exhausted, yet I trouble you with my heart like a young debutante!"

He suddenly felt a clench in his gut that cut through the sleep. The inhibitions he carried fell away, dripping from him like the remaining drops of briny water that still clung to his coat. He unbuttoned it and dropped it to the floor. He then kicked off his boots, and swung his feet up, turning over so that he lay on the narrow bed, his face just inches from hers, their bodies separated by the thickness of the bedclothes she wore over herself.

"Captain, I – this is not—"

"No, Elizabeth, listen to me. I have been carrying a terrible burden that has impaired my judgement."

She looked fearful. "Captain, you are a good man, but I shall not tolerate—"

"Listen, Elizabeth!" His voice was a hiss that silenced her. "Clarence is not the man you think he is."

She looked puzzled. "Will, it was I who told you—"

He was irritated by her misunderstandings, and his tiredness did not allow niceties in his frustration. "For God's sake, listen to me! It's not what you think it is—"

"Captain, you need to leave. Please. I am sorry I opened my heart to you, it seems you have not yet let go of your infatuation."

"Clarence is a *murderer!* He is a murderer, Elizabeth! He murders women and I cannot let you leave with him."

She stared at him for long seconds as the ship rocked. Then she exploded from the bed, grabbing the pot at her feet just in time to retch repeatedly into it, bringing up nothing.

Her eyes filled with tears, the sweat beaded around the edge of her eyebrows. "How can you say such a thing? I asked for guidance for my heart, for you are a man of the world like he is. Yet you stab at him like a rival! Will, I will never go with you. I want to be with Eddy, but I fear marrying him. Is that so hard for you?" She shifted around so that she sat, lotus-style, her back to the wall. She kept the pot modestly over her folded legs.

Hutton remained prone on the bed and fought the extreme tiredness that pulled his eyes closed. "I have carried this since we left port. He threatened to kill you if I told anyone. Since your affair began, he has threatened us all with murder. But I don't believe you are out of danger. He will

346

eventually tire of you and dispose of you as he did so many others."

"Oh, God. Will." Her hand flew to her mouth, and the tears began to well in her eyes again.

"Your own spirit has warned you. You must believe me, this is no rivalry. I am no match for Clarence in any measure. But you have a chance to survive if you can let me get you back to England."

"No, Will. It cannot be true. What proof do you have?"

"Circumstantial, had he not fully confessed all to me already."

"When? Surely not when you were speaking this week?"

Hutton screwed up his face in frustration. "He told me the day your husband died."

Her hand flew to her mouth again, but the other tenderly touched his shoulder. "I am so sorry." Tears rolled again, but she did not lose her self-possession. "You couldn't tell me?"

"I told no-one! I feared that he would carry out his threat."

She buried her face in her hands, the tears flowing freely. "Oh, I have been a fool. A royal fool."

He dared to touch her exposed knee, and she gripped his hand in her own again.

"Elizabeth, he's had designs on you since the beginning. But I fear he has misjudged you, dazzled by your beauty and wit, but not seeing the truth of who you are. He thinks you are as ruthless as he is. Perhaps, once, he was right. But you are no longer like him, Elizabeth. You will live beyond him, for you have your own destiny. I know it more than anything I have known."

She breathed back another great sob, wiping her eyes again. The pot was now a receptacle for the tears that rolled

347

down the curve of her cheekbone, to drop from her jawline. "You must tell me all. Then I shall decide what to believe."

"I will tell you, but I cannot do it now. Meet me tonight. You must come to my room. I promise I shall reveal the whole of it to you. But you must not breathe a word to him. Your very life depends on your ignorance of this."

Elizabeth nodded. Tears still streaked her face, and she looked as unkempt as she had when he entered, but Hutton saw the brightness in her eyes again, where sickness and inner conflict had rendered her dull.

Still sniffing, she lay down again by his side, and ran her fingertips down the side of his face. "You must go, Will Hutton," she murmured. "I will come to you tonight, if I am able."

He swung his feet to the floor and sat rubbing his head and eyes. "Come at four bells of the first dog watch. Wake me if you have to."

"I will. You are a good man Captain, though I cannot always trust your feelings."

"I assure you ma'am, I mean you no mischief in any way. I'm just the captain. And a friend."

She smiled back at him.

He rose unsteadily to his feet, searching for his discarded rubber boots, and bent to collect his dropped coat. The puddle he had left on Elizabeth's bed simply added to the many insults the soiled sheets had received over the past few days.

She gathered the sheets over herself again. "I feel better. Somehow or other, thank God."

"He is watching over you, Mrs Barstow." He unconsciously used her old name as he wrestled with his boots against the rolling floor. In his mind he associated that name with the pious Salvationist he had first met – the thought of her as the virtuous Elizabeth Barstow rather than Lady Elizabeth, the paramour of a mass-murderer, gave Hutton hope that their entire miserable voyage might be saved.

He took his leave of her and wearily stepped back out into the cold wind and flying spray, looking for Eustace the steward.

"Captain! Back so soon?" Mackie's voice boomed from the quarterdeck.

"Mr Mackie! Our passengers are fine, and back in their own rooms."

Mackie raised his eyebrows in mock surprise.

Hutton laughed. "Yes, quite. Could you ask the steward to fetch them fresh water and bedclothes?"

"Sir." Mackie and Morgan exchanged glances. Morgan mouthed 'bedclothes' and laughed.

Hutton turned and saw Reid at the companionway. The young officer still had a spring in his step, but wore the same pale, red-rimmed expression as the others.

"Morning, Captain! Or should I say, afternoon." He skipped up the steps and reported to Mackie, who turned and gave four loud double rings of the bell. Noon had come. It was the cue for the forecastle doors to open and the black and yellow oilskin-clad sailors to pour out like wasps, as they immediately began to ascend the masts to relieve their crewmates.

Durrick came out of the portside cabin door, pulling on his sou'wester, looking as fed-up and dog-tired as the rest.

Hutton hailed him as he passed. "Robert, I am going below, but you may call me if you need me. I have given permission to the passengers to go above decks until four bells. You must enforce their return to rooms if the weather picks up again."

"Yes, sir."

"And Mr Durrick? I want you to resume your watch of Miss Barstow's room."

Durrick pursed his lips but maintained his composure. "The bosun again?"

Hutton noticed Reid listening intently as he stood at the bottom of the steps, waiting to be dismissed by Mackie. "No, actually it is Clarence I am concerned about."

Durrick looked pained, and his tone was more than a little indignant. "Sir, it's no secret among the gentlemen of the cabin that they are at it like rabbits. Once might have been an indiscretion, twice may be a violation of the lady's person, but every day and night for a week! What exactly am I protecting, Captain?"

Hutton was affronted. Durrick had certainly found his tongue since the run-in with the bosun, and the captain was not convinced it was all for the better. "Things do change, Mr Durrick, especially affairs of the heart. I don't expect you to defend the lady's honour – I am sure she may do that for herself – but if someone were to try to take it by force, I would prefer you were at hand. We are all tired, Mr Durrick. But I trust you in this matter to use your discretion."

Durrick was suitably chastened. "As you wish, sir."

Hutton left them and went back into the cabin. He longed for his bed, but there was one thing gnawing at him since the conversation with Mrs Barstow. He rode the bobbing deck to Clarence's door again, and knocked twice.

"Come!"

This time Clarence was dressed, but not for the deck. He remained barefoot and wore short breeches and an open-necked shirt. "What is it, Hutton? Is my water here yet? I'm dry as a damned bone!" He still looked green around the gills, and kept his pot close at hand.

"Mr Clarence, you will find me a bore, but I must ask you something."

"Oh?"

Hutton closed the door behind him. "Mr Clarence, you told me that you mesmerised the bosun—"

"Hypnotised, Will. It is much more refined."

"Yes, quite. But you never did tell me if you hypnotised Lady Barstow. I mean, Lady Elizabeth." He was too tired to have this conversation. He regretted coming.

Clarence looked amused. "Will – are you going to dog me like this for the entire voyage? Because Elizabeth will be my wife one day. You should be grateful I don't ask you to marry us tomorrow morning on the quarterdeck."

Hutton was horrified. As captain he could perform a ceremony, but as a licensed minister he also had the authority to marry them in the eyes of both civic and spiritual authorities.

Clarence must have been watching these thoughts etch themselves on his features as he gave another of his snorting laughs. "Well, that can wait, I suppose." He took a deep breath. "I'll call on Elizabeth and tell her that we are allowed on deck for a while. Did you send for my water?"

Hutton realised the discretion afforded him earlier was a mere trifle – Clarence was back on top. "I did. But Clarence, please. I need to know if you intend to release her before we reach our destination."

Clarence's demeanour changed to irritation. "Look here, Hutton, it's about time I set you straight on a few things. Firstly, Elizabeth is with me. Second, she is with me by her own free will. Third, the only thing I have done to her is give her exactly what she's needed for the last six years. Now she's finally tasting the true passions of her womanhood you'd have to mesmerise her to keep her away from me! In short, Captain, I have done nothing untoward. Everything the lady has done is of her own volition."

His voice hardened further. "It's you and your stupid religion that forces people to act against their will! Once I've shaken her free from the infernal guilt of her upbringing, she will not require your worrying over her like a bloody maiden aunt. No, Hutton, leave us alone! You are barking very much up the wrong tree, in more ways than one! Good day, sir!"

Hutton turned to leave. He wasn't sure whether to be affronted or relieved. He reached for the door handle, then paused. "You haven't seen her for two days, have you?"

"It has been difficult to survive, never mind anything else."

"Enjoy your promenade, then. Good day, Mr Clarence." Hutton pushed open the door, and left Clarence. Five minutes later, he was deeply asleep on his bed, unaware of the room that still tossed around him.

*   *   *

He awoke suddenly at the knocks on his door. His eyes were stuck together, and he wrestled himself awake despite every instinct pulling him back to sleep. He peeled himself from his bed. The ship was still rolling and as far as he could tell, not under way. It was dark, with just the thinnest line of reddish light on the horizon.

"Captain?" Mrs Barstow's voice, soft but sounding stronger than before. He hadn't heard the bells, but he assumed it must be about six p.m. He made it to the door, and cracked it open.

Mrs Barstow stood outside, dressed in a long, unadorned blue dress that was more modest than the last time he had seen her dressed. She had brushed her hair back in a thick ponytail and her face was washed. She smelled of a light perfume rather than the less salubrious concoction he smelt on her earlier.

Hutton cast a glance across the dark cabin, and saw only the slit of light beneath Clarence's door. She turned to follow his eyes, and put her finger to her lips, entering the room and making up his mind for him.

His oilskins lay on the floor, stinking of the sea. He had not seen bathing water for several days, and had slept in his clothes for most of them. His palate cleared by the fragrant Mrs Barstow, he could now smell himself. It wasn't good. He sat self-consciously on his messed up bed, and indicated to her the fixed armchair beneath the window.

She spoke first. "He came to me today. I – I am still in love with him, Captain." She gathered her hands in her lap, and looked down at them. "He is the only spark of life I have on board the ship. I am so much more alive when I am with him. He offers me a future, Will. The future I only dreamed of in the six years since I left my home." Her lip trembled but the tears remained caught in her eyes.

"Then I regret that what I shall tell you this night will not help you resolve your contradictions, Mrs Barstow. Lady

353

Elizabeth. You could leave now, and go to him. You would never need to know what I have to tell you."

"Yes...no. You must tell me, Will. Let my heart choose between my body and my soul."

"No, Elizabeth. Let your spirit decide. Body and Soul will always agree. It is your spirit that must decide."

She looked puzzled at this but did not comment further.

Hutton sighed. "I had to make sure that Clarence had not used his hypnosis on you, as he had on the bosun the night he tried to attack you. Clarence set that up to undermine you."

She looked comically sceptical. "What! Such nonsense, Captain!"

"He told me! I saw it happen before my eyes. I know the key word that induces the bosun's lust for you, and how to switch it off as easily!"

"Captain, I—"

"It's true! I worried that he used similar witchcraft to snare you in his romantic desires. But it was not so. Therefore, you have simply to exercise your will. You may extricate your flesh from his snare, if you turn your mind and will to God again."

Elizabeth looked conflicted. "He has such power over us? Eddy?"

"Well, in a manner of speaking. He has no such power over you, Elizabeth, beyond what you give him willingly."

She sat silently, looking down at her hands, working them nervously. "And what of the rest? He has murdered women?"

"Oh, Elizabeth! If you only knew how he did it, and the monstrous reasons why! He is so cold."

"Then you must tell me!"

354

"Elizabeth. He told me he is the Whitechapel Murderer. He is Jack the Ripper."

Her face went through several iterations of surprise, horror, and finally incredulity. She stopped fiddling her hands and eventually just smoothed out her skirts and stood.

"What is it? Are you leaving?"

"Captain. I walked the deck with Eddy this afternoon and it was most bracing. It completely cured my dreadful seasickness. Though I must admit to some queasiness now."

"I'm sorry, ma'am. It would have been much too dangerous for you to go up on deck during the storm."

"Listen to me, Captain. We spoke to some of the officers. We spoke at length, and they asked me to speak to you."

Hutton froze. "What?"

"Captain, we worry for your health. You have been under terrible strain. I admit I almost believed you this morning. You are a deeply honest and sincere man. But we are sure that your obsessions have caused your mind to falter."

"How dare they speak about such things? That's outrageous!" He began to rise from the bed, but Elizabeth gently pushed him back, her hands on his chest.

"Captain, please. Get some sleep. I am going to Eddy."

"Elizabeth, no! Please, I beg you."

"Captain Hutton! We must rely on you. They said there is another storm coming. You need your rest. And please, leave Eddy alone. He knew you wanted to rival him for my affections. He has trifled with you in jest. It appears you were not in the frame of mind to take such things lightly. He is a formidable adversary, and you have foundered in his play somewhat! That is all it is, Will. He is a fine gentleman, and will be a worthy companion for me when I reclaim my estate."

"But – no! He told me the truth. He threatened you – all of us!"

"Will, I shall hear no more of this nonsense! Please get your rest. We need your stout heart and courage, undiminished by your obsession. I will look after you, if you need it. But I am never going to be with you, Captain Hutton. It is simply not possible. Now, it is you who must choose. I implore you to choose correctly, for all our sakes."

Hutton felt confusion. He wondered if his grip on reality was so tenuous. His mind was reeling with possibilities. "I... I need time to think. I shall rest. Please fetch Mackie."

"I believe he is asleep, Captain. Mr Durrick and Mr Reid are here."

"Let me speak to them. Thank you, Mrs Barstow."

"Please Captain; address me as Lady Elizabeth."

"I'm sorry, my lady."

"Sleep well, Captain."

She left by the door, leaving it open for Durrick and Reid to enter. They came in sheepishly, though Durrick stood the straighter of the two.

Hutton was too tired and emotional to be too angry. He simply felt weary. "Gentlemen, would you explain to me the reason for your mutinous actions?"

Both men immediately protested at his words. Durrick won the upper hand, his voice pitched even higher with emotion. "Captain! How could our concern for you be construed as mutiny? We are trying to help you!"

"Help me by sending a woman passenger to encourage me to resign?"

"What! Did she say any such thing?" Reid exclaimed. "That was never our purpose!"

Durrick continued. "Sir, it was our hope that your lady friend would explain her situation to you, and enable you to let it go. Then perhaps you could get the rest you need, instead of running around after the man and woman all night."

"You impertinent swine! Why did you not come to me personally?"

Before either man could reply, there came a knock at Hutton's door. "What is it?"

"Mackie, sir"

"Come!"

Mackie squeezed himself into the room. There were now three of them standing round the table as Hutton sat on the bed. "Sir, Bosun has the watch. We are finishing the last of the sails. Wind is increasing, Force 5 from the south."

Hutton nodded, and asked the men to sit. "What is the meaning of this impertinence? Are you with them, Andrew?"

"Sir, I am with you. But I am greatly concerned for your welfare."

"What then! Let's have it out, before I decide who will end up in irons!"

The officers looked guiltily at Mackie, who took on the spokesman's role. "Captain, I speak for us all. This man and woman have had a terrible effect on you, sir."

Hutton remained silent, but waved him on.

"Sir, ever since she came on board we have seen your, ah, attachment to her. Then the business with the watch at her door – Mr Durrick was ill-used and worked double watches to comply. Then there were the night vigils you yourself took, at some cost to your own sleep, sir. Then we heard that you have been harassing the man, ever since he took up with the

357

lady. We understand your frustration, sir. But it is not good for a master to miss sleep every night. We have become worried for your health. And then there is the matter of the voyage log. There are some entries in your hand, which...well, they are not the work of a sound mind, Captain."

This may have been the most Hutton had ever heard Mackie say. It provoked a rage in him that was impervious to sense. "Some of you may have forgotten that this is *my* ship, gentlemen. If I decide a course of action is necessary, I shall take it, and direct my officers to comply. And you shall comply!"

His voice rose to a yell. "I have my reasons for the actions I have taken. And I will not be second-guessed by you, nor blackmailed by them!" He jerked his thumb in the direction of Clarence's room.

"Blackmail?" Reid dared to ask. "Surely not? How are they blackmailing you, sir?"

Hutton ignored him. "Gentlemen, I shall overlook your treachery for now, as we have another storm to weather, and a long voyage ahead. I shall concede that I have been tired. I will rest tonight, as you have recommended. But if you ever question my authority or competence again, I shall land at the nearest port and replace every last one of you. Your records shall be stained with your brazen actions on a ship at sea, no less! I would guess that your careers, however promising, will be finished. That will be my final word on this subject, gentlemen. You are dismissed."

Durrick's mouth worked, but he thought better of it and remained silent. Mackie stood, touched his forelock and ushered the others from the room.

As the door opened and shut, Hutton saw Clarence and Elizabeth framed in their own door – he caught her eye before his own door closed again. He locked it, then undressed and wrapped himself in sheets and blankets, the angry sobs following close behind. He was now truly alone.

Chapter Twenty

Off Falmouth
Thursday, 23rd January 1890

The men of the *Irex* dragged with fatigue. Beyond exhaustion, they worked at the extreme limit of their endurance. None of them had ever experienced the like of the storm that had battered them for ten straight days. This was a cataclysm, the winds seeming to come from everywhere at once. All movement on deck was impossible, as the waves swept the decks clean of any man foolish enough to be walking without a tether to the ship.

No-one had eaten a proper meal for two weeks. The galley deckhouse lay in ruins, its weather side staved in and the roof collapsed – it would have been suicidal to attempt repairs while the gales ripped the paint from the steel sides of the ship, and sent blizzards of spray as hard as buckshot into the eyes and skin of any man who didn't protect himself.

While the wind threatened destruction, the sea sought entry to ship by any means. Men worked all night and all day at the pumps, desperately trying to clear the bilges of floodwater which found any and every channel to run below decks, collecting among the cargo of iron and threatening to destabilise the ship. The floods had contaminated the stores, rendered the half-deck uninhabitable and every room in the cabin had been severely flooded.

Movement around the ship was now a perilous high wire act – to get from the forecastle to the quarterdeck, a journey of three hundred feet, now took up to an hour. The men had to climb to the first yardarm on the foremast, then pull themselves hand over hand along the hawsers that connected each mast to painfully haul themselves aft. It was a miracle that no-one had been lost so far.

The other miracle was the ship itself – not a single part of the sailing rig had failed. Each of the enormous steel cross-members had behaved perfectly in conditions at the limit of their design. She was a marvellous example of Clydebuilt pride.

Hutton and the officers worked feverishly above and below decks. Durrick and Reid were glazed-eyed, looking thin and pale as they climbed up and down the masts. They kept their heads cocked to windward, their sou'westers pulled down to protect their exposed faces.

Hutton tried to keep the wind on their starboard quarter while making a run for a sheltered port. He had elected to head for Falmouth, but a disagreement had broken out.

Mackie and Reid confronted the captain – all had suffered greatly from lack of sleep, and their discussion was fractious.

"Captain, are we going to put in? We haven't lost any men yet by the grace of God, but they are sleepwalking. Someone is going to fall."

Hutton was snappy, riven by exhaustion. He had never been as tired in his entire life. "Mr Mackie! Remember who you are speaking to. I know full well."

He focused on the officers with difficulty. "We shall lay off Falmouth and call for a pilot."

Mackie groaned. "Sir, you expect a pilot to come out in this fury? We should run for the port. Anchor in the roads where it's safe. No other ship would dare put out in this."

But Hutton had pressures the others knew nothing about. Clarence had threatened the crew with murder if Hutton tried to put him ashore in England. He had threatened to murder Elizabeth. The captain knew that to put the ship into port would condemn one or more, perhaps even all of them, to death at the Ripper's hands. But perhaps he could put Clarence and Barstow ashore alone, without taking the ship into port...?

Hutton saw Hanson and Murray, at the wheel, listening to this shouted conversation but his mind was too clouded for discretion. "She'll die if we put in. Or one of us. I'd sooner she sank with us than put into port. We must try to get her away with the pilot." In his addled state, he failed to recognise the ambiguity of his words. Murray looked startled.

The captain finally identified the Falmouth light, and put up his light signals to call out the pilot. The men, though utterly spent, thanked God, the stars and whatever other providential talismans they believed in – they would finally be putting in.

It was to be in vain. Twice in the next hour they saw the lights of the pilot boat, an open launch barely twenty-five feet long and rowed by a team of brave men, but twice it signalled to withdraw as the seas were simply too high. The third time, Dick Stearne, who was up in the foremast and had eyes like a hawk's, gave a shout of dismay as he saw the boat capsize.

Mercifully, the pilot's men righted it but that would be the sum of their efforts for the night.

Mackie shouted in the captain's ear again. "Captain, please! It's our best chance. Let's run her into port!"

"Damn you, Mackie!" roared the captain. The men stepped back from him. "We will press on to Portland!"

Disappointment fell like a shroud over the exhausted men and they set to the pumps and the sails again, dejected and reaching the point beyond exhaustion where the officers knew men would be lost.

Hutton went below to tell his passengers that his plan had failed.

Clarence and Elizabeth were in her room as Clarence's had been thoroughly flooded. Yet even here, the carpet was running with water.

Hutton spoke in a monotone "We can't make port tonight." His eyes flickered to the mirror on the opposite wall, and he almost recoiled. The old, ravaged face staring back was surely not his? It was pale, deeply lined and rubbed raw across the cheeks and nose. His beard was an unkempt stubble of black and grey, while his lips looked like split sausages, red, and cracked. His eyes betrayed the strain and fatigue he felt – sunken, red rimmed and bloodshot. He stared into the middle distance.

Clarence spoke to Hutton. "Captain, are you trying to make port? An English port?"

Elizabeth looked at him quizzically, trying to work out the significance of the question.

Hutton replied woodenly. "I am going to put you ashore. Both of you. And then we will continue our voyage."

Elizabeth squeezed Clarence's hand and smiled encouragingly.

But Clarence's face darkened. "Will, you know I have to go to Rio."

"Yes, but she doesn't."

"But Will, I am with Eddy. I will go where he is going."

Hutton looked at them both. He knew they considered him to be unstable, the victim of a mental breakdown; now he must look more pitiful than ever, like a recently-resurrected cadaver. His sodden clothing dripped into the carpeted puddle that was their floor.

"Captain, what do you intend to do?" Elizabeth still harboured a note of concern for him.

"We can heave to until morning, but the storm's eye is still behind us. We risk being overpowered and dashed ashore. I think we should press on and try for Portland or Southampton."

Elizabeth had never seen him so wretched. "He is a shadow, Eddy," she murmured.

Hutton blinked and peeled his eyelids painfully open again, afraid he would fall asleep on the spot. His eyes felt grainy, and he glanced at the mirror again – the redness made them look more yellow than white, the blue irises looking faded around his pinpricked pupils. "I am putting you ashore. You may deal with each other as you will after that. But you will not hold me or my ship hostage, Clarence."

Clarence's eyes flashed with fury. Elizabeth squealed as his hand crushed her fingers. He tried to spring up into Hutton's face, but the motion of the ship deceived him, and he lurched toward the wall instead.

Hutton grabbed his wrist as he fell past, righting him. He snarled into Hutton's face, but the captain didn't flinch.

"So, you would put me ashore in England, would you? It will cost you dearly!"

"Eddy! Stop it! What's the matter?" Elizabeth spoke sharply, either concerned for Hutton's safety, or taken aback by Clarence's manner.

"Elizabeth, this man has lost his mind. He is a hollow fellow, beaten in every way!"

"Eddy, you can't threaten him! He is speaking truth. We cannot stay here. This is a danger to us both. If we are so close to port, why should you not listen to him? You are all I want to take from this ship, my darling. Let us go home!"

Clarence's jerked his hand away from Hutton's indifferent grasp, ignoring his new fiancée. "Hutton, look at yourself! Are you reduced to a mere simpleton, slow of thought and word? You would abandon your passengers to this Maelstrom, and for what? Jealousy? Cowardice? You are a husk, a mere breath of the man I thought you were." He slumped heavily back on the bed next to Elizabeth.

Hutton noted it was the exact place where he believed he had saved her, body and soul, barely more than a week before. The thought gave him purpose. "You are leaving. I will no longer tolerate you aboard my ship. My lady, I give you one last chance to live."

Elizabeth spluttered in surprise. "Captain, I would love nothing more than to leave! However hazardous it may prove, I would sooner leave and live than stay here and die! I am no sailor, Captain, but I fret that our lives should be in your hands!"

Even in his confusion, Hutton knew he had reached his lowest point. He had lost everything – his status, his self-control, his self-confidence. And with that last retort, the lady Barstow had cut his very heart from his body.

He swayed, but touched his cap. "Very well. Goodbye, sweet prince. And you, pretty princess."

His slow-blinking eyes met only the furious glint of Clarence's as he closed the door. He paused outside as they continued to remonstrate with one another, but then moved up to the chart room.

*   *   *

Perhaps an hour later, Clarence sought out Hutton in the chart room. The captain struggled to write up the incident with the Falmouth pilot as the water washed along the floor in tiny tidal waves.

He wrote without emotion. His fatigue had reached an absolute where at any one moment he could either think or do, but not both. He was simply existing.

Hutton had to wait until he finished writing before he could transfer his attention to Clarence. He managed to return the pen and reseal the inkpot, before returning his red-eyed gaze dumbly to Clarence.

"Good lord, Will, you are in a state."

Hutton said nothing, but stared through Clarence into the distance.

"What is your plan, Will? Are you going to ride out the storm and head back out? You know I cannot allow you to return to England. We have spoken about this. Do you not remember?"

Hutton nodded. "Yes, I remember. But we cannot continue our voyage as long as you are on my ship." It was obvious to Hutton. He had to reduce every situation into simple terms.

Clarence was in no mood to bargain. "Listen, Will. You have lost an officer. Durrick is gone."

Hutton's shoulders slumped at this awful news. He began to get up. His weariness was written in every movement.

"Don't misunderstand me, Will. He hasn't merely gone overboard. I had to despatch him, you see." He drew a finger across his throat. "You weren't listening, Captain. You need to understand exactly who you are dealing with."

Hutton stared, uncomprehending. "You...*killed* Durrick?"

Clarence nodded with a note of sympathy. "Perhaps we've done too good a job of convincing you that you're losing your mind."

Hutton swayed as the water ran around their feet. He still held his palms flat on the table, steadying himself.

Clarence's voice took on a cold edge. "Will, I am going to carry out my plan. Consider Mr Durrick an example of what might happen if you try to stop me." He grinned. "I think you understand me now?"

Tears fell from Hutton's red-rimmed eyes but they remained fixed on Clarence's. "I understand one thing. You are a monster. I saw you before all this, in a dream."

He pushed himself back from the desk and turned for the door, lurching unsteadily as the deck moved. "I'm going to put you ashore with your woman. You can both rot for all I care. I'm going to save my ship and my men, and God will help me. You have no such assurance. Goodbye, Prince Albert."

"Captain!" called Clarence "You can't just walk away! I just told you—"

Hutton waved him away over his shoulder and sloshed out into the cabin. The door closed behind him.

The captain shuffled in a daze into the open space of the cabin. Water cascaded down the stairs into the saloon, sucking into the scuppers and down to the stinking bilges, driven by the work of the men at the pump below.

I've lost Durrick. I let the monster take him.

He turned suddenly around and ran straight into his room. He slammed the door behind him, locked it with several frantic attempts, then threw himself on the bed and cried loudly. *What devilry is this, oh God? Why have you forsaken me?* He cursed, then reproached himself. He would remain on the side of the angels, if any had been posted to his aid by an increasingly distant God.

His mind reeled as he plunged into sleep, vivid dreams flooding his consciousness. He was up at the swinging mastheads, seeing the shining heavenly warriors perched aloft, led by a radiant Elizabeth Barstow, a stunning, golden Valkyrie. She smiled at him, her eyes laughing, the way she used to look at him, and raised her sword to do battle with the demonic legions on the deck below. They formed a circle around their master, Clarence. He was once again the black, clawed monster from his earlier dream, clutching the naked body of Lady Elizabeth and sinking his fangs into her frail neck, even as her uncomprehending eyes rolled in terror, her mouth agape in a silent scream. Then Hutton blacked out.

*   *   *

The sound of the bells jerked Hutton awake. They were still being timed and rung on time, though the storm had not abated. He knew he had slept well, but it could have been any time of day in the grey fog kicked up by the constant raging of the storm.

He tried to clear his head, grateful to the point of tears that he had slept at last. His back ached. He gingerly got up, and tried to organise the mess of thoughts that rushed into his tired mind. He thought at once of the chart room. He replayed the conversation with Clarence.

Could it have been another dream?

The painful stab of anxiety told him it was real. He staggered across his room and flung open the door.

The ship still heaved. The deep booms of the waves against the hull told him that the storm was far from over –it may not even have reached its peak.

He turned into the chart room and saw it set as before. Somebody had been in during the night and updated the dead reckoning position. He saw they were barely thirty miles from the Solent, a large, sheltered inlet north of the Isle of Wight with a first class port at Southampton.

He was astounded. He must have slept for at least twelve, perhaps fifteen hours! They would surely make port now. They could restock the ship and rest the crew. They would resume their voyage sometime in February without the accursed Clarence and his blind paramour Barstow.

He realised he hated them both. They had utterly humiliated him, toying with his mind and causing him to question his very sanity. The officers and crew had turned against him. He hated Clarence for his devious manipulations, and the nonchalant evil in disposing of those he regarded as lesser to make a point of his superiority.

Hutton reproached himself; he had endangered the ship by not dealing with his passengers earlier, but now he would settle the matter.

He laboured over the chart for a few minutes, trying to come up with a course that worked. They had missed the chance to run for Portland – it would have needed sharp eyes to pick out the correct light in this hellish weather, and the men of the *Irex* were not in good shape. After such a good sleep, he considered that he was probably in the best condition of them all. To reach the Solent and the port of Southampton, he would need to steer northeast of their current position. He set to work quickly calculating the course to steer.

He wrote them on a scrap of paper for Mackie. Despite the weight of fatigue and responsibility, the chief mate was probably grateful for his crazed captain's prolonged absence.

The thought burned Hutton, even more than the sorrow he felt for Durrick. Close to tears once again, Hutton would have given anything, even his life, to have avoided these days that left him in such tenuous control of his own sanity. He stuffed the scrap of paper into his oilskin pocket. It was time to end this.

He left the cabin, forcing the door open as the wind tried to suck it from his hand, letting it slam behind him.

In the grey light, he saw it was now raining hard, the fresh water mixing with the flying brine. Lightning flashed, illuminating the deck and freezing the flying spray in place; the answering thunder was lost in the booms of the raging sea. The wind was terrific, its shriek the sound of tormented souls. It rose and fell with each gust, and was answered by the groaning members of the ship itself, the lines stretched to their limit and humming their own morose dirge. Spray filled the air, like fog or cloud; there was no physical delineation between sky and sea, air and water – it was a twilight world of both.

Mackie stood clutching the rail. He looked Hutton in the eye but said nothing. He looked more tired than Hutton felt, which was wretched indeed. The mate's face was also rubbed raw from the spray, while his eyes were limned in red, set in deep shadows and bruised from the constant onslaught of wind and sea.

Hutton struggled up the steps until he stood close enough to yell his communication at the mate. "Have you seen Mr Durrick?"

The words were whipped from Hutton's lips as soon as they were out; Mackie shook his head and pointed to his ear. Leaning closer, Hutton had to shout right into it.

"Have you seen Durrick?"

The mate shook his head and shrugged emphatically. Water was being whipped from his oilskins wherever it tried to pool, pouring in a spray like smoke. His sou'wester was plastered to the weather side of his head, and its brim flapped so hard in the wind that it was transparent in motion, like a hummingbird's wing.

Hutton turned his head and the mate leaned his face to his ear, his huge head creating a windbreak that brought a moment of relief from the shredding spray.

"He didn't show up for his watch! Mr Reid stood it instead. I've searched the cabin and below. There is no sign. Bosun and Murray checked forward and he wasn't there! I am very sorry captain, but I think he may have gone overboard. No-one's seen him since last night."

An enormous wave crashed into the starboard quarter and sent a ton of water cascading over them. Hutton stood in the shadow of the bigger man, but Mackie almost crushed him into the rail as the wave pinned them together momentarily. Both men reflexively looked to the helm, where Morgan and another seaman picked themselves up, still clinging to the wheel, white-faced and wide-eyed.

"Andrew!" Hutton was mouth to the mate's ear again. "It was Clarence! He killed Durrick! He refuses to be put ashore."

To his shock, Mackie pushed him away with one meaty hand. He saw him mouth *to hell with you, Captain* and turn savagely away. Another crushing waterfall fell over and between them, separating them momentarily. When the deluge spilled off the deck he saw only Mackie's broad back, pulling on the wheel with the other two men. The ship heeled dangerously to the lee side, and shouts from behind told Hutton that the men above deck were in great danger. As the men struggled to right the wheel, the ship heaved slowly upright.

Then came a very distinct sound, above the hysteria of the wind and the roaring of the waves – a loud crack like a cannonade.

Hutton turned just as a chilling sound rang out above the clamour of the storm - the high, uncontrolled screaming of a man in terrible pain.

He saw several yellow-clad figures wading frantically through the knee-deep water on deck to where another lay, rolling on his back, his head underwater. He saw the man's leg lolling out of the water on deck, bent unnaturally and a flash of blood-red along the thigh.

Hutton lurched down the steps, slipping twice and landing with a splash in the submerged deck. Seaweed pulled at his boots as he waded fast, sending up splashes all around him.

To his dismay, he recognised the injured man as Dick Stearne, the cheerful fiddle player, still whimpering in pain as three men tried to raise him by clutching his oilskins. Hutton arrived and screamed at the top of his voice, hoping the men would hear.

"Take him to the lazarette! Fetch Carroll!"

He heard the order passed around, and the men struggled to carry Stearne to the tiny infirmary in the aft section. They slogged through the repeated assaults by the waves, trying to hold Stearne clear of the floor, but needing a free hand to grip the precious lifeline. Stearne gave piercing cries at every stumble, and blood spurted over the men carrying him, causing the one nearest the wound to vomit and retch as they went.

Hutton searched the heights of the mainmast, trying to isolate the problem. He saw Bosun's Mate Murray on the main yard trying to secure a wildly whipping rope with a block on the end – a considerable danger. He traced the line back to the deck, where Seaman Niccolls was trying to splice a new rope into the broken end with the help of the apprentice Ogilvie. They worked in half-light, with water covering them to their waists as they knelt, feverishly picking the strands with marlinspike and fingers.

He remembered Mrs Barstow's words, about each rope being necessary; *some must work harder than the others.* The bitterness of the thought caught him by surprise. She had caused him more strain than he ever thought possible and it felt like mockery in this desperate situation.

In this case, one rope had snapped with the strain, sending the block like a cannonball into poor Stearne's leg, shattering the bone. Now they had to find port, or Stearne would lose the leg and with it, his livelihood. If he survived the wound.

Southampton was their only hope.

Hutton turned to go back when a massive wave pitched over the gunwale, sending a wall of water rushing toward him. His eyes were blinded by spume, and he sensed rather than saw the wave a split second before it hit. It took his legs out from under him but he managed to get both hands on the line which undoubtedly saved his life. His strained knuckles burned as the wave tried to snatch him from the lifeline. At the point his fingers were giving way, the surge ceased, and he came up, choking and spitting salt water. His panicked breathing rendered him helpless for a few seconds as the water began to ebb away.

He looked around wildly, to see if anyone else had succumbed to the wave. Over on the port gunwale, he saw Niccolls and Ogilvie choking, the latter vomiting seawater. By some miracle they had also escaped – the wave had pinned them to the gunwale rather than scooping them up and tossing them into the boiling sea.

Hutton thanked the sovereignty of God over the elements. A bitter thought followed: God did not exercise sovereignty over the will of men like Clarence. He thought of Durrick and the dead girl in the trunk, even Mrs Barstow. All had fallen victim to the monster.

With that thought, Hutton's mental paralysis fell away. He was free to decide again. With or without help, it was time to finish with Clarence.

He thought of Clarence and Barstow, snuggled up in her room, their only inconvenience a bout of sickness and wet feet if they deigned to touch the floor. Well, that was about to change.

He reached the steps to the quarterdeck and was able to give Mackie the paper with the correct course to steer. Mackie nodded and shouted in his bellowing voice to the helm crew, who moved the wheel several points to starboard.

Hutton went straight to the cabin shared by Durrick and Reid and opened the door without knocking.

Reid lay strapped into his bunk with a leather strop, snoring away the extreme fatigue of his almost constant labours. He was in as poor a state as the rest of them. His closed eyes were red and purple bulges circled with bruises, his lips cracked and peeling, while red patches of raw skin mottled both cheeks, chin and nose.

Poor Durrick's clothes lay on his bunk where he had left them, but of the man himself there was no sign. Hutton felt a stab of indignant anger that he should have been cast off so carelessly by a man like Clarence. The second mate's run-in with the bosun had made him stand taller, but he would have been easily taken in by the gentleman they all admired, whose word they respected above their own captain.

Hutton's flush of shame dissolved his anger as he considered the truth – if he had acted decisively following his first meeting with Clarence, the man would be in irons and possibly in prison right now. His infatuation and fear concerning the widow Barstow had let it come to this, and he miserably admitted responsibility for Durrick's fate.

He rummaged through the mess of flotsam that had drifted beneath the bed and eventually found the partly submerged wooden case that held the revolver. He found it still fitted snugly in its recess like a musical instrument, but the case was waterlogged. Hutton had limited experience with guns, but was assured this was a brand new weapon, presented to the ship at her entry into service by one of the Grubb board members – a Webley, as used by the Army.

After the incident with the bosun, Hutton had returned the revolver to Durrick. The second mate had cleaned and re-stowed it fully loaded. It was a heavy weight in Hutton's hands. He carefully pointed it away from himself and Reid and tried to crack it open. Six fat bullets lay in the chambers, and he tried to wipe the excess water away using the bedsheet. He clacked it closed again with an oily snap. He hefted the weight of it once more, before slipping it into the deep pocket of his oilskin coat.

He thought of waking Reid, but decided the man needed his sleep. Besides, Reid probably shared Mackie's opinion that his captain was mad, and would likely try to stop him. The thought of wounding or even killing Reid in a struggle for the gun made Hutton's stomach churn. He instead slipped out as best he could and lurched next door to the empty stateroom.

Inside, he met only water again, but the bosun's manacles were still on the bed. The key was still in the leg-irons, while the handcuffs lay loose. If he could get Clarence to surrender, he could get the cuffs on him single-handedly...

Ah, Will! What are you thinking!

It was more than just a doubt – it was a stark realisation that this was an impossible feat for just one man, even if he was armed.

* * *

The stairs down to the lazarette were narrow and steep – Hutton shivered at the idea of Stearne's discomfort as he was carried down. He could hear the man's moans as he reached the bottom of the stairwell.

He knocked on the lazarette door and opened it cautiously, still feeling the ship reeling. Down here the motion was less extreme, but the claustrophobic depths of the ship made him queasy.

The three rescuers stood with their backs to him. He could see past them to the table where bright kerosene lamps fully illuminated the ugly break in Stearne's thighbone – it had been cracked by the block on the end of the parted rope. One sharp end of the snapped bone had poked through the skin of the front, while the other end had pierced the back of his leg, leaving him with two ugly wounds that dripped with blood. Thankfully the blood dripped steadily, not in the gushing squirts that Hutton knew meant certain death for a casualty at sea.

Carroll, the former army surgeon, tried to set the break as best he could, fighting to keep his feet and hold down the bile in his throat. Stearne groaned with every touch as Carroll held the break with his thick, hairy fingers, calling for the nearest bystander, to plug the wounds with wads of cotton gauze soaked in antiseptic.

He glanced at Hutton. "Captain".

The others turned and acknowledged him. Hanson was the man furthest from the door. Hutton nodded to them and asked Carroll about Stearne.

"He should be all right, but we need to make port. It's a bad break – it'll have to come off if it goes gangrenous. He could save it if he can get to a proper hospital within two days."

Stearne moaned again as Carroll began to bind the wound. Hutton gulped – the combined smells of antiseptic and the raw meat of the wounded man in the confined room were making him nauseated.

"Hanson, I need you to come with me."

"Sir." The bosun shuffled round to the door.

"Carry on, men. And well done for saving Stearne. Good work."

The others mumbled their modest replies, but Hutton was out of the door and up the steep steps.

Hanson was at his heels. "Captain, what's the matter?"

Hutton thought about how to answer, and settled on the truth. "Bosun, I am placing Mr Clarence under arrest for the murder of Mr Durrick. I need your help in applying the irons."

The bosun was silent, but continued up the stairs right behind the captain until they had reached the saloon again. "Captain. Why have you got it in for Mr Clarence so badly? Is it just because he took your woman?"

The captain sighed, turning to face the bosun. They stood almost eye-to-eye, dressed in their heavy oilskins. Hanson's face looked like the others, except his was craggy and angular to begin with. The red splotches and raw lips made him look like he had been rouged and painted. Perversely, it left him looking softer. Even his red, bloodshot eyes looked less

378

threatening than the hard, stone-grey versions that looked daggers at everyone in better times.

"We enter the Solent in the next hour. He must be secure before we reach Southampton. The lady's life, indeed, all our lives depend on it. He is a vile murderer, Bosun. We must secure him."

The bosun eyed Hutton doubtfully. "Captain, may I speak plainly?"

Hutton thought it was no longer worth pretending he was in command. The next few minutes would decide his fate one way or another. "Speak, Frank. I will hear what you say."

"Sir, the officers think you have lost your mind. The men too, although it's not well-known that the gentleman has got in front of you. I will go with you, Captain, but I need to know it is for more than jealous revenge." He looked at Hutton earnestly, with his own exhausted eyes.

"Bosun, I have his own word that he has killed two people on my ship. When I threatened to put him ashore at Falmouth he killed Mr Durrick. And he says he killed a woman in cold blood. He smuggled her aboard in the trunk."

Hanson's red eyes widened. He suddenly jerked as if pricked with a sailmaker's needle. "The trunk? Oh my God! The trunk – I remember!" He clutched both sides of his head. The memory, suppressed by Clarence's mental meddling, seemed to dawn in his eyes as if he were living the moment again. "The trunk! Jesus! I – it was a dead weight. I said it at the time, but he told me it had a woman inside. There was a woman in the trunk! By God – he killed her!"

Hutton almost fainted with relief. Somebody finally believed him. He felt a surge of joy, the joy of trust in one's own senses and judgement again. He felt it so strongly he

379

could have hugged the bosun like a beloved friend. "Frank, you see it! He has played us for fools, turned the whole company against me, yet we, we two alone know the measure of the man! We must stop him!"

Hanson straightened at this. "What do you want me to do, Captain?"

"I have the revolver. I shall confront him, and lead him to the stateroom. You shall put the irons on him, and we will lock him up until we reach Southampton in the morning."

"Shall I wait for you in the room?"

"No, support me in this, Hanson! I need you by my side. He might yet overpower me. I cannot let him take the revolver."

The bosun nodded. "Should we fetch Mr Mackie, sir?"

"In any other circumstance he would be the first I'd want alongside us, but I fear he is set against me in this matter. He would stop us."

"Very well, sir." Hanson blew through pursed lips, covered in dead skin and crazed like old pottery. "When are we going? Now?"

Hutton nodded grimly. "Yes. It must be now. Thank you, Bosun. Good luck, and may God deliver him into our hand!" He popped open the flap on his coat pocket and withdrew the revolver. He held it in his hand again, getting a feel for its weight and balance.

They mounted the sodden stairs. Their feet slapped through the soaked carpet as the ship continued to roll and took their positions outside Elizabeth's door.

Hutton stood facing the door, about two paces back. He breathed twice to calm his nerves, and held the gun out in front of him, trying to stop his hand shaking. He swallowed before speaking, afraid that his voice might fail him. He adjusted his grip on the revolver, flexed his fingers and curled his finger around the trigger.

Just as he breathed in, the main cabin door to the quarterdeck slurped open, letting in the howl of the wind, and Mackie stamped in, oilskin coat pouring water. He appraised the situation in one mortified look.

"Captain! No!"

"Join me or stand fast, Andrew!" Hutton's voice cracked once, but he found his purpose. "I am doing this now."

"Captain Hutton. I am relieving you of your command. Stand fast!"

"Stand with me, Mr Mackie, and I will forget you said such a thing!"

"Captain, this has gone far enough. You must end this!"

"I *am* ending this. Mr Clarence! Come out. It is time."

The spray was rattling on the skylight overhead, the waves still boomed, but there was no chance that Clarence hadn't heard him. They formed an uneasy stand-off – Hutton pointing the revolver at the door, Hanson close behind, and Mackie about ten feet away, torn with indecision.

At that moment the Barstows' room door opened and Clarence stepped into the orange-tinted light, dressed in breeches and jacket, wearing leather shoes with fancy buckles. His hair hung loose, and he thrust out his chest and stood tall when he saw the gun.

"Will. What do you think you're doing?"

"Mr Clarence, I am placing you under arrest. You will accompany the bosun to the stateroom opposite. Please obey my instructions, or I will be forced to shoot."

Clarence didn't move. "God, this is all a bit dramatic, isn't it? What say you in the matter, Mr Hanson? Mr Mackie?"

Hanson spoke. "The girl in the trunk. Was she dead, sir?"

Clarence frowned with irritation. "Oh, I see. Frankie has come to his senses. It didn't make any difference to you at the time, did it, Frank? Why should you worry about her now?"

Hanson shot a look at Mackie. "I think Captain's telling the truth, sir."

Hutton tightened his grip on the revolver, never taking his eyes from Clarence. "Stand with me, Andrew. If I am wrong, I swear I will turn the ship over to you. But we must arrest this man."

"Eddy? What's going on? What's this about a dead girl?" Elizabeth's voice carried from inside the room, with a note of alarm.

Hutton heard the splish-splash of her light tread approaching the door. "Get back Elizabeth! Stay on the bed! Clarence, step this way. Do it now."

Clarence smiled the wolfish grin that Hutton had seen before.

"Allow a gentleman to retrieve his coat?" He ducked back inside, and Hutton stepped forward. He motioned to Hanson, and stepped back to cover the door with the gun. Mackie also advanced.

They heard Elizabeth's urgent voice inside the room, quizzing Clarence, but he didn't reply. Instead, he stepped back into the light, his fancy overcoat over his shoulders, and one arm round Elizabeth's waist. She was barefoot, and stood barely as high as his shoulder. He positioned her in front of him, but his head and shoulders were exposed above her head. Hutton shifted his aim.

382

"Eddy! What on earth is going on?" Elizabeth's alarm grew into fear.

"Leave her there, Clarence. Step out and follow Mr Hanson."

"Will, enough of this. Mr Mackie, can you please ask him to put down the gun. I will do as he asks, but I don't need a gun pointed at my face. I am a gentleman of my word."

Mackie was barely six feet away. "Captain, please. Whatever this is about, we can settle it in a civilised way. Please, lower your weapon."

"No. Clarence, step towards me. Elizabeth, go back inside."

Elizabeth's face was tense, her eyes wide. "Captain Hutton. This is far beyond madness. You must stop this. You are not well. This is clearly—"

"Mrs Barstow! Get back to your room! We shall settle this now. Mr Clarence, once and for all, do as I say!"

Elizabeth looked exasperatedly at Mackie. "Do something! He has gone utterly mad!"

Mackie remained rooted. "Captain, please—"

The second that Hutton looked away and across at Mackie, Clarence moved. His hand came from behind Elizabeth, arcing over her head and passing a long, thin object into his other hand. It was a sheathed filleting knife, with a blade almost ten inches long. He flicked the sheath off with his free hand, elbowed Elizabeth aside and then stepped forward, sweeping the blade in a violent backhanded arc that cut through Hanson's throat with a *swish* before he could react.

As Hutton turned, in slow time again, he saw a thin white line across the bosun's throat, which a second later erupted with foaming blood, and twin geysers flew from each side of his collar. He fell gurgling to the floor with a splash, eyes stricken and rolling as he raised his hands.

Mackie threw himself forward, but Clarence twisted his wrist and plunged the knife into the big mate's midriff, flicking it back out immediately as he fell toward him, drawing a grunt of shock from him, while Mackie's momentum sent him pitching forward onto the soaking floor at Elizabeth's feet.

Elizabeth found her voice in the two seconds that had passed and let out a short but piercing shriek, before clapping her hands to her mouth and struggling to breathe, wide-eyed. She didn't faint but stood, petrified, as Clarence steadied himself and turned toward her.

The man who was the Ripper glanced quickly toward Hutton, who was repeatedly pulling the trigger to a series of dead clicks.

"That's too bad, Will. I'd have thought you of all men would know the value of keeping your powder dry!" He laughed, a curious sound in the circumstances. It betrayed no mirth, only menace.

He brandished the knife in his hand, watching it with a momentary fascination – despite the damage it had wrought it remained spotless, though his hand and arm were spattered red. "This is an exceptional knife, you know, Will. It'll cut a sheet of paper if you rest it on the blade. It's served me well."

No-one moved. Elizabeth still stood, her whole body heaving with each breath as she controlled her panic. Her large eyes were bulging in fright, and the horror was etched on her pale features as she finally understood. Her hands slowly fell from her mouth, one moving to cover her throat in a reflexive gesture.

Hanson still gurgled, but his blood had mixed with the water to almost cover the floor between them. Mackie was face down between the two passengers, groaning into the soaked floor, his face stained by the mixing of water and blood, his own and Hanson's.

Hutton kept pulling his trigger desperately expecting the kick and roar of the shot, which never came.

Clarence gave him a curious look, satisfied no shot was coming. He turned his attention to Elizabeth. "Now, Elizabeth my dear. I had rather hoped you and I would become man and wife. But it seems our gallant Captain has rather spoilt that. I must thank you for your exquisite favours, but it would be best if I were to be the last man to sample them." He looked back at Hutton, who had ineffectually shot every chamber with no result. "I'm afraid—"

Elizabeth stepped up on the stricken mate's broad back and swung her foot with all the force she could muster directly into Clarence's undefended crotch. He yelled, with pain and surprise, and tried to swing the knife, but a second wave of much greater pain seized him and he dropped it, falling doubled and groaning next to Mackie in another great splash of red water.

She stepped off Mackie and carefully picked up the knife, throwing it into the corner by the chart room. She stood over Clarence, breathing heavily, unsure what to do next. She looked up at Hutton, who was utterly transfixed.

"Well, bloody tie him up or something!" she screamed.

He moved sluggishly at first, but then burst into the stateroom, grabbing the manacles. He tossed her the handcuffs and quickly slapped on the leg irons while Clarence tried feebly to kick out at him. He still groaned in pain, which, by the time the irons had been secured, had become howls of rage and frustration.

Reid had finally emerged from his bunk, blinking in the cabin light, and tried to make sense of what he saw. The whole incident had taken less than a minute to play to its grim conclusion.

Elizabeth was clutching Hutton as the shock began to wear off. She was repeating the words "I'm sorry, I'm so sorry, Will," but he was in no mood for recriminations. He extricated himself and told her to wait in her room.

He looked up and saw Reid. "John! Clarence went mad and killed everyone!" He was still high as a kite on the shock of the moment.

Reid looked, uncomprehending, at the blood-soaked men on the floor, but still regarded Hutton with suspicion, even as the captain implored him to fetch the doctor from the lazarette.

Reid slipped on his rubber boots and splashed through the red mess toward the stairs. He looked back once at the top. "Captain, if this is some mischief, I swear they will have your head for this."

Hutton felt remarkably calm. "I understand, John. But you must attend to the wounded."

Reid looked at the floor again, and set off down to the lazarette.

Looking down, Hutton realised how bad it was. Hanson was obviously dead. The blood had ceased to flow, while his face and lips were already blue. He lolled lifelessly with each roll of the ship.

Mackie looked in the same condition, but his groans still bubbled in the bloody water on the floor. Hutton gently turned him over, and he opened his eyes.

"Captain – I am sorry." The words were soft. "I have no excuse. I should...I should have—"

The blood was pulsing slowly between his fingers clutched over his midriff. There looked to be a narrow but very deep wound across his abdomen, but Hutton hoped against hope that no major blood vessels had been cut.

There came the sound of splashing from below, as Reid came up the heaving staircase, followed closely by Carroll, who froze at the sight before him. "Jesus!"

He ran quickly to Hanson, touched what was left of his neck and looked closely. He held Hanson's wrist for a few seconds, before gently closing the bosun's eyes.

He shifted over to the mate, and took a look under his hands. Blood oozed out, mixing quickly with the water that lay all around. "Can we get him out of the water? I can't put him downstairs, Stearne is there!

Hutton didn't hesitate. "Put him in my room. Lift together. Reid! Come and help us!"

Mackie groaned loudly as they heaved his huge body towards the captain's room in the far corner. They got him through the door and past the desk, and laid him as gently as they could on the bunk.

Carroll pulled open Mackie's oilskins and peeled back his shirt and tunic. The cut was as clean as a surgeon's incision, and at least as big. Blood oozed from the cut, which went very deep. The stink from the wound was bad news.

"It's a very bad wound, Captain. I think his gut is open. He'll be infected immediately. I can do what I can to patch it up, but there's damage in there I can't fix. Not here."

Hutton felt the deep thud in his innards, the clutch of anxiety and failure. "Please, do what you can. If he can make it until morning, we can get him to the hospital. Together with Stearne."

Carroll called over his shoulder, "Captain, can you send for the sailmaker?"

Hutton blinked back tears, for there was only one reason that Colquhoun would ever need to attend a medical case. As sailmaker he was also the maker of shrouds for the dead.

He glanced in on Mrs Barstow, who sat shivering on her bed, hugging her knees to herself. An impressive bruise was forming on her shin, which meant she had done Clarence some real damage.

The manacled murderer was howling from the floor, screaming and spitting curses, while Elizabeth sat listening with a blank expression.

"Are you all right, Mrs Barstow?"

She looked at Hutton with her large, green eyes, the tears filling them and gently rolling down her cheeks. She held out her arms, and he went to her, sitting on the edge of the bed as she cried in great heaving sobs into his stained oilskins, her arms locked round his neck. He thought she was saying "You were right," but it was hard to tell between the other unintelligible sounds she made.

He sat with her for several minutes, but the crying never let up. Eventually, he had to gently unclasp her arms from himself. "I have to get help," he murmured. She nodded quickly, but continued to cry into her drawn-up knees, averting her eyes from him. "I will return soon. Please, remain here."

He stepped back outside where Clarence continued his curses.

"Shut up, damn you!" roared Hutton. "This is all your doing! Don't you understand? You did this!"

Unable to contain himself he kicked Clarence hard in the chest with his thick rubber boot. It felt so good, he did it again, then moved to the head, kicking until Clarence fell silent and Mrs Barstow, clutching her hands over her ears, was screaming at him to stop.

Chapter Twenty-One

Off Scratchell's Bay, Isle of Wight
Saturday, 25th January 1890

The wreck was Hutton's fault in the end, he knew. There was no officer supervising the ship, for Reid had remained below with the casualties and Hutton himself was in an advanced hysterical state. He had taken to the saloon to calm down.

One of the remaining lookouts shouted a warning that a red light was hard on the port bow, and Hutton rushed up on deck to see for himself. Too late, he realised the previous night's plotted position had been estimated too far north. Instead of sailing before the storm up the Solent, they were heading straight for the treacherous cliffs near the Needles on the western tip of the Isle of Wight.

His heart froze as he realised the red light was the warning light of the Needles lighthouse. They were inside the boundary of the fearsome chalk teeth of the rocky outcrop at the western tip of the Isle of Wight. The storm still raged fiercely, and though the helm was well manned, the wind was from directly behind them. There was nowhere to turn.

Too late, Hutton thought. "Brace for collision!"

The shout was carried up the ship forward, the call echoing forward though the shrieking wind tried to stifle it.

Hutton gripped the rail and prayed.

The shock, when it came, was surprisingly light, just a brush with the rocks beneath. Hutton heard the keel thump and screech along the bottom, but the waves lifted her off again and the wind carried her forward. The second shock was far heavier, and stopped the forward motion of the ship dead. Hutton lurched against the rail with a solid impact, knocking the breath from him, but again the *Irex* struggled to live, rising clear of the bottom again. By now Hutton could see men pouring out of the forecastle hatch, carrying what they could; but a third heavy impact knocked them all down like ninepins.

This time Hutton felt the keel rupture, and the *Irex* stuck fast, her back broken. He couldn't stop the tears of sorrow. He had taken the *Irex* on her maiden voyage and wrecked her. It seemed the worst of the many injustices that had blighted their voyage; the ship had performed every task asked of her in the worst of circumstances. He knew her captain had not.

But he had no time to mourn; they were in a perilous situation. The huge waves of the chasing storm were approaching from directly astern, rearing up over the shallows and piling over the decks.

He heard a great crash from aft and realised with horror that the skylight had been staved in. The next wave emptied the bulk of its mass through the gaping hole. He could see straight down into the cabin and saloon, where tons of water now churned, turning the cabin into a miniature lake. The water had nowhere to go but down, and down led to the lazarette where the helpless Stearne lay.

He let go of the rail after the next breaker, and knew he had mere seconds to make the cabin door before the next wave crashed in.

Hutton leapt down the companionway steps, tore the cabin door open and slipped through just as the next cascade fell through the open roof. He waded through waist deep water to Elizabeth's room.

She sat on the bed, over which the water was already lapping. The various surviving articles belonging to her and Clarence floated or lurked treacherously beneath the surface, trying to trip Hutton as he approached her. "Come on, Elizabeth. We need to leave."

She looked up at him with a hopeless expression. "I'm not leaving. My life is finished. I could never live with myself after today."

"Nonsense! Come on!"

"I can't. Leave me."

He took her shoulders. "Elizabeth. You saved our lives. You were the bravest of us."

She stared at him. "No, Will. You were the bravest of us." Then she gave a loud sniff. "But I heard everything. You killed Eddy."

He grimaced in response, his eyes cast down. "I don't know if he is truly dead. I was weak when he was strong, yet when he was weak, I was merely weaker."

Tears welled in her eyes again. "It is I who is weak. Weaker in every way than I ever thought possible. God help me, I mourn him! How can that be? He was a monster. He killed those women! And your men! Everything you said was true! But my heart feels his loss…oh, Captain." She descended into sobs again, overcome by her pain.

Hutton's pity was quickly replaced by anger. Clarence always had a gift of inducing self-loathing in others, even in his death. "No, you are stronger than you ever thought possible." He touched her shoulders. "Elizabeth, put on your clothes, whatever you can salvage, whether wet or dry. Cover yourself up, as much as you can, including your head and face."

He remembered his heavy greatcoat. "Wait here. I'll get you my coat."

He splashed out of her room and into his own, shocked at the state of the cabin which was rapidly filling with seawater.

"Captain."

Hutton leapt with shock. Mackie sat on the bed, sitting up with his back to the wall. He was pale as a marble statue, apart from the livid red patches that covered his face.

"Andrew! Lord have mercy!"

The mate grimaced in pain as he tried to struggle to his feet. His hand was still across his abdomen, but a large bandage was wrapped around it, stained red and yellow. His entire lower body looked like it had been dipped in blood.

"Andrew, can you walk?"

The mate nodded weakly. "I think I can."

"Andrew, get to the galley deckhouse. There is some shelter there. Until the alarm can be raised ashore, we are trapped."

Mackie shook his head. "I will go with you, Captain."

Hutton sighed. "Andrew, you are grievously wounded. Get to cover, away from the cabin. You'll drown here."

In defiance, the mate stood, gritting his teeth and holding his midriff. "I am sorry I doubted you, Captain. I attempted mutiny against you. I am at your service."

Hutton shook his head. "No, Andrew! I absolve you. I shall never mention this to anyone. Please, save yourself!"

Mackie grunted, whether in pain or stubbornness, Hutton didn't know. "I am with you now, until the end, Captain."

"See to Clarence, then. He's in the empty stateroom. Make sure he doesn't escape. I will seek you out there soon."

The mate nodded. "Aye-aye, sir."

Hutton turned and almost forgot his greatcoat, the reason he had come. It was the same one that had covered Mrs Barstow on the day of her husband's death. It still hung from the door, sodden from the waist down but functional. He waded back to Elizabeth's room and handed it to her.

"Stay here until I come back. I have to get Dick Stearne."

The name seemed to rouse something in her. "The violinist?"

"Yes! The very one. He is incapacitated below decks. I have to rescue him."

"I will wait for you. God be with you."

He waded back just as another gigantic deluge of water fell from the ceiling, knocking him flat and throwing him underwater. The shock was fierce, and he came up gasping. He skidded on the cascade of water that swamped the stairs, ending up flat on his behind and up to his waist in water. He hauled himself back to his feet, only to be floored by the next wave dumping its contents through the skylight and down the stairs.

God, is this some kind of joke?

He spat seawater and waded towards the far door. He struggled to pull it open, but the water sucked it closed, until he hauled the door open with one prodigious heave that almost popped his shoulders from their sockets. The water rushed down the stairs ahead of him.

"Stearne!" he called, as he half fell down the steps again. "Stearne! Are you there?"

He opened the lazarette door as water swirled around his feet and, rushed into the small room.

Stearne lay on the table, pale and grey despite the stark red patches on his skin. His leg was supported by a rolled towel, and Carroll had left him strapped to the table to keep him still.

"Stearne! Wake up, man. The ship has foundered."

The man groaned. Hutton suspected he had been given an opiate to ease his terrible pain. He began to unstrap him from the table when splashes from the stairwell told him someone was coming.

He felt an electric chill down his spine, followed by an intense panic. Stearne was forgotten as Hutton cast about desperately for a weapon. He began throwing open drawers, and grabbed a scalpel from one as soon as he saw it.

The door opened the second he turned round, and Carroll fell through it, accompanied by a gush of seawater from the stairwell.

"God Almighty, Captain! What are you doing?"

Hutton trembled with the rush of panic and dropped the scalpel back in the drawer. "I – I thought it might be him."

Carroll gave an ironic laugh. "Clarence? He won't be coming anytime soon. Colquhoun's just sewn him up in a canvas bag."

"He...he is dead, then?" The words echoed around Hutton's head. *I killed him!*

Carroll shrugged. "He was still breathing. But there's not much life left in him. At least he'll be protected inside his shroud."

Hutton felt his knees give way. The doctor lurched forward to catch him, but he still ended up on the floor.

I killed him. I'm a murderer, too.

Carroll shook him roughly to his senses. "Captain! Forget him. He's facing the justice he deserves. Think of poor Hanson. And Mackie, too."

"Good Lord, not Mackie! I just spoke to him…?"

"No, he's like a bloody ox! I sewed him as well as I can, but he isn't going to live long – his gut is sliced open, and it'll infect the wound from inside. But he is awake and moving!"

Just then Stearne groaned, breaking through the chaos in Hutton's mind.

"Let's get him above decks. He'll have no chance here."

They undid the straps, and tried to lift him. He cried out once or twice as Carroll hefted him on to Hutton's back and supported his broken leg as best he could. They staggered toward the staircase like a grisly pantomime horse.

They reached the top, and eventually pushed through into the saloon. The water was now a solid rush pouring from the stairs, fed by the waves crashing through the open skylight above. They struggled and slipped their way up, trying to climb the waterfall. Stearne groaned and cried in distress. The top of the stairs was a torrent, resisting their attempts to climb over. In the end they had to heave Stearne over the top banister and pull themselves up and to grab him before he was swept back down the stairs. The poor man screamed in agony at every drop.

The door to the main deck was lolling open and closed as the water was almost waist-deep on both sides. The cabin filled up with each new wave that crashed in. Hutton knew they had to abandon this end of the ship or they would drown for sure.

Reid was in the chart room, packing the captain's log and chart. He had rolled the main plot chart into a thin brass cylinder, sealing it with a cork stopper, while the log was wrapped in oilcloth and secured with straps.

The young third mate had already made one hazardous trip forward to shoo the crew aloft to the foremast, the point nearest land, and had made the return journey unscathed.

"It's a hard run, sir. I had to time each run between the breakers and then hold on for dear life. Those waves are so strong they almost pulled me away. I think the best way is to run like hell for the mainmast, then climb and use the braces to get to the foremast."

"Very good, Mr Reid. Take Carroll and try to get Mrs Barstow and Stearne to the galley deckhouse. There is space there for a casualty station, and it should be sheltered from the waves, I hope."

Reid shook his head. "Sir, the deckhouse is collapsed. The roof is off. It would be scant comfort."

"There's no way Stearne can climb or stay secure aloft."

"If I could get some men, I could try, sir."

"Make sure Mrs Barstow gets aloft. She can make it alone, I am sure. Leave the log and chart to me. I have to get them safely ashore."

Reid looked at him quizzically, but the events of the night left him in no mood to question his captain again. He handed them over, and the captain cradled them like a newborn.

Hutton fought the water to get to Elizabeth's room. She stood waist deep in the cold water, wearing Hutton's coat, buttoned all the way up.

"Will, I have no stockings. My feet are freezing." She was shivering badly, whether through cold or shock it was difficult to tell.

"But you have shoes?"

She nodded.

"Elizabeth, listen to me. You must do the bravest thing of your life if you want to live."

She looked at him, her large eyes wide, but characteristically free of panic.

"You have to follow Mr Reid along the deck to the mainmast. It is treacherous because of the waves, so you will have to run for your life. There, you must climb up to the main yardarm, make your way to the very end, and then pull yourself along the cable to the next yardarm. Then climb over to the mast again and make your way up to the cross brace and hold on. Help will be coming in the morning, but you must keep covered against the wind."

She considered this information, the fear passing across her face, but then she set herself, still shivering. "I will go with you, Will. I'll wait—"

"There's no time! You can't stay here. You must go with Reid, and go now."

Another flood of water crashed through the skylight, sending a wave into the room, drenching them further.

"Now, Elizabeth. Please!"

She made up her mind and clutched the coat across her chest and up to her throat with both hands. They waded out of the room and Hutton handed her over to Reid, shivering in the deep water that still coursed through the cabin, now falling into the saloon with a steady rush.

She turned to him suddenly. "You are not coming, Will."

Hutton knew it wasn't a question. She had realised his predicament at last.

He shook his head. "I must attend to Mr Mackie. And I need to get Clarence off the ship. He is my Jonah. I won't let the *Irex* die with him aboard."

She launched forward and hugged the captain tightly.

"When will we meet again? I'm afraid I may never see you again." She almost whispered the words, but Hutton would have heard her above the chaos of the storm, even if he'd been deaf.

He wanted to hug her back, but his hands were full with the chart and log; so he kissed her cheek with his broken lips. "I will see you ashore! And if we are separated, I can find you at Missenden House!"

They separated. She touched his raw cheek, but only momentarily, for he knew there was nowhere on his face that was unspoilt anymore.

"You are a good man, Will."

He tightened his cracked lips. "Go, before it is too late! Goodbye, Elizabeth. God be with you."

"Goodbye, Will Hutton." She pulled the hood of her cloak over her head and wrapped it tight to her face like a Mussulman. She turned and pushed through the water towards the door, led by Reid.

Hutton whispered another goodbye in his heart – he knew it was their last meeting, and had no doubt she knew it too.

He stood alone in the cabin, water crashing over him from above and pulling at him from below.

Clarence is my Jonah? Jonah had been a prophet, a good man, hounded by God until he did his sacred duty. Hutton realised he had it exactly backward.

I am Jonah.

He waded over to the spare room, and opened the door in another rush of water. A packed canvas sailbag lay on the floor, floating on the surface, containing the body of Clarence within.

Mackie sat on the bed, puffing in pain. "He's dead, or nearly so. Carroll told Colquhoun to sew him up anyway."

"What, is he still alive?" Hutton's heart leapt.

Mackie nodded weakly, his huge head bobbing slightly, face mostly rubbed raw and ghostly white where the skin remained. "Aye. For now."

"Andrew, can you help me? I want to get to shore and raise the alarm. I will take him with me, so I know he can't endanger us further."

Mackie shrugged. "You should just dump him overboard."

Hutton shook his head angrily. "I have to get him safely ashore with the evidence! No-one will ever believe me. As you well know." The wounded look on Mackie's face made him regret the words instantly. "I'm sorry Andrew. It is a preposterous story to those who have not seen for themselves. Without evidence, I have only my word. I have to have the log, and the body of the man, dead or alive."

Mackie grunted and got up. "How are we doing this, Captain?"

Hutton felt the prick of tears again. The bag sloshing around at his knees contained the worst of humanity, yet tonight he had seen the very best.

"We need to launch the boat, Andrew."

Mackie sighed. "In this sea? Just the two of us?"

Hutton considered. "Very well, let's just get him in the boat. We can decide what to do later, if we can."

* * *

By daybreak, the entire ship's company was aloft in the rigging, at least those that could make the climb. Hutton and Mackie lay in the *Irex*'s only remaining boat, still lashed to the trestle that stood ten feet above the deck, mostly out of reach of the rolling waves. Its gunwales at least offered some protection from the wind.

Mackie slept fitfully, his face grey and lined with pain. Clarence lay unconscious in his bag, safe from the elements. Beside him lay the other evidence Hutton had managed to save – the captain's log wrapped in its oilcloth sheath and the brass tube with the chart. Hutton himself lay at the stern of the boat, dozing from exhaustion despite the cold and his soaked clothing.

The grey dawn lit the surroundings – they were in a shallow bay facing the forbidding chalk cliffs of the island, hundreds of feet high and barely three hundred yards away.

Hutton also saw in full the devastation that had visited the ship; the upperworks lay smashed, while the waves rolled over the entire ship, sweeping anything that wasn't secured to the deck over the sides.

Above him, high on the foremast, some of the men were dotted among the rigging like crows. The sails still billowed in the strong gale, blocking most of his view. On the foremast the men and, he hoped, one woman, were shielded from the worst of the wind by the vast expanse of the mainsails behind them.

At the aft end the quarterdeck was just a mess of water. Their belongings were long gone, washed from every room and nook by the searching tendrils of the sea.

There was a shout from the foretop. The crow-figures began pointing shoreward. Hutton looked across and saw tiny figures appearing along the top of the cliff, silhouetted against the morning sky. Help would be coming soon.

Within minutes there came a loud pop and a hissing sound from the cliff. Hutton sat up and saw a trail in the sky arcing toward the ship, as if someone had thrown a can of smoke. It snagged in the rigging of the foremast, and he watched one of the black figures scramble from the topsail yards to retrieve it. His numbed mind registered that someone ashore had shot a rocket attached to a line. It had been an incredible shot, hitting the bullseye from over three hundred yards away.

He tried to rouse Mackie. The mate was alive, but barely. His lips, torn and peeling like everyone else's, were going blue. Hutton looked down and saw fresh red blood seeping from the bandage beneath the mate's fingers. He did not stir. As the waves continued to roll beneath the gantry, Hutton stepped out and began to unlash the boat.

As he worked, he occasionally looked up. It was now much lighter, and details were clear. A breeches buoy, a tiny frame just big enough to winch one man at a time, was being passed down the line from the cliff towards the ship. It was a wonderful idea, enabling the men to be extracted from the wreck without risking the boiling waves that locked them in the cove. Along the clifftop there were now spectators, dotted in ones and twos and occasional clumps, watching the plight of his ship and crew, but powerless to help.

As he looked back towards the Needles, where the waves crashed ever more furiously against the chalk monoliths and the solitary lighthouse beyond, he saw an impossible sight. Pitching like a porpoise, a long rowing boat was rounding the light and coming toward them. He saw eight oarsmen, pulling for all they were worth, trying to reach the *Irex*.

He again felt tears prick his eyes. The men of the *Irex* were here because of Hutton's own failings as a master and man; but these brave men in the lifeboat had no business being here at all, other than to help them. He considered the murderer in the canvas sack in the boat, and thought of the men who risked all to save life, rather than take it. Humanity offered such bewildering contradictions.

He suspended his work; his own efforts were pointless if a boat was coming. He thought of Dick Stearne and realised the injured must be taken off first. He waited for a chance to drop to the deck.

A big roller went through, and he lowered himself to the soaking deck. He flapped and splashed towards the main mast, and managed to get a firm grip on the belaying post as the next huge wave crashed in, completely engulfing him and ripping his feet from the deck. He held fast, choking out the salt water, and regained his footing long enough to race forward to the lee side of the deckhouse.

It was just as Reid had said – half-collapsed, roofless and offering just enough shelter to make it worthwhile. He squeezed into one of the doors just as the next rush of water barrelled past. Inside he found three men – Stearne, Carroll, and Harry Grayson, lying prone as Carroll worked on him.

Carroll reacted immediately to the presence of a newcomer and recoiled in surprise. "Captain! Good God! We heard you drowned!"

"No, I am with Mackie. He is fading. And Clarence, who still lives. I have to get them off. The lifeboat is approaching from aft. If we can get the casualties away, we can get aloft and wait with the others."

Carroll brightened. "Thank God, Captain! I think Stearne is the better of the two. Harry fell from the braces. Both his legs are badly broken."

Grayson was known on board as 'Old Harry'. Hutton had sailed with him at least five years ago, and he had given his age as fifty-seven. On the articles of this voyage, his age was again listed as fifty-seven. Nobody on the ship would guess he was less than seventy. He now whimpered at every movement, constantly tormented by the pain in his shattered legs which Carroll had bound together as best he could.

As another roller went by, its rush was overtaken by another sound, a raised shout of many voices. They looked up at the foremast through the broken roof and saw the cheering of the survivors aloft. The first of their number had been hauled to safety on the clifftop. The men began to shuffle into orderly lines to await their turn. Among the many shapes clinging to the yards Hutton could pick out Elizabeth, wearing his coat, her legs dangling and one boot missing. Her bare foot swung, looking white and frail in the buffeting wind. Her head was still covered, and she clung hard to the ropes by the foretop where she had climbed.

Hutton felt a deep sense of...what? It went beyond infatuation or even love; it was a profound admiration, the sense that she was simply strong – he did not doubt for a second that she would survive their ordeal, and live on to be a woman of great substance.

He tore his gaze from her, and faced Carroll. "We need to get the injured up to the boat deck. I have Mackie and Clarence there. They must leave first."

It would be hazardous indeed. Hutton and Carroll each took one of the wounded men across their backs, trying to ignore their shrill cries. There was no humane way to carry them, so the men were in agony.

They dodged two breakers and found themselves at the foot of the boat gantry. Hutton took Stearne up first, while Carroll braced himself with his back to the onrushing sea, Grayson helpless as the next wave slammed into them.

Hutton's feet were caught by the wave, and he was knocked from the ladder, holding Stearne to himself with one hand, while the other gripped the ladder for their lives. He somehow held on until the wash subsided. Spitting salt water again, he climbed to the top and laid Stearne in the boat alongside the others. Then he helped Carroll up after they had endured another violent drubbing by the passing waves.

They all lay in the boat now, gasping and struggling for breath, freezing water pouring from every part.

"I swear," panted Carroll, "I am never going to sea again."

They laughed, incredible in the circumstances. Hutton closed his eyes and leaned his head back. They were so close to safety.

He opened his eyes again and looked in the direction of the lifeboat. It still came, barely three hundred yards distant. He began to explain to Carroll how they were going to transfer, when the hardy lifeboat was hit by a huge wave, and immediately swamped. The men were pitched into the sea, oars and all, and the lifeboat turned turtle. Hutton clapped his hands to his head, and Carroll followed his distraught gaze.

The men bobbed up again, small heads black against the foaming sea. After a few minutes of frantic activity, they righted their boat, and soon were pulling again, still coming. Hutton clapped his raw, freezing hands, in spite of the sharp pain it caused. "Look at them! They are still coming!"

"God bless them for heroes!" Carroll countered.

Then two more waves hit the lifeboat, and a third, much larger, dumped them all into the sea again.

Hutton's heart sank as he realised what was going on. As they penetrated the bay, the waves were ramping up over the shallows, making them higher. The men in the boat would have to negotiate the breakers each time they made their back-breaking way over. The chances of reaching the lee side of the ship unscathed and making the return journey with injured passengers were infinitesimal.

Hutton watched as the boat was righted and repopulated, only for them to begin moving away. He didn't blame them. To have come so far was superhuman. But his spirits fell as he realised he had only one chance left.

"Carroll, I must launch this boat. If I can row to shore in the lee of the cliffs I can pull up on the shingle. The injured should be safe there. Can you help?"

The doctor wiped the spray from his eyes with his thick hands. He nodded, wearily.

The two of them let go the lashings. They slid the boat out on its simple davits, but then Carroll baulked.

"Captain, sir, I do not think this is possible. I can't do it."

Hutton didn't quibble. "Then help me lower away."

"But sir, the men!"

"What chance have they got on the ship, Carroll? How will they get up the mast? They'll die here! The storm hasn't peaked yet. The bigger waves will swamp us."

"Then leave me with them, sir. They deserve company, at least." His weak smile was a rueful reflection on what it would mean for himself.

Hutton saw in Carroll the same selfless devotion to duty he so admired in others. It was something that was entirely absent in Clarence. The Ripper had despised it as subservience. Clarence didn't even begin to understand what was in the heart of humanity. The human spirit was noble, a reflection of its Creator, however dim.

He helped Carroll unload the groaning seamen, but when he moved Mackie's body, the mate's eyes fluttered open.

"Captain?"

"Andrew." Hutton's eyes filled with tears.

"Where are we? Greenock?"

"No, Andrew. But you will be safe here. It's just, ah, I need your boat."

"Take it! It's yours. Where are we going?"

"No, Mr Mackie. You need to get out. I am taking Clarence to shore."

"I'll come with you." He stirred, trying to get up, but the effort was too great.

Hutton's tears mixed with the storm-driven spray. He acted before he was overwhelmed with emotion. He cast one

407

final look across the ruined deck of the *Irex* and signalled to Carroll. "Prepare to lower away!"

They shoved the boat free of the gantry, and it hung in the davits. Carroll took the fore end rope, and Hutton stood in the boat with the aft end. Their eyes met for a moment, two men with dwindling chances of survival, but driven by a sense of duty.

"Goodbye, Captain!" yelled the doctor. "You are a brave fellow."

"Goodbye, Carroll. You are a noble fellow yourself!"

Carroll gave a salute "Godspeed!"

"Lower away!"

The boat dropped precipitously as Carroll tried to time his release between the huge breakers. Hutton tried to follow and the boat landed heavily in the swell. He loosed off the boat and grabbed the oars from beneath Clarence's bag, tipping it over. The man inside the bag groaned.

"Help! I'm blind! I can't move..!"

"Oh, shut up, Clarence!"

Hutton could hear the next wave coming. He pushed off the steel side of the ship with one oar and began rowing to put the small launch's head to the wave, his back to the oncoming peril.

Mackie propped himself up but his gaze was fixed behind Hutton, his eyes telling the story that Hutton didn't want to hear.

He felt the prow of the boat rise up, and keep rising as the roaring of the wave drowned out all sound. The boat tipped almost to the vertical, until Hutton was hovering above Mackie, who was slumped at the opposite end. The sailcloth bag between them screamed and the lumps of Clarence's hands and knees bulged through the canvas as he struggled.

Within the next second, Hutton felt himself falling through space, and then the extreme shock of complete immersion in the freezing water paralysed him.

He felt the boat land on top of him, but the wave carried him over, tumbling in whatever direction, he couldn't tell. His body was panicking, and he desperately wanted to breathe in. He felt the gritty, sharp bottom of the sea against his neck.

His lungs burned. He felt light in his eyes, but the pain in his chest was unbearable.

Jesus! I am in your hands...
Sarah – I'm sorry —
Sarah

Chapter Twenty-Two

Isle of Wight
Thursday, 13th February 1890

The weather was benign for the first time since Blake arrived. There was a brisk wind but the sun was up. The white puffy clouds against unfamiliar expanses of blue created a pleasant bucolic idyll, complete with the sounds of bleating sheep and the cries of the seagulls wheeling overhead.

The exchange of hostages was to take place almost in the shadow of Osborne House, the palatial island residence of Queen Victoria. It was in the extreme north of the island, near the famous yachting centre of East Cowes.

The original plan had been to meet at the court house. Lloyd had delivered new instructions that morning. The lonely location they had chosen was deeply disquieting and suggested the government men had an endgame planned.

Blake knew his only alternative was to run, but his own desire to know the truth overrode his desire to escape.

Yet he knew it was a vain hope to expect the answers he sought. Neither Blake nor Rennie were convinced by Playfair's sincerity. Even if by some chance they walked away from this meeting, he doubted the fabled Mrs Barstow would be accompanying them. But this had to end, and if there were any chance at all of gaining their freedom from Playfair and his cronies, it was worth taking.

Blake sat in the coach with Rennie. He had forced Peabody to miss the meeting despite his friend's strenuous protestations. He set the magistrate to collate the paperwork for the findings report, which Blake had already written, and wind up the proceedings.

Blake had returned a compromised finding to save his friends, including the kidnapped Elizabeth Barstow. He recorded all the deaths as accidental, the missing presumed drowned, while Clarence's existence was completely erased from the final report. Nineteen men still remained under the watchdog eye of the matron at the National Hospital, but their stories would not be told.

He felt a deep shame at his compromise, but he refused to consign good men like Rennie and Peabody to the gallows for the sake of an unwanted truth. The official record may have been covered up, but it drove him to uncover the real truth for the sake of his conscience..

They had cleaned up Thornthwaite, who was compliant enough now his freedom was secured. He was wearing his 'Marston' clothes, though they still had no idea who he really was. He now sat between Rennie and Blake in the roomy coach belonging to the Hollis family.

Mrs Hollis had insisted that her coachman, their trustworthy companion of the past few days, should bring them to and from the appointment. Blake had protested strongly, trying hard to dissuade her without explaining that they did not expect to return; though her protracted farewell to Rennie implied that the lady of the house knew far more than she was admitting.

They had shared a touching goodbye – it had brought more tears to Blake's eyes, who had considered himself irredeemably stoic until these trying times.

Rennie had held the woman's face in his hands. "If I come back, I'm going to ask you to be Mrs Rennie," he had said softly, and she had looked him in the eye and nodded, holding back tears of her own before sending him away with heartfelt kisses and a lingering hug.

Christopher Hollis had been released back to the constabulary with a stern letter from Blake warning Sergeant Trevannion of serious repercussions should young Hollis suffer any ill will or damage to his promotion prospects. They had laughed about it, picturing the pompous Trevannion frustrated by that particular kink in his fiefdom. None of them doubted that Hollis would go far, maybe even as far as Scotland Yard, given his family connections. The constable had remained untainted by Blake's adventures, unaware of Clarence and his true identity. Blake considered the Hollis family safe from reprisal, though nothing would stop Thornthwaite from taking his own revenge. It was a bitter thought.

Blake looked at the impassive Thornthwaite next to him. His face was freshly bandaged, though it remained black and blue around the eyes. The handsome young lawyer, or whatever he was, would have a very different appearance from this time on.

Each of the men was occupied in his own thoughts until they heard the sound of an approaching carriage. Blake beckoned Thornthwaite down, and stepped out of the coach, straightening his hat and coat. He looked down the lane at the two-horse coach labouring up the slope.

It stopped about thirty yards down the lane from them. Both sides of the lane were thick hedgerow, and the sticklike trees offered another layer of concealment. It was indeed a secluded place.

Blake moved Thornthwaite ahead of himself, in clear view of the other carriage. It was Lloyd who stepped down from the driver's seat, his blond hair distinctive, and still wearing his fancy coat.

Blake was accustomed to noting oddities, and his spirit sank further when he saw that Lloyd was driving rather than seated inside. It meant his adversaries were keeping their circle of trust very tight.

Lloyd walked over, shielding his eyes from the sun, trying to decipher Thornthwaite's features from the shadows and bandages. He approached until he was standing close enough to speak. "John?"

Thornthwaite spoke thickly in response. "Yes, it's me."

"What the devil have they done to you?" He cast Blake an accusatory glare. "You were supposed to bring him unharmed, yet you have brutalised him again!"

Lloyd had a pronounced lisp due to his missing front teeth, a consequence of his own meeting with Rennie in the hotel room.

Blake could see Rennie's shoulders shaking with mirth inside the coach. It emboldened him. These men had tried to kill them in turn. He would give them no satisfaction at this final reckoning.

"Mr Thornthwaite here was involved in another disagreement with Mr Rennie. I believe you have some experience of this too, Mr Lloyd."

Thornthwaite scowled. Lloyd ignored the jibe and beckoned his comrade towards him and began to lead him back to the waiting carriage.

Blake was concerned. "Excuse me gentlemen, have you not forgotten something? This was supposed to be a trade."

Lloyd ignored them, and so Blake began to trot after them. "Gentlemen—"

Lloyd turned and pointed a blunt revolver at Blake's chest. "Sir, return to your coach. I shall bring further instructions presently."

Blake held his palms open, and backed away. He reached the coach, standing by the open door where he could see Rennie, who remained concealed inside.

"Gordon, I think this may be the end. I would like you to know that I have valued your assistance and, indeed, friendship more highly than you can imagine."

Rennie grinned back from the contrast of the dark interior. "Thank you, Mr Blake. You've given me the best story of my life, though I can't think when I might be publishing it. It's been an education watching you work."

"I certainly could say the same about you, Mr Rennie. How is the merry widow, by the way?"

Rennie betrayed the first hint of vulnerability Blake had seen in the man. "Ah, you know, Mr Blake. That's a story I'd be very happy to write if we get out of this. I have every reason to hope we will."

Blake was impressed that Rennie could remain optimistic while his own mood was dipping. "I believe we might be advised to make our excuses." He glanced up at the coachman, who was smiling contentedly.

The coachman winked. "Spot of bother, sir?"

414

"I'm sorry?" Blake was bemused.

"Sir, the mistress is quite keen that you should return in one piece."

"The mistress?"

"Mistress Hollis, sir. She was quite insistent."

Blake was puzzled. "Are you intending to help in this matter?"

"Sir, my loyalties are to Colonel Hollis, God rest him, and his family. I'm a sort of...family retainer, you might say. I'm just saying – if the deal goes sour for any reason, I'm here to help."

Rennie's voice came from inside the coach. "Always good to know a fine woman with the right connections, Mr Blake!"

Blake frowned at him. "Do you know about this, Rennie?"

The Scot gave a mighty wink. "Let's just say I have complete faith in the fair Mistress Hollis and her staff."

He never misses a thing, thought Blake.

The coachman alerted him. "I think he's calling you over, sir."

Blake looked over towards the other coach where Lloyd was waving impatiently.

"Would you mind, Mr — er..?"

"Symonds, sir."

"Please, Mr Symonds." Blake climbed back in and the coach set off at a slow walk. They drew up very close to the other coach.

Lloyd stood with hands on hips, his habitually peevish expression verging on outright annoyance. "Mr Blake! What the devil is this?"

Blake shrugged an apology. "I thought it would make the transfer easier. I can't imagine the lady would like to stand around in the cold any more than we would."

He made no move to alight from the coach, but instead glanced across at the other coach – it was plain black and the screens were drawn. "Where is our hostage?"

Lloyd said nothing. He leaned around Blake to peer inside the gloom of the coach. He wrinkled his nose when he caught sight of Rennie.

"The reporter's here, my lord." Lloyd beckoned to Rennie. "Come on. Out you come."

"Aye, if it's all the same to you, I'd rather sit right here."

Thornthwaite got out of the black coach and walked up to theirs. Blake tried to glimpse the other occupants through Thornthwaite's open door, but could only make out one person. Lloyd's use of 'my lord' suggested that Playfair was alone.

"She's not here, is she? Do you even have her?"

Lloyd ignored him and ordered them out of the coach. "I'm not going to ask again."

Blake hesitated but Rennie just shook his head.

Lloyd pulled the revolver on them again. Thornthwaite looked on smugly.

Blake appealed to his former prisoner. "Look here, Thornthwaite! Tell me what the devil is going on and we'll come out. You have my word."

It was Lloyd who answered. "Well, Mr Blake, it rather seems you're going to have a nasty turn of luck. You see, we have evidence that you discovered some very prejudicial information about the Royal Family in the course of your inquest."

416

Blake nodded. "Indeed. That is no secret."

Lloyd smirked, the same smug grin that Thornthwaite used. "Yes, but you don't realise that we also uncovered evidence that you are here to meet some foreign spies in order to sell on your information. Fortunately, we arrived in time to disrupt your corrupt and treasonous arrangement."

Too late, Blake realised the depth of their deception. He tried to keep his calm. "I see you have been busy, Mr Lloyd."

Lloyd gave a fake bow of acknowledgement. "Our dear Sergeant Trevannion has received a tip-off to that effect and will be along shortly. Sadly, when he arrives he will only find the poor, dead bodies of the treacherous coroner and his crooked friends. You see, your deal went sour – the foreign agents decided to kill you rather than pay you for your trouble. Of course, this means your inquest will be tarnished, and will need to be sealed in the interests of the Crown. Terribly sad, really. So, to conclude: it ends here for you, Mr Blake. Could you and your reporter friend please step down so we can do this quickly? You too, coachman. I'm afraid you picked the wrong fare today."

Blake looked across at Rennie, who shook his head and mouthed *Wait.*

As Blake turned back to look at Lloyd, the blond man's head practically disappeared in a thick red spray, while a deafening boom nearly broke Blake's eardrums.

He was still trying to gather his senses when Thornthwaite's chest and neck also seemed to explode with a cloud of dust and red mist in another ear-cracking blast. The carriages lurched as the horses started, and crows erupted from the trees overhead in a chorus of cries.

417

There followed the sound of feet landing on the hard-packed ground of the lane, and Symonds appeared at the window, leaning down to retrieve Lloyd's revolver. Blood ran all over the frozen ground, steaming in the cold air. Steam also billowed from the broke-open shotgun that Symonds cradled in one arm. He pocketed the revolver and popped two new shells into the shotgun, cracking it closed with a snap. He looked in on Blake and Rennie, who were both sitting still, deafened and half-dazed.

"All right, gentlemen? Bloody good job there was just the two of them, eh?"

Blake's mouth moved but no sound came out.

Rennie reacted first. "By God, I like this fellow! Your mistress was absolutely right!" He roared with laughter. "Family retainer, my arse! Come on Blake. Let's pay His Lordship a visit."

He hopped down from the far door, avoiding the carnage outside. Blake followed, taking the long way around the coach and horses.

Rennie was knocking on the carriage door, covered by the heavily-armed Symonds. "Open up, Your Lordship! Don't try any funny business. We're armed."

Rennie gently closed his fingers round the handle, then yanked it open.

Playfair sat in the corner of the carriage, facing them, hands up and palms open. Opposite him, hidden in the dark interior, sat a woman dressed in very fine clothes. For one heart-stopping moment, Blake feared it might be the Queen herself. But as his eyes adjusted to the inside gloom, he saw it was a young woman, and from her looks he could only assume it was the long-awaited Mrs Barstow.

"Whatever you think you're doing, just stop right now!" Playfair still had plenty of bluster despite the sudden reversal. "She's coming back to the House with me! She's seen what's at stake here, and how far we are willing to go."

He spoke harshly to the girl. "This changes nothing, my lady. I brought you here so you might see that you have no choice but to agree to my offer. I remind you, my lady, you still have nothing to bargain with. Should you wish to cast your lot with these murderers and scoundrels, you shall be seized along with them and only the gallows shall await you!"

The woman's eyes were wide, beautiful; but she didn't acquiesce. Instead she regarded the men outside, controlling her fear with a self-possession that made Blake marvel.

"Who are you gentlemen?"

Blake stared, realising he had the penultimate piece of the jigsaw. He held out his hand to her. "If you are Mrs Elizabeth Barstow, then we are here to release you."

"Like hell you are!" exploded Playfair. "To hell with this absurdity, Blake! I told you that you are finished! Yet you are still playing games!"

"No, sir!" The colour was up in Blake's cheeks. This was more excitement than he could possibly stand. "It is *your* ridiculous game that has gone on long enough. I gave you what you wanted. I bowed to your wishes. And you were to repay us with death and dishonour! For what? For the protection of your sacred estate and its wretched progeny! I tell you that your vile protégé shall never sit on the throne of England. Not now. My evidence shall ensure it, and you shall ensure our safe passage!"

The girl's face brightened. "So, you are Mr Blake?"

He gave a slight bow, and her smile could have lit London.

419

"You know about Eddy? Clarence, the Prince?"

Blake smiled in relief. "Yes. I believe we do. But we need you to corroborate a few things."

Playfair fumed but didn't say a word.

Blake stepped aside from the door to let her out, and she stepped into the sunlight, dazzling in an expensive, fully trussed gown with a velvet cape and hood over beautifully coiffed hair. The only blemishes were on her face - the remnants of bruising under her eyes, while her painted lips were still slightly dried. Her eyes were large and bright, though there was a bloodshot stain on the white of one eye. Evidently she had been dressed up by the royal couturier – not the usual treatment for a kidnap victim or a prisoner.

"I would wager you have a story to tell, ma'am."

"I would be glad to tell it, Mr Blake, but I need to leave this island at the earliest possible opportunity," she replied coolly.

Playfair roared from the inside of the carriage. "This is not over, Blake!"

Rennie stuck his head inside, glaring at Playfair who was still cowering in the corner. "Oh, but I think it is over, Your Lordship! You see whose arse is hanging out in the wind now? Take a look, pal!" He pulled the door wide to display the mess to the reluctant Lord.

"What is our dopey police sergeant going to find when he arrives? He's expecting to find two dead bodies? He's going to find your men, apparently killed by foreign spies!"

Playfair's red face lost some of its colour as it began to dawn on him. He had been caught in his own trap.

Rennie wasn't finished. "But it gets better! We also have a Home Office Lord with his pants round his ankles who is missing a certain young lady who knows too much – what did
420

you call it? – 'prejudicial information'! Looks like our foreign spies got exactly what they came for."

Playfair turned visibly paler as the import of the situation began to strike home.

Blake wasn't nearly as convinced as Rennie appeared to be. They may have been killed in self-defence, but these were still officers of the Crown. His mind reeled at how they might ever get out of this alive.

He studied the Lord, curious as to why he appeared threatened. Surely he had the full organs of state at his disposal...

Rennie was revelling in the simplicity of his own theory. "Ha! Well, this won't play well down at the gentleman's club now, will it, Your Lordship?"

Playfair glared but his eyes betrayed wavering purpose as he pondered Rennie's words.

As he saw that look, Blake suddenly realised the real truth.

"You are working alone, my lord, are you not? This entire murderous scheme of yours is of your own devising! There is no government sanction for your plan, is there? You concocted the entire affair."

Playfair said nothing, but the blood slowly drained from his face.

Blake felt the euphoria rise in his chest, the certainty of triumph. "This is your own little powerplay? You enlisted the Lord Chancellor's office and the Solicitor General while playing your own game to recover the Prince's lost honour, is that it?"

Elizabeth's forehead wrinkled at these words. "Mr Blake?"

"Yes, ma'am?"

"You wanted to know my story – well, I can vouch for yours. Lord Dunsfold has acted secretly throughout. He was planning to marry me off to the Prince, dispose of the evidence against him, spike your inquest, and thereby earn himself the grateful thanks of the Crown and a seat at the highest table."

One look at Playfair's outraged face was enough to confirm her story.

The wheels of Blake's mind turned rapidly as the case fell into place.

"Don't forget, my lord, we still have the proof of Clarence's true identity, safely in the hands of our trusted friends, ready to go to the foreign press at the drop of a hat. We have my detective friend's evidence tying Clarence to the Ripper murders. And I promise you, we will find Henry Rudd's correspondent Dr Foster, and corroborate his evidence with ours.

"Finally, we have young Elizabeth here, a living witness to Clarence's crimes aboard the ship. There's enough evidence to guarantee our safety for many years to come."

Blake finished with a flourish. "And as my friend Mr Rennie has pointed out, your own scheme has ensnared you! I doubt you'll be able to organise a charity luncheon for the Sailors' Home once the dust has settled here. As far as your game is concerned, my lord, it appears to be checkmate. I trust you will have organised a worthy cover story by the time Sergeant Trevannion gets here."

Playfair was trembling with rage. His face had turned puce, and the veins stood out in his neck and forehead. But he said nothing.

"I would say, lady and gentlemen, it is time for us to take our leave!"

Blake knew the one weak link in their story was Trevannion, who would doubtless do whatever he was told. But it mattered little against the cards they now held.

"I need not remind you that if you take any action to harm any of us, now or in the future, you can be sure you will be held personally responsible for any and all information that finds its way onto the front pages of the world's newspapers. Good day, my lord!"

Blake touched his hat at Playfair through the window, who looked like he was about to have a seizure.

Symonds shut the door on the miserable lord, unhitched the horses from his coach, and scattered them with two shots of the revolver over their heads.

Rennie led Elizabeth round to the other side of their coach and hopped in, facing her. Symonds climbed back up to his own driver's seat and got his own horses moving. He broke them into a fast trot as the other three collapsed in a delirium of joy at their escape, none more so than Rennie.

"You know, I'd love to see his face when the police get there! Oh my God, I'd pay good money to see that!" He giggled like a child. The pressure was gone in a marvellous release. He banged on the coach roof. "Mr Symonds! You are a true prince among men! Take me home to your beautiful mistress and start making arrangements! There's going to be a summer wedding!"

"Righto, sir!"

Blake had to intervene. "Mr Symonds, first we must take Mrs Barstow to the ferry at Cowes. Fast as you can!"

"I will, sir."

He turned to Mrs Barstow, turning a little pink. Whether from the excitement or her level gaze, he wasn't quite sure.

"Ma'am, I received your letter."

"Thank you, Mr Blake. I am sorry for the melodrama. I was quite upset."

"What happened to you, ma'am?"

She shook her head, collecting her thoughts. "I wrote the letter when I gave up hope that Captain Hutton had been rescued. The major took a great risk to accommodate me, and I was very grateful that he did not breach my trust in him. But when I arrived at the ferry in Ryde, I was accosted by Mr Lloyd." She gave a slight tremor at his name, having seen the steaming remains as she was whisked past.

"They brought me straight to Osborne House! I'd only heard of the place before, but it is simply breathtaking. I was well looked after – after all, they actually wanted me to marry Eddy!" Her face fell as her eyes focused far away, recalling.

Blake interjected. "Eddy – this is Clarence? He is alive? Is he really the prince?" The questions tumbled from Blake's lips. He had to know, and time was short.

Elizabeth sniffed once, her lip trembling slightly. "Yes. He is the Prince, he is the Ripper, and he is the vilest man I have ever known. If the devil himself came down, he couldn't be a better liar, deceiver and evildoer. Perhaps he was the devil all along." She set her lips in a hard line, and gently wiped her eyes. "But for a time, I was hopelessly in love with him." The tears welled again.

"But, he is still alive? At the House?" Blake cursed himself for asking again, but he had to insist.

"Yes, Mr Blake!" she retorted sharply. "He is alive. But the circumstances are very different. He is an idiot."

424

Blake watched her, confused. She was wiping away the tears again, using a silk handkerchief that was probably worth a month of his salary.

"By God, this gets better and better!" Rennie was practically hugging himself at the turn of events.

She sniffed again, and composed herself. Her words had an angry edge. "He lives, but barely. He has lost his mind. Whether he half drowned, or whether it was the assault he received from Captain Hutton, he has become a timid simpleton. God in his wisdom has reduced him from a vile, manipulative murderer to a simple child in a man's body." She gave an ironic smile. "I could no sooner marry him in his present state than how he was before. When I told Mr Playfair that, I suppose my fate was sealed. But I hadn't reckoned with your efforts, Mr Blake. I can only thank you."

Blake looked away modestly. "I had the best help I could have asked for, ma'am."

"Thank you Mr Blake. I am privileged to have received the mercy of good men such as yourselves. I have been attended by gallantry throughout this distressing time, and I thank God that you were as tenacious and honourable as Major Owen, and most of all Captain Hutton. He was the finest of men. A brave sailor and a selfless example to all."

Blake cast his eyes down.

"What is it, Mr Blake? I am sorry if I spoke out of turn?"

"No, no, of course not ma'am. It's just – I am ashamed to say ma'am, that I had to make a bargain with Playfair. A condition of your release was that I had to place blame solely on Captain Hutton for the loss of the ship and the men. I regret that my finding is already written."

Her reaction was far stronger and more unexpected than Blake had anticipated. She seemed to cave in on herself, and her face crumpled in grief, huge tears springing from her eyes and running globs of black liner down her cheeks. She whipped out the handkerchief and held it to her mouth and nose, heaving great sobs that shook her whole body. Even Rennie fell silent.

Neither knew what to do. Rennie had a natural gallantry about him, but her grief seemed so powerful and yet so personal that intervention would have been churlish, if not merely patronising.

They sat in awkward silence as her grief shook the interior, until after long minutes it had subsided into occasional heaving sobs. She folded the handkerchief around and around, trying to dab away the blotches of eye make-up that had run. She finally threw her head back and breathed deeply.

"He was the best of men, Mr Blake. I inadvertently increased his burden by my own foolishness. He worked tirelessly to save others, and yet because of me, his life and now his reputation are forfeit. Dear God! Is there no justice?" She blew her nose, a most unladylike gesture for one dressed in such finery. But it was obvious she had no care for such trivialities.

"I will remember him. I will ensure he is remembered. He has a wife. She should know the truth. I shall write to her, for I knew him better than anyone aboard, and the burdens he carried." She dropped her hands in her lap. "Please, I just need to get home."

"Where is home for you, ma'am?"

"I shall go home to Great Missenden. Missenden House, the seat of the Bayes-Montagus."

Blake and Rennie exchanged glances. "I'm sorry, I was given to believe that—"

"Mr Blake. I am Lady Elizabeth Bayes-Montagu and I am returning to the home I left six years ago."

E.B.M. Elizabeth Bayes-Montagu, realised Blake. He produced an envelope from his coat inside pocket and weighed it in his hand. It was the balance of Rennie's hotel bill, ready to be paid in full. He exchanged a glance with Rennie, who smiled and nodded.

"Then, my lady, here is enough to ensure you can travel. You should have plenty for sending a telegram ahead if you should wish." He held out the envelope until she took it from him, folding it into the fan pocket of her sumptuous dress.

"Thank you, Mr Blake. And to your associates. I cannot thank you enough. I realise from your conduct today that this process has cost you much, but you have uncovered the truth that others sought to conceal. I hope it was worth it. I owe you my freedom, for which I shall always be grateful. If you should ever need a patron, you have one."

It was an incredibly generous gesture. Blake felt the flush from his cheeks to the crown of his pate. Even Rennie was silenced – a first as far as Blake knew. They both muttered "Thank you ma'am," for there were no other words.

* * *

They saw Elizabeth through the ticket hall and safely on to the ferry. She stood at the rail of the ship, studying it and running her hand along it as if seeking a connection to the

427

ship she had abandoned three weeks before, probably reliving some of the moments she had endured.

No-one passed her without pausing to admire her in her finery, and for a moment Blake felt a panic that the woman travelling alone might be vulnerable. But she straightened up from the rail, searching them out and waved brightly to them, a broad smile on her face for just a moment. He knew she would be safe.

With a blast of the steam whistle and a belch of black smoke, the ferry's massive paddles began to turn, and the smell of burning coal drifted over to the pier where Rennie and Blake stood. They watched as the ship moved away into the choppy but sunlit sea – it was turning into a beautiful afternoon.

Though he would have loved to take the ferry himself and leave the island far behind, Blake had one more important task to perform. The two men walked back in silence to where Symonds still sat up on the driver's seat of the coach.

Blake smiled, knowing Rennie would be in safe hands as well. He turned to thank the men who had saved his life.

"Thank you, Mr Symonds. We owe you our lives. I shall commend you to your employer Mistress Hollis as an exceptional servant."

Symonds just gave a tight smile. "You have no idea, Mr Blake! I should thank you for allowing me to have some excitement. First interesting day out I've had in years." He looked up at the receding ferry, still pulling out of the port in a belch of black smoke. "And I will thank you for something else – for giving the boy Christopher some proper work to do. He's just going to get fat and slow working for that useless sergeant, you know."

"He'll make a good detective, and soon."

They shared another look, their smiles doing the talking.

"Good luck, Mr Blake."

"Good luck to you, Mr Symonds."

Blake turned to shake Rennie's hand, but found himself at a loss. Rennie instead gave Blake the first bear hug he'd received since his schooldays, a grand and intimate gesture that Blake wasn't expecting, but it seemed a most appropriate response.

"You make sure you give me your address, Mr Blake. I intend to correspond."

"And I too, Mr Rennie. What will you do?"

"God, isn't obvious? I'm going straight back to Brading to marry Mistress Hollis! Then I'm going to live as a man of leisure and drink to the old Colonel's health all my days!"

Blake chuckled. "I fear you will bore of such a life, Rennie."

"Aye, but I'll take it 'til the end of the summer at least!" He grinned, that gap-toothed smile that Blake genuinely loved to see.

"I will miss you, Gordon Rennie." Blake's tears smarted in his eyes.

Rennie grasped Blake's hand warmly in both of his. "And I will never, ever forget what you gave me on this little island. This is the best story of my life. And I reckon it's only just beginning." His eyes glinted too.

"Well. I shall be in contact. Good luck, Mr Rennie."

"I'll look forward to it. Good luck yourself, Mr Blake."

They released their handshake with awkward solemnity, and parted – Rennie into the coach, and Blake to the nearby station.

The train only took about half an hour to Newport – there were only two stations enroute. Blake got out and hailed one of the cabs, and as the sun still rippled down on him through the shadows of spider-legged trees, he realised this was how it had all begun – a cold cab-ride to the court house.

He entered the court house as he had almost every day for the past ten days. He returned Jeremy's greeting, but kept his coat on this time. As he walked the colonnade, he felt excitement fill the pit of his stomach.

He reached the doors of Court Room No.1 and paused, collecting himself; then quietly pushed open the door.

Peabody sat at the large table in front of the bench with his back to the door, sifting the papers – from the look of it he was almost done.

Blake walked up the aisle, and when he was almost at the table, Peabody turned to look. His face dropped for a second as the recognition sank in, before he leapt from his seat with a shout and hugged Blake round the neck. "My God! I'd given you up for dead!"

Blake let his hands enfold Peabody's stout frame in return. "It's over. We are free men. I released the girl. Rennie is fine, and Playfair is finished. If there were any justice I could do to the tale, then you would hear of it. But for now, please do sit."

Peabody was in tears. "Dear friend, you are alive, by the grace of God! But tell me – is it true? Have you fixed this devilish affair once and for all?"

Dear friend. The tears sprang up again, but Blake didn't care. Peabody was blubbing freely and clinging to his arm. It felt wonderful.

"Yes, Stanley, I have fixed it for good."

430

Epilogue

Near Amersham, Buckinghamshire.
Friday, 20th April 1934

It was a beautiful spring day, unseasonably warm after a long, harsh winter. The sun beamed a full, yellow light that had been missing for so many months of winter, smiling life and energy upon the folk who milled in front of the ornate chapel in the impressive grounds of Missenden House.

The first buds of the late spring were showing at last, and the idle chatter of the well-wishers and those paying their respects turned invariably to weather, growing seasons and horticulture – the neutral staples of upper-class British conversation when awkwardness must be avoided at all costs.

The man who had sat at the back of the chapel noted the remarkable life of the woman to whom he had come to pay his respects. A former society beauty and socialite, she had thrown open her estate with a largesse uncommon in the austere days of the post-war world. Her ongoing generosity reflected her girlish years as a pious, if misguided, Salvationist.

According to the plump lady who regaled him with stories of the fine lady's past, she had left the family home at eighteen to work among the poor. She had married down (of course, darling, I mean, where was she going to find a proper *gentleman* in the slums!) Then she had attempted to elope to the Colonies. A disastrous voyage had ended in shipwreck, which saw her return as a young widow, (and she was carrying a *child*, heaven help us! Of course, it could never remain in the family, you know, so it was given up for adoption to Lord and Lady somebody-or-other who never could have children, which was a crying shame because they were *such* a handsome couple...) Subsequently, she settled back into the life of a society lady, her natural place (after all, hadn't she been entertained at Osborne House after the shipwreck? *Osborne House*, darling!) She had thrown herself into the Suffragist movement, becoming a leading speaker and activist (which didn't impress *everyone*, of course, dear) She used her considerable fortune and inheritance to improve the lot of the poor, and patronised several excellent schemes to renew the plight of the slums. She endowed sailors' societies, and even granted pensions to the widows and orphans of sailors. She learned to fly in later life, and flew her own aeroplane regularly to Europe in the Twenties. (She was no shrinking violet, dear! Oh, she was a fine woman, and beautiful as Aphrodite! But she never married again, darling! And it's not like they weren't queueing at her door. Everyone believed her heart was queered by Salvationism!) She continued to live a life of adventure and abandon, raising many eyebrows in society. (She was never really one of us, you know, dear. But a delightful girl all the same. Died far too young if you ask me...)

Having finished her gossipy monologue, she held up her eyeglasses to peer at him.

"And what about you, dear boy? Are you one of the Rawnsfords? How do you know our dear departed Lady Elizabeth?"

The man looked down at her. He was tall and athletic, and still had thick, dark brown hair though he looked around forty. He had a wide, sensual mouth like his mother's, but he fixed her with his father's eyes, pale-blue and almond shaped. His smile had a wolfish quality which slightly chilled the old woman.

"Well, madam, it appears that I am family. I have come here today to be reacquainted with my mother's estate and to claim what is rightfully mine."

Author's Note

This story is based on an actual event – there really was a sailing vessel *Irex* that was wrecked on her maiden voyage off the Isle of Wight on 25th January 1890.

Although that event was real, and some names and places may be familiar, this book is entirely a work of fiction. The people, characters, conversations, events and locations exist only in the author's imagination. Any resemblance to actual persons, events or characters is entirely unintentional and completely co-incidental.

Clarence's story of the naval collision is inspired by the Camperdown Incident off Tripoli in 1895. This very real naval tragedy transpired five years after this story takes place. Clarence's version is not intended to be a direct correlation to the actual incident and exists only in the realm of fiction.

Fans of Ripper lore will know that the Duke of Clarence connection has been discredited by researchers – the excellent Casebook website at www.casebook.org is a very diverting resource which kept me up into the early hours for several weeks. Despite this research, I felt the theory was fuzzy enough around the edges to contain the conspiracy I have concocted to accommodate it.

For those interested in the golden era of clippers and sailing carriers that connected the entire planet and provided the lifeblood of the British Empire, I would wholeheartedly recommend the engaging work of Basil Lubbock. Even though his books were first published in the 1920s, they have not been bettered.

The National Maritime Museum at Greenwich is another excellent resource. Although the magnificent clipper *Cutty Sark* was unavailable to me during the writing of this book, there is an equally majestic example of those steel-built cargo ships moored at Penn's Landing, Philadelphia – the *Moshulu*, which I was able to examine at close quarters.

The National Trust Needles Battery and Museum on the Isle of Wight provided the inspiration for this story and is a highly-recommended visit for anyone holidaying on the island.

Though I have taken pains to avoid them wherever possible, any mistakes in the text are my own, as are any historical inaccuracies and anachronisms.

Carl Rackman
Surrey, 2016

Acknowledgements

Writing a book is one of those things everyone thinks they can do if they only had time.

I used to be one of those people, and the process of writing a novel has been something of an eye-opener. It's not about imagining the story, or building the characters or even the writing. For me it was about making the huge commitment to write and keep going – the other stuff came to hang off that.

I would never have been able to make that commitment had it not been for the excellent support of my family, friends and supporters who encouraged me through the various stages of writing, editing, refining and finally publishing this book.

My wife and daughters have been unfailingly supportive through all the late nights and mood swings as my faith in my writing abilities swung wildly from stratospheric to non-existent with each new chapter. I owe the existence of this book to them.

My father-in-law and brother-in-law both told me independently that I should write a book. I took their advice and am very glad I did.

My parents have been unflappable supporters of my writing, and read the story in irregular and ever-changing instalments from the earliest drafts. My mum is still the first to read any of my work and remains my greatest fan!

I must devote a great debt of gratitude to my wonderful friend and neighbour Steve Cantwell, who read the first draft of Irex. His reaction convinced me that I could be a writer for real. Our many reader/writer meetings over cups of coffee and hot chocolate at our local café have evolved into a rich editorial partnership that has seen his input grow in the production of all my books. Thank you, Steve.

I also thank Jane Sleight, who trod this self-publishing path long before I did – her help, advice and critique were invaluable in making sure that this book eventually entered the digital and physical marketplace.

I hope my growing readership enjoyed *Irex*. I invite you to follow me for more! I can be found online using Twitter (@CarlRackman), Facebook (@rackmanbooks) and website (www.rackmanbooks.com). I also have an active author page on Amazon.com (Carl Rackman).

Carl Rackman

30632693R00246

Printed in Poland
by Amazon Fulfillment
Poland Sp. z o.o., Wrocław